REBECCA TOPE lives on a smallholding in Herefordshire, with a full complement of livestock, but manages to travel the world and enjoy civilisation from time to time as well. Most of her varied experiences and activities find their way into her books, sooner or later. She is also the author of the Thea Osborne Cotswold series.

www.rebeccatope.com

By Rebecca Tope

A Cotswold Killing
A Cotswold Ordeal
Death in the Cotswolds
A Cotswold Mystery
Blood in the Cotswolds
Slaughter in the Cotswolds
Fear in the Cotswolds
A Grave in the Cotswolds
Deception in the Cotswolds

❖

Grave Concerns
The Sting of Death
A Market for Murder

The Sting of Death

REBECCA TOPE

Allison & Busby Limited
13 Charlotte Mews
London W1T 4EJ
www.allisonandbusby.com

Hardcover first published in Great Britain in 2002.
This paperback edition published in 2011.

A CIP catalogue record for this book is available from
the British Library.

10 9 8 7 6 5 4 3 2 1

ISBN 978-0-7490-0889-5

Typeset in 10.75/14 pt Sabon by
Allison & Busby Ltd.

The paper used for this Allison & Busby publication
has been produced from trees that have been legally sourced
from well-managed and credibly certified forests.

Printed and bound in the UK by
CPI Bookmarque, Croydon, CR0 4TD

For my mother
Sybil Tope

CHARACTER LIST

DREW SLOCOMBE – alternative undertaker
KAREN – his wife
STEPHANIE and TIMOTHY – his children
MAGGS BEACON – his assistant
DEN COOPER – police detective

ROMA MILLAN
LAURIE MILLAN – her second husband
CARLOS PEREIRA (Spanish) – her first husband
JUSTINE PEREIRA – her daughter by Carlos
HELEN STRABINSKI – her sister
ANGUS – uncle to Roma and Helen
CONRAD – younger brother, died in childhood
NINIAN – older brother
LOLITA (LOLLY) – Roma's dog

PENN STRABINSKI – Helen's daughter, Roma's niece
SEBASTIAN STRABINSKI (Polish) – Helen's husband,
Penn's father
MIRIAM – Sebastian's sister, Karen Slocombe's mother
GREAT-AUNT HANNAH – Polish sister of Penn and
Karen's grandmother

PHILIP RENTON – farmer at Gladcombe Farm
SHEENA – his wife
GEORGIA – his daughter
RALPH – his employee
YVONNE RENTON – his mother

AUTHOR'S NOTE

The geography in this story is a mix of reality and invention that sometimes requires challenging feats of logistics. Pitcombe, Bradbourne and North Staverton must be on the extreme westerly side of Somerset for it to work. This, we must therefore assume, is the case.

When the idea of bringing Drew and Den together first arose, in 2001, it also became regrettably apparent that their names are uncomfortably similar. So Den is often referred to as Cooper, in the hope of avoiding undue confusion.

This reissue, nearly ten years later, highlights many subtle changes, both in the world and in my style of writing. But I find the tone has remained largely unaltered in subsequent novels, and I have very much enjoyed revisiting Roma Millan in particular.

There have been some revisions made along the way. In the original hardback version, I found some instances where people not merely travelled like lightning, but were literally in two places at once. I hope I have ironed all these out now. Never, before or since, have I attempted to portray so many different viewpoints in one book. It has produced a hectic, headlong story that I hope will entertain, amuse and horrify.

CHAPTER ONE

'What on *earth* does she think she's doing?'

Penn was staring in bewilderment at a figure at the top of the field. 'Is it some sort of ritual?'

'She's zapping wasps, I think,' Laurie explained mildly. 'There's a nest of them close to her precious bees and they're robbing the hive. It led to all-out warfare, and she goes up when she can to lend her support to the bees.'

'Um – how?'

'Well, if I've got it right, she spreads a trickle of honey on the roof of the hive, and then when a wasp starts drinking it, she hits it with a piece of wood. She says she killed sixty yesterday.'

'Is that enough to make a difference?'

'I wouldn't think so.'

Penn's gaze was riveted on the veiled apparition, over a hundred yards away. Her aunt was a constant mystery to her – sometimes so sensible it hurt, other times completely mad. A young golden cocker spaniel sat at a judicious distance watching its mistress warily.

'Doesn't she get stung?'

'Scarcely ever. She's very good at it, you know. Her honey won all the prizes in the show last week.' He smiled, a parody of the proud husband.

'You've really taken to this rural life, haven't you? It's working out a lot better than I expected it to.'

'Roma wouldn't have allowed it to fail. You know what she's like.'

Penn chuckled. 'Yes, I know what she's like,' she agreed. 'After all, I've known her all my life.'

'And I'm just a newcomer on the scene,' he supplied lightly, putting out a hand to prevent any protestation.

Roma Millan was enjoying herself enormously. Everything people told you about wasps was completely wrong. It didn't make any sense, for example, to talk about 'making them cross'. It was hard to see how a wasp could be any more provoked than to have a hunk of wood brought down on its fellows in a relentless offensive, just when some irresistible honey had been provided by a kind deity. And yet there was no sign of anger. They flew past her shoulder, over and around her, to get to the bait, and sat meekly lapping at it while death came out of the sky.

'Serves you right,' Roma muttered, as a particularly large insect was flattened under her sure aim. 'You should leave my bees alone.' She had refined the force of her blows, so as to reduce the risk of damage to the roof of the hive. The bees seemed unconcerned at the thumps – she almost permitted herself to believe they knew she was there to help them.

The truth was that she was worried about the bees. They couldn't get on with their normal work while having to man all defences against the wasps. It was war, pure and simple. Struggling pairs of combatants rolled on the ground beneath the hive – wasp and bee locked together, trying to sting each other, like soldiers in a pre-mechanised war. The only sure solution would be to track down the wasps' nest and get a professional to destroy them. In a six-acre field, with several hundred yards of hedge, this was a tall order. Meanwhile, she couldn't bear to let the poor bees fight it out unaided.

Penn's energetically waving arm eventually attracted Roma's attention, as she brushed a trickle of sweat out of her eye. 'Oh!' she muttered happily to the spaniel. 'Better go and say hello. Come on, Lolly.'

She didn't hurry – it was too hot for that. Penn would come to meet her in a minute, when she'd judged that Laurie wouldn't feel abandoned. Her niece's features came slowly into focus as the gap between them diminished, the curves of her face reliably distinctive. Penn had one of those faces, Roma had long ago discovered, that always took you by surprise. You only remembered a shadowy form of it, so the reality seemed to possess an extra dimension and vivid colours. Penn's brow was high and convex, her cheeks as plump as a baby doll's. Her skin was a deep honey-brown after a sunny summer. When she smiled, her mouth was a wide expanse of teeth and full lips. Roma thought she was lovely, a fortunate blend of her mother's rich colouring and her father's Polish bone structure. *Pity Justine never looked so nice*, Roma caught herself thinking with a stab of irritation. Trust her sister to produce the perfect daughter, leaving Roma with a much inferior model. All this talk about genes and designer babies made Roma laugh. Nature would always be several jumps ahead. Justine, the child of an achingly handsome Spaniard and the not unattractive Roma, had turned out sallow, under-sized and un-coordinated.

Aunt and niece embraced lightly, the affection

restrained. Roma looked over Penn's shoulder at Laurie. 'I told you she'd be early,' she said. 'She's always early – keen to see her old auntie, like a good girl.'

'What were you doing with the bees?' Penn asked quickly. A shade *too* quickly, Roma noticed, aware of the way Penn worried about the threat of comparison with her cousin Justine. 'It looked awfully violent.'

'I was helping them fight off the wasps. Futile, I know, but it makes me feel better.'

'Are the bees in serious trouble?'

Roma shook her head. 'Not really, in the long term, but it's a dreadful nuisance for them, and it's sure to interrupt their work. By this time next month, the wasps will have mostly died off. I should probably feel sorry for them – they haven't got anything like the organisation of the bees. But I don't – I hate them. I like killing them just for the sake of it.'

Penn tutted, her shock only half-simulated. 'I never took you for a killer,' she smiled. The spaniel was jumping up at her, demanding attention. Penn took little notice.

'We're all killers in one way or another – aren't we, Laurie?' Roma said.

Her husband raised an eyebrow, and took a half-step backwards. 'Steady on,' he protested. 'Speak for yourself.'

'Tush!' Roma derided him, and began to say something more, before stopping herself. 'Well – let's go and have a cup of tea, then. Or lemonade. I think there's some left in the fridge.'

The threesome sat in the tight little courtyard between the back of the cottage and the wall surrounding the vegetable garden, Roma defiantly positioning herself in full sunshine, the others, including the dog, edging sideways into a patch of shade. Penn made routinely approving remarks about the garden and the glorious location they'd found for themselves, and waited for the questions to begin.

'What did you say this woman was called – your long lost cousin on your father's side?' Roma finally enquired. 'It all sounds a bit peculiar to me.'

'She's called Karen, and she's the daughter of Daddy's sister, Aunt Miriam. You must have met her now and then?'

Roma blinked slowly. 'I suppose I did,' she agreed. 'Wasn't there a funeral? Somebody's father? I got roped in to mind all you infants, while everyone went off to the church.'

Penn considered. 'Probably that was Karen's granddad. Aunt Miriam's father-in-law. My dad would have gone, because – well, because he does things like that. He'd have wanted to be with his sister. So if my mum was busy, you'd have had

14

me to look after as well. I hardly remember it – nobody seemed unduly sad.'

'Miriam looked like you do now,' Roma said slowly. 'Same round cheeks and bouncy hair. I remember Helen talking about her sometimes, saying what a good friend a sister-in-law could be. I'm sure I only met her once or twice. Funny how long ago all that seems; another lifetime. So this long lost cousin is Miriam's daughter?'

'She isn't really long lost; I've known where she is. We used to have holidays together when we were really little. I stayed with them once for a whole week. Karen and I played with dolls a lot, and our mothers cooked. You're right, they were good friends for a few years, Helen and Miriam. I remember my dad joking about it, saying they liked each other more than him.'

'But it didn't last long?'

'They moved away, that's all. There wasn't any falling-out or anything.'

'Well, it's a nice coincidence that she lives only a few miles from here. You can visit us both on the same trip. Very convenient.' Roma leant her head back, getting the sun full on her face, eyes closed. But the questions continued. 'Is she the same age as you?'

'Older. I seem to remember she was six when I was four. She's got two kids now.'

15

'Married, dare I ask?'

'Oh, yes. All very traditional in that respect, from what I can gather. Except—' Penn spluttered into laughter. 'Well, I suppose they *are* rather unusual, after all.'

Roma waited, eyes open again, but unfocused. In the shade of the tangled wisteria, Laurie seemed to have dozed off.

'Her husband's a sort of undertaker. He runs his own business, doing something New Agey – natural burials in a field behind the house.'

'Good God! You mean Drew Slocombe? I know Drew, you idiot. He's the sweetest boy. Not the least bit New Agey, either.'

Penn closed her eyes for a moment. When she opened them again, she shook her head slowly, in resignation. 'I might have guessed,' she sighed. 'You've been here five minutes and already you know the entire population in intimate detail.'

'We've been here for almost a year, and Drew is one of the few people I've actually befriended locally,' Roma corrected. 'He's one of those easy people you feel you can talk to about anything after five minutes' acquaintance. He obviously has a soft spot for older women – in the nicest possible way, of course. We took to each other right away.' She hoped Penn couldn't see the brief wince at the memory of her last conversation with Drew. It still brought a surge of hot embarrassment, two weeks later.

'Laurie? Did you know she was carrying on with a young undertaker?' Penn asked. 'Who just happens to be married to my cousin, into the bargain?'

'Nothing to do with me,' Laurie disclaimed, without opening his eyes. 'She does exactly as she likes, you know that.'

'So – tell me how you happened to meet him,' Penn invited.

'He was a guest speaker at my Probus Club. Did it very well, too. No mealy-mouthed euphemisms . . . called a corpse a corpse—'

'And a spade a spade,' Penn supplied, erupting into another musical laugh. 'I assume he has plenty of use for a spade. God, Auntie, this is all very bizarre.'

'It's not bizarre at all. You'll see when you meet him. He's a perfectly normal young man.'

Karen Slocombe was taking the sudden reappearance of her cousin with complete equanimity. 'She'll stay an hour, talk about the kids, and her job and how we last saw each other in 1979, and that'll be it. That's how it always is with cousins – you know you've got something in common, but you're damned if you can work out exactly what it is.'

17

Drew chuckled. 'I wouldn't know. I've only got one cousin.'

'Yes, I remember. A simpering child called Nanette. Interesting name.'

'Boring person. So, are we giving this Penn some lunch? And is Penn short for Penelope?'

'Yes to lunch; no to the name. The story, as I remember it, is that our grandfather was helped by Quakers when he first came here from Poland, and quite quickly became one himself. When his son – Uncle Sebastian – had a daughter, Grandfather was ill, and they thought he was going to die. So they named her after William Penn, the Quaker, to please him.'

'Did he die?'

'No, you know he didn't. He lived another twenty years. He'd only just died when I met you. Don't you remember?'

'Now you mention it,' Drew said vaguely. 'I get confused when I've never actually met any of the people concerned.'

'We should make more effort to keep in touch with them,' Karen said seriously. 'We owe it to the children. My mother's only seen Timothy twice.'

Drew sighed.

'I know,' she sympathised. 'It's all such a performance.'

'Let's get the cousin over with first,' he said. 'One relation is quite enough to be going on with.'

They'd finished Karen's home-made leek soup before Penn mentioned to Drew that Roma Millan was her aunt. 'She says she knows you,' she added.

'Oh, yes,' he nodded with enthusiasm. 'I know Roma. She and I get on very well. The first time I met her, she asked me exactly how long it takes for the flesh to come away from the bones, assuming the body isn't in an airtight coffin.'

'And did you know?' Penn's face paled slightly, but she seemed determined not to be disgusted.

He laughed and shook his head. 'Not really. And I don't think she was genuinely interested. She was just showing off to the other Probus ladies.'

'That sounds like my auntie,' Penn agreed.

'We had a long talk a couple of weeks ago – did she tell you?'

Penn shook her head. 'I don't think so.'

'Oh, well . . .' he let the sentence tail away.

Karen's failure to join in the conversation was due to a preoccupation with helping her two-year-old daughter Stephanie finish her soup without getting most of it on the table. In a high chair on her other side, Stephanie's little brother Timothy banged a spoon.

'Family life,' Drew sighed, half-apologetically. 'You probably didn't bargain for all this.'

'They're sweet,' Penn mumbled. 'It's very nice to meet them.'

'Well, we quite like them,' Drew said. 'Though we do have our moments.'

Karen wiped Stephanie's face, and handed her a thick slice of bread spread with Marmite. 'That should keep her quiet for a bit,' she said.

'I's always quiet,' Stephanie announced reproachfully. Everybody laughed, including Timothy.

'You are,' Karen confirmed. 'You're amazing.'

'It's a coincidence, though, you being Karen's cousin, as well as Roma's niece,' Drew pressed on. 'One of those small world things.'

Penn shrugged. 'England's fairly small, when you think about it. Roma was looking for a rural retreat, and because she was based in Bristol all her working life, it's not surprising she looked in this area. Laurie's lived mostly in Devon, so it's familiar territory for him, too.'

'They seem to like it, anyway.'

'It's absolutely fabulous, apart from traffic noise, and aeroplanes going over. It's a lovely view of the hills, whatever they're called.'

'Brendon,' Drew supplied, before Karen chipped in determinedly.

'How's your dad, Uncle Sebastian? I used to

like him. He always seemed to have a special way with children.'

'Because he's never properly grown up,' said Penn. 'He's a perpetual little brother. Your mum has a lot to answer for. He still tries to get her approval.'

Karen looked at her own children thoughtfully. 'These are only a year and a half apart. It probably won't be the same at all. My mum's four or five years older than your dad, isn't she?'

Drew let their talk wash over him, thinking about Roma Millan, and continuing to marvel at the fact that her niece was Karen's cousin. There seemed to be something fatalistic about it, something that would maintain his link with Roma. If so, he was grateful for it. Roma intrigued him in several ways. She seemed so robust and clear-sighted at their first encounter, but during their talk of two weeks ago, she'd revealed deeper layers, where she was much less sure of herself. The revelation had been deliberate. She was asking him for something, appealing to him in some unspecified way. He wondered whether Penn held any clues as to what this might be.

Conversation became uncomfortably arduous again as Timothy demanded everyone's attention while he ran through his repertoire of animal noises. 'We'll go and sit in the garden,' Karen ordained, as soon as the salad and cold meat had all gone. 'These two won't be such pests there.'

Another reproachful look from Stephanie made Karen take back the remark. But they adjourned to the garden anyway.

Drew commented on the influence of the Polish genes in the appearance of the cousins. 'You really are very alike,' he observed. 'Like sisters.'

'We were saying how odd cousinship is,' Karen said. 'Or is it cousinhood? Anyway, here we are with all these genes in common, and we know almost nothing about each other. And I for one have almost no idea what Poland's like, even though my grandparents were born there. I've never been, have you?'

Penn nodded. 'I took a year out after school and spent three months there. I stayed with Great-Aunt Hannah – Grandma's sister. I suppose she must be your great-aunt as well. An amazing character. I still write to her.'

'How old is she?'

'Oh, not very old. Early seventies. She makes me feel very connected to that part of the family. Tells me all the births and deaths and marriages.'

'Why wasn't she a refugee as well?'

Penn shrugged. 'More people stayed than left, you know. The family aren't Jewish – they weren't in much actual danger.'

Karen shook her head. 'It all seems a million years ago, the war and everything. Mustn't it be awful to live in a country that everyone instantly associates with events of sixty years ago? You say *Poland*, and all anyone knows about it is that it was invaded by Hitler. I suppose everyone there regards it as ancient history, as well.'

'More or less,' Penn said vaguely. Her attention had been caught by the contents of the field behind the house. 'Is that your cemetery?' she asked Drew.

'Peaceful Repose Burial Ground,' he corrected her. 'Fifty-two burials already.' The pride in his tone was unmistakable. 'Just about enough to live on, if we're careful.'

'Only if I grow nearly all our food,' Karen pointed out, waving towards the further end of the garden. 'I'm getting very good at it. Everything we've just eaten, apart from the butter and meat, was home-grown.'

'Fantastic,' Penn applauded, half-heartedly. Her main attention was still on the graves in the field. 'They don't show,' she said, and then laughed at her own words. 'I mean . . .'

'I know. Even though we haven't banned formal headstones, like some places do, most people opt for a piece of natural granite or sandstone, and we're not arranging them in straight rows. The trees are a good camouflage,

23

too. Amazing how quickly they're growing.' He surveyed his acres as if seeing them afresh. 'We haven't even been here two years yet, you know,' he boasted.

'It's lovely,' Penn told him. 'No wonder Aunt Roma's so impressed. It's absolutely her kind of thing.'

'She wanted to book a plot—' Penn's expression of horror stopped him. 'Why, what's the matter?'

The visitor put a hand flat against her sternum, and didn't speak for a few moments. 'She's only fifty-nine. And she never talks about dying. It seems like tempting fate,' she gasped breathlessly. 'It gave me an awful feeling, you saying that. Just superstition, I know.'

'It is, yes,' he said firmly. 'Just thinking about dying doesn't make it happen, you know.'

'Right,' Penn said shortly. 'I'm sorry. I hate to think of her dying before she's patched things up with Justine, you see.'

'Justine?' Karen repeated. 'I remember a little girl called Justine. Auntie Helen brought her to some family gathering.' She frowned, trying to remember.

'Roma's daughter,' Penn confirmed. 'They fell out five years ago – it was all rather horrible. Roma can hardly bear to say her name now.' With a visible effort, she changed the subject and

24

told Karen and Drew about her aunt's vendetta against the wasps, making them laugh more than the story warranted, all three eager to lighten the atmosphere.

'This is a bad area for wasps,' Karen remarked. 'Stephanie's been stung twice in the past week, poor little thing.'

Again Penn's violent reaction was startling. 'No!' she gasped. 'That's absolutely terrible.'

Karen raised her eyebrows. 'No, it isn't,' she said. 'It only hurt for a minute, and she forgot all about it in no time. She's not allergic or anything.'

'But people can *die* from a sting. And you don't always know if you're going to react badly; from one sting to the next, you can become sensitised.'

'Phooey,' said Karen, unmoved. 'One person in a million, maybe. There's no sense in worrying about it, anyway. If it happens, it happens.'

'You can get special medical kits, with an antidote, if you go into anaphylactic shock. You should get one,' Penn pressed, her expression still full of concern.

Karen's face hardened, and she looked away over the field, forcing down the annoyance. 'Well, it's only a short season. I don't expect I'll bother,' she said lightly.

Never happy in an atmosphere of conflict,

Drew sought to moderate things. 'Karen doesn't approve of the over-medicalisation that goes on these days,' he explained. 'I think she's right, on the whole. Never before have human beings been so healthy, and yet they seem to worry constantly about their physical wellbeing. It's irrational, when you stop to think about it.'

Penn blinked. 'Well, er – I suppose that's so,' she stammered. Drew had the impression he'd struck a nerve. When Penn had first arrived, he'd characterised her as an intelligent young woman, confident and relaxed in a new situation. When he'd learnt of her relationship with Roma Millan, he had recognised a similarity immediately. Not in looks, as with Karen, but in general outlook and approach to the world. Now he began to revise this judgment. She was much less grounded than he'd first assumed; the initial behaviour seemed more of a façade than the real woman, and a very thin façade at that. She was nervous, flustered and irritated. Casual remarks could upset her. He watched her closely for a moment, observing a struggle to relax. He also had an impression that she wanted to say something to him.

An urgent wail from Timothy effectively removed Karen from the scene, leaving Drew attempting to mollify their visitor. He returned to the subject of their mutual acquaintance.

'Your aunt's retired then, is she? She's never

mentioned anything about her work to me.'

It was a dismal failure. Penn's face tightened even further, and her hands curled into fists. 'She was a teacher,' she muttered. 'The same as me – only I'm in FE. All my students are over sixteen, thank God. But Roma was in primary.'

It was difficult to see why that should cause such agitation. Drew grinned his most disarming grin. 'Of course – I should have known. She's just like my old French teacher, Miss Harrison.'

'And was Miss Harrison dismissed for abusing the kids?' Penn flared, her eyes wide and hot. 'Because that's what happened to Aunt Roma. That's why she's hidden herself away down here, trying to forget about it and start a new life. She had a lot of good years left in her, and they took it all away from her – for *nothing.*'

Karen looked over from where she was sorting out the children. Penn stood up, brushing non-existent fluff from the legs of her trousers. Drew teetered on the plastic garden chair, not sure whether to stand as well or stay in place.

'I'd better go,' Penn said. 'I'm sorry to have been so touchy. I'm not usually like this. It's just . . .' She clamped her lips together, and pressed a finger and thumb into the corner of each eye, in a gesture Drew recognised as designed to stem the flow of tears.

'It's just—' she looked at Drew urgently. 'Can

I trust you about this? Trust you not to think I'm mad?'

He looked up at her, mildly. 'I shouldn't think you're mad,' he smiled. 'And even if you are, there's probably a reason for it.'

'It seems mad, to be coming to you, a complete stranger, and pouring out my troubles.'

'Happens all the time,' said Karen, overhearing this last remark and giving an encouraging laugh. 'Must be something in his face.'

'Well,' Penn tried again. 'It might be nothing at all. I'm probably drawing all the wrong conclusions. It's Justine, you see.'

'Ah,' Drew breathed.

'She's gone missing.'

Karen and Drew exchanged a long deep look, containing concern, confusion, and, from Karen a resigned, *Oh God, here-we-go-again.*

'You'd better try telling us about it then,' said Drew, pointing at Penn's chair in a silent instruction to sit down again.

CHAPTER TWO

In the kitchen, Roma was extracting honey in a gadget designed to leave the honeycomb intact, so the bees could simply fill the cells up again, without having to reconstruct the complex wax foundation. The design of this gadget left something to be desired, and however carefully she worked, the result was always sticky deposits of honey on almost every surface. Her shoes stuck to the floor, and her fingers were sweet and gluey. The pervasive other-worldly smell of the fresh honey mixed with the wax made her feel drunk. There was something so excessive about it, the bounty of high summer, endless outpourings of it, filling ranks of jars, clear and glistening. It was magical and Roma loved it.

From the doorway, Laurie asked 'Nearly finished? I'm getting hungry. When are you going to allow me in?'

'I can't stop now,' she puffed. 'There's much more than I expected.'

'Can't you keep it in that plastic bucket, instead of decanting it into all the jars?'

'Best to do it all in one go.'

'And anyway, you're enjoying yourself,' he supplied. 'I must admit it does look like fun. I wish you'd let me help you.'

'You'd only get covered in the stuff. Give me another twenty minutes, and I'll let you get to the fridge. Go and have a sherry or something.'

'I hope I'm going to be allowed to make mead out of some of that,' he said, before turning away.

'You might. Though I warn you, it's nothing like as nice as it sounds.'

'Mine will be,' he called from the living room.

Half an hour later they had bread and cheese and wine laid out in the courtyard, and the sun blazed down on Roma's unprotected head.

'I don't know how you can bear it,' Laurie said, as he always did. 'I'd have sunstroke in five minutes.' He tugged lightly at the brim of his straw hat.

'It's my natural element,' Roma boasted. 'It

brings me to life. I put it down to being born in January and spending my first five months of life yearning for some sun. Since then, I've never been able to get enough of it. Carlos was the same – being Spanish, I suppose. It was one of the few things we had in common.'

Laurie smiled neutrally, showing no sign of discomfort at the mention of Roma's first husband. 'Not like me then,' he said serenely.

'Not like you,' she nodded. 'Although the child was more your type. Funny, that.' *The child* was as close as Roma could usually get to referring to her daughter. Laurie had learnt to accept this without demur. It was in any case unusual for Justine to be brought into the conversation in any way at all, and Laurie was alerted to the implication that this was a meaningful moment. Roma went on, musingly, 'She always shrank out of direct sunlight, as if she was some kind of vampire.'

'Chalk and cheese,' Laurie remarked.

'From such accidents of incompatibility, tragedy is born,' Roma said melodramatically.

'And there's precious little anyone can do about it,' he tried to soothe.

She sighed. 'I wish I could stop thinking about her, once and for all. She doesn't need me any more. We just keep wounding each other, time after time. She was a truly awful

31

adolescent, confronting me on every tiny thing. I couldn't understand it, except to put it down to a genetic inheritance. Her father's always been very unstable. I think that's why the doctors agreed so readily to section her when she was really bad.'

Laurie had heard some of this story before, but it was no easier to listen to this time. 'Don't go over that again now,' he pleaded. 'It doesn't do any good.'

Roma didn't seem to hear him. 'I actually do wish I could forget all about her,' she went on. 'Animals let their offspring wander off across the savannah and everyone's happy. It's the natural order of things. What's the matter with us that we feel we have to hang on to responsibility and concern throughout our entire lives? It doesn't make sense.'

'I know what brought this on.'

'What?'

'Penn. You often start thinking about Justine when you've seen Penn. I've noticed it before.'

'Really?'

'Definitely.' He reached over and touched her arm. 'It makes sense, after all. There's bound to be an association, even though Penn's always so careful not to mention her cousin.'

'She is, isn't she. I don't think she's lapsed once, in five years. It's always been me who's raised the subject, and that hardly ever. It's remarkable, when you think about it. Such control!'

'You think they see each other?'

'They were always good chums. I shouldn't think that's changed. But who can say?'

'Helen would know,' he ventured. 'She'd probably love to fill you in on the whole thing.'

'My dear sister's dying to have another go at me, and tell me how it's all completely my own fault, and I'm the worst mother in the history of the world.' She sighed. 'It's only because you've always been here that she's restrained herself. She's scared you'll rush to my defence and tell her off. She'd hate that to happen.'

'We never really know who the strong one is, do we?' he said obscurely. 'I can't believe your sister would care a damn about anything I might do.'

A flight of swallows swept joyously across the field behind the house, dancing in the air in a show of such soaring exuberance that the human beings were silenced in awe. Roma spoke slowly, after a few minutes. 'You notice that sort of thing so much more as you get older, don't you?'

'One of the many compensations,' he agreed peaceably. His wife's response startled him.

'*No!*' she said in a choked voice. 'There are no compensations for old age. That isn't what I meant. The young might be too busy to see what

33

the birds are doing . . . but they've got time to make up for it.'

'But—'

'I know. It sounds like a contradiction. It's idiotic of me to kick against something that happens to everybody, that's practically the definition of being alive at all. But I can't help it. It's completely beyond my control.'

'Well, never mind,' he soothed. 'You're not even sixty yet, for heaven's sake. You've got another thirty-five years at least.' He turned his face away from her as he spoke, looking out across the garden and the fields beyond. The expression he hid from her was very different from that suggested by his words.

Penn had done her best to give the full background to Drew and Karen, and they'd done their best to accord her their undivided attention. It wasn't easy. Time went by, the children grew fractious, and Drew remembered some paperwork he'd left undone from the previous week.

Penn described how she and Justine had always been close. They were only six months apart in age, and their mothers were sisters. 'But we look completely different,' she said emphatically. 'We both take after our fathers, you see. Hers Spanish, mine Polish. We used to joke about that; how our mothers couldn't have settled for plain ordinary

Englishmen. And we had our foreign surnames to unite us, as well.'

'Did you go to the same schools?'

She shook her head. 'No, we didn't. We pleaded to be allowed to, but it never happened. We lived just too far apart for it to be feasible.'

When Penn got her first teaching job, after college, Justine had been living close by. They'd laughed about the coincidence, but they both knew that Penn had deliberately applied for posts in the area, she admitted now. 'I suppose it must be the family connection; she's just always been my best friend. And she needed me at the time. She was having a very rough patch and it was important for me to be there for her.'

Drew let her prattle on, following the thread, but making no response. The sooner the story got itself told, the happier he'd be. It wasn't too long before Penn realised she ought to summarise. 'She lives in a funny little cottage now, on a farm. She's never had a proper job, you see, never had much money. She does pottery.'

'Pottery,' Drew echoed. 'Does she have a workshop, then? And a kiln, and all that?'

'She has now,' said Penn shortly.

Drew felt as if he was being led in a very convoluted zigzag where a straight line would have worked very much better. 'When did you last see her?' he asked impatiently. 'And what makes you think there isn't a nice ordinary explanation for her absence?'

'Today's Sunday,' Penn held up her forefinger. 'I last saw her on Tuesday evening. So that's – five days? I'd made an arrangement to see her on Thursday, for lunch, and she didn't show up. I phoned her, and there was no reply. I emailed her – still no reply. Then I went to the cottage and she wasn't there. I've got a key, so I let myself in, and had a look round. It seemed to me that she'd dropped several things at short notice, meaning to come back to them. It's very seriously out of character.'

'Email?' echoed Drew. 'She can afford a computer, then?'

'No, no. It belongs to Philip – the farmer. Except he doesn't really farm now. All his animals were slaughtered in the foot and mouth outbreak. He's some sort of dealer. Anyway, Justine goes to the main house to use his computer. She helps with their child, so she's in the house quite a bit.'

Drew tapped a finger thoughtfully on the arm of his chair, trying to think what else to ask. 'You haven't gone to the police?' he checked.

Penn shook her head. 'They wouldn't take much notice. She's an independent adult, and there's no sign of violence.'

'Have you got any mutual friends? Anyone else who might have some idea of where she's gone?'

'Only the Rentons.'

'And they haven't seen her either?'

Penn closed her eyes in a *give me patience* gesture. 'No,' was all she said.

'How much does she have to do with them? Rather a lot, by the sound of it.'

Penn paused, as if mustering her thoughts. 'It's quite complicated,' she said with a frown. 'Philip doesn't keep much stock, as I said. Just a few sheep, I think. He buys and sells straw, great lorryloads of it, and does a bit of dealing in fodder. Justine's cottage is a long way from the house; a quarter of a mile at least. And she has the use of a small barn, as well. For her pottery.'

Almost lazily, he elicited the rest of the story. It didn't strike him as of very much interest, and he felt no sense of excitement or challenge. Justine babysat the Rentons' daughter, Georgia, and did some secretarial work for Philip on his computer. In return she was charged a very low rent, and allowed to use the computer for email and internet access. Sheena Renton was a workaholic sales manager, commuting to Bristol and away from the farm most of the time. Her life seemed filled with a never-ending succession of new initiatives, launches, promotions, assessments. 'Justine makes fun of all the jargon,' Penn said with sudden relish. 'She can be very funny when she's making mock of someone.'

In the end Drew went into the house to fetch tea, and threw himself dramatically on Karen. 'Save me!' he hissed. 'She's never going to go at this rate.'

'Not a very fascinating mystery then?' she asked, from her cosy place on the couch, with a child on each side. 'I had a feeling it wouldn't be.'

'I think she's making something out of nothing. Although . . . well . . .'

'Drew Slocombe!' she accused. 'You've been hooked, haven't you? Don't pretend to be bored. I know that look.'

'No, really. I think it'll come to nothing.' Drew glanced impatiently at the window onto the patio. 'I'm supposed to be doing that piece for the Natural Death Centre. I'll never finish it now.' He scratched his hairline with frustration. 'What shall I do?'

'Leave it to me,' said Karen. 'I think I know the very thing.'

And she did. She carried Timothy outside, and plonked him on Penn's lap. 'Sorry I've been so selfish with him,' she beamed. 'He's having his bath in a little while, so this is your last chance to play with him. It'll do me a favour, too. Stephanie likes a bit of special time with me, especially on a Sunday.'

Penn got the message. After three minutes of

clumsy dandling, she made a big show of not realising the time, and gathered up her things.

At the front gate, to which Drew had accompanied her, she turned. 'You don't think she's in trouble at all, do you?' she accused.

'Well . . .'

'I didn't want to tell you this, because I'm sure you'll think it's rubbish. But I do rune readings for people.' Drew said nothing. 'And when I did Justine's, on Thursday, I got *Hagalaz* which means radical disruption. Then the symbol for breakthrough – complete transformation – and then the Blank.' She looked at him fiercely. 'And that means death. Those last two in combination are the most powerful thing you can draw. And believe me, Drew, I'm good at the runes. My readings are always accurate. So when Justine didn't turn up for our lunch date, I was sure something had happened to her.'

Drew sighed. 'I said I'd do what I can to help. I'll go to her cottage tomorrow evening, and see what strikes me about it. I can't say more than that, can I?'

'You might say you believe me,' she flashed, before getting into her car and driving off with the briefest of waves.

Penn hadn't missed the glance that Drew and Karen exchanged when she first mentioned Justine. There'd been something avid, especially in Drew's eyes – something almost predatory. He'd wanted to hear the whole story, leaning slightly towards her. 'Just because a person disappears doesn't mean they've been murdered,' he said. Penn thought he lingered on the word *murdered* as if saying *rapture* or *merriment*. In short, he'd reacted very much as she'd hoped he would. Drew Slocombe was obviously obsessed with violent death, preferably with a mystery attached, and Penn had handed him the very thing he craved. The eager hungry look in his eye had betrayed him and belied the charming boyish manner he adopted.

The brief reference to person named Maggs had been intriguing. 'She's a marvel,' Drew said, as if repeating something he'd said countless times. But Penn had gleaned very little more about her than that. A young female partner in the undertaking business, who apparently had many skills and talents, and who of necessity would be made party to the Case of the Missing Cousin, as Penn suspected Drew had instantly labelled her story.

Everything had been kind and calm and sympathetic, but there had been a moment when the summer sky suddenly turned heavy and sinister. The blue intensified, the air thickened, until she could hardly breathe. She hadn't known Drew well enough to predict his response, and it was never easy to manipulate people into doing what you wanted. She had almost lost his attention at one point, despite the promising beginning. She'd said too much, waffling on about the Rentons and pottery and how far back she and Justine went. He'd clearly been impatient for her to go, and more than half inclined to dismiss the whole story as a lot of groundless anxiety. The bit about the runes had been a gamble. Her experience had been that the most surprising people took these things seriously, especially when the readings often did turn out to be amazingly accurate.

And she had eventually secured his co-operation. When it came down to it, of course, he could hardly have refused. She was Karen's cousin, after all.

Karen too was aware of the persuasiveness of the cousinship. 'I feel rather responsible,' she said to Drew, on Monday morning. 'You're only appeasing her because she's family.'

'I don't expect I am,' he said. 'To be honest, I had Roma in mind more than you.'

'Charming.'

'Wait till you meet her. You'll like her as much as I do. She's a real original.'

'Bit off, getting sacked for hitting a primary school kid, though,' Karen said. 'I thought Penn was a bit over the top about that. It's absolutely not on these days.'

'We don't know the details,' Drew objected. 'The kid probably had it coming. And you can see she's not a woman to stand any nonsense. Very old-fashioned she'd be as a teacher. Stern but fair, that sort of thing.'

'And what was that stuff about not speaking to her daughter for five years? Sounds very extreme. How do you know she'll be pleased with you for cooperating with Penn? She might be glad Justine's disappeared.'

'That's possible,' Drew agreed diplomatically.

Karen crunched a piece of toast, while peeling a banana for Timmy and dribbling pieces of discarded bread across the floor with the side of her foot. None of this prevented her from continuing the conversation.

'No, listen. Think about it. Presumably she – Justine – must know there'd be people worrying about her. Penn, for a start. And the people on the farm. So either she's a selfish cow who doesn't care if she upsets people, or something caused her to rush off before she had a chance to tell anybody.'

'Maybe Penn was driving her mad and she's just gone off for a break.'

'You think Penn's a bit . . . smothering?' The word came out with a mouthful of toast crumbs.

'She could be,' Drew conceded. 'After all, she doesn't appear to have a bloke. She wastes a lovely summer day visiting an ageing aunt and a cousin she hasn't seen for decades.' He cocked his head at her, deliberately caricaturing the situation.

'Well, I don't know about that,' Karen began, before realising he wasn't serious. 'Oh, go to work, will you.' She threw the banana skin at him.

He caught it deftly and added it to the overflowing compost bucket in the corner. 'Ah, there's Maggs. Now I'll have to tell her the whole story as well. She can come with me this evening, if she's not doing anything.'

'Go on then,' Karen flapped him away. 'I've got nappies to wash.'

Maggs greeted him warily. 'Nothing from the hospice, then?' she enquired, as he opened the office door for her. 'Dragging on a bit, isn't it?' The hospice was overseeing the dying of a Mr Graham French, who was destined for a grave in Drew's field when the time finally came. Drew had visited him three times, liking him more on each occasion, and the protraction of his passing was stretching nerves on all sides.

'Just shows, you never know,' Drew said routinely.

'Hmmm. I thought they would have given him the killer dose by this time. It doesn't seem kind to let it take as long as this.'

'He's not in too much pain. Maybe he asked them not to. I got the feeling he's quite happy to let it take its time, when I saw him last week.'

'Scared, I suppose,' hazarded Maggs.

Drew shook his head. 'I don't think he is, oddly enough. There's no sign of it in his eyes. He says he's had a good life, done most of the things he set out to do, and really loves the idea of his atoms turning into grass.'

'The perfect customer,' Maggs nodded.

'Or would be, if it wasn't for the Wicked Daughter.' Mr French had two daughters, Mrs Jennings and Mrs Huggett, the Good one and the Wicked one respectively. Mrs Huggett didn't like burials, hated the idea of a semi-permeable cardboard container which would allow entry to worms and water and other substances below ground. She had phoned Drew and berated him for his disgusting practices. Mrs Jennings, on the other hand, was entirely supportive of her father, and had written Drew a note to that effect, giving her phone number and making it clear that she would be one of his more hands-on customers when it came to preparing the body for burial.

'I'm going to be quite sad when he does

die,' Drew admitted. 'He's a really nice man.'

'Occupational hazard,' Maggs said, with scant sympathy, effectively curtailing this topic of conversation.

Drew had some difficulty in broaching the subject of the missing Justine. Maggs had been very much more closely involved with his last brush with mysterious death than Karen had, and was party to most of its more embarrassing aspects. The fact that yet again the central characters were all female was sure to cause his business partner some amusement.

He decided to come at it obliquely. 'Had a visit from Karen's cousin yesterday,' he began. 'Did I tell you she was coming?'

Maggs frowned. 'Can't remember,' she said. 'Did you do that piece for the Natural Death outfit?'

'I made a start. The cousin stayed hours longer than we expected her to.'

'Visitors can be a pain,' she said vaguely, turning her attention to the post that had been sitting inside the office door. 'Hey, look! The Briggses have paid at last. And they want to know if we can supply a hazel tree over the grave. Hazel – we haven't had one of them yet, have we? Don't they grow nuts?' She grinned. 'Doesn't that mean that if you eat the nuts, you'll be eating bits of Old Lady Briggs?'

Drew had had enough. 'Maggs,' he blurted, 'are you doing anything this evening?'

She turned her clear black eyes on him, widening them to show the very white whites. It was a trick she had, that Drew always enjoyed. He looked at her, her brown skin several shades darker after two months of summer sunshine, her ample contours clearly outlined in a tight T-shirt and stretchy pedal-pushers. She'd worked for him for nearly two years now, and they understood each other to the core. 'Why?' she invited.

'Um – detective work,' he said quickly.

She tilted her head sideways. 'Oh?'

'This cousin – her name's Penn – she's worried about another cousin, Justine—'

'Whoa! Too many cousins. Explain.'

'Right. Well, Karen's mother and Penn's father were brother and sister. *Are* brother and sister, I should say. So they're first cousins.'

'Penn – this person's called Penn?'

'Right. After William Penn, the well-known Quaker.'

'Who founded Pennsylvania. Got it. And . . .'

'And Penn's mother is Roma Millan's sister. You know Roma Millan – the woman who sells the honey in Pitcombe.'

Maggs shook her head. 'We get our honey from the supermarket.'

'Shut up and listen. Roma has a daughter

called Justine. So she's first cousin to Penn as well, but on the other side of her family. They're quite close buddies, it seems – see each other all the time. I suppose the cousin bit doesn't really matter, the point is, Justine's gone missing in the past two or three weeks, and Penn's getting very worried. Splurged it all out, just as she was leaving. And then stayed about two more hours filling in the background.'

'Hmmm,' Maggs adopted her sceptical face. 'Did she already know you were Drew Slocombe, Ace Detective, on the side?'

He thought about it. 'I doubt it. Only if Roma told her, and I wouldn't think *she* could have heard anything. They haven't lived here long and it's not as if I've been headline news recently.'

'So out of the blue, this cousin of Karen's asks you to track down another cousin. She must have had some idea that you were into this sort of thing. You don't just ask people to help search for missing persons unless you think they've got some sort of special interest or talent for it. Or if you do, you go to somebody you already know and trust. What about Justine's father? What about—'

'Okay,' he stopped her. 'I get the message.' He tapped a front tooth with his pencil. 'You think I'm being set up?'

'I think it's possible. But carry on; I'm with you so far.'

'Good. Now – we're going to a village called Tedburn St Mary, the other side of Exeter, this evening, to Justine's cottage, to see if we can discover signs of disturbance, or anything to suggest she left under duress, as they say.'

'Hasn't Penn already had a look?'

'She says she wants a second opinion.'

'What's she like, anyway? I need to know more about her if I'm going to be involved in this.' She stuck out her chin. 'I never signed on as an amateur detective, you know. This is something you got yourself into, nothing to do with me.'

He chose to concentrate on the original question. 'She's pretty – very like Karen, actually. Neurotic, gets into a state about the slightest things. We couldn't say anything without her working herself up. Wasps, teachers—'

'Lots of people are scared of wasps and teachers,' Maggs remarked. 'She was all right about the field, then?'

'Not really. When I said Roma was thinking of booking a plot, she freaked out then, as well.'

'Sounds boringly normal to me,' dismissed Maggs.

'She reads runes,' said Drew slightly desperately.

'Hmmm,' said Maggs, and then asked, 'What does Karen say?'

'Something along the lines of *Here we go again.*'

'I don't blame her.'

'But we'll do it anyway, won't we?' he said. 'You wouldn't leave me to cope all on my own?'

'Course I wouldn't,' she winked at him. 'I was beginning to worry that we were never going to do anything but bury people and argue about chapels.'

He raised a forefinger sternly. 'The chapel argument has been settled,' he told her. 'We're definitely not having one.'

'That's what you think,' she muttered, turning to go to the filing cabinet.

CHAPTER THREE

Monday morning was an unwelcome dawn for Detective Sergeant Den Cooper. It was his first day back at work after a fortnight's holiday on Corfu. The whole thing had been a horrible mistake. Greece was intolerably hot in July and August, the girl he'd gone with had rapidly let her mask slip and turned into a whingeing monster with no interest in anything that Corfu had to offer. They'd trudged down to the same beach every day, swum for an hour, spent three hours in the same taverna for lunch, gone back to their room for a siesta, and then sought out a succession of ad hoc night-time entertainments which seemed to get worse by the day. He had come home burnt, fat and depressed.

But he wasn't at all enthusiastic about going back to work, either. He'd been based at Okehampton Police Station since first qualifying as a Constable, and it was stalely familiar by this time, nearly seven years later, despite having progressed to Detective Sergeant during that time. Most of his colleagues had moved on and he was aware of a reputation as a plodding worker, conscientious but uninspired most of the time. It was Cooper who went the extra mile to ensure that there was no lingering doubt about a villain's guilt, Cooper who was kind to old people, tolerant of juvenile miscreants and who got to convey bad news to relatives. Cooper who had had a messy love life, and was showing little sign of getting that side of things sorted.

The station seemed to have been put under a sleeping spell when he presented himself for duty. Another hot day, all the windows were open, hoping to catch the light breeze that the building's position generally enjoyed. No phones were ringing, no computer printers chattering.

'Everything quiet then?' he asked Julie, on the front desk.

'As the grave,' she sighed.

'So you haven't missed me?'

'Didn't even notice you weren't here, to be honest. You may as well take another two weeks for all the work there is.'

'You should be glad. Not many places can claim to have a redundant police force these days.'

Julie reached down and produced a paperback book. 'Funny you should say that. I picked this up in one of the tourist places. It's an old novel, set in a village down near Teignmouth. They arrest this girl on suspicion of setting fire to a hayrick, but they don't like to lock her up, because the jail hasn't been used for years and it's full of hen shit. Not like Teignmouth these days, eh.'

Den smiled. Julie's passion for bygone fiction was legendary. She'd read everything, and drove everybody mad by comparing present experiences to something she'd just come across in a book. It got her into trouble at times. *Julie, for heaven's sake, why can't you live in the real world?* was a commonly-heard complaint.

'Teignmouth's a dump,' he agreed. 'Not too many hayricks round there now, either. What was the penalty, by the way?'

'What? For burning the hay? Oh, transportation for a first offence. Hanging if you did it more than once. Though it seems the judge had some discretion about that. Scary, anyway.'

'I don't know.' Cooper was wistful. 'If they hadn't arrested anyone for years, it must have worked pretty well as a deterrent.'

'Maybe.' Julie looked up at him, as everyone

had to. 'You don't look as if Corfu did much to refresh you,' she observed.

'Corfu was fine; the company was disappointing,' he summed up.

'Oh dear. New girlfriend not up to scratch?'

'You see a different side of people on holiday.'

'So – ?'

A year or two ago, he would have resented the interest. He'd struggled to keep his private life separate from work. Now it didn't seem to matter any more. 'So she is now an ex-girlfriend,' he said baldly.

'Well, she's got plenty of company, hasn't she? That must be quite a big club by now.'

He sighed and picked at his nose where the skin was peeling. 'I'm giving up on women,' he announced. 'It's obviously never going to work.'

'You're probably right,' came the unsympathetic reply.

Philip Renton drove jerkily, impatiently overtaking at every opportunity, only to find himself forced to a crawl behind yet another maddening old person, apparently out for a leisurely spin. Surely it wasn't his imagination – there really were more of them every time he went out.

Recklessly, he pulled out from behind the

latest old dodderer, forcing the Saab into third gear and revving ferociously as he passed the Fiat Uno. He threw its driver a savage look, which went entirely unheeded. Coming towards him was an oil tanker, travelling much faster than Philip had first judged, leaving scant space for him to return to his own side of the road. Swinging the wheel, he made it, cutting up the Uno in the process. The tanker sounded its horn in a long reproach, and Philip scorched away, grinning manically to himself.

Ahead the road was temporarily clear, and he reached ninety before having to slow again behind a caravan. A glance in the mirror showed no sign of the Uno, but if he couldn't pass soon, it would catch up with him, and the driver was unlikely to feel very well-disposed towards him after his demonstration of impatience. At the very least, Philip would feel humiliated at his lack of progress.

It would all be perfectly all right, of course, if only they'd put some money into improving the roads. This stretch was crying out for some dual carriageway – with all these stupid dips and bends making it so tricky to overtake on single lanes. But the car knew its stuff, and he shot past the caravan the instant an opportunity arose. This was more like it, he rejoiced – and only six or seven more miles to the motorway now.

He hadn't wanted to do this trip, anyway. He'd planned a lazy Monday tidying his office, and sending out some advertising copy to a few of the local papers. The straw harvest had been good, and his stores were growing rapidly, as he bought up the product of fifty or sixty farms across the South of England. The trick, as always, was going to be to get ahead of the competition, persuade his customers to order enough for the whole winter's needs, at a price that could turn out to be inflated. The whole business was based on risk. A long cold winter, with animals lying in that crucial week or two longer than usual, could make straw a highly sought-after commodity. Those who bought extra stocks now might make a modest profit by reselling it later. But a short mild winter would leave them with a surplus that nobody wanted. Philip was a clever salesman – he let people think they'd got a bargain, as well as being foresighted enough to lay up secure stores for the winter to come. Considering he was new to the game, he'd taken to it very successfully. Unsettling, then, the way it came over him every few days how much he disliked it; how much he craved to go back to the days when he'd been a *real* farmer, with real animals and none of this nonsense with giant lorries and all this wheeling and dealing.

'So restock, why don't you?' his wife and

others asked him repeatedly. 'Everybody else has.'

It was true that all his neighbours had bought in new herds of dairy or beef cattle, new flocks of sheep, too. They seemed to have got over the agony of 2001. Philip, it seemed, could not.

He'd been called out by Ralph Gardner, all the way up the M5, nearly as far as Tewkesbury. Ralph wouldn't take the responsibility of passing 150 acres of wheat straw as best quality, because there was ragwort growing in amongst the corn. Although straw was seldom used as fodder, there were always going to be animals nibbling at it, if it was left outdoors where they could reach it, and ragwort could kill horses and cattle. Philip had been irritable. 'Well, is there or isn't there? Tell him we won't buy it if it's not clean.'

'It's just in one corner of one field. He says he'll keep that stuff separate.'

'So what's the problem?'

'I don't trust him. And I haven't got time to stand here watching him while he combines the field. If you speak to him, put the fear of the Devil into him, he's not likely to try anything.'

Ralph was part of Philip's network, negotiating on his behalf, arranging transport, scheduling pick-ups and drops, but he was always careful to avoid taking responsibility for hard decisions.

Sheena wouldn't be back till late – probably

they'd turn up together somewhere around seven. The evening meal would be some microwaved junk that would have made Philip's father gag. Philip had grown up on Gladcombe Farm, his father a specialist in dairy cows and sheep, the yard full of hens and geese and two or three collies. But the entire stock had been wiped out the year before in the cataclysmic foot and mouth epidemic, Frank Renton had hanged himself in the barn, and Philip was left to pick up the pieces. He'd taken up the dealing, and let his wife, with her high-powered career, bring in three times the cash that he could earn.

The old cottage, home to old Sid Pike for sixty years, had been one of their residual assets. Sid had reluctantly gone to live with his daughter near Taunton, and Justine Pereira had been taken on as tenant. The arrangement had worked smoothly, Justine doing fill-in childminding for young Georgia, when both parents were out in the evenings or at weekends. Justine worked at her pottery in a small barn, keeping herself afloat financially. As far as Philip had been aware, she had no objection to the babysitting. She took Georgia for walks, played with her, told her stories, and in many ways acted more like a loving mother than Sheena did.

He'd been warned, of course, that having a young female lodger was asking for trouble.

Ralph had been the first to put it into words: 'If she's pretty, you'll be running off down there every chance you get,' he'd predicted. 'And if she's not, there'll be other problems. Depression. Loneliness. What's she doing, living all by herself like that, anyway?'

Philip had dismissed it all. 'Keep up, mate,' he'd admonished his colleague. 'Women these days, they're a different breed. She's an artist, putting everything into her work. No time for any goings-on.'

'And *is* she pretty?'

Philip shrugged. 'Not particularly. Very thin and pale. Big strong hands, from working the clay, I suppose. Straggly black hair.'

'Hmmm,' was Ralph's knowing reply.

Justine had lived in the cottage for almost two years now. Trouble had accompanied her, after all. But not at all in the way Ralph had predicted.

Well-trained by her old-fashioned father, Penn sat down that evening to write a short letter:

> *Dear Karen and Drew*
> *It was a great treat to meet you at the weekend, as well as Stephanie and Timothy. They're a real credit to you. Lunch was delicious, and we were lucky*

with the weather, weren't we. It's probably going to rain for a month, now!

I'm sorry to dump all that stuff about Justine onto you, but I would appreciate anything you can glean about her whereabouts. It's ever so good of you to take an interest in something that must seem very peculiar. I'll catch up with you tomorrow evening, to talk it over again.

Once again, many thanks for your hospitality.

With my very best wishes

Penn

Roma let the dog jump out of the car ahead of her, watching it fondly for a moment before scooping up her shopping and ducking out of the vehicle herself. Laurie was inspecting runner beans inside the front gate. 'Aren't they lovely!' he said. 'They grow them for the flowers in some places, you know, and hardly bother with the edible angle.'

Roma ignored him. 'You'll never guess what's just happened to me,' she interrupted.

He looked at her, noting the bristling quiver of her shoulders. 'Dangerous driving accusations?' he hazarded.

She narrowed her eyes at him. 'How did you guess?'

'Sheer luck.'

'Well, it's ridiculous. Lolly knows to keep still when we're driving.'

'You won't get any sympathy from me. Who saw you?'

'Some officious young constable with nothing better to do. He actually *chased* me, pushing me off the road into a layby. That was far more dangerous than having the dog on my lap.'

'There was a woman stopped for eating a piece of toast while driving, not so long ago. Dogs on laps are obviously well beyond the limit of tolerance these days. If you persist in doing it, you'll have to take the consequences.'

'Don't be so boring.' Roma tossed her head. 'Everything's gone safety mad, these days. They all think they can live forever if they just follow all these lunatic rules. Haven't they any *idea* of how it all actually works?'

Her husband sighed softly. 'Evidently not,' he murmured. 'Come and have some coffee. You're not going to be charged, are you?'

'Certainly not. They wouldn't dare.'

'No – they probably wouldn't,' he agreed.

But Laurie knew her well enough to realise that she'd been quite badly stirred up by the incident. He could imagine the righteous indignation on the face of the policeman, the subtle scorn directed at this middle-aged madwoman. It happened to Roma over and over again: the rash assertion of her unconventional ideas so often brought her face-to-face with other people's contempt. And contempt was very wounding, all the more so because it was generally what she herself felt towards the world at large. The ongoing restless unfocussed power struggle that she waged against authority and institutions was exhausting and, Laurie felt, quite unnecessary.

The protracted battle against dismissal from her teaching job had badly shaken her, but hadn't noticeably altered her general attitude. Laurie had been as supportive as he knew how to be, but he knew he'd been disappointing. They had only been married a year when the business started and the shock to him had been very nearly as bad as it had to her. They both knew she was effectively on her own in this and other crises, not least because of her prickly reaction to his clumsy attempts to help.

She wasn't always like this, of course. Absorbed with her bees or her fruit bushes, on long companionable walks, reminiscing about her early years, she was the best possible partner. Funny, shrewd, uninhibited – Laurie knew how to appreciate her good qualities and to turn his face away from the flipside of her nature. If there were taboo areas between them, well, he'd just have to live with that. Nobody was perfect, after all.

'It's turning out nice,' he commented. 'They said it'd clear up.'

'Hmmm,' was her unconvinced reply. 'We've seen the best of the summer, all the same. There's rain forecast for tomorrow. It all goes by so quickly. The creeper'll be turning red any day now.'

'Nonsense,' he protested. 'It's got three weeks yet, at least.'

'Well see,' was all she said, leaving Laurie with a feeling that she wasn't just talking about the changing seasons.

That afternoon, with the sun making a poor effort at breaking up the persistent cloud layer, Laurie heard the phone ringing from where he was making a new rock garden, some distance from the house. Ten minutes later, Roma came out looking for him.

'Did you hear the phone?' she asked, her voice unnaturally tight.

He nodded. 'Anything interesting?'

'It was Penn. She's been getting herself in a state about Justine . . .' The name emerged with trails of emotion attached to it. Laurie could almost see it floating over the lawn. He knew from the constriction in his own chest that they were about to embark on something that any sensible person would work hard to avoid.

'Oh?' he said.

'Some story about the wretched girl being missing. It sounds quite odd, but then I don't know any of the background. Why has she come to me about it? Especially now, when she could have said something yesterday. You know, I had a feeling she was keeping something back. Even more than usual, I mean.'

'Justine's missing?' he echoed. 'It sounds as if Penn's very worried. Who else would she turn to for help?'

'She's not *turning* to me. She wanted to tell me she's asked Drew to help find her. As if she needs my blessing.' Roma frowned, a hand on her throat. 'There's obviously much more to it than she's told me.'

'Drew?'

'You know – that boy with the burial ground. Married to Penn's cousin. She went to see him after leaving us yesterday.'

'But why tell him about Justine?'

'Oh, he's got a bit of a name for solving mysteries like this. In the right line of business for it, I suppose. He more or less offered, the moment Penn let drop that . . . Justine . . . was missing.' It didn't seem to be getting any easier to articulate her daughter's name.

Laurie cocked his head sideways, as if hoping to catch some omitted piece of data. 'Am I being very dense? I don't seem to be following this very well. How long has Justine been missing, and did you know about it before today?'

Roma moved unsteadily to a slatted garden table, and leant on it. Laurie experienced a surge of anxiety. 'Are you all right, my darling? Here, sit down. You've gone all pale and wimbly.' He forced a flippant laugh, more for his own reassurance than hers.

She echoed the sound and stood up straighter. 'I'm perfectly all right,' she said firmly. 'I don't know what came over me. It's just turning into one of those days, where you wonder what the hell's going to happen next. I could kill Penn for involving me in this. Why should I *care*? I haven't seen the blasted girl for five years, anyway. For all I know, she's been missing ever since then. It's the same as if she was dead – same effect, at least.'

'It's not the same, though,' Laurie told her, summoning up the strength to voice his thoughts. 'If she was dead, you'd have to give up hope of things coming right between you. And—' he fixed her with a fierce look '—don't tell me you haven't wanted that. You've been waiting for her to phone or write with an olive branch, or to turn up with a new little grandchild astride her hip. Even after five years, you can still pretend it's all just a temporary interruption to your normal relationship. You'd have to forget all that if she was dead.'

'Well, she isn't dead. Of course she isn't. Who said anything about her being dead, anyway?'

'You did,' Laurie reminded her. 'And I'm beginning to think that Penn probably did, as well. I can't think of anything else that would knock you so off balance. So sit down and tell me the whole thing from the beginning.'

They settled side by side on a wrought iron garden seat, casting brief glances at each other's face, but mainly addressing the lawn and the field beyond. 'Justine's been living on some farm near Exeter, apparently. And Penn visits her a lot.'

'And you didn't realise they saw each other frequently?'

Roma shook her head. 'I had no idea. I didn't think their paths had crossed since we . . . well, since we fell out. For all I knew, she was still in London. That's where I've imagined her.' She threw a look at her husband. 'Penn didn't tell you any of this, did she, when she came here last week?'

'Most definitely not. She wouldn't have done that. It would be demeaning.'

'Would it?' Roma frowned. 'How?'

'Well, going behind your back, giving me information that I wasn't allowed to share with you. Maybe not demeaning. Unethical. Divisive.

And since I never met Justine, it wouldn't have been very appropriate.'

Roma inhaled deeply. 'I'd certainly have been furious if I'd found out,' she acknowledged. 'Anger's always the easy option, isn't it.'

'We all know how hurt you've been by the rift,' he said gently.

Her breathing began to thicken, and he saw the tightening of her jaw. 'And there I was, trying to keep up the act of an uncaring monster,' she laughed shakily.

'That doesn't matter now. Please tell me what Penn said. The whole thing.'

'She apologised for worrying me, to start with. Said she'd hoped it would all turn out to be nothing, and I never need know about it. Clever of her, come to think of it. Whetting my curiosity like that. The rest is what I've just told you. She and Justine have been close friends since . . . well, all along, I suppose. She went to have a look at the cottage, last week, after Justine failed to turn up for a lunch they'd planned, and didn't answer her phone. Apparently, there's no sign anywhere of Justine . . .' She swallowed painfully.

'Didn't she ask the farmer if he knew where she was?'

'She says she did, but he was impatient and unconcerned. Apparently the cottage is some

66

distance from the main house, and Justine didn't see a great deal of them. But she hinted that she doesn't think he's telling her everything.'

'So why not call the police and let them extract the truth from the chap?'

'She's convinced they'd show no interest, because Justine's a responsible adult, and there's no suggestion of foul play. So instead she's asked Drew to help. That's why she phoned.'

'I'm beginning to see,' Laurie nodded. 'So, what did you tell her?'

'To calm down and not jump to any conclusions. What *could* I say? I can't see any use in invoking the law. But you're right that this Philip needs to be spoken to again. I wondered if you might be the person to do that.'

'What? You're teasing . . . aren't you?' He looked at her intently. 'This has nothing to do with me. I'd make the most awful mess of it – you know I would.'

Roma pursed her lips, her mouth suddenly an old woman's display of pleats and puckers, the upper lip leathery and brown. Far from repelling him, it had the effect of increasing Laurie's fondness for her. She was always so tough and decisive, but the weight of getting through the years was inexorably dragging her down. It seemed a shame that this had happened – whatever *this* might be. He knew she didn't want to be bothered with it, but to get on with her gardening and beekeeping in peace.

'It's rather a pity Penn chose to confide in you,' he suggested. 'Don't you think?'

Roma tossed her head dismissively. 'Not at all,' she asserted. 'If my daughter's in some sort of trouble, it's only right that I should know about it.'

'That's not what you said ten minutes ago,' he observed.

'I know,' she admitted.

'Well, I hope I've made it clear that I'm not going to do any detective work for you,' he said flatly. 'I'm not up to anything like that, and I can't believe any good would come of it. If the girl's in trouble, it's a matter for the police. And if she's deliberately done a bunk, she won't thank us for ferreting her out.'

'But . . .' Roma sighed. 'Oh, well, I suppose you're right. Come on – we'd better have runner beans with those chops, I suppose.'

'Of course,' he confirmed, in mock indignation.

CHAPTER FOUR

Justine had lost count of the days, drifting in and out of a nightmare state where she dreamt of being attacked with a hammer, or buried alive in the desert for the ants to eat. How long could people live without water? She tried to assess the damage that was being inflicted on her body. The blood thickening, moving more sluggishly, carrying its essential cargo less and less efficiently. Hands tied behind her, she had nonetheless managed to make a complete investigation of her prison, and hazard a guess as to where she might be.

It was a small stone house, with trees growing all around it. It didn't seem to have been lived in for a long time. It was very dark and it had taken her hours to adjust to the gloom. When she did, it was to see thick cobwebs everywhere, drifts of dust and dead leaves around the edges of the ground floor rooms. There was a kitchen, with a sink and taps. She struggled to turn the taps with her mouth, licking desperately at the rusty orifices where water should emerge. But the supply had been turned off, or the pipes ruptured by frost. Nothing but a very unpleasant metallic taste met her tongue.

Upstairs had two small rooms, neither with running water. If there was a lavatory or bath anywhere, they must be in an outbuilding, to which she had no access. All she found was a large damp patch on one outer wall, where glistening beads of moisture still lingered. It was foul and disgusting, but she scooped them into her mouth when the thirst became unbearable.

Having her hands tied behind her back had been the first intimation that this was not some weird kind of game. To start with, that's what she had assumed: that her abductor was in fact only teasing. It had taken her slow befuddled brain far too long to grasp the seriousness of what was going on. Then, with wrists lashed tightly together, she'd gone berserk, running in a horrible bent position as fast as she could away from this inexplicable danger. In no time, she'd fallen over, rolling painfully onto a shoulder, an instinctive move to save her face from injury.

But she still hadn't given in. She'd started to scream, hoping there'd be someone in the farmhouse to hear her, while knowing there wouldn't be. The scream had been a mistake. A cloth had been clamped over her nose and mouth, a sweet terrifying smell filling her head and quickly knocking her out.

And thanks to that unconsciousness, she had no idea what had happened next, or how long it might have lasted. She could have been driven fifty miles or five hundred yards.

When she came to, she was being dragged backwards by the arms into this loathsome place, and then thrown down on the floor. Astonishment had taken precedence over all other emotions. Dazed, her head ringing, heart pounding, she could only stare at her assailant and stammer, 'But why . . . ?'

'It's for your own good,' came the breathless reply. 'You'll understand one day that there wasn't any alternative.' There was something pleading in the voice.

Wildly, Justine had looked round. 'Will you bring me food? I'll die here otherwise.'

'We'll see about that,' was the only response. After closing and locking the door, the hammering began. It seemed to last a long time, while Justine stumbled crazily from one room to another, looking for a chance to escape. Gradually the house became darker and darker, and she understood that boards were being nailed over all the downstairs windows.

Derelict though it might be, the house seemed all too sturdily built. The cob walls looked to be over a foot thick, and the windowpanes far too small to crawl through, even if she could break them without lacerating herself, and then push aside the wooden barricades. Another door at the back was locked, and a high bolt rammed home for good measure. She didn't notice the cessation of the hammering in her distraught state. All she heard was the receding sound of the car engine, as she was left all alone in her lightless prison.

Drew was not deceived by Maggs's cheerful humming as they drove slowly down the bumpy farm drive. 'Strange places, farms,' he said. 'I get the distinct feeling that we're trespassing.'

'It is a bit spooky,' she agreed. 'But we're calling on Justine Pereira, that's all. Friends of her cousin, with an interest in her pots. Probably happens all the time.'

'I doubt it – the place is almost impossible to find,' Drew objected. 'Lucky we left early, or it would have been dark before we got here.'

Early was an understatement. Maggs had become more and more excited through the morning, unable to settle to any useful work and driving Drew mad with constant surmisings as to what could have happened to the missing Justine. So at three o'clock he'd clapped his hands and announced they were going right away. Phone calls would be diverted through to the mobile and with luck they could make people think they were in the office – or at least out in the burial field. It was by no means unusual for them to have absolutely nothing to do for days on end, even though Drew was regularly asked to officiate at non-religious funerals, and they devoted considerable effort to publicity and promotion of their services. This particular week threatened to be a quiet one, with Mr French the only customer likely to require their services. And even he could linger on for ages yet.

'It'd be more fun in the dark,' said Maggs with bravado. 'All these great big trees, look! And what a nice view down there.' She peered between two large oaks to the fields beyond. 'Is this all part of the farm, do you think?'

Ahead of them was a broad farmyard surrounded by buildings. There was a stone house to the right, its front door opening directly onto the cobbles of the yard. In front of them was a large barn, twice the size of the house, made of whitewashed cob. A large square opening suggested it had an upper floor; stout double doors at ground level were firmly closed.

'Wow!' said Maggs. 'Look at all this.'

Behind the barn, more sheds and open-fronted buildings were visible, some containing stacks of hay and straw. There was no sign of any livestock, not even a dog.

'I think we go down here,' Drew decided, spotting a continuing track to their left.

'You could get seriously lost amongst all this.' Maggs couldn't stop her awed inspection of the complex buildings. 'Half of them don't look used.'

'It's just a normal farm,' said Drew.

'Well, I think it's scary.' They'd driven fifty yards down the narrowing track before a small cottage came into view.

'Bloody hell! These ruts are going to wreck the exhaust,' Drew complained.

'Nah,' Maggs scoffed. 'The van'll cope with this, no problem.'

They'd chosen to use their all-purpose, much-loved van, rather than Karen's little Fiat – wisely, as it turned out.

'That must be it,' she said superfluously. 'You'd think she'd be scared to live here all by herself.'

'Scared?' He raised his eyebrows at her. It wasn't a word she uttered often, and now it came twice in a single minute.

'I don't mean *I* would be. But most women are wimps.'

Drew knew better than to comment on that.

They let themselves in through the front door with the key they found under a brick, as described by Penn. 'Not very secure,' said Maggs.

'Not much need to be,' muttered Drew. He was already inside, stepping warily into a room that turned out to be the kitchen. The air smelt stagnant, with a hint of something rotten. Vegetable, rather than animal, he decided with relief. Drew's nose was flawless in such matters. He rather thought a cabbage had been left to decay in a rack somewhere. There was a Rayburn – stone cold – and a good-sized pine table. Two handmade rugs hung on hooks above a cupboard that seemed about to fall to bits.

'Hey!' breathed Maggs. 'Isn't this great!'

'Is it?'

'Look at this floor! These flagstones must be hundreds of years old. And the shelves – real oak. Practically as old as the floor, I should think.'

'Dusty,' observed Drew. 'And chilly. Must be freezing in winter.'

'Not with the Rayburn going,' she corrected him. 'Let's see what's through here.' She dived through an open door into a larger room. It had two good-sized windows, one looking out on the area at the back of the house, and one onto the track where Drew's van was parked.

There was an original oil painting on the wall depicting a female nude in the act of stepping into her knickers. It was very good, as far as Drew could judge. He could feel the texture of the woman's legs, the thinness of her ribs, the gloss of her black hair. Peering closer, he found a signature that looked like 'C. Perrier'.

Ranged along the back wall was a pile of cushions, at least eight of them, large and well filled, which presumably served as a couch. It seemed surprisingly old-fashioned for someone in her twenties. Drew could just remember his mother going through a phase of removing all furniture from their living room and replacing it with cushions like these. A hardback book was lying on the floor, open and face down, as if someone had been reading it only moments before. A closer inspection revealed it to be *White Teeth* by Zadie Smith. Justine had evidently nearly finished it: the book was open at page 417.

'Nice picture,' said Maggs without enthusiasm. It seemed she preferred the kitchen. A half-filled mug of cold scummy coffee sat on the floor near the book.

'Okay,' said Drew. 'Time for the detective bit.'

Maggs cocked her head. 'We-e-e-e-ell,' she

began, 'she was sitting here, drinking coffee and reading. No telly, you notice. Then someone came to the door. She got up and they told her something that meant she had to leave in a rush. She didn't ask them in, because then she'd have given them a drink as well, and there's only one cup. What's that noise?'

They traced the hissing sound to a radio, plugged in and switched on, but off station, so there was nothing but atmospherics. 'Maybe someone jogged it,' suggested Maggs. 'Maybe there was a struggle.'

'No other sign of it,' Drew pointed out.

'Well, what would there be? There isn't much to be knocked over. The cushions look a bit bashed about.' On closer inspection, Drew agreed with her, although there was nothing that couldn't be explained by a person lolling across them and burrowing down to get comfortable.

'Didn't you say Penn had already had a look round?' Maggs asked. When he nodded, she went on, 'So isn't it strange that she left the radio like this? Wouldn't she have turned it off?'

'Maybe she only glanced in here, just to check that Justine wasn't asleep on the cushions.'

'Or dead,' Maggs added.

'Right.' He heaved a small sigh. 'Let's try upstairs.'

Justine's bedroom also had a large window,

but contained considerably more furniture than downstairs. The bed was covered with a pink and white quilt, which to Drew's inexpert eye looked handmade. Certainly not by any means an ordinary duvet. A small upholstered chair was piled high with clothes, some of them inside out, and all of them crumpled carelessly. A table in the window held a pedestal mirror, a scattering of make up, various lotions, cottonwool pads, hairbrush and nail varnish. It was all coated with a fine film that Drew concluded was more face powder and talc than normal house dust. A bookcase overflowed on to the floor, with piles of volumes leaning against the wall. They mostly seemed to be current fiction in hardback. Picking one up at random, he found REVIEW COPY – NOT FOR RESALE stamped on the title page. So Justine worked as a book reviewer, did she, as well as making pottery? He could see no sign of any notes or newspaper cuttings, no paper and pens and no computer.

'Hmm,' said Maggs. 'She's a bit of a slob, isn't she.'

'Certainly doesn't bother to make her bed,' he nodded. 'But then who does these days?'

Maggs opened a wardrobe and rummaged for a minute on the floor, beneath four or five long dresses and skirts, and a thick winter coat.

'Doesn't seem to be anything down here,' came her muffled voice. 'How about on top?'

Drew had to move the clothes from the chair and climb onto it, to see the top of the wardrobe. 'Two shoeboxes, one larger box, a handbag and a pillow,' he reported. 'All covered in dust. Not been touched for months.'

Drew retreated down the narrow stairs, noticing how the smell of rotting cabbage grew stronger. When he turned to look over his shoulder, Maggs wasn't behind him. 'Where are you?' he called.

'Just coming,' came her voice, slightly muffled.

After a brief search, Drew found the source of the cabbage smell in a cupboard under the white porcelain sink.

He didn't notice Maggs coming downstairs, his head averted from the collection of mouldering vegetables. 'Oh, see what I've found!' she suddenly crowed, having been rummaging in a pile of clutter on the pine table. She brandished a mobile phone triumphantly.

'Okay,' Drew murmured. 'Point taken. Most women never go anywhere without their mobiles.' He was by this time in very little doubt that Justine Pereira, daughter of Roma Millan, cousin of Penn Strabinski, had not intended to leave the house for more than a few hours – certainly not for a week.

'We think it looks fishy then, do we?' Maggs said. 'On the whole. Generally speaking?'

Before he could concur, the doorway went dark and they both turned to see why. A broad figure was blocking out the light, so they could not at first distinguish much detail. Maggs made a sound rather like *Ooh-er!* while Drew remained silent.

'What the hell are you doing here? Who are you?' The man's voice was deep, his indignation unmistakable.

'We've been looking for Justine,' Drew said. 'That is . . .'

'We've been worried about her,' Maggs interposed fluently. 'She hasn't been answering her phone, you see. And she's missed one or two appointments. So we thought we should come and make sure she's all right.'

The man asked the obvious question. 'How did you get in?'

Maggs and Drew glanced at each other; they hadn't rehearsed the answer to this one. 'A friend of hers told us where to find the key,' Maggs offered. 'You must know how careless Justine is about things like that.'

'You know her?' His eyes narrowed disbelievingly. 'Who are you, for God's sake? I've never seen either of you before in my life.'

Drew couldn't explain afterwards why he'd

instinctively withheld any mention of Penn. She hadn't asked him to, and her name would surely have smoothed the way quite effectively. He could only suppose that it was something to do with her connection to Karen, and a prudent feeling that it was wise to reveal as little as possible.

'My name's Slocombe and this is my business partner,' he said. 'You won't have heard of us. We're old friends of Justine's from before she came to live here. We know her mother, actually.'

The man finally came into the kitchen and stood where they could see him properly. He was tall and muscular with a heavy jaw and thick dark brows. 'Well I'm Philip Renton,' he said, 'and I own this place. Justine is my tenant and I can assure you there's no reason at all to worry about her. I know for a fact that she's gone off for a little holiday. Camping, I think she said. So you can go back to wherever you came from and assure all those friends and relatives that everything's fine. She'll be back soon. I'll tell her you dropped by, shall I?'

Drew spent a long time considering the face before him. The eyes hardly moved, as if the brain behind them was working overtime, and all the man's attention was turned inward. There was no discernible warmth, no simple fellow feeling.

'We came quite a long way, you know,' Maggs

said reproachfully. 'The place doesn't really look as if she went camping.'

Renton laughed. 'You think she should have tidied up first? Are you sure you know our Justine?'

'I think she'd have taken her phone,' said Maggs robustly.

The man glanced down at the mobile. 'That's her old one,' he said. 'She'll have the current one in the car, in case she needs to use it. But she won't want it in the tent with her. She'd want a break from all that rubbish.'

'Car?' Drew echoed. Penn hadn't mentioned a car. Somehow it cast a different light on things.

'Yes, *car*,' the man insisted. 'Beige Metro, ancient thing it is now, but it seems to go all right. Passed its MOT only a few weeks ago, as it happens. After a bit of welding work.'

Despite the sudden thawing into something close to chattiness, Drew continued to feel that the man was monitoring his own words with enormous care. There was a lack of spontaneity in his delivery, a distance, as if he were speaking to them down a phone or from a platform. But at least he didn't seem angry or suspicious any longer.

'We'd better go.' Drew turned to Maggs. 'Do you think we can find our way back to the main road?'

'Course we can,' she smiled. Drew wanted to hug her for the way she hadn't put her foot in anything. She hadn't mentioned Penn or given anything away about where they came from.

'Come on then,' he smiled back. 'Sorry if we alarmed you,' he told Philip Renton. 'Perhaps if you would be so kind as to tell Justine we were looking for her? I'd be very grateful.'

'No problem,' said Renton, following them out of the cottage.

'What time is it?' Drew asked, as they bumped the van back down the track.

'Five past five.'

'Let's go to Okehampton and see if there's a police station there. I think we have something to report, don't you?'

She stared at him. 'Gosh! It's not like you to call in the cops. But if you're going to, why not try Exeter? It's nearer and on the way home.'

He hesitated. 'For one thing, there are people in the Exeter police who'd probably know me, and for another, I don't fancy driving through town just as the rush hour's starting. The van'll overheat if we get stuck in traffic. Anyway, it's a nice evening for a bit of a drive.'

'I still think it's funny. Why does it matter that someone might recognise you?'

He chewed his lip. 'Well, they might get silly

about me and detective work. It's just a gut feeling – *another* gut feeling, if you like – that it'd be easier. It's not far, anyhow.'

'Okay,' she said slowly. 'I just hope you know what you're doing. I've always thought you preferred to leave the police out of things if you possibly can.'

'Nonsense. Don't I always keep on the right side of the law?'

'When you have to,' she conceded. 'But this – what are you going to tell them?'

'What did you think of that farmer chap?' he asked, rather than giving a direct reply.

'Odd,' she said. 'Not too happy to see us. Distracted about something. But he's a farmer. Aren't they always distracted about the weather or the price of beef or something?'

'Did you pick up any clues about his relationship with Justine?'

She scratched her head and screwed up her face. 'Not really,' she admitted. 'He seemed to know quite a lot about her. All that stuff about the car. He didn't seem worried at all.'

'Mmm. Thanks, by the way, for not mentioning Penn.'

'That's okay. I could tell you wanted her kept out of it. Don't know why, though.'

'Just a sort of hunch. Except I don't think Mr Renton was saying more than he had to, either.

The whole thing was an exercise in minimalism, when you think about it.'

Maggs wriggled her shoulders. 'Could be he really thought we were thieves or squatters or something, and we'd run away at the sight of him. He might have been so thrown when we said we knew Justine that he couldn't think straight.'

'Oh, he was thinking straight, all right,' Drew said firmly. 'That's what's bothering me.'

They found Okehampton Police Station with no difficulty, on the hill leading down into the town. 'Looks like a school,' Maggs observed.

Drew examined the building. 'It must have been one once,' he agreed. 'You wouldn't think they'd need all that space, would you?'

The generous car park had clearly been the playground at one time, and the entrance once thronged with chattering pupils. 'Lucky they're still open,' Maggs muttered. 'It's well after half past five.'

A very tall man met them inside the main door, dressed in a short-sleeved green shirt and cord trousers. He looked as if he'd recently been exposed to too much sun. He glanced around the reception area and seeing it unmanned, sighed and stopped. 'Good evening,' he said. 'Can I help you?'

'Er, well . . .' Drew began. 'This is going to

sound funny, but we think you should know about a young woman who's missing.'

'Oh yes, sir? A relative of yours?'

'Only a very distant one,' Drew said. 'By marriage, that is. Though I've never met her,' he added hastily.

'Really? That sounds rather odd. Perhaps you'd like to come through and tell me about it?' Drew and Maggs exchanged one of their looks, sharing bewilderment. They'd both expected to be given a form to fill in and nothing more than that. The tall man noted their reaction.

'I'm sorry. I haven't introduced myself,' he smiled. 'Detective Sergeant Cooper. I'll take your names and details in a moment. You seem surprised about something.'

'Well,' Drew forced a laugh. 'We didn't expect you to take us so seriously.'

'We're really not like the police you see on telly,' Cooper told him. 'You've taken the trouble to come here. The least I can do is listen to what you have to say. Don't you think?'

Maggs gave a little bounce on her toes, a sign that she was pleased. 'Oh yes,' she said. 'Oh, definitely.'

DS Cooper had been on the brink of going home after a dull and depressing day, when the unlikely duo came in through the front entrance of the station. An open-faced youngish man, neatly dressed and of middle height, accompanied by a plump dark-skinned girl, unself-consciously wearing clothes that showed every curve; an intriguing pair. Cooper was instantly impressed by the girl in particular. Clear-eyed and very young, she seemed completely at ease. She also seemed to have a very relaxed relationship with the chap.

It took a few minutes to establish who they were and the nature of their partnership. 'You run a funeral business?' he repeated incredulously. It would probably have taken him a solid week of guessing before he'd come up with that. And yet, now they'd told him, he could see that it fitted Slocombe's well-scrubbed look, his gentle smile and air of having seen more of life than most. The girl was far more complicated. How in the world had she stumbled into such a business? He hoped he would get the chance of finding out more.

'It isn't at all relevant to what we're here about,' Slocombe assured him. 'It's got absolutely nothing to do with it.'

Deftly, Cooper extracted the salient points. Drew did most of the talking, turning to Maggs for confirmation now and then. The detective made notes every few seconds, circling some words and linking others with heavy lines. Finally, he summarised.

'Your wife's cousin asked you to help her find this Justine Pereira, after she'd failed to locate her herself. You can't be sure, but it seems possible that she arranged to visit you yesterday with this specifically in mind. You freely agreed to this request, and you took your business partner with you on an exploration of Miss Pereira's home. You find signs that she left in a hurry. Her landlord, a farmer, confronts you, and tells you there's nothing to worry about – she's gone off camping of her own accord and will contact you when she returns. So why come to us?' He wrinkled his brow exaggeratedly.

'Gut feeling,' Drew ventured.

'We couldn't just leave it there,' Maggs added.

Cooper smiled. 'No,' he agreed. 'I do see.'

'I'm not really sure that I do,' admitted Drew. 'It's something and nothing, isn't it. Not just the atmosphere on the farm – which really is odd – but before that. I've never met Penn before, but she got under my skin somehow. There was an edge to her, as if she had to hold on tight to herself. And then this farmer, Renton, was the same. You could tell he was being careful what he said, that he had to think about it first.'

Cooper had little else to do, otherwise it might have gone differently. He liked these people and trusted the bloke's judgment. 'I assume you regularly get involved in people's lives,' he said thoughtfully. 'You see them at times of crisis, the same as I do. You get a feeling for what's a natural reaction and what isn't. That kind of thing?'

'Right!' Drew responded. 'That's right. You've put your finger on it. This Renton chap – he was behaving like a man in a crisis. And yet, if he was telling the truth, he hadn't anything to worry about. I hadn't thought it through until now.' He turned to Maggs for her endorsement. 'Had you?'

She ducked her chin, uncharacteristically self-effacing. 'Well . . .' she began. 'I just thought he was a bit tense, I suppose. I was more bothered about Justine's things, left the way they were. And the mobile. I didn't believe what he said about the mobile. I think he just made that up on the spot.'

'Er—' Cooper prompted. 'I don't think you've told me about that.'

They quickly made amends. 'Why would someone keep their old phone anyway?' Maggs concluded. 'And it was all charged up, ready to use. It was the mobile that finally did it for me.'

Both men looked at her. The detective nodded slowly. 'Good point,' he said. Then he sat up straighter. 'Look, there isn't a lot we can do, with no evidence of any foul play or violence. But I'll put an alert out and get in touch with Miss

Strabinski to see what she can add. From now on, there'll be a lot of people watching for Miss Pereira and her car. Have you got a description of her?'

Drew and Maggs both shook their heads. 'She's small,' said Maggs eventually. 'And drives a beige Metro. An *old* beige Metro.'

'How do you know she's small?' Drew asked her.

'Her clothes in that wardrobe, for one thing. And the shoes in the bedroom were only about size 4.' Maggs glanced down at her own size 6s, with a tiny sigh. 'Oh, and she's got black hair, quite long.' She glanced at Drew smugly. 'There was a rather unhygienic hairbrush in the bathroom.'

'I don't remember going into a bathroom.'

'You didn't. I dashed in while you went downstairs. You can learn a lot from bathrooms.'

'Did you find anything else?' Cooper asked.

Maggs shrugged. 'Just soap and shampoo – oh, and a fairly new-looking toothbrush.'

They drove home briskly, Drew finding himself irritated at being so upstaged. 'Why didn't you mention the toothbrush right at the start?' he demanded. 'You were playing games with him *and* me.'

'It just seemed such a cliché,' she defended.

90

'And I thought she might have another one, an old favourite, that she'd taken with her. I still think she might. I mean, for a person to leave without even a toothbrush does seem very dramatic.'

'There wasn't a handbag anywhere,' he reminded her. 'Which would a girl choose first, if she was in a tremendous rush?'

'That isn't really the question. If she thought she'd be back by bedtime, she'd just take the bag. I bet she leaves it in her car most of the time, anyway. My mum does that – drives Dad crazy. She puts it under the passenger seat. I'm forever having to go out and fetch it for her.'

'The policeman was nice, wasn't he,' Drew interrupted.

'Tall. Not the most cheerful bloke in the world.'

'There's something about very tall people, isn't there,' he mused. 'They always seem unusually *dignified*, somehow. Especially when they're thin as well.'

'He's got a bit of a pot,' she noted. 'Must be fond of a beer.'

'Seemed a good listener.'

'Sensible, too. Weren't we lucky to find him!'

'Weren't we,' he agreed, with only slightly less enthusiasm.

* * *

Karen was much more interested in his findings than he'd expected her to be. Since the children had arrived, she'd become a somewhat less reliable confidante than before. The long discussions they'd had in the early days, where she followed every twist and turn of his thinking, were now very rare. They both knew that Maggs had in some ways taken Karen's place, and although most of the tensions arising from this development had been accommodated, there were still moments when it mattered.

'I wish I'd come with you,' Karen said, having heard the story. 'After all, Penn is my cousin.'

'Justine isn't, though,' he corrected her. 'And you didn't miss much.'

'Except that nice policeman,' she chuckled. 'He sounds quite something.'

'He was unusual,' Drew agreed. 'I think we just caught him on a quiet day, when he was glad of anything to relieve the boredom.'

'Surely not. I thought they were all working their socks off these days, with crime levels soaring and all that.'

'Evidently not in Okehampton. Not this week, anyway.'

'He won't really do anything, though, will he? What're you going to tell Penn? You ought to phone her. She'll be wondering what you thought of the cottage.'

'Tomorrow. I'll do that tomorrow. Sorry I was too late to help with putting the kids to bed.'

'I kept them up a bit late, hoping you'd come in time. Timmy had a long sleep this afternoon in the garden.'

Karen's garden was increasingly prodigious as the summer wore on. She'd encroached on the burial field at one end, cutting down a straggly hedge and planting a row of fast-growing willows a generous fifteen yards further back, gaining herself a space for beans, brussels sprouts, cabbages, sweetcorn and potatoes. Drew had been happy to let her. He had ten acres to play with, enough to bury thousands of people, enough to last a lifetime, even if business became seriously good. And since their income was significantly below the official poverty line, the food she produced was more than welcome. 'I'll soon have enough surplus to make regular sales,' she said proudly. 'I can do veggie boxes.'

Drew had his doubts about that, but said nothing. Veggie boxes involved efficient paperwork, a lot of driving to deliver the boxes, and a lot of complaints and demands from bothersome customers.

'Did you ever meet Justine?' he asked suddenly. 'As a child, I mean?'

Karen's gaze lost focus as she examined memories from early childhood. 'We had a party,

I remember. It must have been my mother's birthday – thirty, possibly. Uncle Sebastian came with Auntie Helen, Penn's mother. And they had another little girl with them, a bit younger than Penn. I remember I was fascinated by her; she had very black hair and a narrow little face. She looked like a picture of Mary Lennox in a book I had. You know – the girl in *The Secret Garden*. She seemed thin and sad like Mary. She was probably only two or three. I have a feeling somebody said her mother was away, so Auntie Helen was looking after her for a while. It seems like a million years ago. I wasn't a great deal older than Steph is now.'

'Your family!' Drew exclaimed. 'It's like one of those ten-volume sagas. I thought, you being an only child, there'd be nothing much to it. How come it's taken me so long to realise?'

'There *is* nothing much to it. It's a perfectly ordinary group of people.'

'Maggs said she must have long black hair,' he remembered. 'And she's small, to judge by her clothes and shoes. Seems to fit your memory of her.'

'Her father was Spanish, isn't that what Penn said? That would explain the hair colour. She sounds very bohemian.'

'Lonely,' Drew pronounced. 'At least, solitary. There was something sad about the place where she lives.'

'I wonder where she is,' Karen said with feeling. 'It's good of you to get involved, Drew. Especially as it might get you into trouble with Roma. You realise that, don't you?'

He frowned. 'I hadn't seen it like that,' he admitted. 'You mean because she hasn't been speaking to Justine?'

'She might feel rather iffy about you interfering, if the whole subject of Justine is taboo. You ought to go and talk to her about it, if you don't want to lose her friendship.'

'She's not that special to me, you know.'

'Oh, I think she is,' Karen twinkled. 'But that's okay. I know what you're like by now. It doesn't worry me.'

'No reason why it should,' he said uncomfortably. There were still grey areas in his dealings with other women that had never been properly thrashed out between them.

The phone interrupted. 'Hospice here,' said a brisk female voice. 'I understand you're dealing with Mr Graham French? Well, he died at six o'clock this evening. We'll keep him overnight, but perhaps you could come for him tomorrow? The family will be in touch in the morning.'

'Thanks.' He sighed as he replaced the phone. He'd really liked Mr French.

* * *

Roma Millan's sister Helen had mixed feelings of her own about the virtues of family life. Just at the moment, she could definitely have done without the whole business. The post had brought no fewer than three letters from assorted relatives, and they all seemed to want something from her. She had hoped, when she firmly decided that one child was quite enough, that the responsibilities of blood ties would weigh lightly on her shoulders. She had no image of herself as a caring dependable person, and if she forgot people's birthdays they never seemed surprised or offended.

The letters were from her husband's sister, Miriam; her daughter, and Angus, her father's much younger brother. Angus was the only one who wrote regularly from his isolated Devon village. He'd bolted there, after his breakdown, like a frightened rabbit, and although nobody ever laid eyes on him, they all received frequent communications in which he complained about how poor and cold and hungry and ill he was. Helen sent him cheques when she remembered, but he didn't always pay them in. She supposed he seldom visited a bank, and would prefer cash, but Helen didn't have spare cash very often.

Miriam wrote old-fashioned chatty notes, which sounded just like her speaking voice. She ran a small holiday hotel in North Wales, and like Angus, was rarely seen in person. She was now asking Helen, with some urgency, for advice on making her new man a partner in her business. Helen was both irritated and flattered.

Penn, her daughter, wrote her usual cool page, printed out on the computer, and containing little more than a list of social events, films seen, outings, plans for the coming few weeks. Most people would have kept in touch by telephone, but Helen was out a lot, and would probably never remember to return missed calls. More than that, mother and daughter both acknowledged that they had so little to say to each other that such calls would be full of awkward silences. Much safer, they'd concluded, to maintain the illusion of a relationship with these routine sheets of paper. But this one was different. *I'm going to see Aunt Roma on Sunday,'* Penn wrote. *'And then I'll call in on my cousin Karen, who lives quite close by. You always said I should.'* Then it went on:

> *'By the way, I haven't seen Justine for a bit. In fact, she missed a lunch with me that we'd planned, and now she's nowhere to be found. I've been getting really worried. I feel a bit of a fool to get worked up about her, but Justine has always seemed so vulnerable, and I've got this overwhelming*

feeling that she's in trouble. She's never done anything like this before. She always tells me if she's going anywhere.

'But it's probably nothing. Don't worry about it. It's only that if you have heard anything, you might let me know? Thanks.'

Helen sighed. Justine definitely was not her responsibility, and she didn't have the least intention of worrying about her.

CHAPTER FIVE

Tuesday morning's post brought the note from Penn, which Drew read over his coffee and toast.

'Why bother with a letter when she knows I'll be speaking to her today, anyway?'

'Manners, I suppose,' suggested Karen. 'And I think she's got too much time on her hands, all these weeks of holiday from college.'

'I don't remember that being a problem for you when you were teaching.'

'No, well I had you, didn't I?' she gushed playfully. 'Penn doesn't seem to have anyone to distract her.'

'I could phone her from the office, tell her everything we found yesterday. That could give her something to think about.'

'You won't have time,' Karen reminded him. 'You've got all the preparations for Mr French's funeral. They'll want it this week, won't they?'

'Thursday,' he said distractedly. 'I should think.'

'And it might be better to wait for her to phone you. Then she'll be paying for the call.'

'Good thinking,' he said, wishing they didn't have to watch the pennies quite so closely.

'Look, there's Maggs,' Karen changed the subject. 'Will you do the removal right away? Do you want me to take the phone?' After a somewhat hostile beginning, where she'd refused to act as unpaid secretary for Peaceful Repose, Karen had very gradually permitted the boundaries between the business and the house to blur, so now she would cover for the times when Drew and Maggs were both out. They had lost business and annoyed several people in the early days, when the phone had sometimes gone unanswered.

'If you can cope,' he accepted. 'You're not going out, then?'

'I might this afternoon, if the weather bucks up, but I'm planning a lazy morning. Stephanie's doing some drawing, with any luck.'

'We've got to go and collect Mr French,' was the first thing he said to Maggs, in the office. 'He died at six o'clock yesterday.'

'Okay,' she said with no sign of emotion. 'Let me get the doings.'

She unhooked a tailored black jacket and well-pressed trousers from the back of the door and slung them over one shoulder before disappearing into the adjacent cool room to change. Coming back two minutes later, she gathered up a printed pad of 'removal dockets' that Drew had copied from Plants, the undertaker he'd worked for before setting up on his own. Most of the intricate bureaucracy had been dispensed with, but he'd found it necessary to keep a detailed record of removals. On it they noted any jewellery on the body; the name of the doctor who certified death; the exact date and time; mileage travelled, plus full name and address of the deceased.

A folding trolley was kept permanently in the back of the van, as well as the zip-up bag into which the body would be placed, for purposes of delicacy and discretion. Drew had a recurring dream where the van was involved in an accident and dead bodies spilt horribly out all over the road, naked and mutilated in some scenarios.

'Let's go, then,' Maggs chivvied him. 'The daughters'll be after us if we don't bustle.'

The hospice was nearly twenty miles away, so they were out of the office until close to eleven o'clock. Although accustomed to driving around with a dead person in the back, there was always some slightly dampening effect on conversation as a result. Maggs lolled against the back of her seat, apparently lost in thought, and they said little to each other. Drew found himself wondering what Mr French's last words or thoughts had been. He often wondered how it must be to die, and encouraged stories from relatives which went some way to enlighten him. 'He didn't go peacefully at all,' two or three wives had said fiercely, as if they'd been badly deceived. 'He fought it every inch of the way.' Only one person had gone into such graphic detail that Drew had felt he'd been there himself. It was a woman recounting the death of her mother. 'She howled all night, making a terrible unearthly noise. Full of fear and horror, as if she knew exactly what was happening and couldn't bear it. The nurses gave her painkillers, but it didn't make any difference. I sat in the downstairs room and listened *for nine hours*. She was like an animal in a trap or someone being tortured. And yet when I went to look at her, every now and then, she was lying there, eyes closed, quite relaxed. It was all going on inside, beyond anyone's reach.'

She'd shuddered. 'I'll never forget it. Nobody ever said it could be like that.'

Drew tried to convince himself that the woman hadn't really been terrified or in awful mental agony. It was just some strange physiological response to the closing down of her system, like the spasmodic kicking of an animal. But it left him uneasy.

The most common story, which he'd heard dozens of times, was the one where the person died unexpectedly at the very moment when their attentive relative had gone out for a few minutes or gone home for a rest. 'It was as if she did it *on purpose*,' said one daughter. Drew generally assured them that this was probably true. 'I think people do prefer to die alone,' he sometimes said. 'Funny as it sounds. Or perhaps they just feel they've been released somehow, when their loved ones aren't there. While they're being watched over, there's some kind of link that keeps them hanging on.' His customers invariably responded well to this sort of remark, as if greatly relieved to have his permission to discuss the taboo subject.

'I wonder if Justine's dead,' said Maggs, breaking the long silence.

'The police chap didn't seem to think so.'

'He'll be contacting Penn, don't you think? For a proper description and the car number. It ought to have been her who reported it in the first place.'

'I wonder whether she'll mind that we went to the police,' Drew suddenly thought. 'She won't have been expecting us to do that. And I imagine she doesn't want me to talk about Justine to Roma.'

'What?'

'Because of the rift between them. Didn't I mention that?'

'No. What happened?'

'I have no idea. One of those messy family things. They haven't spoken for five years. I sometimes think that's the default position, actually. Look at Mr French's daughters.'

'They do at least speak to each other. As far as we know, anyway.'

'Well, this thing with Roma and Justine seems to be quite heavy.'

Maggs was suddenly excited. 'Hey, that's probably got something to do with it, then. Justine going missing, I mean. Don't you think?'

'I can't imagine how. It's old history, whatever it was that caused the fight in the first place.'

'You really don't know what it was?'

He shook his head. 'No idea. Though I suppose Penn must know.'

Den Cooper had the phrase *something and nothing* going round his head. A young woman missing, reported by people who'd never met her, and yet had become sufficiently concerned to make a special detour to a police station.

On the face of it, the person who ought by

rights to have come in was the girl's cousin, Penn Strabinski. Slocombe had supplied part of her address with some hesitation, claiming that was because he had difficulty in remembering it. He didn't have her phone number. It was all oddly tenuous. But Den had been in the job long enough to know that it was a good idea to listen to stories like this; that breaks with normality very often did signal breaks from the accepted codes of conduct. And then there were the mobile phone and the toothbrush. Oh yes, there was plenty of substance here, just below the surface and Den was more than happy to give it his attention, at least until something more urgent came along.

He found P. Strabinski easily enough in the phone book, and was on the brink of calling her, when he decided that a face-to-face visit might be more effective. Leaving a copy of his five-line report on the DI's desk, and logging himself out, he drove off towards Crediton, where Slocombe had said she lived. Den was fond of this quiet back road, remembering it from his boyhood, when he had a best friend who lived in the village of Bow. Memories of summer days spent cycling to and fro always surfaced when he used this route.

Events of the last year had done much to sour these associations, however. Foot and mouth disease had ravaged the area and the police had been closely involved in the implementation of the appalling culling that had traumatised virtually everybody for several ghastly months, more than two years earlier. Many of Den's lifelong friends had lost all their animals and the whole nature of farming had changed. Although superficially back to normal after two years, he knew that the spirit of west Devon had been weakened, that reliance on providing leisure activities for uncomprehending townies was the best many people could hope for by way of a livelihood. He knew, deep in his bones, that he couldn't go on as he was, either; not just because of outside changes or his hopeless love life, but because he was getting so little fulfilment from the job. Perhaps that was the real reason he'd been so attracted by this something and nothing story. It fitted his mood.

Penn Strabinski came to the door warily. As always, there was the flicker of shock at Den's height before the acceptance came. He could almost hear the thought processes. *Goodness, what a tall man. Oh well, tallness is okay*, was roughly how it went.

He introduced himself and presented his official ID card, before explaining that he was looking into the apparent disappearance of a

Miss Justine Pereira, who he understood was a relative of hers.

Her sudden loss of colour came as quite a surprise. She put a hand to her throat and seemed to find the next breath hard to manage. 'That comes as a shock?' he queried.

'Oh,' she gasped. 'Not really. I mean – I didn't know the police were involved.' She stared anxiously at his face. 'You haven't found her, have you?'

He smiled. 'Not yet,' he said, thinking there was considerable ambivalence in her words and manner. Almost as if she did not want him to have found the missing Justine. But he was quite prepared to discover he'd got this wrong. 'I understand you've been worried about her,' he went on.

'Drew!' she realised. 'Drew's been to see you. And he gave you my address. At least . . . it wasn't Aunt Roma, was it?'

'Hold on! Perhaps I could come in, and you can tell me all about it? All I seem to have so far is a name and some vague suspicions.'

She hesitantly led him into a small and rather dark room in her little terrace house. 'You live here alone?' he asked casually. The place was sparsely furnished, with little left lying about. Nothing unusual or handmade caught his eye; the furniture was plain and serviceable. No gleam of polished oak or lovingly burnished silverware. *Unloved* was the word that came to mind.

'That's right,' she said. 'I did think of getting a lodger to help with the mortgage, but then I managed to get some extra marking work, which helped. And I've got a few private pupils over the summer, cramming for their Common Entrance.'

'You're a teacher?'

'Well, my main job's at the FE college, but the pay isn't too good, as you probably know. Luckily, there's usually some extra stuff for the asking.'

'Like the cramming.'

'Right.'

She seemed to be relaxing slowly, as he'd hoped. He remembered Drew Slocombe's comments about tensions and undercurrents, and thought he knew just what the undertaker had meant. Something certainly wasn't right.

'I gather you've had a look round your cousin's cottage, since she went missing? What was your impression?'

She sucked her lower lip. 'Well, it was untidy, but then that's not unusual. It did look as if she'd gone out in a hurry. But I'm more worried by the lack of word from her. A phone call at least. And it's out of character for her to miss a date with me. We were having lunch together last Thursday in Exeter and she never showed up. That was when it all started. By Saturday I was quite alarmed, so on Sunday, when I went to visit Karen and Drew, I decided to ask him to help.'

Cooper cocked his head at her. 'Rather than come to the police?'

'I didn't think you'd take any notice. She's a responsible adult and there was no sign of a struggle or anything. And I suppose it isn't really very long since I saw her.'

'When was that exactly?'

'Um . . . the Friday before last. That's when we fixed up the lunch and a bit of a shopping spree. She was looking forward to it.'

'Did you know that her landlord, Mr Renton, says she went camping, on the spur of the moment?'

Again she went white and breathless. 'Oh.' She forced a grating laugh. 'That makes me look very stupid, doesn't it.'

'You didn't ask him where she was?'

'He's never there. I . . . um . . . well . . .'

Den narrowed his eyes in puzzlement. 'Go on,' he encouraged.

'Camping,' she repeated carefully. 'How funny. In the Metro, I suppose? That's really odd.' She seemed to be regaining composure. 'Right. Well, Philip ought to know. It looks as if I've wasted everybody's time, doesn't it. Philip told Drew she was camping, did he?'

'That's what Mr Slocombe says. The farmer found him and his assistant exploring the cottage and confronted them, probably thinking they were intruders. When they told him they were looking for Miss Pereira, he explained that she'd gone off for a few days on her own, presumably with a tent.'

'Did he say where?' A look of annoyance crossed her face. 'And who is Drew's "assistant"?'

'A young woman, who works with him. You don't know her?'

'I remember now that he mentioned her. I haven't met her.'

'She's . . .' he caught himself, with a faint self-mocking smile. 'She seems quite a talented person. Observant.'

'So why are you still bothering to investigate?' she asked sharply. 'If Phil says she's gone camping, surely that's the end of the matter?' She paused, another idea popping up. 'And why on earth did Drew go to the police, once he'd been told she was all right? What the hell was he playing at?' The annoyance was thickening into something a lot stronger.

'You'll have to ask him that,' said Den primly. 'Meanwhile, since I'm here, it would be helpful if you could supply the model and registration number of Miss Pereira's car. And a photograph of her, if you have one.'

'You're going to carry on searching for her, then?'

'Just to put our minds at rest,' he said easily. 'She might be a responsible adult, but she also sounds rather vulnerable. Wouldn't you say?' Without waiting for a reply, he went on, 'And perhaps I could have her mother's address as well?'

This time, Penn's reaction was to flush crimson. 'What? Why the hell do you want that? Her mother hasn't set eyes on her for five years or more.'

'Doesn't know you've been worried about her daughter, then? I understood that you visited her at the weekend. You never mentioned it to her?'

Penn chafed, eyes darting from point to point in the room. 'Well, I did phone her yesterday, as it happens. I hadn't the nerve to mention Justine face-to-face. Aunt Roma tends to get into quite a state if the subject arises.'

'And what did you tell her?'

She lifted her chin and looked directly at him. 'I said I was worried about Justine, who'd apparently gone missing, and that I'd asked Drew to help me find her. She knows Drew, you see. I thought I should at least warn her.'

'Warn her? You think there might be bad news on the way for her?'

'Well, I did think something like that. But now . . .' she almost shouted at him, 'now we know she's gone camping, everything's all right, isn't it? You can just forget the whole business.'

'We'll very likely do that in a day or two,' he soothed her. 'Just bear with us while we give the matter a bit of attention first. If you'll give me those details, I'll be on my way.'

He found himself whistling, albeit rather a mournful tune, as he went back to Okehampton. There most definitely was some sort of case to answer here; something unusual and complicated. There were so many undercurrents you could be swept out to sea by them if you didn't watch out. And – happiest thought of all – he had every reason to see Drew Slocombe again. Drew Slocombe and his charming, good-looking, observant girl assistant.

Laurie Millan was never very comfortable in his own company. He paced the living room restlessly, waiting for Roma to come home from the shops. 'Got herself arrested this time, for driving with the dog on her lap,' he muttered. He didn't know what to do with himself while he waited. He'd already carefully laid out a pad and pen on the dining table, to make it look as if he were about to write a letter. The moment Roma's car turned in through the gate, he would sit down and start writing, glancing up as if distracted from something absorbing, as she came in. It was important that she should never realise just how needy he was at times like this.

She was taking much longer than expected. Even if she stopped to natter with one or two women she knew, she wouldn't be as late as this. Fiercely he quashed the idea that she'd had an accident. Somebody would have phoned him by now, if that was the case. She was just thoughtless, dawdling around the country lanes, maddeningly self-sufficient, not considering him at all. It made him angry and very frustrated because he could never reveal his anger. This was one of their many unspoken agreements.

When Pereira had buggered off, after years of towering arguments and broken crockery, Roma had rapidly discovered the many pleasures of living alone. It had been a revelation. Life became peaceful and easy, and she vowed, loudly and often, that nothing would ever induce her to live with a man again. For thirteen years, she stuck to her vow. Then Laurie had come along, and slowly persuaded her that he would never get in her way, would give her company without making demands; would listen to her complaints, and make no attempt to change her views. He would cook for her, and sleep with her, and go on holiday with her. All he wanted in return was someone to accompany him on his dream retirement to the country. Someone who would make the house feel alive, and give him something on which to fix his attention. Roma had protested that it was unfair; that all the benefit accrued to her, but he'd insisted, and eventually she could not resist the offer.

His persona was of a mild, harmless chap, in a tweedy jacket and carpet slippers; that was why Roma had married him. He was a sort of glorified servant, a butler-cum-gardener, who also provided reliable companionship and a listening ear. Nobody paused to ask themselves what was in it for him. Or if they did, they found easy answers in the present-day balance between the sexes. Men were essentially drones, after all. They earned their billet by being affable, pleasant company, keeping out of the way, and never *ever* showing the slightest hint of violence. This last was punishable by the most cruel sanctions. One thoughtless slap, and they were cast into the outer darkness, sans virtue, sans money, sans hope, sans everything. Laurie never forgot that. He would never never slap Roma, that much was certain. The fact that she had slapped that horrible little beast in her school carried no implications for how she behaved towards him. He wholeheartedly supported her in her view of the matter – that society had gone mad, that there was no justice, and it was a perpetual unforgiving scandal that she had lost her job over it.

She arrived eventually, breezy and liberally besmirched with black smudges on hands and face. Laurie looked up from his writing pad, a questioning smile on his lips. 'Did something happen?' he asked mildly.

'Oh, not really. There was a man with a flat tyre, on the bypass, and I stopped to help him. It was raining,' she added, as if that explained everything. 'He had no idea where the doings were. It was like my old Renault – remember? You had to turn a bolt from inside the boot, and that released the spare tyre from underneath. Impossible to guess, if you didn't have the handbook. Poor chap was going mental, bashing the thing with a club hammer he happened to have with him.'

She spoke breathlessly, good cheer sparking from her, at her piece of charity. Laurie sighed. 'It could only happen to you,' he said fondly. 'Was he grateful?'

'I suppose so. A bit embarrassed, me being a woman. The old habits aren't quite dead yet, more's the pity.'

'Did you get my stamps? And the lightbulbs?'

'Of course. Everything that was on the list.' She was unstoppable in this mood; so proud of herself, so sure she had life by the ears and could make it go any way she wanted. Laurie could only hope that it would last. 'I'll go and get some soup started, shall I? Must be nearly lunchtime.'

'It is,' he agreed, slowly packing away his small collection of writing materials. 'And it looks as if the rain's stopping at last.'

Sheena Renton had been late home on Monday; so late that Philip was already in bed and made only a token grunt in greeting. Tuesday morning, however, seemed unusually relaxed, given her normally hectic schedule.

'Good God, it's eight fifteen!' Philip cried, on waking. 'Why are you still here?'

She stretched lazily. 'Nigel said we could take a few hours off after last night. The meeting didn't finish till past ten. We got everything sorted, though. I feel great.' She looked at him through her lashes and pouted. 'You haven't got to be anywhere, have you?'

He couldn't pretend to miss her meaning, although he really didn't like sex in the morning. Too sober, too relaxed, too much light streaming through the window. But Sheena was deftly determined and her conjugal rights were satisfactorily claimed.

'Isn't it great without Georgia,' she purred afterwards. 'At least for a few days.'

'Mm,' he concurred, before rolling back the duvet and flopping heavily out of bed. 'Cup of tea?' he offered.

'Okay.'

By the time he got back with two mugs of tea and a few rounds of buttered toast, she was asleep again, rather to his relief. He quickly dressed and left her to it, the tea cooling beside her.

He wandered aimlessly out of the house and stood in the empty yard. It was eighteen months or more since there'd been any animals on the farm, but he could still hear the ghostly sounds of cows and calves and pigs. They'd been culled as 'dangerous contacts' with a foot-and-mouth-infected pig farm, because Philip's father had bought in three new sows just at the wrong moment. He hadn't been able to forgive himself for it, despite everyone insisting he couldn't possibly have known the risk. He'd forced himself to participate in the slaughter, as some kind of penance. But not penance enough, it seemed. Only self-destruction had relieved him of his misery and remorse, his helpless rage and loss of hope.

Philip had watched impotently, his own

memories just as terrible. He too had taken part in the cull. The cows had gone passively enough, but the pigs had been frantic. He still heard their screams in the night and supposed he always would.

Sheena used the whole catastrophe as justification for returning to her full-time-plus job, even though Georgia had been barely a year old at the time. Philip had wanted to talk her out of it, but could never find a convincing argument. He'd thought it was obvious: a mother's place was with her child. But Georgia made no complaint, despite a gruelling routine under the care of a day nursery where the staff seemed to change every week. Gloria, the blowsy woman in charge, never seemed to remember which one Georgia was when Philip turned up to collect her. He knew it wasn't the right way for a child to grow up; she was so quiet and withdrawn it was often as if she wasn't in the house at all. The only times she seemed animated and happy were when Justine was around.

The household became a haphazard business, with food snatched at odd times and Justine drafted in to babysit at short notice much more often than originally intended. It had begun to feel as if they were mere automata, running round in mechanical circles, with no idea of why, until Philip had woken up one morning uncomfortably convinced that it couldn't go on like that any longer.

Sheena was right that it was much more relaxed without Georgia; in some ways, at least. Never an attentive mother, she had jumped at the suggestion that the child spend a week or two with her granny on the Isle of Wight. Leaving all the arrangements to Philip – after all, it was his mother, who had moved to the island with a close woman friend after she was widowed – Sheena hardly seemed to notice the absence of her little girl. Philip observed this with a painful knot of tangled feelings, but made no comment. Time enough for all that when his wife decided Georgia should come home again.

At least he'd dealt with those people looking for Justine without rocking any boats. He was pleased with himself about that. The next problem was going to be Penn. But Philip's policy was always to take things one step at a time. It was surprising what you could do, how much you could bear, if you broke it all down into manageable slices. It had been like that through the foot and mouth nightmare. He'd gone through the daily motions, inventing routines for himself, slowly incorporating ideas for the new business, making new contacts, until it came to

Christmas and he could look back and feel he'd triumphed over the horror of it all. He'd done it then; he could do it again now.

Helen Strabinski was losing the battle against her curiosity. Something was obviously going on, to do with Roma and Justine and Penn, and she wanted to know what it was. The drizzle was depressing, thwarting the plan she'd had to do some outdoor work. She'd promised she'd have a dozen stills for the tie-in book the BBC were producing, to accompany a gardening series. The garden in August was supposed to be full of lush sunlit borders, dahlias and gladioli and red hot pokers, all epitomising high summer. Instead, everything was damp and bedraggled and completely unsuitable. She could get on with a few indoor mock-ups, but she wasn't in the mood. It never really worked, anyway.

Instead, she resolved on paying an unannounced visit on her sister. If she took her camera, she could claim to be searching for a cover shot for a new *Glorious Gardens* magazine; yet another glossy monthly to squeeze onto the shelves. A number of photographers had been invited to submit possible shots for the cover, and Helen was determined that they'd choose one of hers. She thought Roma's beehives might add an original touch – if she could pluck up the nerve to approach them.

It was a forty-mile drive, but there wasn't a lot of traffic on the small roads she chose. Twice she stopped to take pictures: first of an old barn with its roof falling in, and later of a field full of glossy-looking red-and-white cattle. Made a change from the ubiquitous black-and-white ones, she judged.

Roma had always been one for dramas, of course, since they were children. Six years older than Helen, she'd forged her way through school, making enough of a mark for teachers to shudder slightly at the name of Willowfield. 'Not Roma's sister?' they'd asked hopefully, only to sigh when she nodded. 'But I'm not at all like her,' Helen had learnt to say, brightly.

It was true – she was nothing at all like her sister. Roma had been fearless, argumentative, noisy. Helen was altogether different. And their brother had been different again – older than them, neurotic even in his teens, and very poor company.

Laurie was standing in the doorway, before she was even out of her car, as if he'd been watching out for her. There was no car in the driveway, suggesting that Roma was out. 'Hiya!' she greeted him cheerily. 'Thought I'd drop in for a bit. Sorry to arrive so late. Must be nearly teatime, but you don't have to feed me.'

His face looked dark, somehow, as if in shadow, and yet he was standing in the open. He smiled a welcome, but nothing changed in his eyes. 'Helen,' he said, as if he hadn't been able to remember her name at first. 'Haven't seen you for a while.'

'Roma writes to me,' she said. 'I gather things are a bit frazzled at the moment.'

'Are they?' Laurie looked alarmed. 'Not that I've noticed.'

'Well, Penn said . . .' She stopped herself. Something in Laurie's face made her insides clench for a moment. A bleakness, mixed with a flash of anger, told her to shut up and wait for Roma.

But she had to talk about something. 'Is Roma well? No more of that sciatica?'

'That was ages ago,' he dismissed. 'It only lasted a week or so. She hasn't got time for anything like that. She's insanely busy all the time.'

'She always has been. It makes her feel important,' Helen said automatically. 'Though it's a bit difficult to see how she manages it, stuck in this quiet spot.'

'Bees, shopping, garden, gossip, reading circle—' he rattled off, marking each on his fingers. 'And there's much more. Every time she comes home, she's made a new friend, and heard their entire life story. I can't keep up with it all. She makes me feel old.'

'Poor Laurie. Isn't it like you expected?'

He forced a laugh, and raised his eyes to the hills beyond the garden. 'Oh, it's fine. It's a lovely spot, and I don't let anything disturb me. She's getting me a greenhouse for my birthday. That'll be fun.'

Helen found herself wishing the weather was better. 'I did wonder whether I could take a few pictures of the hives,' she ventured.

'Oh?' He didn't seem very interested. 'Bit murky for that. There won't be many bees working with it like this. House-cleaning weather, Roma calls it. The workers knuckle down to making new cells, mucking out debris, that sort of thing. I assume you'd like a few actual bees in the pictures?'

Helen shivered. 'Not particularly,' she said.

Laurie looked at her. 'Oh, that's right – you're scared of them, aren't you. Roma mentions it from time to time. Seems funny, her being so fearless with them. Did something happen to put you off them?'

It was Helen's turn to stare. 'Surely she told you?'

He cocked his head questioningly. 'Told me what?'

123

'Our brother, Conrad. He died of bee stings when he was small. I was only a few weeks old. Roma must have been six. She was there at the time. If there's anything odd, it's her becoming a beekeeper now. Some people might think it very perverse.'

'I'm certain she's never uttered a word about that,' he said wonderingly. 'Poor little chap. How did it happen?'

'He was playing with a dog from next door. A great big daft thing, an Old English sheepdog. It knocked the hive over and the bees came charging out, furiously angry. He had a hundred stings, and died of shock. My mother was distraught, of course.'

'How awful for *you*,' Laurie said, passionately. 'She can't have had much emotion to spare for a baby after that.'

'Oh, well, I think I was a sort of haven. If anything, she over-protected me, hung over me in case some other dreadful accident happened. It was far worse for our older brother. I don't think he was ever quite right afterwards.'

'You mean the invisible Ninian? The one who went off to Japan and was never heard of again?'

Helen laughed. 'That's the one.' She was quiet for a few moments, and then went on, 'You can imagine the frenzy every time a flying insect came into the house. Bee, wasp, bluebottle, they all caused havoc. The whole family behaved as if they were the most lethal objects imaginable. Like poison darts, or something.'

'Well, Roma's not a bit scared of them now. Not bees or wasps.'

'No, well. Roma regards fear as an intolerable weakness.'

'That's true,' Laurie agreed quietly.

Roma arrived home to find them sitting in the small conservatory with tea and biscuits. 'Oh, it's you!' she breezed. 'Couldn't think whose car it was. Giving yourself a day off?'

'Something like that,' Helen smiled. 'Laurie's been looking after me.'

'So I see.'

'This place is lovely, even when it's raining. You were clever to find it.' Helen gazed over the garden and field, much as Laurie had done earlier.

'It suits us,' Roma nodded. 'It feels much more remote than it really is. You can't hear any traffic – have you noticed?'

'What about people? Have you made any friends? Laurie says you get plenty of chance for a gossip.'

'I never gossip,' said Roma stiffly. 'But I do discuss things with people in the village. I joined the Probus Club, and we have very interesting meetings. There are two or three women I get on fairly well with.'

'You always were one for women friends,' said Helen. 'Do you still keep up with Caroline? And Fenella Frobisher. I used to *hate* Fenella Frobisher when she came to our house.'

'We write two or three times a year,' said Roma. 'They've got quite boring, to be honest. All about grandchildren and Caribbean cruises. They don't seem to *care* about things any more.'

'Getting old,' said Helen unfeelingly. 'Though I did think you and Caroline would go on marching and protesting till you dropped. I'll never forget seeing you on telly when there was all that carry-on at Greenham Common.'

Roma sighed. 'A million years ago,' she murmured.

Laurie disappeared into the kitchen for ten minutes, before inviting the sisters to join him for an early supper. He'd laid out an impressive assortment of salads, with cold chicken and hard-boiled eggs. 'Wow!' said Helen. 'You're a magician!'

'He's very good with food,' said Roma complacently. 'We'll eat in an hour or so. Come and see the garden first. You've got your camera, I see.'

Helen remembered her picture ideas and

glanced at the sky. 'Can I do a few shots with the beehives in the background?' she said. 'I don't need to get too close, with the long lens.'

'They won't hurt you,' Roma said coolly.

Helen spent twenty minutes trying to capture the roses and mallow and potentilla in the foreground, with the hives still visible in the distance. She seemed to be having problems. 'What's the matter?' Roma demanded.

'The depth of field's all wrong,' Helen muttered. 'The hives are so out of focus, nobody's going to know what they are.'

'Can't help you there,' shrugged Roma.

'I know!' Helen squatted down low in the long grass just inside the field beyond the garden. 'These grass heads are gorgeous when you see them up close. And it's long over there too, by the hives.'

'Careful!' Roma teased. 'Don't get too close.'

Helen threw her a savage look. 'It's not something to joke about,' she spat. 'It'd serve you right if you got stung to death yourself, one of these days.'

'Well I won't. You can bet everything you've got on that.'

'I probably can, too,' Helen glowered. 'But that's my shot, all the same.' She eyed the hives. 'I probably need to be about twenty feet away.' Bravely she covered the distance, leaving Roma to watch in amusement. She refused to acknowledge to herself that the bees were always tetchy in August, with their honey stores to protect and the atavistic awareness of the impending end of the summer. The hive-robbing wasps wouldn't have improved things, either. There was, in short, a fair chance that her sister would get stung if she approached too closely – especially if she was wearing any sort of perfume.

But all was well. Lying on her stomach, the camera held awkwardly in front of her, Helen took her time in framing her shots. At last she returned triumphant. 'Brilliant!' she enthused. 'There was even a butterfly in a couple of them.'

'I should charge you a fee for using my props,' said Roma sourly.

'I had a letter from Penn,' Helen began, over the salads. "She seems worried about Justine.' Helen had promised herself that she would not be intimidated by Roma's sensitive areas. Where other people tiptoed around her and obeyed unspoken taboos, Helen steeled herself and plunged in. Having survived the bees, her courage levels had risen. Roma might be her big sister, argumentative and irritable, but she seldom turned the full force of her rage or sarcasm onto Helen.

'Oh, yes. Nobody seems to know where Justine is. Penn even got me worried about it for a few minutes. But really, I think it's a fuss about nothing. If there'd been some sort of disaster, we'd have heard about it by now. The thoughtless creature has just gone off without telling anyone. To be perfectly honest . . .' she paused, apparently having second thoughts. 'Well, Penn seems to have been seeing an awful lot of Justine. I wondered whether she felt she needed a bit of space.'

Helen sifted this jumble thoughtfully, overlooking the implied slight against her own daughter. 'I'm surprised you think you know anything about your daughter's motives. It's at least five years now, isn't it? She's probably a completely different person by this time.'

'Have you seen her?' The question was abrupt.

'Once. She came to us for a weekend with Penn, a couple of years ago. Her hair was so short, it was like an animal's coat. She looked very strange. But Penn tells me it's long again now.'

'Hmm,' Roma uttered, as if quite uninterested.

'So you're not bothered that she's gone missing?'

'It doesn't make any difference to me, does it? She's been dead to me for years anyway.'

'Dead? Do you think she's dead?'

Laurie, at the end of the table, cleared his throat. 'She doesn't really mean that,' he said softly, as if the suggestion upset him. 'She's more worried than she'll admit.' He twinkled fondly at his wife, but she did not seem inclined to twinkle back.

'Don't speak for me, please,' she said. 'I wouldn't dream of telling anyone how you were feeling.'

'Sorry,' he put up his hands defensively. 'You're quite right.'

'But are you worried or aren't you?' Helen demanded. 'Why haven't you gone to the police? Why's it all been left for Penn to investigate?'

'It hasn't. There's a chap doing it for us.'

'Oh?'

'It sounds a bit odd, I suppose. He's married to Karen, which is a coincidence, because I happen to know him as well.'

'Karen? You mean Sebastian's niece?'

'The very one. I imagine you knew her as a child. So it's all in the family.'

Helen went dreamy for a moment. 'I haven't seen Karen for – must be twenty years.'

'Well, go and see her now, why don't you? She lives in North Staverton, this side of Bradbourne. It's only about six miles. She's bound to be there. She's got two small children.'

'No,' Helen decided. 'I won't go now. But I'm

130

glad I've caught up with what's going on. I hate feeling left out.'

'Nothing's going on,' Roma said irritably. 'It's typical of Justine, getting everyone running round in circles. She always was thoughtless.'

'Poor Justine,' Helen muttered. 'She could never do anything right, could she.'

'She was perverse. She deliberately went against me, every chance she got. It was so *stupid*. That's what I can't get over. Like a brainless sheep, insisting on getting tangled in the densest brambles, when there's a perfectly good path right beside it. That's just how I see Justine – ramming her head into bramble thickets, just because I told her not to.'

'She was just a normal teenager,' said Helen quietly. 'You over-reacted at every little thing. You made her far worse. All that foolishness about her turning out like our poor Uncle Angus. Either that or Carlos. You wished bad things on her with your nonsense. You made it happen.'

'I lost interest,' said Roma brutally. 'I got terribly terribly *bored* by it.'

'Don't fool yourself,' Helen said. 'It certainly wasn't boredom that caused all the trouble. What's more, the way I heard it, it wasn't even you who made the break in the end.'

Roma scowled and said nothing to that. Helen began again on a lighter note. 'So what happens now? I don't think Penn's going to let it drop. It's not particularly common for a woman of twenty-six to go off without telling anybody.'

'It's a lot less common for her to be abducted and murdered,' Roma flashed back.

'Well, I hope for Penn's sake that she shows up soon. My dear daughter doesn't cope very well with mysteries. She gets scared.'

'She didn't strike me as scared when she came to see us last week. She seemed to be on rather good form, actually.'

'Well, she would with you,' said Helen. 'Not that you'd notice if she was having a breakdown in the middle of your patio. You've never been aware of how anybody was feeling.'

'Phooey,' said Roma, with finality.

CHAPTER SIX

Karen was watching out for them when they got back with Mr French, and came into the office with Timmy on her hip as they were unloading their cargo into the cool room next door. 'You've got to go out again,' she said urgently. 'I've got the name and address here.'

'What? Another removal?' Drew still used some of the jargon of the funeral directing business, despite his attempts to recreate it in a more approachable and informal fashion. 'Someone in a hurry?'

'It all sounds a bit messy,' she grimaced. 'It's a middle-aged woman who's been recovering from an operation at her daughter's . . .'

'If she's recently had surgery there'll have to be a post mortem,' Drew interrupted.

'No, it seems there won't be,' Karen went on. 'The operation was a month ago and she'd been making very poor progress. The doctor's signed her up, so she's all clear for you.'

'Then what's messy about it?'

'I'm not sure. The daughter was a bit coy.'

'Oh, it'll just be the usual,' Maggs breezed. 'People worry about every tiny leak. We'll cope.' She grinned at Drew. 'Fancy – two in one day and it's not even lunchtime.'

'Take the mobile,' Karen told them. 'I'm going out this afternoon. I'll switch the phone through before I go.' She turned to go back to the house. 'Roma Millan phoned as well,' she remembered. 'She wants you to pop round and see her sometime. This evening, for preference.' There was a wistful note in her voice. It had been a long time since she'd been free to 'pop round' to anything with any kind of spontaneity.

Drew and Maggs completed the removal without incident and Maggs went to work in the cool room, washing the body and dressing it in the smart outfit provided. Drew made phone calls to the doctor and the family, making sure the paperwork was in order. 'Unusual,' he remarked, 'issuing the certificate so easily.' But he spoke lightly, well aware of his role in the complex machinations involved in disposing of a human body. Burial was easier, with fewer forms to complete, and a generally more relaxed attitude. Even so, a doctor was inviting raised eyebrows by certifying a death as non-suspicious in these circumstances.

'The family desperately wanted to avoid a post mortem,' this practitioner now told Drew. 'And it's all perfectly kosher. I've seen the woman every day for weeks and it was obvious she wasn't going to recover.'

Drew's next task was to make the firm point to both families involved in the impending funerals that since he and Maggs were not equipped for embalming, the funerals would have to take place within three days. He established dates and times with them, both burials taking place on the same day. The sense of being busily occupied, even slightly pressured, was gratifying. The sporadic income from Peaceful Repose Funerals, plus even more sporadic engagements as an officiant at non-religious cremations, meant that Drew and his family were forced to live very simply. The prospect of over a thousand pounds coming in for what was essentially a single day's work, lifted his spirits. They'd be able to take the kids out for a day, buy Stephanie some new shoes, and stock up the freezer with some meat.

He didn't give Roma or Justine or Karen's cousin Penn a thought until late afternoon. He'd gone out into the burial field to mark out the sites for the two new interments. The next morning, if it didn't rain, he could make a start on the digging. Since his gravedigger had let him down, over a year earlier, he'd done the job himself, manually. The Peaceful Repose style was to keep graves as shallow as was practicable, but it was still an onerous job. Two in one day would leave him with a stiff back. Once in a while, members of the dead person's family would do it themselves, but Drew was still required to advise and assist.

Preparing for a funeral always gave him a buzz, even after years in the job. Unlike any other rite of passage, it gave no opportunity for second chances. Even a wedding could be done again if disaster struck. But a funeral only happened once, or so you could safely assume. It absolutely had to be given every chance of success. Drew always felt an obligation to give a perfect service. This meant attending to the details, even in the simple back-to-basics package that he offered his customers. The body had to be respectably contained, whether in coffin, shroud or willow basket. The procession from the cool room to the graveside had to be dignified and orderly. The lowering into the grave had to avoid clumsiness. Whatever words or prayers or music the family might choose to accompany the burial had to be respected. Drew and Maggs had sometimes been forced to bite back giggles, and avoid each other's eye, at some of the more mawkish offerings at this stage, but they'd never disgraced themselves. He knew he could seem old-fashioned and slightly pompous in his insistence on the necessity for respect, but his worst nightmares all involved being caught out in frivolity during a burial.

It was the bee that reminded him of Roma. As he bent to pull away a clump of overlong grass from the spot he'd chosen for Mr French's grave, his fingers must have closed on a bee. The result was a painful sting, just below the first joint of his right forefinger. He could see the barb still in his flesh, with no sign of the offending insect, even though he was sure a bee always died after stinging somebody. Pulling out the sting, he expected the pain to subside, but instead it seemed to get worse. Red hot and acute, it felt much sharper than he remembered from previous experiences.

He went back to the house and presented himself to Karen. 'I've been stung,' he whined. 'It really hurts. What're you supposed to put on bee stings?'

'Are you sure it was a bee?'

'Not really. It must have been quite small.'

'Well, you'll have to ask your bee lady, won't

you? She's probably got some patent remedy.' Her lack of sympathy was characteristic. She was generally brisk about illnesses and ailments, apparently acting on the premise that the less attention you accorded them, the quicker they went away.

'Roma? I forgot – she wants to see me. Should I go now, do you think? Maggs can cope without me for half an hour, till she goes home.'

'What about supper?' Karen did her best to maintain regular meals, resisting the growing tendency to let mealtimes move unpredictably across the day. But August was a sloppy month, especially to a former teacher. Drew didn't think he'd be missing very much if supper went ahead without him.

'I'm not sure how long I'll be,' he said.

Karen shrugged. 'We'll just have some cheese and salad then. You can help yourself when you get back.'

'Look! It's going all red,' he noticed. 'Do you think it was one of those killer bees you hear about?'

'No such thing,' she scoffed. 'That's just an urban myth.'

'That's all right then,' he said, unconvinced.

'Why didn't you tell me about your brother Conrad?' Laurie murmured smoothly, barely changing his tone, as he sat with Roma in the lounge, the patio doors open to the sweet-smelling garden.

'What? What are you talking about?' she stared at him wildly, her thick grey hair seeming to crackle with the energy of her astonishment.

'He was stung to death by bees. Don't you ever think about him?'

'He was a brat,' Roma said shortly. 'I was actually quite pleased to be rid of him.'

'Roma!' For the first time, she saw horror and disgust on his face at something she'd said, and a sour disappointment seeped through her.

'It's true,' she insisted. 'I was six. I didn't think the death of a child was anything to get so worked up about. Children didn't seem particularly special to me at the time. Still don't, I suppose, in a lot of cases, though I've got enough social conditioning now to understand a bit more about how people feel when their child dies. Listen,' she said fiercely, pushing her face close to his. 'Don't you go judging me by some mindless tabloid morality. I hoped you'd be able to keep an open mind, to take me as I am, however deviant the rest of the world might think me. I hoped you'd be an *ally*.'

He looked at her boldly, stalwart in the teeth of her rage. 'Roma, you know I am completely your ally. But the fact remains you're a creature from a different world to me. If I'm sometimes slow to react as you want, it's because I can't always keep up with you. It's my failing, not yours. But what about your parents? They must have been shattered.'

'Thank Christ you didn't say *devastated*,' she applauded, with a brief smile. 'Yes, of course they were. They felt and behaved very much as you'd expect. And I was angry and jealous and – oh, furious. It's always been the first emotion I reach for at times of crisis. I almost burst with it. But . . .' she thrust her face at him again, '—I did *not* feel guilty. Contrary to what you might be deep down suspecting, I didn't push the little fool into the hive. I actually wished I had, because they got rid of the dog, and I loved him considerably more than I loved little Conrad.'

Laurie slowly closed his eyes. 'I don't know what to say,' he mumbled.

'Don't say anything. It's not worth the effort. It happened fifty-three years ago, if anybody's counting. And until today, I don't think I've thought about Conrad for at least a year. Probably a lot longer.'

'So there's no significance to the fact that you now keep bees?' he asked. 'I mean, it's interesting psychologically, don't you think?'

'I realise you got all this from Helen,' she said calmly. 'And she will have told you how both our parents would go berserk if a bee ever came into the house. She might not have mentioned that I always liked them, even before Conrad died. The people next door kept them, and I would lie in the grass beside the hive and watch them going in and out. They got rid of them, of course, as well as the wretched dog. I promised myself that I'd keep my own one day. It took a long time to get there, but I did. Satisfied?'

'Perfectly. It's rather a happy ending, in a way,' he said, emolliently.

Drew's finger was still sore when he reached Pitcombe and parked beside Roma's garden wall. Her cottage was a short way out of the village, surrounded by fields. All was quiet as Drew walked up the front path. It was a warm evening, with the heavy languor of high summer that seemed to occur more in memory than reality. Perhaps because it was rare and unexpected, he sensed an undercurrent. Such humidity surely presaged a storm before long? The very silence carried unsettling suggestions.

In response to the doorbell, Roma appeared around the side of the house, and led him back into the lounge through the french windows. Laurie was comfortably settled in a soft chair and Drew hurriedly begged him not to get up. The two men knew each other only slightly. Drew imagined, rather to his surprise, that there was a glint of relief in Laurie's eyes at his appearance.

'I've been stung,' Drew began, his finger still tingling. 'It really hurt.'

Roma glanced at the proffered finger. 'It always hurts more if it's close to a joint,' she said. 'It'll soon be better.'

Drew stifled a sigh. Women these days could be heartless creatures. 'Karen says you wanted to talk to me,' he said.

'We had a call from the police,' Laurie said quickly. 'We weren't expecting that.' The reproach was unmistakable.

Drew didn't reply, but looked at Roma for elaboration. She squinted up at him from her chair. She wore a very low sun-top, her skin tanned but wrinkled. 'Sit down,' she said, nodding at the settee. 'I'll get us some nibbles in a minute.'

'I'll do it,' Laurie offered, already levering himself out of his armchair. As he bent forward, shifting his weight onto his feet, he emitted a low grunt and put a quick hand to his middle. It became a frozen moment; Drew concerned at the obvious stab of pain, Roma studiously looking away, Laurie struggling to recover himself. In those three seconds, Drew understood that whatever might ail the man was not to be mentioned or even acknowledged. So powerful was this unspoken instruction that he had little difficulty in dismissing it as insignificant. Just a twinge of indigestion, a fleeting stiffness, nothing more. Laurie stood upright and walked steadily out of the room. Roma met Drew's gaze unperturbed. She even smiled slightly. 'It's a lovely evening, isn't it,' she said. 'After such a dull day.'

Drew nodded, knowing she didn't really want to discuss the weather. He also knew her well enough to suspect that she would find it difficult to come out with what she wanted to say. She reminded him sometimes of his mother: a brisk and impatient manner on the outside covering a host of hidden uncertainties and anxieties.

'This policeman,' she began. 'You put him onto me, I presume?'

Despite himself, Drew felt under attack. Her face remained impassive, but the words were clearly accusatory. 'Well . . .' he mumbled. 'I suppose I did in a way.'

'You went and reported my daughter as being missing? Is that right?'

He took a deep breath. 'I thought there was enough to justify reporting it, yes. She obviously left her cottage in a big hurry.'

'Did you speak to Penn first?'

'No I didn't.' He lifted his chin. 'She asked me to go and look round, to confirm her worries about your daughter. She involved me and I just took it from there.'

143

'Hmm.' She tapped her fingers on the glass-topped table beside her chair. 'You took it much further than I thought you would. And the police seemed more interested than might be expected. I must admit I was cross with you when I got that phone call. I'm still not happy about it.'

'But if she is in trouble, surely you want to know about it? And Penn . . .'

'Penn's a fool most of the time.' Roma clapped a hand to her chest in an ambiguous gesture. 'I shouldn't say that – she's always been good to me and manages to keep on the right side of everybody. But I don't think she's got a very subtle mind. She often seems to get the wrong idea about things. I can't imagine why she sent you off like that. If she's seriously worried about my daughter, she ought to have gone to the police herself.'

'I think she assumed they wouldn't be very interested. That's what she said.'

'Anyhow, it's done now. I think I managed to convince them that I have absolutely no idea where the wretched girl's got to. It's damned bothersome, all the same.'

They both turned as a clatter announced Laurie with a trayful of savoury snacks and a large jug of home-made ginger beer that he announced as his speciality. Drew helped to distribute glasses and plates and helped himself to an assortment of nibbles. He was surprised at the selection: not mere crisps and peanuts, but more the kind of thing to be found at a smart cocktail party, carried round by girls in silly costumes. 'You haven't made these, have you?' he asked Laurie.

Roma answered for him. 'No, we got them from the little delicatessen in Bradbourne. We have rather a weakness for this sort of thing. Try the cream cheese whirls.'

Drew needed no urging, and was enjoying the various taste sensations when there was a sound from the garden, where the light had almost gone. Before he could work out what it was, a thin voice called, 'Hello? Is anybody there?'

'Who's that?' Roma responded sharply. Drew heard disbelief in her voice. And fear.

'It's me,' said the visitor, appearing slowly around the corner. 'I rang the doorbell, but I don't think you could have heard it.' A young woman was standing there like a character from a fairytale. Her black hair hung down her face like a gypsy's and her face was streaked with grey smudges and seemed to be bruised. Her bare legs were caked with mud up to the hem of a grimy cotton dress. Nobody spoke for a long moment, before the girl said again, 'It's me, Mum,' and burst into tears.

Maggs locked up the office, making sure her two exanimate clients were covered in damp cloths before she went. It was only the second time ever that there had been two bodies in the cool room simultaneously and the effect was to make it seem decidedly crowded. The warm evening was bad news, and the cloths were her own idea, as some small defence against the natural processes that would inexorably advance during the next two days. There was never going to be any chance of the sort of industrial refrigerator used by most undertakers, not even of an air conditioning unit. The most she could hope for was a large stone slab, acquired from some old farmhouse dairy, which would certainly be a help.

Mr French was her bigger worry, thanks to his chemotherapy. The wholesale poisoning of his system, at a point in his illness where all chance of recovery had long evaporated, made her angry. It also made him malodorous. It always struck her as an unnecessary extra burden for the families if their loved one had begun to smell of putrefaction even before the burial. In a warm August, the problem could only be exacerbated.

She fetched her bike from its place beside the back door and wheeled it into the road. She still lived with her parents, six miles distant, and the Yamaha knew the way without any conscious direction on her part. It was her usual habit to spend the journey letting the wind slap into her

146

face, enjoying the sensation of naked speed and thinking of nothing. It was an essential cleansing process that she had learnt early. After her first few weeks working for a funeral director, her mother had reproached her for the stream of graphic stories she'd brought home with her.

'I don't mind you doing the job, if it's what you really want,' she'd said. 'But I really don't want to hear too much about it. And your father says it makes him feel sick.' Maggs had done her best to comply. Her parents were in their late sixties, having adopted her as a small child. It had been as successful as such a transaction could ever be. She respected and admired them, was grateful for their care and concern, but she secretly grieved for her natural parents, that feckless mixed-race couple who had somehow failed to get it all together.

She had friends, but none of great intimacy. The job created the same kind of barrier as it did for Drew. It made people uneasy. They would look at her hands and flare their nostrils like nervous horses. Maggs didn't mind. She loved the work and wholeheartedly shared Drew's zeal for the alternative way of doing business. She was popular with the families and knew exactly how to pitch her dealings with them. She dreamt of expanding Peaceful Repose out of all recognition, in a future time when the majority of funerals were conducted their way. She would be a pioneer, a teacher of forthcoming generations of undertakers. And in the process, incredible as it might seem now, she would make a lot of money.

Absently, she mounted the bike, gunning the engine, enjoying the sensation of power beneath her. Stephanie appeared in the open doorway of the Slocombes' house and waved to her, as she often did. Maggs was increasingly fond of Stephanie, despite some disagreements with Drew about being used as an unpaid childminder. Every now and then she allowed a fantasy scenario to enter her mind where she and the little girl became joint owners of a big improved Peaceful Repose Funerals while Drew took early retirement and got out of their way. An all-female business had a lot of appeal for her.

Turning her attention back to the road from her answering wave to the child, she had to abort her intended departure with a hurried slewing, to avoid a car inches from her front wheel. It had quietly come to a standstill beside Drew's gate and a very tall man was unfolding himself from the driving seat.

It was the friendly Okehampton policeman and the sight of him did strange things to Maggs's insides. Nine or ten thoughts struck her simultaneously: she wasn't wearing her crash helmet; she was dressed in completely the wrong clothes; it was amazingly pleasant to see him again; it was very scary to see him again; he was *fantastically* tall; she'd be able to talk to him all on her own, without Drew; he must have some exciting news about the Case of the Missing Cousin; and, damn it, it was Karen's cousin they were looking for, so he'd probably want to see her, not Maggs.

'Hello,' she said carelessly. 'What brings you here?'

He pushed out his lower lip in a boyish grimace of comic embarrassment. 'The usual answer to that would be "I was just passing . . ." but—' he swept the small country lane with a rueful glance, 'you wouldn't believe me.'

'No,' she agreed.

'So let's say I was intrigued by your cemetery. I've never seen a wild burial ground, or whatever you call it.' He focused on the signboard beside Drew's gate. 'Peaceful Repose, eh? Sounds cool to me.'

'We like to think it is. Do you want me to show you round? I was just going home, actually,' she added superfluously.

'Don't let me hold you up.' He scratched his chin, embarrassment still evident. 'It was only a whim.'

'Any progress on finding Justine?' she finally asked. 'Did you go to the cottage?'

He shook his head. 'I went to see her cousin. Miss Strabinski.'

'And?'

'Well, something's not right. I agree with you on that. But that isn't enough for a real investigation. Just a couple of lines in the log and keep our eyes open for the missing woman. I'm not very strong on hunches as a rule. There's not usually time for them, anyway. But this one's niggling me. There's something so – well, *foggy* – about it. I phoned the mother, incidentally. She didn't sound very friendly.'

'Drew's there now,' Maggs said carelessly. 'He likes her a lot. It's a thing with him, older women.'

'Oh? But isn't there a wife?' He glanced towards the cottage, where sounds of Stephanie and Timmy giggling wafted through the open door and windows.

Maggs grinned. 'Yes there's a wife. It doesn't bother her. He's always the perfect gentleman. Well, nearly always. No, but honestly, Karen's got no reason to worry. They're a great couple.'

He didn't say anything more for some moments. Maggs watched him as he took a few restless steps along the grass verge and back again, expecting him to light a cigarette. He had that tense deprived air of someone desperate for a fix of his preferred substance. 'We could go for a drink,' she offered unthinkingly, responding to this perceived need.

'Oh no.' He shook his head. 'I'd be keeping you. Aren't you expected at home?'

She chuckled. 'They've learnt to expect me when they see me, in this job,' she assured him. 'On call more or less all the time, me.'

He frowned in sympathy. 'Sounds worse than the police. What do you do for a social life?'

'Go without, mostly.'

'Then let's do the drink,' he said, suddenly decisive. 'Lead the way.'

She took him to a roadside pub some distance from North Staverton and Peaceful Repose, shamelessly showing off her biking technique, staying a mere hair's breadth inside the speed limit. But she was wise enough to don her crash helmet, making a performance of it, before setting off.

They sat under a cherry tree in the pub's garden and drank the local ale. He told her about his recent holiday and she wistfully regretted not having been abroad more than twice in her life. They each came up with amusing incidents from their working lives, observations about human nature and the reactions of their families to how they lived their lives. 'My mum's learnt to leave me to it, at last,' he said. 'Considering she lives in the same town, I hardly ever see her. She's always running around on some new project. I don't know what it is with middle-aged women these days.'

'HRT, probably,' Maggs grimaced. 'Do you know how they make that stuff? It's an absolute disgrace. Totally sick.' She almost spat the words and he glimpsed the strong character beneath the dimples.

'My ex-girlfriend used to get upset about that, too,' he remembered. 'Something about pregnant mares.'

'They have to keep them hidden in some remote part of the American desert, for fear of animal rights activists,' she said narrowly. 'I'd put a bomb under their cars myself, given half a chance.'

'Steady!' he cautioned her. 'Don't forget I'm a cop.'

'Right!' she laughed. 'Are you a good cop?'

'Not really for me to say.' He tipped his head sideways in mock consideration. 'Probably not as good as I thought I'd be by this time. Likely to remain a sergeant forever at this rate.'

'Maybe you should move?' she suggested. 'Okehampton seems a bit of a dump.'

'There's a lot of different kinds of dump,' he remarked. 'I'd rather live on the edge of Dartmoor where there's still some genuine sense of community than in a Teesside inner city. A mate of mine moved to Middlesbrough. He calls it God's arsehole.'

Maggs spluttered. 'How rude,' she said.

With an unarticulated unanimity, they finished their drinks and prepared to leave. A sense of something begun, foundations established, marked the evening. Neither wanted to risk spoiling it. Maggs sat astride her motorcycle and watched him drive away, his long body filling the driving seat, his hair brushing the car's roof. 'Goodness, he's tall,' she murmured to herself, before riding buoyantly home.

CHAPTER SEVEN

Sheena and Philip Renton seldom coincided. Their busy working lives described complex ellipses that necessitated a small army of staff to perform all the delegated tasks of cleaning, cooking, washing, gardening – and taking care of little Georgia. Sheena earned almost three times as much as her husband, which in her eyes gave her carte blanche to be away from home for almost all the hours of daylight.

But when she did eventually come home that evening, her husband was waiting for her, sitting in the large kitchen with a cold beer in front of him.

'All right?' she asked him automatically. 'Had a good day?'

'You ought to be asking me if I've had a good *week,*' he grumbled. 'It's about that long since I saw you long enough to talk about anything. I don't count this morning,' he added with a weak smile.

'Surely I spoke to you then?' she said lightly. 'And I'm sure I saw you the day before yesterday. Anyway, with Georgia out of the way it's a great chance to do some catching up. I went to Swindon this morning to stir them up a bit. Just because it's August, they think they can switch off and do bugger all.'

He looked at her closely, wondering when they'd last taken any real notice of each other. They'd only been married eight years, after all. Wasn't that a bit soon for such routine apathy? They almost never went anywhere together or discussed anything halfway serious.

'I mean it,' he tried again. 'I've got things to tell you.'

'Shut up, Phil,' she snapped. 'I've got stacks to do. Haven't you got somebody you should be phoning? Did you call that Roger chap back?'

'There were people here yesterday looking for Justine,' persisted.

'Oh? Did you tell them she's away? Where did she say she was going? What did they want her for?'

'Seemingly Penn's been worrying about her.

She hasn't turned up for something she said she would. I don't know where she was going.'

Something in his tone hooked her attention. She frowned at him. 'Hang on. Has something been going on here that I should know about? When's she coming back? Georgia's due home – tomorrow, is it? We'll need Justine at the weekend. I'll be in Edinburgh.'

'I thought you'd forgotten all about Georgia,' he said harshly.

She tossed her head. 'She's fine with your mother. I don't see any point in worrying. Maybe we could ask her to keep her a bit longer? Have you phoned them? I bet they're having a whale of a time.'

Philip looked away, grabbing blindly for his bottle of beer and swigging from it. 'For all you care, Mum might as well keep her permanently,' he accused.

She didn't rise to the bait. There was enough truth in his words to keep her silent. Letting herself become a mother had been the biggest mistake she'd ever made, and she had never been able to hide the fact from herself or from Philip. The child had no doubt been aware of it too. A solemn, well-behaved little girl, she'd quickly learnt not to cling. Instead she went willingly to the day nursery and assortment of babysitters that her parents found for her, quietly playing with bricks or crayons. It was as if the whole family had made a pact to hurry through these inconvenient years of infancy as rapidly as possible, because once Georgia grew up, everything would be so much better for them all. They could have holidays together then, in a civilised fashion, and Georgia would no longer be such a nuisance.

Sheena was almost grateful to her daughter for the way she seemed to understand. Whenever she experienced a pang of guilt at her lack of maternal feeling, she would ask the child, 'Are you okay, sweetie?' and Georgia would always nod briskly and proffer a drawing or toy as if to demonstrate her contentedness. She made it easy for her mother to pursue her own course with none of the anguish of many a working mother.

How she'd managed to get onto such a treadmill, Sheena couldn't now quite recall, but on it she was, and it was thrilling, most of the time. If she could swing a couple more meetings, using every female trick available, and then some, she'd be all set for a major step up the career ladder. Two steps, probably. *Ladder*, she repeated to herself. Not a treadmill at all. Treadmills just went round in a big circle, and dumped you back where you started. She was no hamster. She was a climber. She was going to scale the heights, and look back over her shoulder at all the sad little people down on the ground. Having the baby had been a bad mistake, and for a few months, Sheena had worried that she'd never regain her momentum, but it had all worked well enough, once she pulled herself together.

Phil was useless, of course. Show her a man who wasn't. And he was always lying to her. It wasn't so much the lies she objected to, as the minimal effort he made to be convincing. It was demeaning to have him tell her two contradictory things about how he'd spent his day, when any fool could see that neither story was true. She supposed he'd been having some sort of fling, as several people had warned her he would if she didn't make more effort as a wife. But she didn't think it would ever turn into anything serious. Philip was hers for life; they'd been through too much together, with that unspeakable foot and mouth business, followed by his dad's suicide. Phil depended on her for his stability and security, and if the sex was perfunctory between them, then that really wasn't so important. She liked living at Gladcombe, having so much space, and so few other people around. It wasn't a real farm any more, of course, but that at least meant less mud and muck and midnight crises. If Philip could make enough money at his forage dealing to satisfy his own self-esteem, then that was plenty for her. In fact it very often seemed to comprise the best of all worlds.

She realised he hadn't answered her question. 'Have you?' she repeated.

'Have I what?'

'Phoned your mother to see how they're getting on.'

'I did try a couple of times, but there was no reply. They'll have been on a beach or something. Mum'd soon let us know if there was a problem.' He took another swig of the beer and got up from the chair. 'I think I'll just . . .' he moved towards the door, '. . . um, go and see if there's enough oil in the car. The red light came on this afternoon.'

She let him go, her thoughts again on her forthcoming meetings. Any babysitting difficulties could be resolved nearer the time. Philip had a point, anyway. While the weather was nice and everything apparently going smoothly, Georgia may as well stay another week or so with her granny.

The phone started ringing out in the hall. Normally Sheena would leave the answering machine to deal with it, but she was already heading for the stairs and passing close by the instrument. She picked it up without really thinking.

'Sheena? It's me. How are you, dear?'

It was Yvonne Renton, her mother-in-law,

apparently conjured by the recent conversation and Sheena's last thoughts.

'Hi, Mum, we're fine. Sorry we haven't managed to speak to you all week. Phil says he did try, but . . .'

'Not to worry, then. I'm just the same as always. No need to keep ringing me.'

'But we really should, seeing you've got Georgia with you.'

'Pardon?' The voice was suddenly sharp. 'What did you say?'

'Georgia. How is she? Is she being good? Can I have a word with her? We've just been talking about you both and wondering – well, wondering if you might keep her a bit longer . . .'

The older woman's voice cut through her words. 'Georgia isn't here, Sheena. Surely you knew that? Philip phoned me last week and cancelled the whole arrangement. I must say I wasn't at all happy about it. I'd been planning and preparing it for weeks. I hope she's over her flu now? That's really what I phoned to ask.'

Sheena couldn't think. Her brain seemed to have been anaesthetised. All she could feel was embarrassment. She'd been so inattentive as to miss some crucial piece of information. Philip had obviously told her what was happening and she'd forgotten, or never even heard him. But flu? Surely she would have known if the child had flu?

Instinct reassured her that everything was all right. Philip must be playing some kind of stupid game and she'd quickly get out of him just what was going on. In any case there was no sense in alarming her mother-in-law, although it might be too late to think of that.

'Sheena? Are you there?'

'Yes, I'm here. I've been away all week, you see. I only just got in and haven't had a chance to speak to Philip yet. I didn't know about the flu. Last I heard, Georgia was going off to you. It sounds bad, I know, but it's all going crazy at work and I haven't had a chance to check in here.' She was babbling, aware of how it must come across to Philip's mother, but willing at the moment to paint herself in a bad light rather than admit she'd been lied to.

'You know, Sheena,' the older woman said conversationally, 'I do sometimes wonder whether you deserve that child.'

'Well, thanks for that,' spat Sheena. 'I'll get Phil to phone you after I've spoken to him.'

'Yes, you do that,' the woman was saying as Sheena put the phone down.

Penn felt a desperate need to keep busy. Time had dragged all day, with no phone calls, no visitors, nothing to distract her from her obsessive thoughts. She would have liked to phone Roma or even the newfound Cousin Karen, but she couldn't think of a convincing pretext. If there'd been any news about Justine, someone would have contacted her. The tall policeman had said something vague about putting out a description and that was probably as far as any police effort would go.

By early evening she'd reached the conclusion that she ought to go away for a few days. Then she could come back refreshed to resume her life. At least, that was her most optimistic scenario. There were much darker visions at times. When she tried to consider the situation dispassionately, she repeatedly bumped up against any number of complications and hazards. Had she been clever enough? Had Drew Slocombe been convinced by what he'd found in the cottage? For the hundredth time she ran through it all from every angle. She was determined that it would work out, no matter how high the cost. Penn Strabinski had always been a determined character, always getting what she wanted. There had been setbacks, of course, but she wouldn't even contemplate failure at this point. There was far too much at stake now and definitely no going back.

But it would be sensible to absent herself for a few days, all the same. There was nothing more she could do until things quietened down again and everyone went back to their accustomed grooves. Not until then could she embark on the next stage of her plan. The next and final stage.

The only affectionate greeting Justine received was from Lolly. The little dog jumped off Roma's lap and flew to welcome the newcomer. Bending stiffly, Justine took the animal between her hands. 'Hello, little thing. What's your name, then?' She glanced enquiringly at her mother.

'Lolita,' supplied Roma gruffly. Justine snorted in derisive amusement.

Drew found himself meeting Laurie's gaze, which seemed entirely as bewildered as he himself felt. Then he looked again at the girl. 'You're Justine?' he asked faintly. He thought he'd recognised the figure from the oil painting in the cottage he'd searched.

'That's right,' she confirmed. 'And I'm very lucky to be alive. I've been locked up for days with no water and my hands tied behind my back.' She spoke angrily as if at least one of those present were directly responsible for her plight.

Laurie seemed to come to his senses. 'You poor girl!' he exclaimed. 'You look dreadful. Come and sit down. Can I bring you anything? Would you like to go and have a good wash?'

As if at a signal, Roma finally joined in. 'What

on earth have you been doing?' she demanded. 'What's been going on?'

'Don't bully her, woman,' Laurie said. 'The poor girl's in no state to answer questions.'

'But . . .' Roma considered snapping back, but a renewed burst of weeping from Justine distracted her. 'Oh, for heaven's sake,' Roma tutted. 'You'll have to tell us *something*. Do you need a doctor? Are you hungry? Do you want me to get a bed ready?'

'Bed,' the girl whispered. 'I haven't slept for days. Only odd snatches.'

'Right. I'll go and find some clean sheets, then.' Roma started to leave the room, then turned back. 'Did I hear you correctly? Somebody *kidnapped* you, did they?'

Justine nodded. 'I'm in the most awful trouble, Mum. Otherwise I wouldn't have come. I know you don't want me. But—' she looked desperately from face to face, pausing worriedly at Drew and addressing him directly: 'Whatever you do, don't tell Penn I'm here.'

Karen had watched Maggs go off with the tall stranger and spent a few moments wondering who he could possibly be. The small mystery irritated her, as did many things recently. Everybody seemed to be having a much more interesting life than hers, and there was little prospect of changing that, at least until Timothy started school. Drew's erratic career was full of unpredictable variety, most of which Karen never heard about. She watched the burials taking place in the field behind the house, but almost never got directly involved. Her only solace, pathetically, seemed to be the vegetable garden that occupied so much of her time.

Stephanie and Timmy were wonderful, of course. They were funny and interesting and entirely adorable. They played peacefully together and were in robust good health. But Karen had been a teacher in a primary school and was accustomed to the pressures and rewards of hectic days and visible success. Life now felt thin and unstimulating by comparison. Essentially, she supposed, she felt guilty for not achieving more. And then guilty for being so boring and stupid for not enjoying what she had and making the best of it.

Much of the problem lay with Maggs. Although the two women got along well on the surface, Karen had intercepted many a pitying or even contemptuous glance. She had become a lesser person simply because she'd produced children, and childless women made no secret of this. However hard Karen worked at retaining her lively wits, at the same time as making a good job of raising the kids, she knew she'd lost status in the eyes of the world. It was irrational, unfair, often unacknowledged – but real just the same. She was aware of herself as a shadowy figure, on object of reduced attention from almost everybody.

Turning away from the window with a sigh, she went to find food for the children's supper. Stephanie was lying on the floor, feet crossed in the air, chin resting on one hand, drawing carefully with the other. Karen nudged her with her foot. 'That's no way to do your drawing,' she chided. 'You should sit up at the table.'

The child ignored her, peaceably continuing to draw. Irritation swept through Karen again and she jabbed Stephanie's ribs harder. 'Get up!' she ordered.

'Ow!' squealed her daughter. 'You kicked me!'

Timothy looked up from the couch where he'd been watching television, thumb in mouth. He blinked reproachfully at his mother. Stephanie slowly got to her feet, picked up the drawing things and slid on to one of the upright chairs next to the table. She didn't say a word. Karen closed her eyes and inhaled deeply.

'Sorry, Steph,' she managed. 'That was bad of me.'

Stephanie gave a very adult shrug. It was a seminal moment for Karen. Dismissed by her own child, as well as by everyone else. *That's it*, she vowed silently. *I'll show them all.* She didn't know how she'd do it, but she wasn't going to let herself be ignored any more. Just wait till Drew gets home, she fumed.

Sheena went carefully out to the yard, looking for Philip. Her head felt swollen and impossibly sensitive. Inside it there were lightning flashes, as the implications of her mother-in-law's words struggled to be understood. Only one thing was clear: Philip had lied to her about Georgia's whereabouts. And that made no possible sense.

She found him coming around the corner of the house from the covered area where they kept their cars, and stood in front of him, trying to focus on his face.

'Where is she, Phil? What have you done with her?'

'Who? What?' He widened his eyes and reached out a hand to her. She backed away from him.

'Your mother just phoned. Georgia isn't with her. She hasn't been there at all. Tell me what the bloody hell is going on.' Her voice sounded strange to her own ears, but her husband's expression reflected back none of her panic.

'She's perfectly all right,' he said, quickly. 'It was idiotic of me not to tell you, but there didn't seem much point.' He smiled tentatively. 'I didn't think you'd be too pleased about it, so decided to let it wait until they came back.'

'What?' she almost screamed. 'What are you talking about?'

'Come on, Sheen. Cool down. There's no need to get in a state. Christ, you hardly notice the kid when she is here. It doesn't matter to you if I change the arrangements.'

She held her breath and inwardly counted to five. 'It does matter, actually. I'm her mother. I do in fact want to know where she is at all times.'

'Well, I'm sorry. I just had a better idea, that's all. Honestly, darling, she's perfectly all right.'

'I don't believe you.' She realised as she spoke that it was dreadfully true. Philip was too relaxed, making too big an effort to keep his shoulders loose, his face bland. He should at least be alarmed by her discovery. Such insouciance was unnatural. But if he was intent on playing some horrible game, she saw no option but to co-operate. She turned to go back into the house, flipping one hand at him to follow her. 'Okay,' she snapped. 'You can prove it to me. Call the number where she is and let me speak to her.'

'I can't. She's camping,' he said. Sheena was reminded crazily of a television sitcom, where people dig themselves deeper and deeper into trouble by inventing more and more extreme lies to cover their mistakes.

'Camping,' she repeated woodenly. 'Where? Who with?'

'Justine!' he announced, and for half a second, she believed him. 'I let Justine take her. She begged me. You know how fond they are of each other. There didn't seem to be any harm in it.'

Sheena savoured this story, watching his face. He grinned self-deprecatingly and spread his hands. It was a good performance, but there was a parodic feel to it – an actor depicting rueful confession of a rather minor misdemeanour.

'Is that really true?' she demanded. 'Why didn't you tell me before? Why all the secrecy?'

'I thought you might be jealous,' he said. 'Of Justine. Having all that time with your daughter. Silly,' he tried to laugh. 'You hardly even thought about her till now.'

'Because I thought she was *safe*. I thought she was being organised to death on the Isle of Wight. Which is how she likes it. How could you do that to your mother? Even I wouldn't be that rotten.'

He shrugged. 'She didn't really mind. It was going to be a sweat for her.'

'But . . .' she felt the first real thrusts of fear. 'Where is she now? Where's Justine? When are they supposed to come back? Tell me the truth, Phil. You've *got* to tell me everything.'

He pushed past her into the kitchen and sat down on one of the wooden chairs, leaving her to choose whether to stand or sit. She opted to remain vertical, leaning lightly against the edge of the sink, her back to the window. 'It's quite a long story,' he said. 'And you're not going to like it.'

'Tell me,' she repeated. But she allowed herself to glance at the clock on the wall, and to note that she had five minutes before the conference call with their American sister company. If she missed it, she'd lose so much ground, it would take six months to recover. She gritted her teeth, and glared at her husband. 'Am I right to be afraid something's happened to Georgia?' she demanded.

'Of course not,' he said emphatically.

'If I can believe that, then the rest can wait,' she said. 'Can't it?'

'Absolutely,' he agreed, with transparent relief. 'You get off to your telephoning. I know how important it is to you.'

Her mother-in-law's words echoed in her head. *I do wonder whether you deserve that child.* Something told Sheena that she would never manage to live with herself if she let it drop now. Her child had been with a girl who'd had strange people come looking for her, for nearly a week, and her husband was trying to tell her something he knew she wouldn't want to hear. Some story she couldn't begin to guess at. Only a monster would go off to a conference call at a moment like this. She might be an inattentive mother, but she wasn't a monster. She stifled the groan that threatened to turn into hysterics if she didn't keep strict control.

'I can't,' she said. 'You know I can't. Something terrible's been going on, and I've been blind and deaf and unforgivably stupid. So tell me the whole thing. Please.'

He wouldn't look at her, but instead swung his gaze from floor to window and back again, in a jerky arc. 'Sit down then,' he told her. She obeyed, wondering when the numbness would turn to something much sharper.

'I've been having an affair with Justine,' he began. 'For about two months now. We're lovers.' He said the word roundly, as if it held a vital key to what came next. As if it was the one sweet note in a discordant song.

Sheena clenched a fist on her thigh. 'Why does it feel as though that's the least of my worries?' she grated.

'Well . . . we've been talking about going away together, taking Georgia with us,' he said quickly.

'Don't be ridiculous,' she dismissed. 'You'd never leave this place. You're fooling yourself, and that wretched girl. Look, phone her, will you? Tell her to come back right away.' She tried to quell the tremor in her voice. Philip simply stood there, shaking his head slowly.

'Don't tell me she hasn't got a mobile?'

'She left it behind. I haven't spoken to her since she left.'

Sheena's fear returned. 'What?'

'I think something might have gone wrong,' he admitted. 'I thought she would have got in touch by now.'

'When were you going to tell me about this?'

'Soon, I suppose. When we had it all properly organised.'

'So what kept your mouth shut when you realised you had no idea where our little girl was? When for all you knew they were both dead in a ditch somewhere? I can't believe anyone could be so appallingly irresponsible.'

He doesn't deserve the child, either, she thought. *What a pair we are!*

'It'll be all right,' he said desperately. 'They'll turn up.'

'I'm phoning the police *now*,' she said. 'What was all that stuff you told me earlier on? People looking for Justine? What did you really tell them?'

'That she's gone camping,' he said loudly. 'The truth.'

'So why are people looking for her?' Sheena repeated. 'Philip, I've had the feeling for the past half hour that something is terribly wrong.'

'No, no,' he persisted. 'Look, don't call the police this evening. It'll be dark in a bit. They're not going to do anything until tomorrow, are they? Wait till then. Justine might phone us this evening, anyway. Georgia won't come to any harm.'

She clenched her fists ineffectually. 'I don't see any point in waiting. They'll ask why we delayed.' She looked into his eyes, trying to read him. 'Are you truly not worried?'

'Truly not,' he said, unblinking.

She glanced at her watch. She had only missed a few minutes of the conference call. It would probably go on for at least an hour. Philip had given her a firm assurance. She continued to watch him. 'Aren't you afraid for Georgia?' she asked one last time, with genuine curiosity. 'Doesn't it occur to you that you might have handed her over to a psychopath? Or that they've both been murdered? Why aren't you showing more concern? Why aren't you as scared as I am?'

'I'm scared,' he laughed tightly. 'Believe me, I'm scared. But not for Georgia.'

Drew felt very much in the way as Roma and Laurie slowly began to realise that Justine needed

173

more than a drink and somewhere to lie down, but it didn't seriously occur to him to leave. After all, he had been asked to find the girl, and her sudden reappearance was far too interesting for him to miss whatever might happen next. Roma came back from making up a bed, finding Justine sunk exhaustedly into Laurie's usual chair, showing no sign of wanting to climb the stairs.

Roma was stiffly furious, from the look of her. She had introduced Drew, adding, 'He's been looking for you, as it happens.'

Drew's immediate thought was that Maggs should be there. It seemed all wrong without her. She'd have enjoyed it enormously. As for him, he simply felt embarrassed.

Justine's eyes narrowed 'Looking for me? Why?'

'He won't hurt you,' said Roma, contempt clear in her voice. 'I should think he's as curious as I am to hear what you have to say for yourself.'

Justine let her head flop back. 'I don't think I can,' she said faintly.

'Start from the beginning,' Laurie advised calmly. 'If you're feeling well enough, that is. You're probably thirsty, aren't you?'

'I'd love some orange juice or something,' she admitted, seeming very small in the deep chair. Bare feet added to the waiflike image. Drew had a sense of struggle to maintain a fragile poise. Roma didn't move to fetch the drink.

After a long minute, Laurie got up heavily, and went out of the room. As he passed Justine, he looked into her face. 'Everything's going to be all right,' he said kindly.

Roma tutted, and returned to her interrupted defence of Drew. 'You needn't worry about Drew. He's family, more or less.'

'What?'

'His wife is Penn's cousin. On her father's side.'

Justine snorted, as if this were the final straw. 'And that's supposed to make me trust him, is it? Penn's insane, you know,' she went on earnestly. 'She tried to kill me. That's what I've been trying to tell you.'

Roma tutted again. 'Rubbish!' she said vigorously. 'Penn's been very worried about you. She asked Drew to try to find you.'

'Are you a detective?' the girl addressed Drew directly for the first time. He looked into the dark eyes, which were the same colour and shape as Maggs's, he noticed, but with none of the humour or energy.

'Not really,' he said. 'I seem to wander into complications from time to time, that's all. I'm actually an undertaker. That might account for it. I'm drawn into people's lives at times of crisis.

And when someone dies, their secrets start leaking out.'

'Who said anything about anybody dying?' Justine seemed angry. 'Why did Penn go to an *undertaker*, for God's sake.'

'I think my profession was irrelevant at the time. It was just a coincidence. All she knew was that I'm married to Karen.' It sounded unconvincing to Drew, even as he spoke. It had been the weak spot all along, as Maggs had been quick to point out.

'Actually, she did know you were an undertaker,' said Roma. 'That's how I knew who she was talking about. She said you were New Agey.'

Drew gave this some thought. 'I wonder who she'd been talking to, then? Karen wouldn't have given her that impression.'

'You are rather famous, you know,' Roma informed him. 'It's not the local press any more. Even I saw the piece about you in *The Guardian* not so long ago, and I hardly bother with the papers. Penn probably saw it, and made the connection with her cousin's surname.'

Laurie came back with the orange juice, and handed it solicitously to Justine. 'They're not interested in me,' she said to him in a little girl voice. 'They keep talking about Penn.'

Roma smacked the table with the flat of

her hand, not hard, but more than enough to indicate her frame of mind. 'Perhaps Penn's more interesting,' she said unpleasantly.

She doesn't like her own daughter, Drew realised. The hints had been there, from Roma herself, but now he experienced it for himself, and it came as a shock, even though he wasn't inclined to like Justine very much himself, the way she was behaving at the moment. Had she always been hard to like, or had Roma's antipathy created a person who had come to expect the whole world to feel the same as her mother did? It seemed to Drew that the answer to this mattered quite a lot.

'Nothing's changed, has it, Mum?' Justine said. 'You still think I'm a waste of space.'

'Prove to me otherwise,' Roma invited. 'Go on, I'm waiting. You turn up here looking like a Bosnian asylum seeker on a bad day, and then start whingeing about God knows what. Please, tell us why you're here.'

'Penn kidnapped me and held me prisoner in a foul derelict hovel,' Justine said, looking from face to face as if expecting to be disbelieved. 'She locked me in, and left me, with my hands tied behind me. I only had horrible water that came through a hole in the roof. If it hadn't rained I'd be dead by now.' She held out her wrists for inspection. They were banded by weals and raw places where the skin had rubbed away.

Roma met Drew's eye. Each raised brows, in silent question. Drew felt the room dividing into factions, him and Roma against Justine and Laurie.

'Where? Where did she leave you?' Roma demanded.

'I had no idea at the time, but when I finally got out and found a road, it turned out to be a place near Glastonbury.'

'So how did you get out?' Drew asked. 'Did you unscrew the hinges?' Unscrewing the hinges was Drew's own personal contingency plan, should such a fate ever befall him.

'I tried,' she turned to him earnestly. 'But the screws wouldn't budge. There wasn't a screwdriver, so I had to use a knife. I broke two blades before I gave up.'

Roma cleared her throat. 'This sounds like a rather weak B-movie,' she remarked. 'Are you sure you haven't lost your grip, dear?'

'I knew you'd say that.' Justine laid both hands palms upwards in her lap, deliberately calm. 'How do you think I got these marks, then?'

'She's obviously had a terrible time,' Laurie insisted nervously. 'We should hear her out.'

'Thank you.' Justine threw him a smile. 'She thinks I've staged the whole thing as some bizarre act of cruelty against her. Don't you?' she challenged her mother.

Roma sniffed, like an offended headmistress. 'I still have no idea *what* to think,' she said imperiously. 'So far you haven't made any sense at all.'

'Perhaps you should keep quiet and listen,' said the girl, wincing as she altered her position. You say everyone's been looking for me – right? I said, didn't I? They're out to get me.' She grew wild-eyed, turning her head to face them all, one by one.

'Nobody's out to get you,' Roma contradicted her impatiently. 'You sound like a madwoman. Who might *they* be, anyway? Have a bit of sense.'

'They've been worried about you,' Laurie explained soothingly. 'Penn in particular. She told Drew you'd gone missing and then phoned us here. She thought you were in trouble.'

Justine coughed inarticulate indignation at this. Laurie smiled understandingly, adding, 'Then Drew went to your place and saw your landlord.'

Justine turned to Drew. 'Really? What did you think, when you saw the cottage?'

'I thought it looked as if you'd left in a hurry.'

'Right. I did. She tricked me into getting into my own car, with her driving . . .' She shook her head, apparently at her own folly. 'Then she parked in the woods, and *attacked* me.'

'How?' Drew was fascinated.

'She pushed a pad into my face that smelt disgusting. Chloroform, I suppose. She must have had it all ready.'

'Where's your car now?' Drew pressed, remembering the description of it.

'Still tucked away in the woods, probably. When I woke up, we were getting out of *her* car and I was gagged, with my hands tied. I was so groggy and so totally astonished I didn't put up much of a fight. Then she left me.'

'So how *did* you get out?' Roma asked, scepticism vivid on her face.

'I managed to make a hole in the wall, beside an upstairs window. The place was made of cob and there was a soft bit. I climbed out, scrambled down a tree that had a branch within reach. It's lucky I'm so small, but it was still a tight fit and I've got bruises all round my middle, where I had to force myself through. And then I fell about twenty feet and banged my knee.'

'And then you walked forty miles with a bad knee and your hands tied behind you, until you got here,' Roma supplied.

'No. I hitched, actually, and walked the last half-mile.'

'How did you get your hands untied?'

Justine shuddered. 'I almost pulled my arms out of their sockets, wriggling them round to the front. Believe it or not, it can be done. Then I chewed through the rope. It took hours.' She threw her mother a scathing look. 'That was *before* I made the hole in the wall.'

Drew gazed at her, aware of an increasing desire to believe her. But the part about Penn was altogether incredible. There had to be lies or fantasy mixed into the story.

'And how did you manage to find this place?' Roma pressed on ruthlessly.

Justine paused, flushing pink. 'I looked you up, ages ago, on the Ordnance Survey. I knew how to get to you.'

Roma was momentarily silenced, but Drew noted the effect Justine's words had had.

'I think that's enough questions,' said Laurie. 'The poor girl's dead on her feet. She needs a hot bath and clean clothes. Probably a doctor as well.'

Justine shook her head. 'I'm okay,' she said. 'Just terribly tired and stiff.'

'The person you hitched with,' Drew put in, more gently than Roma's interrogation had been. 'They must have been concerned about you.'

'It was a young girl,' Justine told him. 'She was in a hurry and didn't want to get involved in anything awkward. I told her I'd fallen over a stone in the road and scraped myself. People believe whatever you tell them.'

Roma gave a sarcastic laugh. '*Some* people, maybe,' she remarked.

Laurie mumbled an inarticulate reproach and Drew suppressed a sudden urge to defend the girl against her intractable mother. This was an unfamiliar Roma and he began to regret having so unthinkingly taken her side. There was a long moment of silence.

'So what happens now?' Roma finally inquired. 'Are you afraid that Penn will seek you out, and force you back into captivity?'

'I'm hoping you won't let her,' Justine's voice was stronger. 'But she'll tell you everything I've said is made up. She'll say I'm in the habit of fantasising, and must be off my head.'

Roma's face clearly revealed her reaction to this. 'Penn's always been perfectly straight with me,' she said. 'She's been an ideal niece, all her life. We get along very smoothly.'

'She's extremely devious, and she's got something going on that she doesn't want you or me or anyone to know about. She set this up, you know – my disappearance. She thought it all through, step by step.'

Drew let a small sound escape his lips as he thought of all the wild theories Maggs would probably come up with at this point. Everyone looked at him. He tried to pretend he was coughing.

'But why?' Roma returned to the point. 'Why on earth would she do that?'

'I spent days trying to think of an answer to that,' Justine replied. 'And all I could come up with was that she's always hated me, and this is some sort of mad revenge.'

'She never hated you. She adored you. She followed you around, worried about you. You were the greatest of friends, right from the start.'

'No, Mum. We fought like cats. We competed over every single tiny thing. But she can't leave me alone. She always has to score one more point over me.' Her face crumpled suddenly. 'But I did think she liked me, that we were friends. I still can't believe she wants me dead.'

Roma took a long breath. 'Well, somebody's obviously cracked in all this,' she summarised. 'I'm even beginning to think it might be me. Nothing you just said makes the slightest sense. It's totally at odds with the way I've always seen the family.'

'I don't think anybody's mad,' said Drew, tentatively. 'It's like this in families; people see things differently, remember things differently, too. When you get the whole picture, you can usually see how everyone's perception fits in.'

'Come on, Drew!' Roma protested. 'Either Penn locked Justine up in a remote shack or she didn't. If she did, then Penn's got a screw loose, and if she didn't, then Justine's either telling a terrible lie, or else she can't distinguish fact from fantasy. You're not telling me there are any other interpretations, are you?'

'Obviously there are,' Drew said. 'Penn could have very sane and sound reasons for doing what she did. She could be following orders from someone else. Or she could have shut Justine in by mistake . . .'

Justine laughed unpleasantly. 'No, she didn't do it by mistake,' she told him. 'It was all very very deliberate.'

CHAPTER EIGHT

'Den?' Julie flapped a sheet of paper at him, the moment he walked into the police station. 'There's a new development at that farm out at Tedburn – the one that reported the missing woman. Apparently there's a missing child as well, now. Exeter were going to take it, but they noticed your name's down as having some involvement there this week. Wonders of computers, eh?'

'What?' He snatched the paper from her. 'When did this come in?'

'Ten minutes ago. Danny said it'd wait until you got here. The parents seem pretty sure the missing woman has got the kid, and there's no obvious danger. Just a weird story. You'd better go and see them.'

He frowned in puzzlement. 'Nobody's mentioned a child up to now. Whose is it?'

'Georgia Renton,' supplied Julie, pointing to a line on the sheet of paper. 'Aged three. Daughter of Mrs Sheena Renton, who called us. Says she thought the kid was with its grandma, but found out from her husband that he let the Pereira girl from the cottage take her on a camping trip.'

Den sighed, well accustomed to garbled jottings from telephone conversations. 'It really isn't our patch,' he reminded her. 'I think we ought to leave it to Exeter.'

'No, but this Renton woman asked for you by name. They want to see the same person again.'

He could not quite avoid a small glow of pleasure at being personally chosen. 'Oh well, can't disappoint them, then.' Privately, he resolved to call Drew Slocombe or his young partner before turning up at the farm. It might be unprofessional, but the whole case had a maverick feel to it – *something and nothing* – even if things now seemed to be escalating. The child sounded to be more mislaid than dangerously lost. Given the wishy-washy collection of vague facts and half suspicions, it seemed to him quite reasonable to involve the undertaker, not to mention the captivating Maggs.

* * *

Maggs listened with total attention as Drew recounted the bizarre evening at Roma's house. 'Phone Penn,' she ordered him. 'See what she's got to say for herself.'

'I can't. At least, I can't mention Justine. She's genuinely scared of Penn finding out where she is. She doesn't seem to trust Roma to keep her safe.'

'Probably with good reason. She doesn't sound much of a mother.'

'I think Roma's the one person in all this that's okay,' Drew defended. 'She might have made a bit of a mess of her relationship with Justine, but otherwise I think she's a hundred per cent. Look at the way she's got her life sorted.'

Maggs pursed her lips. 'This I must see,' she decided. 'I can't make proper connections if I haven't met the people.'

'I've told you everything there is to know about them,' he assured her.

'Don't be silly, Drew. You know what you're like with older women.' She looked him in the eye, and he could hear the unspoken words, *Remember Genevieve.*

'Well, you can't just show up and put them under your expert scrutiny, can you?'

'Maybe not,' she mused. 'But I could probably think of something. I could pretend to be a gypsy selling clothes pegs.'

'You're too black to be a gypsy,' he told her. 'You could be one of those wretched disadvantaged youths who sell dusters and gadgets that don't work and cost ten pounds. Except they always seem to be male.'

'I could be a rambler, in need of a cup of tea. Don't they live near the Quantock Way or whatever it's called?'

'They do, actually.' He inspected her critically. 'I suppose you could manage to look like a rambler. They do come in all shapes and sizes.'

'Go on – say it. Too black for a gypsy and too fat for a rambler. I've gone off the idea, anyway. If Justine's been found, there isn't any more for us to do, is there? It's just some messy family disagreement, and we should mind our own businesses.'

'We probably should,' he agreed. Then he met her eye, and they giggled like children. 'But we don't wanna do that, do we?'

Laurie continued to be solicitous towards Justine, fetching drinks and snacks for her, as she reclined with Lolita on the couch in the conservatory watching Roma working in the garden, playing with Lolita. The dog's obvious pleasure in the visitor's company had irritated Roma. When Lolly refused to go outside with her mistress, choosing instead to lie on Justine's legs, Roma was more than irritated.

'Don't get in a state about it, Ma,' Justine said tiredly. 'She'll soon get fed up with me. You know what dogs are like – all over people for a bit, but she knows where her best interests lie.'

Roma swallowed her resentment, and headed for the dahlias.

'Feeling better today?' Laurie enquired. 'How's the knee?'

'I'm covered in bruises, and everything aches, but I'll mend. I can't stay here much longer, I know. Mum doesn't want me here. She doesn't feel any differently towards me now than she did five years ago.'

'She's immensely relieved that you're all right,' he confided. 'She really did think you might be dead.'

'And she cared?'

'She definitely cared,' he assured her. 'I've never seen her so upset.'

'Really? Well, she soon got over it.'

'It's a front. Quite a lot of what you see of Roma is a front.'

'You like talking about her, don't you? She's lucky to have you. Luckier than she deserves.'

'Pooh!' he said dismissively. 'I'm the lucky one. She doesn't really need anybody; I'm just here on sufferance.'

'She *married* you, Laurie. Surely that shows some degree of commitment?'

'That was me. I insisted. She said it made no difference to her, either way, except it made it easier to get her hands on my money if I died without warning.'

'Haven't you made a will?'

'I have now. I hadn't then.'

'Well, I still think she's fallen on her feet. After the way she behaved with my dad, I didn't think she'd ever make a go of marriage. She's far too self-absorbed.'

'The way I heard it, they were as bad as each other. Two people who should never have got together. Somebody should probably have stopped them.'

'It was mad passionate love at first sight,' Justine said. 'Wild horses couldn't have kept them apart. The surprising thing is that they only managed to have me. I gather everyone expected them to have about ten.'

'I wouldn't know about that,' said Laurie primly.

'Except, of course, she never really took to motherhood. I was a very bad baby, who obviously hadn't read the right books. Nothing I did fitted with the theories. I refused to be controlled by her.'

'Dangerous,' hissed Laurie, sucking his teeth.

Justine shrugged. 'It felt like the only choice I had, at the time, if I wanted to survive. I wouldn't do it any different, if it happened all over again.'

'Well, now's your chance to make your peace,' Laurie suggested.

Justine pulled a face. 'Haven't you seen how she is with me, even now? That's what I've been talking about. It's hopeless. She'll never change, and I can't do it all on my own. I'm not staying here for longer than I can help. Maybe I could go to Daddy.' She stared wistfully out of the window.

'It's up to you,' said Laurie weakly. 'You young girls, I can't work you out at all. My boys seemed so much more straightforward.' He sighed.

'I'm not a young girl, Laurie. I'm twenty-six. Old enough to know what I want and where I'm going. I do too,' she said fiercely. 'I'm a very talented potter. Funny, don't you think, how nobody's even mentioned that. As if it was some childish little hobby that I must have grown out of by now.'

She got up stiffly, and walked the length of the room and back. 'I don't feel so bad today. But it makes you realise how unreal those films and stories are where the hero gets beaten black and blue, and ten minutes later he's racing down the street after somebody. And next day, he's as good as new. It isn't at all like that in real life.'

Without warning, Roma strode into the

conservatory, making her husband and daughter both jump. 'We have to do something about Penn,' she announced. 'Where is she? What does she think is going on?'

Justine went pale. 'You're not going to tell her I'm here, are you?'

'I won't if you insist, but I can't see the harm. Surely she's more likely to be afraid of you, now. If your story's true, you can report her to the police, get her charged with holding you against your will. If she knows you've got away, she'll be shivering in her shoes.'

'I need to know why she did it,' Justine said doggedly. 'I asked her, over and over, and she kept saying it was all for my own good. I think she might be in trouble of some sort, and kidnapping me was a diversionary tactic. If that's right, then I might cause even more problems for her by going to the police.'

'I thought you hated her. I thought you'd be delighted to land her in as much trouble as you possibly can?' said Roma.

'It's difficult to like somebody who nearly killed you,' Justine said, 'but until I know what's going on, I suppose I should reserve judgment.'

'Very noble,' Roma said sourly. 'And very confusing. We can't go on like this, you know.'

'Like what?' scowled Justine. 'What exactly is it you can't stomach?'

Roma clenched her fists dramatically. 'All this bad feeling, for one thing. And putting yourself between me and Laurie. You'd only been here two minutes before you'd managed to set us against each other.'

Justine laughed caustically. 'Then it must be a very flimsy sort of marriage, that's all I can say.'

Roma closed her eyes as if praying for patience. 'As I said,' she repeated, 'we can't go on like this.'

Drew took the call from DS Cooper, leaning forward eagerly to wave at Maggs in the cool room, as he realised who it was. He listened to Cooper's story with growing amazement. 'Penn did mention a little girl,' he remembered. 'Justine looked after her sometimes. But—' he stopped, not sure he should reveal his knowledge of Justine's whereabouts. 'But she didn't say anything about them being together,' he finished lamely.

Maggs had come to his elbow, eyebrows raised interrogatively. Drew winked at her, while jotting down the detective's mobile number. 'Okay,' he said. 'We'll keep you posted if we hear anything. But we're going to be busy today and tomorrow. We've got two funerals.' He couldn't keep the note of pride out of his voice, despite knowing it was unlikely to impress. Most funeral directors could comfortably manage five or six funerals in a day.

'What was all that about?' Maggs demanded, as soon as he'd replaced the phone.

'Our tall policeman, calling to say they've had a report of the Rentons' child going missing. He's on his way there now.'

'And you never told him that Justine's turned up?' she accused. 'Why on earth not? He's sure to find out and then he won't trust us any more.'

'There was something about Mr Renton claiming the child is with Justine, when it obviously isn't. I thought I should tread carefully for the time being.'

She sighed melodramatically. 'I don't get it,' she grumbled. 'Aren't you worried about the kid?'

He rubbed the back of his neck consideringly. 'I'm not sure. It's a very peculiar business. The whole thing's peculiar. You can't really believe anything anyone says. Justine's story is like something out of James Bond; Penn's a mass of inconsistencies; the Renton bloke struck me as definitely shifty. And now the woman can't keep track of her own daughter.'

'Not to mention Roma Millan, who sounds as if she's got some dark secret rotting away in a corner somewhere,' Maggs reminded him. 'We still don't know what it was that made Justine and her mum such enemies.'

'Well this won't get the graves dug,' he said,

suddenly weary of it all. 'First things first. Even if we did have something to suggest there's been a real crime, we haven't got time to do anything about it until after tomorrow. And somehow I get the feeling that neither Penn nor Roma really want us to be involved from here on.'

'They've gone off you, have they?' she teased. 'Poor old Drew.'

He gave her a lofty look. 'To work, woman!' he ordered. 'I want Mr French all sealed and odourless by lunchtime. Mrs Jennings said she wanted to dress him this afternoon.'

'No problem. He's not as bad as I thought he'd be.'

'She's probably got a fairly strong stomach after all that hospice visiting.' Accommodating the wishes of relatives, while at the same time trying to protect them from some of the grimmer realities, was all part of the job. He and Maggs were both inclined to let people have their way, where other undertakers would make difficulties. As a matter of principle, they saw no reason to shield people from the essential facts of death. But there was always a dilemma when it came to smell. Death was inescapably smelly, a fact which seemed to escape almost everybody until confronted by it. At most funeral parlours, synthetic sprays were used, as well as scented flowers and embalming, plus cool temperature control. Peaceful Repose managed little in the way of such emollients. But they did worry about it, especially in August.

The Rentons greeted Den Cooper rather more anxiously than he'd expected. It had taken him almost an hour to reach them and they clearly regarded this as inferior service. 'Isn't a missing child serious enough for you?' demanded the woman shrilly.

'I'm sorry, madam,' he placated her. 'According to the report I received, you aren't unduly afraid that any harm has come to her.'

'We don't *know* that. How can we possibly know?' Sheena looked from her husband to the detective and back again. Den thought she seemed bewildered, as if something definitely didn't add up. He knew how she felt. He turned his attention to the farmer.

'Could we take it from the beginning, sir?' he appealed. 'When did you last see the little girl?'

Philip Renton folded his arms across his chest. 'Last Thursday morning,' he said firmly. 'She was in Justine Pereira's car, waving to me as they drove away.'

'And where were you?' Den asked Sheena.

'At work, of course,' she said scathingly. 'I have a very challenging job. I thought my husband was taking Georgia to stay with his mother on the

Isle of Wight. That's what he told me.' She glared angrily at Philip.

'But instead the plan changed and she went away with Miss Pereira, without your knowledge?' Den was adept at reflecting back at people the unlikeliness of their stories. This one was more unlikely than most.

'He says he and Justine were planning to go away together, taking Georgia, and this must have been some sort of trial run,' she explained through gritted teeth.

Den looked at Philip Renton. He had an elbow on the table, his brow leaning on his hand, the picture of a shame-faced husband caught in the act.

Den decided to skip the side issues. 'So neither of you has heard anything from or about your three-year-old child for six days?' There was no need to lace his words with reproach; the flat summary was enough.

'I was certain she was with her grandmother on the Isle of Wight,' Sheena said loudly. 'I only found out last night that I was lied to, and that Philip hasn't any idea where Justine has taken my daughter.'

'Last night?' Den queried. 'You knew last night that she'd gone, and you only phoned the police this morning?'

'Yes.' She glared again at her husband. 'He

persuaded me that it would do no harm to leave it until this morning to call you. But I lay awake all night, worrying.'

'Right,' said Den. 'Mr Renton, where did Miss Pereira say she was going?'

'She didn't name an exact place. She took a tent and said they'd find a nice spot for camping, and then she'd phone me in a few days to say how they were getting on. Look, officer—' he glanced at Sheena, including her in his assurances 'I'm sure there's no need to worry. Justine and I . . . well, we're very fond of each other. She won't do anything to hurt Georgia. You know how complicated it can be to get to a phone if there's no mobile signal. She'll turn up again any day now.'

Den tapped a fingernail against his teeth. 'There is, of course, the other matter of Miss Pereira having been reported missing. You told Mr Slocombe on Monday evening that Miss Pereira had gone camping, didn't you?'

Renton nodded, with a look of self-assurance. 'That's right.'

'But you didn't say she'd taken your daughter with her?'

'Why should I? That had nothing to do with it. They weren't looking for Georgia.'

'And you were worried that it might get back to your wife?'

198

Renton flushed faintly and looked again at Sheena. 'Something like that. At that stage, you see, I was still hoping Justine would come back with Georgia and we could all carry on as normal for a while.'

'He's not telling the whole story. You can see he isn't,' Sheena burst out.

Renton's face reassumed its practised blandness at this accusation. Den was reminded of an habitual criminal he'd frequently had cause to interview, who adopted just such an expression under interrogation. It was a knack that many young boys acquired, but generally seemed to lose as they grew up. It shrieked *Liar!* to those on the receiving end, but frustratingly succeeded in obscuring the truth. There were times when torture seemed the only effective option, Den had often thought, grimly.

'So what went wrong with your plan?' he asked, staring hard at the man.

Renton's composure faltered for a second. 'N-nothing,' he said. 'There wasn't a plan. Not really. It's true that we've been "having an affair".' He mouthed the phrase as if it offended him. 'Nobody claims to think that this is the perfect marriage, after all.' An intake of breath made him glance at Sheena, his expression giving the lie to his words. Den thought he glimpsed a yearning pain underneath the studied blandness.

He nodded for the man to go on. 'But it was all still at the talking stage, as far as taking anything further was concerned. It's not something to be undertaken lightly.'

'Not when there's a little girl involved,' Den agreed.

'Oh, she wouldn't have been a problem,' Renton said unpleasantly. 'I don't suppose she even knows that Sheena's her mother. She saw much more of Justine and the day nursery women than she ever saw of her own mother.'

A dramatic hiss warned the men that Sheena had had enough. She launched herself at Philip, fingers curved rigidly like claws, and before Den could stop her had raked four long scratches down both of Philip's cheeks. Immediately, she fell back, Den belatedly clutching her shoulders, and stared at her handiwork. Blood slowly welled through the broken skin, surrounded by white weals. Her victim cautiously put a hand first to one side, then the other. 'Shit!' he breathed.

'You asked for that,' she panted. 'It bloody well serves you right.' Den silently agreed with her, but was duty-bound to react otherwise.

'Mrs Renton, I must warn you that violence is unlawful. Please give me your assurance that there'll be no repetition of what just happened,' he said formally.

After a moment she nodded and muttered,

'You needn't worry. It won't happen again.'

An awkward silence followed, while Den tried to make sense of everything they'd told him. He spoke slowly. 'It still isn't altogether clear whether or not we are dealing with a missing child. It doesn't appear that she was abducted, since her father willingly allowed her to go. There's no suggestion that she's been taken abroad or that she's come to any harm. As far as I can understand it, there was no firm date for her return. Essentially, the only cause for concern is that Miss Strabinski has been worried about her cousin and thinks she left home very abruptly, possibly under some coercion. She doesn't seem to be aware that the little girl is with Miss Pereira. And when she heard that you'd claimed that her cousin had gone camping, she was very surprised – and somewhat annoyed.' He eyed them both carefully. 'Have I missed anything?'

'Only that I want my daughter back – *now*,' insisted Sheena.

'Penn got it wrong,' Renton added. 'She's making a fuss about nothing. It isn't any of her business, anyway.'

Den was reminded of something Drew Slocombe had observed, about Renton seeming to monitor everything he said before letting the words emerge. It was rather like someone speaking a foreign language, that tiny hesitation

201

before every phrase. Or someone overcoming a stutter. Maybe, he conceded, that's all it was. Or just an odd mannerism.

'But Penn was here on Thursday, too, wasn't she?' Sheena remembered. 'I met her as I was driving out. It was early, just after eight.'

This time, the silence was full of tension. Watched by his wife and the police detective, Renton was obviously at a loss for a reply, for the first time. But he recovered quickly. 'No,' he said, bewilderment plain on his face. 'Or if she was, I never saw her. She must have come and gone again in a couple of minutes.'

Den looked out of the window onto the yard. 'Would you notice a car going to the cottage?' he wondered. 'Where exactly is the track?'

'They do have to come into our yard for a very short way,' Renton explained, pointing out the route. 'In through the gateway where you came in and then sharp left down the track to the cottage. We don't sit here all day watching out for vehicles. You can't see the yard from the living room or my office.'

'And there isn't a dog,' Den noted. 'So Miss Strabinski could have been there for some time and you wouldn't have known. What time did Justine and the little girl leave?'

Renton shrugged. 'Mid-morning,' he offered. 'I have no idea of the precise time.'

'You work from here, I take it?'

'I'm in and out. I have to go to check quality on the ground and attend sales and so forth. But I'm here a fair amount of the time, yes. I was here last Thursday.'

Den made a few lines of notes. 'One more thing,' he remembered. 'Could I possibly have a recent photo of Georgia?'

The couple seemed to forget their differences and stared at each other in dismay. 'Oh!' breathed Sheena, 'Well, I suppose we *must* have one somewhere . . . ?' She looked helplessly at Philip.

'Justine took a few of her, sometime around Easter. I remember there were daffodils.' He shrugged. 'I have no idea where they might be. Presumably in the cottage.'

'Maybe a video, then?' Den suggested. 'We could probably have a few stills made, if you could let us have . . .'

'No, we haven't got a video camera,' Philip cut across him. 'We don't really do photography at all, you see.'

'And you never took her to a professional?' Den's disbelief was growing. Surely everybody took pictures of their children? Especially girls, especially the first child. What was the matter with these two that they seem never to have bothered?

'Oh, I remember!' Sheena suddenly crowed. 'Your mother sent us one, didn't she? Georgia's nearly three in that. She hasn't changed much since then. I'll fetch it.'

The photograph had been slightly bent, pushed carelessly into a drawer. It showed a small girl sitting on a blue carpet, wearing dungarees. Her hair was short and wispy, her eyes very large, her expression serious. Den's impression was of a child very small for almost three. 'Thanks,' he said. 'It always helps to have a picture.'

'You're going to search for her then, are you?' Sheena persisted.

'We'll definitely search for Justine Pereira,' he told her. 'Because it seems very likely that we'll find your little girl with her, don't you think?'

'I hope so,' the woman responded flatly.

'Now I'm going to have a look around her cottage. One of you would be welcome to accompany me. In fact, that's the usual procedure.'

Neither of them seemed inclined to act as chaperone. 'We trust you,' said Philip casually. 'The key's under a big stone to the right of the front door.'

Without further discussion Den walked down the track to the small house, thinking as he did so that he'd had cause to visit numerous such dwellings during his career. A great many farms had originally included workers' cottages on their property, and although a lot had been sold off or allowed to fall derelict in recent times, a lot still remained. This one was typical in many ways. Set at some distance from the main farmhouse, allotted its own fair-sized garden, just big enough for a family – and almost completely unmodernised.

He looked into every room, noting the untidiness, the air of having been left abruptly, but with no signs of violence. He found the mobile phone and the toothbrush, as Maggs had described. He left with a feeling of having learnt almost nothing.

Karen had no clear idea of what she would say when she phoned her cousin Penn, except that this was the only person she felt might offer her some sense of being involved in the business of Justine's disappearance.

'You only just caught me,' came the response. 'I was going out.'

'Thanks for the nice note you sent,' Karen began. 'I hope we can keep in touch, now you've made the first move.'

'Has Drew made any headway in trying to find Justine? I was hoping to hear from him before now.'

'What? Surely they've told you?' Karen was incredulous. 'I assumed somebody would have called you right away.'

'What? What do you mean?' Penn's voice was strained, even panicked.

'They probably just didn't get around to it. Drew was at Roma's last night, when Justine walked in. I haven't heard the whole story, by any means. I was just going to bed when he got home and fell asleep before he could say much. He promised to fill in the details this evening, but I'm not holding my breath. Yo be honest, I thought you could probably tell me all about it.'

'Are you sure about this?' Penn seemed to be having trouble breathing. 'I mean . . . did he really say it was Justine?'

'Of course. Who else would it be? It was all rather exciting, apparently. She hadn't seen Roma for years, as you obviously know. And Roma wasn't too happy to see her. Drew's busy today or I could go and ask him for the rest of the story. He's got two funerals tomorrow.'

Penn was no more impressed by this boast than Detective Sergeant Cooper had been. 'Look, Karen, I'll have to go. I'm catching a train down to the coast and I haven't got long. Thanks for the call, it was really nice of you. I'll be in touch when I get back. It'll only be a few days. Say Hi to Drew for me, okay.' The haste was almost indecent and Karen felt the rejection. 'Go on, then,' she said curtly. 'Have a nice time.'

The only response was a snort. Somehow Karen had the impression that Penn did not expect to enjoy herself.

Penn was indeed not optimistic about enjoying herself. Neither did she know what she ought to do next. She was indeed catching a train, as she had told Karen, but not for another hour. As she had fallen into the habit of doing in recent months, she reached for her bag of rune-stones. Originally treating them as a novelty when one of her students had given them to her, she had become increasingly impressed by their usefulness. The interpretation of each symbol was a real intellectual challenge at times, and she rationalised her interest as being a topic of serious study. Justine had gently mocked her at first, of course. 'Look, it isn't fortune-telling, or anything like that. It's just a sort of *pointer*. It directs your attention, focuses your thoughts,' Penn had insisted.

She shook the bag, then stirred the smooth oval shapes with a finger, and withdrew three stones, laying them out from right to left, as the booklet had instructed. The first two were very similar: one showed two triangles joined at one point, making a sort of bowtie. The one to the right of it was another bowtie, this time on legs – the symbol for The Self. Penn shrieked as she realised the implications of the third stone. Once again, as she had described to Drew on Sunday afternoon, she had drawn Breakthrough followed by the Blank. And this combination meant Death.

She scattered the stones with a violent hand, doing her best to ignore her thumping heart. It was pure coincidence. Those two had been on top of the bag from the last time. The whole thing was stupid anyway. How could it *possibly* mean anything?

But she couldn't suppress the shaking that had gripped her; the sudden certainty that she was destined for something terrible. Penn Strabinski was, in short, decidedly frightened.

CHAPTER NINE

Drew was limp with exhaustion, having dug both graves by early afternoon.

Maggs looked up at him fleetingly as he came into the office, and wrinkled her nose. 'You smell,' she told him.

'Well, let's hope we don't get any visitors, then,' he puffed, wiping his face with a hanky. 'I'll cool down in a minute.'

'You should have left it until this evening,' she chided him. 'Instead of choosing the hottest part of the day.'

'Never mind. It's done now.' He flopped into a chair and waited for his breath to return to normal. Maggs seemed restless. 'You did know the Frenches want to use the church tomorrow, didn't you?' she said. 'And there's that flower festival thing at the weekend; they want us out by three at the latest, so they can get started on the decoration and stuff.'

Drew sighed. 'I wish they wouldn't.'

'What?'

'Keep wanting to use the church, especially in summer. We can quite easily do it all at the graveside just as meaningfully.'

'The Frenches think there might be fifty people,' she observed. 'Personally, I'd rather they used the church.'

'In America they cheerfully get a hundred or more to the graveside.'

'With rows of chairs and a catafalque all laid out on artificial grass,' she snapped back. 'And probably only in places where they can be sure it won't rain.'

'Really? They really use a catafalque?'

She leant back in her chair. 'I don't know for sure,' she admitted. 'That's how it looks in the films sometimes. If you don't like using the church, you should crack on with building us a chapel of our own.'

Drew sighed again. 'I've told you a thousand times we can't afford it,' he said. 'And anyway, it's not the way I want it to go. Once we had a chapel, there'd be "Abide With Me" and fancy coffins, and processions and it'd all be back to the bad old ways.'

'Not necessarily,' Maggs said sternly. 'It's up to you to offer them alternatives.'

It was a recurring disagreement, that never seemed to move any further forward. Drew was aware of being unreasonable in his desire to keep the burials as plain as he possibly could. He firmly believed that the majority of church services meant nothing whatsoever to the people involved and were little more than a nod towards the old conventions. He wanted people to construct their own heartfelt ceremonies in the open air, with minimal fanfare. However much Maggs might try to convince him that most people just weren't up to such creativity, he stubbornly resisted the idea of building their own chapel. The furthest he was prepared to go was some kind of open-sided shelter where people could gather when the weather was seriously inclement.

But his heart wasn't in the argument today. He couldn't shake off the memory of Justine Pereira, bruised and scratched and telling such a wild tale of what had befallen her. He'd stayed until well past nine, before realising he'd already been there far too long and should leave mother and daughter to resolve their differences as best they might. He'd barely managed to convey any of the story to Karen before she zonked off to sleep. Now Maggs was too busy to talk about it, too. She was annoyed with him for failing to pass the accusations against Penn to her new police friend.

Normally he would be more than happy to have two funerals to prepare for. Maggs had taken on most of the work for the burial of Mr French, while Drew handled Mrs Stacey. The old lady with the unsuccessful operation was a sad story, which he'd heard now from both the doctor and the lady's daughter. She wasn't so old, either – seventy-two, with all sorts of hopes and plans still for the future. She had heard Drew speak a year or so ago, when he'd been actively promoting his services to a variety of clubs and lunch groups, and had made sure that her daughter knew she'd be wanting a place in his cemetery when the time came. Efficiently, she had noted the phone number and included her wishes in her will. Everything was straightforward, apart from a continuing small doubt as to the rightness of proceeding without a post mortem. It happened regularly enough for him not to be tempted to raise any direct questions, however. The doctor was the final arbiter; it was his job to distinguish natural from unnatural deaths. But since the trauma and general loss of trust arising from the Harold Shipman story, most doctors were treading more warily. Everyone was now aware of just how simple it was for them to certify a death as unsuspicious, and it was a matter of self-protection to remain well on the right side of the law.

Mrs Stacey was a sad case for a number of reasons and Drew sighed as he envisaged the scanty attendance at the graveside the following day. An unmarried daughter, busy with a go-getting career; two or three friends, confused and perhaps resentful about the unorthodox funeral; a nephew who had phoned to ask for directions, and Maggs. Drew had offered to say a few words as the coffin was lowered, and the daughter had gratefully accepted. 'It will seem awfully strange,' she'd admitted. 'No music or anything.'

Drew was only faintly optimistic that she would in the event find it a genuinely moving experience. It didn't sound as if her mother had managed to convince her that this was a far better way of ending her time on earth than some scrappy formulaic cremation.

The day continued cool, with a light breeze and grey skies. Drew found himself thinking about Justine Pereira and the bizarre story she'd told the previous evening. He wondered how she and Roma were getting along now, and whether they'd come to any accommodation. He found himself stabbed by compunction at having concealed the latest twist in the tale from Detective Sergeant Cooper, who obviously trusted him and wanted his co-operation. Drew had not missed the spark that had been struck between Maggs and the tall policeman and felt almost fatherly towards her as a result. She could do worse, he told himself, having watched her work through a number of unsatisfactory boyfriends, not one of them lasting more than a few weeks.

'I'm going to phone Roma and see how they're getting on,' he announced suddenly, making Maggs jump.

'What?' She was carefully marking the positions of the two new graves on their chart of the burial ground, using a ruler to keep it accurate to the nearest centimetre. 'Look what you've made me do,' she reproached.

'Sorry. I was thinking about Justine.'

'Oh. So was I, sort of. Make them tell the police, then, will you? It's their duty, after all. You can't just leave them in the dark. It's perverting the course of justice.' She uttered the phrase in a sing-song, enjoying the sound of it.

'I'll tell them I think I'll have to say something if they don't. And then you can call your friendly detective, if you like.' His generosity was amply rewarded by the sudden twinkle in her eye.

'Right then,' she said carelessly.

'And I suppose I ought also to be a bit firm with them about the missing child? Try to get them to take it seriously.'

'How do you know they won't?'

He rubbed his neck again. 'I don't, do I? It's just a feeling. I mean, it seems as if we're the only people who know the whole story. Everyone else is working in the dark.'

'We don't know the whole story,' she corrected him. 'We don't know where the little girl's got to. And when the police find out that Justine's turned up without her, they're going to be taking her disappearance a lot more seriously.'

'Yes,' Drew agreed, with a frown. 'Of course they are. With good reason. Somehow I didn't see it like that. Bloody hell, Maggs, they won't be happy about this, will they? With me not saying anything this morning.'

'Better late than never then,' she observed. 'Shouldn't I just phone Den right away, before you talk to Roma?'

'Go on, then. Make his day.'

Penn repacked hurriedly, adding clothes and necessities to cover more days than she had originally planned for. She'd have to rush for the train now. If it was true that Justine had turned up, then things had obviously changed dramatically and she had to be prepared. There was really no knowing what might happen next or where she stood. Even without the disquieting rune reading, she was clearly in trouble.

With everything so uncertain, it seemed wise to remain out of sight for the time being. There was only one person who might safely be approached at this stage, and even he might be unpredictable. All the same, the idea struck her that a brief call to him wouldn't hurt. She keyed in the number and waited with crossed fingers for him to be the one to pick up at the other end.

She was in luck. 'It's me,' she said. 'Look, I'm going away for a bit. Down to the coast. It's all getting much too messy. You can keep in touch on my mobile number, okay?'

Having replaced the phone, she stood for a moment, waiting for the trembling to subside.

The train was surprisingly prompt in arriving and she joined the short queue for taxis just outside the station. She knew of a hotel that would probably have a room, even in the high season. They wouldn't remember her – it had been three years since she last stayed there, during a dutiful weekend escorting her maternal grandmother on a trip to the seaside. The old lady had been in her late eighties and had died not long afterwards. Penn had rather resented the task, demanding to know why her mother or aunt couldn't have done it instead. But Helen had conveniently developed sciatica, and everyone knew there was no chance of Roma putting herself out in such a cause. Roma had been impatient of her mother's forgetfulness and deafness and constant need to go to the lavatory.

The hotel was set two or three streets back from the sea front, in a tree-lined avenue filled with similar establishments. It was an ideal place to hide, although Penn was some decades younger than almost all the other residents. She smiled self-consciously at the girl on Reception. 'I'm hoping to persuade my father to join me here,' she explained. 'But there's no sense in forcing him. I take it you could find a room for him if he suddenly puts in an appearance?'

'I'm sure we can manage something, Madam. How long would that be for, do you think?'

'That's a bit difficult to say at the moment. I'll be here for a week or so, I suppose. Am I being a terrible nuisance?' she simpered. 'I'm afraid it's one of those complicated family things.'

The receptionist became confiding. 'To be honest, we've got quite a few empty rooms. People don't come to the seaside the way they used to. If it wasn't for the weekend conferences, we'd be virtually empty most of the year.'

'Oh dear,' Penn sympathised. 'But lucky for me. I'll keep you posted, anyway.'

'Thank you, Madam.'

* * *

Den was a few miles away from Gladcombe when his mobile warbled. Assuming it was the DI or someone from the station, he flicked his hands-free button and barked 'Cooper.'

For a second he didn't recognise the voice at the other end. When he did, he very much regretted the tone he'd used. 'Maggs? What do you want?'

'At last! Have you had the phone turned off? I couldn't reach you – and this isn't something I can put in a text.'

He examined the phone. 'I think it was on. Maybe reception's bad round here,' he said vaguely. 'What's the matter?'

'I've got something to tell you,' she replied stiffly. 'I'm really phoning with a message from Drew.'

'Oh?' He tried to soften his voice, but with little success. There seemed to be some obstruction in his throat.

'Yes . . . the thing is, Drew was at Roma Millan's, in Pitcombe, last night, when Justine walked in. She's still there now. She's had a terrible time, or so she says. Something about being kidnapped.'

'When? *When* did this happen?'

'Last night.'

'Why didn't he tell me before now? I spoke to him this morning. Why wait all this time?'

'He says Justine was in such a state, she obviously wasn't going anywhere. He wasn't really sure what to do.'

'Even when I told him the Renton child was missing?'

'He didn't think you sounded too worried, and he was thinking about Justine to the exclusion of all else. He was very slow to understand the implications. But we've had a think, and realised you have to know the whole thing.'

'Is the child with Justine?' As soon as he asked he knew what the answer would be. It was obvious.

'No, it doesn't look like it. That's worrying, isn't it.'

'It bloody is. Well, thanks for telling me now. I'll have to go and see her right away.'

'Sorry, Den,' she pleaded. 'We just didn't think it could be that serious.'

'Let's hope it's not,' he said tightly.

Pulling into a lay-by he called DI Hemsley, reporting succinctly the tangle of findings so far. 'I'll go straight to Pitcombe now,' he said. 'We'll have to hope Justine knows where the little girl is.'

'What about the Strabinski person? She started all this, as I understand it. Could she be playing some game?'

'Very likely,' Den agreed. 'She's a bit odd.

Nervous. Could be she knows more than she's saying. And there's the undertaker,' he went on in a rush. 'Plus his assistant. They seem to be getting pretty deeply into this, though I'm not best pleased at the way they left it till now to tell me they'd found Justine.'

The DI clicked his tongue warningly. 'Civilians,' he said. 'Don't let them get too involved. Sounds like amateur detective stuff to me.' He paused, and Den could picture him doodling while he considered every angle. 'This is a weird one,' he summarised. 'Better get the press in on it – can't do any harm. Have we got a picture?'

'Yeah, but it's not very good.'

'What are the parents like? Emotionally, I mean.'

'Fairly flat. Stunned, I guess. He's got the lid tightly on, and she doesn't seem to know what to think. They're not as scared as you'd expect. At least . . .' he remembered Renton's scratched face. 'Maybe they are. But not in the usual sort of way.'

'How many missing children cases have you handled, Cooper?'

'None, sir. It's just . . .'

'People almost never react as you expect,' Hemsley told him. 'It won't really have hit them yet. They've been pinning all their hopes on the Justine girl. Any minute now they'll have to start thinking paedophiles, opportunists, all that, if my gut's anything to go by.'

'Let's hope it's wrong then, sir,' said Den gloomily.

Hemsley hummed a wordless reply. 'Come back here first and collect Timms,' he instructed. 'Sounds as if you might need her.'

Roma's jaw was clamped so hard she felt one of her molars protest under the strain. *Bloody hell*, she thought. *Can't even have a good rage these days without getting toothache.* It wasn't exactly rage, though – more a fit of frustration at the way everything seemed to be crowding in on her. Less than a week ago, she'd been minding her own business with her bees and dog and husband for company. And not a care in the world. Now there wasn't any escape from a whole string of worries.

The reappearance of Justine was at the heart of it all, of course. Trailing anguishing memories and accusations, the girl showed no sign of having matured or mellowed over the past five years. If anything, she was even more impossible than before. Laurie didn't help, either, with his heavy reproachful sighs and clumsy attempts at diplomacy. All he succeeded in doing was aggravating Roma's already fragile temper.

'You don't *know* her,' she'd said several times. 'You've never even met her until now. Believe me, I've got good reason to regret that she ever discovered where we live.'

He'd refused to listen. 'She's a perfectly nice girl,' he insisted. 'I don't know what you can possibly have against her.' And Roma hadn't even tried to enlighten him.

Since Drew's phone call about the Rentons' missing child, everything had become infinitely worse. Without even pausing to think, Roma had flown to Justine's sanctuary in the spare room, and confronted her. 'What's all this about a little girl?' she demanded. 'The police think she's with you. What the hell have you done with her?'

Justine had been convincingly bewildered. 'What?' she stammered. 'Are you talking about Georgia? Isn't she at the farm?' And then, after a moment's thought. 'Jesus Christ. Has Penn abducted *her* as well?'

Roma hadn't known what to make of the horrified expression on her daughter's face, but she swept on anyway. 'Penn wouldn't hurt a child,' she protested. 'Wake up, for God's sake, and stop this insane behaviour. You'll be ending up in a mental ward at this rate.'

'Oh yeah? You're thinking of having me sectioned, are you? Well, it wouldn't be the first time, would it?' It was a palpable hit, sending them both spinning back through the years, reliving similar hysterical scenes between the two of them. Roma's hands had dropped to her sides.

'Of course not,' she said wearily. 'But we can't go on like this, can we?'

'We're not going to,' Justine told her. 'I'll be out of your way in a couple of days. I only need time to think what I should do. But Georgia . . .' she returned to the subject worriedly. 'We'll have to find her, Mum. She's only a little thing and she won't be able to cope if she's somewhere strange, with people she doesn't know. Why aren't the police searching for her?' She turned her large dark eyes on her mother.

'Because they think she's with you. Or they did until now. Drew Slocombe's telling them that you're here, as we speak, and we'll probably get a visitation within the hour.'

Justine groaned, before gathering herself together. One hand over her mouth, eyes closed, she took several deep breaths. 'Good,' she said, after a minute or two. 'I'll tell them everything.'

'They won't believe you,' Roma warned her.

'My goodness, Mother, you almost sound worried about me,' the girl taunted.

Now, an hour or two later, with the police due any moment, Roma was unable to suppress her mounting concern for her daughter. Laurie had had another go at her, full of reproach at her heartlessness, and the image of the missing child, of whom Justine seemed inordinately fond, refused to go away. Try as she might, Roma couldn't think of a reassuring explanation as to what had happened to the child.

'What are her parents like?' she asked Justine. 'They sound awfully irresponsible.'

'Busy,' was the brief reply. 'They should never have had her. Neither of them spends any time with her. Sheena probably hadn't even noticed she'd gone.'

'Irresponsible,' Roma repeated. 'But they must have thought she was all right, surely?'

'I don't know, Mum,' Justine sighed. 'I have no idea what's been happening there over the past week.' She glanced down at her damaged wrists. 'I was otherwise engaged.'

'It has to be Penn,' Roma concluded. 'If your story's true.'

'Careful!' warned Justine. 'You don't want to start believing me, surely?'

The conversation languished before it got to the same old track again. The eventual arrival of a car containing two plain clothes officers came as a relief to them both.

Roma let them in, cocking an amused eyebrow at the mismatched couple. A very tall young man accompanied by a short, stout middle-aged woman. They introduced themselves as Detective Sergeant Den Cooper and Detective Constable Bennie Timms. 'We've been expecting you,' Roma said, with a subtle hint that they might have been a bit quicker.

There was no doubt that they were seriously interested in whatever Justine might have to tell them. They sat in the big kitchen, facing Justine across the table, leaving Roma to take a seat on the outer edge of the group. The tall man checked her name, address, date of birth and car registration number, filling in a pre-printed sheet, which seemed ominous to Roma.

'You're aware that the police received a report of you as a possible missing person, early this week, are you?' he asked her daughter.

Justine nodded, with a faint smile. 'I wasn't missing, exactly. I'd been abducted. By the person who reported it, strange as that may sound.'

Den's eyebrows jerked up. 'Drew Slocombe abducted you? Is that what you're saying?'

Justine made an impatient sound and smacked the table lightly in irritation. 'No, of course not. Penn. My cousin, Penn Strabinski. All this is her doing. She's probably got Georgia hidden away somewhere. Christ knows why, though. She must have gone barmy.'

'You know the little girl's missing?'

She nodded. 'Drew phoned my mother a little while ago. You told him, apparently.'

Roma was impressed by her daughter's composure, in spite of herself. She showed no sign of apprehension, no guilt or prevarication. From the police point of view, she must be coming over as a very good witness.

The woman leant forward. 'Miss Pereira – do you have any reason to be concerned for little Georgia's welfare?'

Justine smacked the table again. 'Of *course* I do. I'm horrified that she's been gone all this time. I knew her parents were useless, but not this bad. What did they tell you? Why aren't you combing the countryside for her?'

Den spread his hands and looked her full in the face. 'They told us you'd got Georgia, that you'd taken her camping. Her father says he waved you off last Thursday morning. But he told her mother the child was with her grandma on the Isle of Wight, because he didn't want her to think you were having such close contact. He says he's been having an affair with you.'

Roma had a good view of her daughter's reaction. Disbelief, amusement and finally horror were all clearly to be seen. 'He lied to you,' she said furiously, breathless with repressed emotion. 'The man's a slimeball.'

'You didn't take Georgia camping?' Bennie

Timms kept to the point that most interested her. 'Not even for a night or two?'

'I did not.' Justine's calm was almost painful to witness. 'On Thursday morning I was chloroformed and forcibly imprisoned in a derelict house somewhere near Glastonbury. I spent four days there without food and almost no water, until I managed to escape. The first thing I did was drink some foul green stuff from an old water trough. I was so thirsty.' She looked from one to the other. 'My cousin Penn was responsible,' she said firmly.

Den Cooper's eyebrows took on a life of their own as he tried to digest this story. 'Er . . .' he began. 'Well. Hmm. So why didn't you report this abduction when you got free? If it's true, it's a very serious charge to make against someone. I mean . . .'

'You don't believe me,' Justine supplied. 'I didn't think you would.' She proffered her wrists, turning them to show the abrasions and bruises encircling them. 'How do you think this happened, then?'

'Why don't you tell us?'

'She tied my hands tightly behind my back. I've got bruises across my shoulders, ribs and hips as well, where I forced my way through a small hole I made in the wall. And before you ask, I really have no idea why she did it.' A look of painful doubt crossed her face. 'She said it was for my own good.'

'She says you and she have always been good friends. Like sisters. She asked Drew Slocombe to try and find you. He went to your cottage and thought there was enough evidence of disturbance to cause concern, so he and his partner reported your disappearance.'

'There you are then!' she triumphed. 'He was right. There *was* cause for concern.'

'So where's little Georgia?' put in DC Timms, slightly desperately. 'Is she in the derelict house as well?'

'Jesus, I hope not!' Justine exploded, before quickly calming down. 'No, she can't be. That wouldn't make any sense.'

'None of this makes any sense,' Cooper muttered irritably. 'All we know for sure is that there's a little girl lost in the middle of it somehow.'

'It's got to be Penn,' Justine repeated thoughtfully. 'It couldn't be anybody else.'

'Workers on the farm?' Timms suggested. 'Suspicious local characters? People do snatch small girls, you know. How well was she supervised? Could she have wandered off somewhere?'

'Didn't you ask her parents all that?'

'Of course, and they told us the child was with you.'

'And you believed them?' Justine grunted. 'Well, she's not. And I'm as worried about her as you are. There could be paedophiles living inconspicuously in one of the villages close by, but I doubt it. She wouldn't have wandered off on her own. She's a timid little thing, small for her age. I've got some good photos of her at the cottage. I suppose we could go and get them.'

'Can you show us this derelict house?' Cooper suddenly demanded. 'We should check it out, even though you don't think she's likely to be there. It would help to confirm your story at the same time.'

Justine grimaced. 'I doubt if I could find it again,' she admitted. 'It was dark when I got out and I just scrambled down tracks and country lanes until I reached a proper road.'

'Where's your car?' Den asked, watching her reactions closely.

'Tucked away in the woods near my cottage, I presume,' she said readily. 'I worked out that Penn must have hidden it there; her own was parked a few miles from where I live and she must have manhandled me from mine to hers while I was out cold.'

'But *why*?' Drew almost pleaded. 'Why would she do all that?'

Justine fingered her bruised ribs gingerly. 'She must have wanted it to look as if I'd driven off in my own car, like Philip said.' She frowned at them suddenly. 'That's funny, isn't it. As if he might have known what she was up to. That hadn't occurred to me until now.'

Den shook his head impatiently. 'I'm sorry,' he said. 'But let's try and keep it simple for now. You'll understand that we'll have to search this house thoroughly, now we've found you here, in the light of what Mr Renton told us.' He looked at Roma. 'I take it you won't have any objection?'

She shrugged. 'No search warrant I presume?'

'It wouldn't take long to get one.'

'Go on,' she said. 'The little girl isn't here. Justine might have a wild story to tell, but she isn't a child abductor. At least I can vouch for her on that.'

'Thanks, Mother. I love you too,' Justine muttered.

Twenty minutes later Cooper and Timms conceded that Georgia Renton was not anywhere on the premises. At Roma's suggestion Laurie had taken refuge in the garden when the police first arrived, but he insisted on going with them on their search. 'Just to make sure they don't break anything,' he said stiffly. Roma shot him a penetrating glance. *Don't you crack up on me too*, she silently begged. Laurie had been increasingly withdrawn over the past twenty-four hours, apparently shocked and upset by the skirmishing between mother and daughter. When the police had finally gone, he found Roma in the kitchen.

'I'm sorry, dear,' he said softly. 'But I don't think I can take much more of this. If you don't mind, I think I'll take myself off in the morning for a few days. I've been making one or two phone calls and have a place to go to. Don't worry about me.'

He looked grey and suddenly old. She reached out a shaking hand to him. 'But you can't just disappear,' she said.

'No, no, I'll keep in touch. Just humour me, Roma. Please. I know it's pathetic, and you can't abide weakness. I know I'm letting you down.' He put a thin hand on his chest, pressing hard for a moment. 'But I think it's the best thing to do. It won't be for long, I promise. Just until all this business is settled.'

The wave of fear that washed over her was disabling. She struggled for breath. 'All right, dear,' she managed. 'I won't try to stop you. It'll all be sorted out in a few days, you know.' She forced a shaky smile. 'Everything does always come right in the end.'

A strange expression crossed his face. 'Of course it does,' he agreed. 'In the end we all die.'

Roma turned away from him sharply, making no reply.

* * *

Den had always enjoyed the company of Bennie Timms. At an unusually late stage in her career she had applied to transfer to CID and had been received with enthusiasm by her superiors. Female detectives were in short supply and her special talents of empathy and insight rendered her invaluable in cases involving children. It had come as no surprise to Den when the DI assigned her to the investigation into the whereabouts of little Georgia Renton.

'So what do we think?' he asked her, as they drove out of Pitcombe. 'Someone's telling blatant lies here. Complete fabrication from start to finish.'

'Hmm,' she said cautiously. 'I'll answer that when I've seen the parents.'

'Fair enough. I'll rephrase my question. What did you think of Justine Pereira?'

'I think she's on something,' came the surprising response. 'Not necessarily Class A – more like Valium or Prozac. Maybe antidepressants. She's got that cloudy look about her, as if she doesn't dare look the world full in the face.'

Den whistled. 'I didn't notice that at all. Would that make her more likely to lie to us?'

Bennie shrugged. 'Possibly not. And I think she really does care about the kid. Something was hurting in that department. And did you catch the messages between her and her mother? Giant-size can of worms there, or I'm a cucumber.'

'I'm with you on that,' he confirmed. 'Actually, I can cheat a bit there. I happen to know they haven't set eyes on each other for five years, until now. Some big bust-up that made them hate the sight of each other. Drew Slocombe mentioned it.'

'We ought to find out what it is,' she said. 'I'd guess it has to do with children in some way.'

'Drew might know. Or his wife.' Den remembered Hemsley's injunction not to involve the undertaker any further, and sighed. 'I bet Drew could give us several pointers if we asked him.'

'Then why don't we?'

Den explained briefly, concluding, 'the DI has a thing about amateur detectives. Must have had a nasty experience with them.'

Bennie laughed. 'Oh, yes he did. When he first started as a DC we had a murder, out in the sticks towards Hatherleigh. Danny was convinced a local recluse had done it. To be fair, there was a lot of incriminating stuff. But there was this young lad, bright sixth form kid, went ferreting about on his own and came up with the weapon, motive and perfect forensic evidence. Walked in, dumped it all on the front desk with a rude note for Danny, and walked out again.'

'Embarrassing.'

'Very. So you'd best advise your undertaker friend to use a bit of tact if he's going to try and help. Personally, I think we need all the support we can get. I quite like the public to get involved, so long as they don't take risks.'

'Me too. At least they know the background better than we ever do.'

'So what d'you say we ignore Danny and start tomorrow bright and early with a visit to North Staverton?' she suggested.

'Great idea!' he agreed, not least because it would mean another chance to spend some time with Maggs.

'Meanwhile, where do we go from here?' she asked. 'It's nearly four already. Hasn't the DI ordered a full search of the farm for the kid? It all seems very *pedestrian*. As if nobody seriously thinks she's come to any harm.'

'He'll have sent a couple of lads to search the outbuildings, probably. And there'll be some high-powered efforts going on in the office – computer searches for known paedophiles around here, contacting anyone whose name's come up in the past few days.'

'What if it's a kidnapping? Is there someone in the house with the parents? There might be a call if she's been taken for ransom. How well off are they?'

'Reasonably. Hemsley's probably put a tap on their line. It's not all down to me, you know.'

She tapped his arm. 'No, Den, I know it isn't. But I still don't get it. Why isn't there more of a hoo-ha about it? Normally there'd be all hell breaking loose over a little girl going missing.'

He thought hard. 'I guess because we can't believe she's in genuine danger. They're all lying; that's how it feels. There's some game going on, with the kid being passed around like a parcel. We thought Justine Pereira must have her. Wrong. So now it's got to be the Strabinski woman, or her mother, or even Justine's father, who's around somewhere. Maybe the granny on the Isle of Wight, who's got something against Sheena Renton and wants to give her a fright. They all have to be interviewed.'

'I don't like it, Den. I think you've got it horribly wrong and I'm going to tell Hemsley so.'

'Fine,' he nodded, uneasily aware of how little he actually cared.

Karen made a special effort over the evening meal, feeling unaccountably guilty towards Drew.

'Something smells nice,' he commented, coming into the kitchen.

'My chicken thing,' she smiled. 'We haven't had it for ages.'

'Can I do anything?'

'You could slice the beans if you like. If your stung finger's up to it, of course. Steph helped me pick them. And go and get some mint for the spuds.'

'Mint,' he said worriedly. 'Do I know which is mint?'

'Take Steph with you. She's pretty good at herbs.'

'She's a genius.'

'Not a bit. She just has a good teacher.'

The banter came as a relief to them both. As if responding to the lightening of the atmosphere, Timmy began humming tunelessly, rocking in his high chair, chest stuck out comically.

Everyone made short work of the meal and sat back contentedly. 'I phoned Penn,' Karen said idly. 'I thought I should keep in touch.'

'Oh?' Drew felt little immediate interest. 'How was she?'

'A bit strange, actually. She's a funny creature, not at all as I remember her as a child. Everything anybody says seems to set her off.'

'Why? What did you say?' A flicker of anxiety disturbed his contentment.

'When I told her Justine had turned up she got very agitated.'

'Oh, God.' He closed his eyes. 'I didn't tell you, did I?'

236

'What?'

'That Justine particularly didn't want Penn to know where she was. I never got round to giving you the story.' He stared at her, unable to believe how much he'd withheld from her. 'There was much more to it than the little bit I managed to tell you.'

'I fell asleep,' she laughed, determined to sustain the harmonious mood. 'It wasn't your fault.'

'No, but it matters. Justine says that Penn . . .' he glanced at the children, '. . . that she coerced her into something. More or less accusing her of abduction.'

'Good grief. How bizarre. You don't believe her, do you? After all, it was Penn who first raised the alarm about Justine being missing.'

'Somebody's certainly not being straight,' he agreed. 'But Justine did seem to have been badly treated. She's got bruises to prove it.'

'It can't possibly have been Penn,' Karen said with certainty.

'You could be right, but it's a bit unfortunate that Penn now knows where Justine is. I should probably phone them and let them know.'

'Don't be silly.' Karen's voice had acquired an edge. 'They're *friends*, for heaven's sake. What are you afraid will happen?'

He hesitated, reluctant to annoy his wife. It

made such a pleasant change to have her full attention, combined with such a good mood. It wasn't that she had grown sour or complaining since having the children; it was simply that she'd been distracted away from the partnership they'd once enjoyed. It was nothing more than the natural normal progression from newlyweds to parenthood, and he never for a moment wished he could change anything. But once in a while he thought wistfully of the early years, when they'd talked far into the night and Karen had been so full of energy and humour and enthusiasm. She'd worked as a teacher until Stephanie was born and then returned for a term before realising that Timmy was on the way. Somewhere in those turbulent few months she'd lost the bloom of youth. A bounce had gone out of her that he feared would never return.

Now she was doing her best to share in his latest adventure, which did after all involve her cousin. She had her own ideas as to what could be going on and he owed it to her to listen.

'You're probably right,' he said. 'The whole thing's a storm in a teacup. Except for the missing child,' he added, with a worried grimace.

'Child?' she echoed.

'That's right. The police seem to think Justine's got her landlord's child with her. But there was no sign of it yesterday when she turned up at Roma's, and she made no mention of it.'

'What sort of child? How old is it?'

'A girl. Three and a bit.'

'So where is the poor little thing? What do the police think? I assume Maggs told you that the tall handsome policeman came looking for her yesterday when you were over at Pitcombe? I only worked out who he was much later. He wasn't in uniform, but if he's CID, he wouldn't be, would he.'

'You're joking! She never said a word.'

'She's shy about it, probably. They went off together.'

Drew was surprised at his own reaction: annoyance and a sense of betrayal. Why on earth hadn't she said something? She'd had every opportunity. 'Well, well,' he puffed, lost for words.

'But they do know about Justine turning up, don't they?'

'Maggs phoned this afternoon, yes. Den was a bit short with her, apparently. But we've done our duty.' He chewed his upper lip. 'I phoned Roma as well and warned her that the police will want to see Justine. They've probably been by now.'

'So where on earth can the child be?' Karen broke out, with real trepidation. 'Don't you think it's worrying?'

'I suppose I do,' he agreed. 'Although . . . well, somehow I can't help feeling the kid's okay. She might be with Penn.' He snatched at the suggestion, finding it rather compelling as he thought about it.

'She isn't with Penn,' Karen asserted energetically. 'That makes no sense at all.'

'Well she must be somewhere,' Drew yawned. 'And I've done all I can for the time being.'

CHAPTER TEN

Drew woke at six thirty next morning to the sound of Timmy's chirruping. Like any dawn chorus, it managed to be both enchanting and annoying at the same time. Drew groaned softly.

'Never mind, the mornings are getting darker now,' came Karen's comforting whisper. 'By October, he'll be sleeping till eight.'

'Roll on October, then,' sighed Drew. 'My finger's still stiff, you know.' He held it up for inspection, showing her where the joint was swollen and red.

'It's better than yesterday,' she judged. 'I've been thinking about this business with Justine and Penn,' she went on, nestling comfortably against his ribs. 'And I suddenly wondered if my

Mum knows what's going on. She's awfully out of it, in her Welsh mountains.'

'Would she be interested? Justine's nothing to do with her.'

'She might. She keeps up with Uncle Sebastian and Auntie Helen, and she always seemed to like Penn.'

'Families,' sighed Drew. 'You know, Roma accused me of having romantic ideas about the family.'

'Oh? Does that mean she's cynical about them?'

'I think it probably does. She's too self-sufficient to care much about distant relatives.'

'Then why does Penn keep visiting her? What's the attraction?'

Drew smiled. 'I forgot you still haven't met her. She's a very magnetic personality. Charismatic, even. She stomps round, doing whatever she likes, telling people just what she thinks, but she's funny, as well. She's one of those people who are much more complicated than they first appear. I think, deep down, she's got a good heart.'

'As your granny used to say,' Karen supplied automatically.

'But there's a darker side as well, which she tries to ignore. From what I saw on Tuesday, I guess Justine's expert at rubbing her nose in all the things she's trying to avoid.'

'Nasty. I knew I didn't like Justine, even though I only saw her once.'

'I quite liked her,' he murmured. 'After a while, not at first. She grew on me.'

'Has Maggs met Roma yet?'

He had to think for a moment. 'No, I suppose not. Why?'

'Oh, I don't know. They sound as if they might have things in common.'

'D'you think so?' He gave the idea some thought. 'Can't really see it myself. But they would probably like each other.' He listened to his baby son for a few moments, before going on, 'Justine's a potter. When this is all settled we should go and have a look at her stuff.'

'What if she's put in prison for kidnapping? Would she be allowed to sell her pots then?'

He angled his head awkwardly to look at her. 'Is that what you think? That she kidnapped little Georgia?'

'I don't know,' she sighed. 'But if it's a choice between her and Penn having done it, I'm pretty sure I'd opt for Justine. Penn was always so *straight* when she was little. She had a huge sense of fair play. I know I hardly met Justine, but I find it easy to believe she's devious and sly.'

'You can't judge people by one glimpse of them as a child,' he reproached her. 'Even if she was sly then, that doesn't prove anything now. I was a little monster when I was six or seven. I bit my teacher in kindergarten. I stole my mother's engagement ring and wouldn't tell her where I'd put it for six whole months, just to torment her.'

'Stop, stop!' she protested. 'Let me keep some of my illusions.'

'But you see the point.'

'Sort of, but I don't really agree with it.'

'Circumstances force people to change. There's so much we don't know about Penn as she is now. Has she got a man, for example? What was all that stuff about runes?'

'What?'

'Oh, you missed that. As she was leaving here on Sunday she gave me some nonsense about drawing Justine's runes and getting an ominous reading.'

'Like the Tarot, you mean?'

'Search me. But it didn't sound particularly rational.'

'I never said she was rational. But then Justine doesn't sound any better. I just think that if you have to believe one over the other, I'd go for Penn. That's all.'

Timmy's burblings were acquiring a note of urgency, impossible to ignore.

'Here we go then,' muttered Karen, pulling away from Drew and getting lightly out of bed. 'Don't forget you've got a busy day today.'

* * *

Maggs was obviously on good form as she slewed her bike to a halt beside the Peaceful Repose signboard and wheeled it jauntily up the front path. The prospect of two funerals in one day was cheering. It made her and Drew feel needed, as if their services were being welcomed by the world at large.

'Hiya!' she greeted him. 'Everything all right?'

'Certainly is,' he nodded, still warm from the cosy chat he'd enjoyed with Karen.

'I had a thought just now,' she went on. 'Did you hear any more from the wind chime people?'

Drew groaned melodramatically. 'No, thank goodness, and I don't want to. They seem to have accepted the inevitable, at last.'

'You'd never have thought they could be such a pain, would you?'

Drew nodded a rueful agreement. The strife over the wind chimes had been one of his few real conflicts with a purchaser of one of his graves. Unthinkingly, he'd readily agreed that they could hang a set of tubular chimes from a tree close to the grave. Almost instantly, he regretted it, when he and Karen were kept awake throughout the next night, which happened to be particularly breezy. 'Who'd have thought it could be so maddening?' he'd said wonderingly.

First thing next morning, Karen had marched out and removed it. 'You'll have to tell them it won't do,' she said. 'It's disturbing the peace.'

'I will,' he'd promised.

But the customers were very unhappy about it. They called him a philistine and a dictator. They insisted that no sane person could possibly object to the charming sounds the thing made; that their dead sister had loved them, and always had one outside her window. She wouldn't rest in her grave without it.

Drew had tried a compromise – offering them the option of putting the chimes up when they visited, and taking it down again when they left. This wouldn't do at all, they said. It was for *Barbara*, not for them. Fortunately, Drew was supported by three other families, who maintained that wind chimes would interrupt the serenity of the field, and they didn't want to hear them clanging away when they came to visit. What's more, in two cases, the deceased person in the cemetery had nursed lifelong antipathies to the things. 'Granddad always said they bore no relation whatsoever to genuine music,' insisted one family.

Drew had been bruised by the argument, and amazed at the surprises that could creep up on you when you least expected them.

'The French daughters seem to have settled

their differences,' Maggs went on comfortably. 'Did I tell you?'

'Did you tell me what?'

'The nasty one phoned yesterday while you were digging the graves. She said she'd had a dream, where her Dad came to her and told her he was really happy to be buried here and she should be pleased for him.'

'I don't believe it. She's making it up.'

Maggs widened her eyes. 'What a thing to say! She sounded as if it was true. I thought it was nice,' she said sentimentally. 'Anyway, it should mean they won't start fighting this afternoon. It's going to be a good one. I can feel it in my bones.'

'What if she had another dream last night where he changed his mind and wanted to be cremated instead?'

'He wouldn't do that.'

'Maggs,' Drew said slowly. 'You don't actually believe the dead come back in dreams, do you?'

'Oh! Surely you're not trying to tell me it's all wishful thinking?' she cried, in mock distress. 'But it happens so *often*. Remember little Mrs Finch? And that sweet woman whose mother told her what hymns she wanted? Oh Drew, don't spoil it.'

'Softie,' he accused teasingly. 'You'd better just hope I'm not right about the nasty daughter.'

'It'll be fine, Drew. Things always go right for you,' she assured him.

He'd heard it before, and had long ago abandoned any efforts to dispute the underlying assumption. But he didn't think it was fair, all the same. Just because his children were both alive and well, his marriage in reasonable shape, and his business thriving, he didn't think it justifiable to snipe at him. Maggs herself, after a shaky start, had forced life to work for, rather than against her. But Drew had glimpsed the pocket of resentment that she harboured against people who never even paused to realise how easy their lives were. And he knew that in her book, he came into that category himself.

'Well this isn't going to get us anywhere,' he said briskly. 'Mrs Stacey at ten thirty; Mr French at one. Things to do, partner. No time for idle gossip.'

The ringing of the telephone seemed to confirm his words and Maggs reached to answer it with a cheeky smirk.

Sheena had felt a powerful need to escape after that morning's visit from the police. She'd found it so unendurable at the farm that she'd gone into town, to her office, smiling bravely at her colleagues and then plunging into sales figures, finding to her relief that it was perfectly possible to forget what had happened so long as there was something else to focus on. She knew that most people would find this inhuman, even insane – that they could never understand how rows of dry figures could in any way oust the horrors of her own child being lost, but so it was. Somebody, she told herself, would be looking after Georgia. Somebody always did, after all. If not Justine, then somebody else.

She worked until mid-afternoon and then went out into the street looking for something to eat. There was a teashop on the corner, but at the door she stopped, seeing clusters of people at the tables who might have read the reports of the missing child in the morning paper, or seen it on television. They might recognise her and whisper, which would be intolerable. So she crossed the street and went into a small newsagent's, where she bought a packet of crisps.

She did not go back to work, but instead climbed into her car, her mobile firmly switched off, and just drove aimlessly for over an hour. Finally, aware that she could no longer avoid the many grim realities at Gladcombe, she turned for home. If she drove slowly, it would be nearly six when she got there. The sun would be sinking on the second day since everything began to unravel. All she had to do was to take it one minute at a time and eventually there'd be answers, things would come right, Georgia would be found safe and well and Philip would beg her forgiveness.

Driving through the sunlit countryside, she tentatively permitted her thoughts to return to recent bewildering events. It had, of course, absolutely served her right. She'd been a lousy mother. She didn't deserve little Georgia who'd been so good and quiet and neglected and unprotected. She'd seen the looks the child had occasionally given her: wary and bewildered as if she couldn't understand why there was always such a distance between them. Why her mother never seemed to keep still long enough for a long lazy cuddle. Why she never had a story read to her or a game played with her. Sheena couldn't pretend to herself that she'd been anything like an adequate parent. She hadn't liked the role, had chafed under the responsibility and the constant nagging knowledge that Georgia needed and expected much more from her than she was ever going to get.

Justine had been a godsend. Although refusing to act as full-time childminder, she'd been taking on more and more evening and weekend babysitting. She and the little girl had obviously established a rapport, laughing together, wandering off hand in hand to pick flowers or watch birds. Sheena had felt nothing but relief as she heard the laughter. Georgia came in tired and went to bed unprotesting on the light summer evenings of the past few months. Several times Justine had put the child to bed, even if Sheena had been at home and perfectly capable of doing it herself. Justine had read a bedtime story, tucked her in and kissed her.

The idea that somehow this same Justine had kidnapped the child was very hard to swallow. Now it seemed there was some other explanation – some other person had gone off with her child. This was unaccountable, but nonetheless true. She wasn't even particularly angry about it. It seemed too strange for that. She was numb, shocked. She'd become a victim and she did not like that at all. Inside her was a dark mass, composed of tangled feelings that were better unacknowledged. It wasn't so difficult to act the part of the panic-stricken mother, tinged with rage at the person responsible, plus a dash of the guilt that all mothers are supposed to feel. Even Philip seemed to be convinced. But Sheena couldn't pretend to herself that this was anything close to the reality.

Penn woke late and for a moment had no idea where she was. The room was featureless: pale cream walls, sunlight flickering through light blue curtains; a television attached to the wall in a strange unfamiliar way. *Hotel* she remembered. *I'm in a hotel.*

She hadn't brought a watch or clock with her, and had no idea of the time. It had to be nine or later, judging by the strength of the sunlight. The only way to find out was to switch on the TV and she fumbled with the remote control that was lying on the bedside cabinet.

Her guess had been spot on. The channel she selected at random informed her that it was nine o'clock and therefore time for a news summary. Before she could properly concentrate the smiling announcer had begun to read the headlines. 'Police are increasingly concerned for the wellbeing of three-year-old Georgia Renton, apparently missing since last Thursday from her home near Exeter. There is growing evidence that Georgia has been abducted. Her parents are unable to account for her movements since Thursday, due to a misunderstanding as to who was taking care of her. The police are urgently requesting any information concerning the child.' A photo showing Georgia in blue dungarees was briefly flashed up, as the woman finished the item.

Penn snorted to herself. The report was nonsensical as it stood. The parents didn't know where she was; the police didn't know where she was – so why hadn't the blindingly obvious explanation occurred to them?

* * *

Having comprehensively failed in all enquiries and searches via the telephone and computer, DI Hemsley ratcheted up the investigation considerably that morning. 'Cooper – back to the farm. Take a search team with you and concentrate on buildings, the Pereira girl's cottage, woodlands. Make the parents think we're pulling out all the stops. They know we've located Justine Pereira, minus the child. They're going to be a lot more worried on hearing that, I shouldn't wonder.'

'Have you tapped their phone?' Den asked.

Hemsley nodded uncomfortably. 'Don't like doing it without telling them, but given all the doubts about them, it seemed sensible. No results, though. Nothing in or out. Except maybe that in itself is a result. Wouldn't you think they'd want to tell people the news? And wouldn't friends and relations have seen the media by now and be clamouring for details?'

'They're very odd people,' said Den.

'So off you go. I want to feel we've got somewhere by lunchtime.'

Den left the search team working through the numerous farm buildings, and set off down the track to Justine's cottage. The Rentons had evidently spent a restless night, receiving him with pale tense faces, but still apparently in firm control.

'Decided to take this seriously at last?' Philip said with heavy sarcasm.

'We've never doubted that this is serious,' Den told him. 'We've been putting in a great deal of effort following up on everything you've told us. This morning we're giving the whole farm an inch-by-inch search, starting with the outbuildings. I would like to see Miss Pereira's pottery workshop, if you'd just come and open it for me.'

'It isn't locked,' Sheena said. Den gave her his full attention. She was restless, twitchy, almost dancing on the spot.

'Mrs Renton,' he started to say. 'Are you . . . ?' He wasn't sure what he wanted to ask her. *Are you all right?* sounded crass, in the circumstances.

'I need to know how much longer this is all going to take,' she burst out. 'It's a week now. Where *is* she?' She looked at her husband, not the detective, as she said this. 'Do you think somebody's hurt her? Surely nobody would do that? Not Georgia.'

'Nobody's hurt her,' said her husband wearily. 'I keep telling you, there'll be a rational explanation.'

'But *what*?'

He'd merely shaken his head at that.

Justine's pottery workshop was a surprise. It was bigger inside than he'd expected from the overgrown shed it had appeared from the lane; a good eighteen feet long by nine or ten wide, with a sturdy bench running down one side. A fair-sized kiln stood on a low brick platform at the end, a potter's wheel sat proudly in the middle of the floor space, and free-standing shelving holding scores of pieces of pottery ran down the side opposite the bench. The majority of items were made of terracotta, and a red dust filmed the floor, walls and surfaces. Plastic buckets with lids were ranged beneath the bench, and jars with paintbrushes standing in them were clustered in one area. Coloured pictures were tacked up on the walls, presumably for their design potential. Some were abstract, some close-ups of flowers or stone walls, some were of natural scenes, mainly favouring trees or mountains. In short, Den concluded, this was the workplace of a very committed and active potter.

Unlike the cottage, here everything seemed to have been tidied up, washed, lidded, stacked, as if the owner had intended to be absent for a time. But perhaps that was a necessary discipline of the work? If you left the lid off a bucket of clay, it would dry out. Dimly recalling pottery classes at school, with the teacher boning on endlessly about putting everything away, and making sure the air could get to some things and not others, Den nodded to himself.

Even if Justine had fully intended to come back next morning, she'd probably have left it all just the way he saw it now.

Before leaving, he gave the finished pots a closer inspection. On the red terracotta were slashed thick black designs. A lot of the pieces seemed to be plant holders, but in strange shapes, defying gravity, pots leaning out from other pots, so a single piece had space for five or six plants, all facing different ways, large and small, high and low. Although no expert, he could see that considerable talent had gone into the making of these objects.

But there was nothing to suggest that a small girl had ever been in here. Justine might be an affectionate babysitter, but she hadn't let Georgia play with clay, as far as he could see. No small misshapen efforts, no low-level corner where a child could have her own worktable. Pottery for Justine Pereira had clearly been a serious adult matter.

Leaving the shed, closing it carefully behind him, he stepped out into the lane again. Something prompted him to turn right, continuing down towards a clump of trees rather than returning to the farmyard. There were signs of vehicular use, with marks of large tractor tyres just visible on either side of the grass that grew down the centre of the track. A well-built dry-stone wall ran along one side, unusual in a Devon setting. The trees were good-sized, mainly oak and ash, as remnant of a much larger stretch of woodland, he surmised. The track ran directly into it, and presumably through it to whatever fields lay beyond. He was just about to turn back when a glint of metal caught his eye, a short way into the wood.

He knew right away that it must be a car, and remembered Justine's assumption that her Metro must be hidden amongst the trees. Striding quickly down the last few yards of the track, he found a beige Metro tucked between two large trees, its nose tilted downwards. Another two feet and it would have been in a rough brambled area from which it would never have driven out again unaided.

Intrigued, Den tried the driver's door, which opened at his touch. Inside, the floor was muddy, the seats scattered with an assortment of objects – newspapers, sweet wrappers, tapes and their empty plastic cases, a jacket and a paperback book. There was also a black handbag, which he examined carefully. It contained a jumble of paper: receipts from petrol stations mostly, plus a purse, diary, cheque book, a bubble pack of pills and a pair of dark brown tights. Before removing the bag for safe keeping, he automatically noted that there were no seat belts on the back seat and that the one on the front passenger side appeared to be jammed at full stretch and therefore useless.

This, assuredly, was Justine Pereira's car. If it had been used to drive a small girl away on a camping trip, then the child could not have been securely strapped in. There were no toys, nothing obvious to suggest that Georgia had ever been inside this car. 'Forensics'll have to see this,' Den muttered, carefully closing the car door again.

Initially he intended to go straight back to Philip Renton and confront him with his discovery. It made nonsense of the man's story and Den wanted to see his face when he realised he'd been caught out. But caution prevailed. There was a chance that things could get out of hand and he ought to be prepared. He went to find two of the officers searching the buildings and told them of his find.

'Pete, you call a forensics team,' he ordered. 'Ben, you'd better come with me.'

When Philip Renton opened the door, Den spoke curtly. 'Excuse the intrusion, sir, but I seem to have found Miss Pereira's car in the woods down there—' he waved in the appropriate direction. 'There's a forensics team on its way, who'll be examining it for the traces of your daughter. Meanwhile, perhaps we could have another word with you?'

Without waiting for invitation, he stepped into the house, followed by Constable Ben Wilson. Renton was pale but composed. 'I'm afraid I don't understand,' he said calmly.

Den led the way into the living room, with a window overlooking the yard. 'Mr Renton, you'll be aware that this development throws considerable doubt on the story you've told us. If it's true that you watched the car leave, containing Justine and your little girl, how would you explain the fact that the same car is now in the wood on your property?'

'She must have come back,' Renton said with a shrug, that was aborted just too late. 'I'm sorry, Sergeant, but I was telling you the truth. I waved them off last Thursday morning. Are you *sure* it's the same car?'

'I am. Miss Strabinski gave me the registration number, and this one is the same.'

'Penn knew the car number?' Renton blew out his cheeks. 'Amazing.'

Den ignored this. 'How was your daughter secured in the car?'

'What?' Renton met his gaze his eyes steady. 'Well, I suppose she wasn't. She was kneeling on the back seat, waving at me through the rear window. I don't think Justine's seatbelts work very well.'

Den was struck by the impression that this

259

latest news had done nothing to increase the father's anxiety. 'So,' he continued, 'how does this affect your thoughts on where your daughter might be?'

Renton shook his head. 'I have no idea,' he confessed. 'Perhaps the car wasn't performing properly and she came back, dumped it, then set off again. There's a bus that passes the end of the lane every afternoon. She might have taken that instead.'

'Why would she dump it down in the woods, where nobody could see it?'

'So we wouldn't worry,' returned the man glibly.

'Why not leave a note or try to get your help with the car? Why would she be so desperate to get away?'

Renton sighed. 'Who can say? Justine was never easy to predict. She might have got some idea in her head. Georgia might have thrown a tantrum at the thought of the holiday not happening after all. I don't know,' he finished, uselessly.

Den concluded that he was getting nowhere. 'We'll have to wait for the forensic findings,' he said. 'Meanwhile I'd be grateful if you could stay here. I must say I'm very surprised to find Mrs Renton away from home at such a time.'

'She needs to be doing something. It was

driving her crazy cooped up here. I think she's best out of it, quite frankly. She'll come back when she's ready. She's only gone to the office.'

'I take it we can contact her by phone if necessary?'

'Of course.' Renton leant confidentially towards Den. 'She's worried about her latest sales drive, you see. She doesn't think they can manage without her. Either that, or she's scared they'll manage so well they'll decide she's not such a big cheese after all. The job always did come first.'

Den's growing suspicion that there was something close to insane about the whole Renton family was strengthened by this bizarre little speech. He indicated with a jerk of his head to Ben that they should leave. 'If there's no more you can tell us about the car, we'll return to our search,' he said.

'There's no more I can tell you,' Renton insisted. 'I'm as mystified as you are, Sergeant. All we want is for you to find our little girl safe and sound.'

Roma felt drained. Laurie's abrupt departure immediately after breakfast had been a bad shock to her system, hinting as he had of illness as one reason for his escape. Roma did not cope well with illness of any description. Those who knew her best would go further and claim that she was completely terrified of it.

'What's the matter with Laurie?' Justine had demanded. 'He looked awful.'

'Oh, it's all got a bit much for him,' Roma tried for an airy tone. 'He says he's going off for a few days' peace and quiet.'

'He doesn't look very well to me,' Justine persisted. 'Is he going to see a doctor?'

'Certainly not. He's perfectly all right. He just doesn't like this sort of disturbance.'

Both women knew they were on the thinnest of ice, through which they could not afford to fall at this particular moment. Reluctantly, Justine backed away. 'Okay,' she muttered.

Now she was back in her room, confronting Roma yet again with curt questions. 'So what about the Rentons? And Penn?'

Roma took a moment to savour the mixture of irritation and relief she felt. Anything was better than discussing Laurie. 'I think the police came close to believing you,' she said. 'That woman especially. She was watching you the whole time.'

'And you?'

'And me what?'

'Do you believe me?'

Roma heaved a sigh. 'It isn't quite that simple. But I don't see why you'd stick to such a daft story

262

if it wasn't true. And I think you are genuinely bothered about the little girl. And I tend to think you haven't been carrying on with the Renton man. Not having met any of these people, it's difficult to form a proper judgment.'

'You know Penn.'

'Yes, I do know Penn. You're asking me to believe some extraordinary things about her.'

'I know I am. I hardly believe it myself. Last time I saw her – before all this – she was perfectly normal. Although . . . well, I had the feeling there was something she wasn't telling me. She kept giving secretive little smiles, like a soppy schoolgirl in love with the teacher. I assumed she'd met a man.'

'Maybe that's it. She's fallen in love with some criminal, and he's put her up to all this.' Roma revived slightly at this idea. 'Wouldn't that explain everything? They had to get you out of the way so he could abduct little Georgia.'

'But why? Nobody's said anything about a ransom demand or anything like that. And it's a bit elaborate for your average paedophile.' Justine clenched her fists impotently. 'God, I can't just sit here while the poor kid might be going through all kinds of hell. I've got to *do* something.'

'Try to remember where that derelict place was,' her mother advised. 'There's still a chance that's where she'll be.'

Justine shook her head. 'I know she's not there. No, I need to go upstairs and have a really good think. My head's all over the place.'

Roma nodded. 'Good idea,' she approved. 'You're still not in a fit state to go anywhere, anyway, with all those bruises. I'm going to the shops for a bit; we haven't got anything for supper. I'll leave Lolly with you for company.'

'Right,' agreed Justine flatly.

By eleven on Thursday morning, DI Hemsley had called DS Cooper back to the station, leaving a forensics team to examine the Metro. 'We need to have another think about all this,' he said. 'We still have no direct evidence that there's been any violence against the youngster and only Mr Renton's word that she was last seen in the company of the Pereira girl. Now she's turned up without the kiddie, we have obvious cause for serious concern. That's why I fed it to the media last night. They'll always co-operate when there's a little one involved. We now have only one obvious line of investigation before we start a no-holds-barred, full scale search for her.' He looked at Den. 'This Strabinski woman. Is there a chance she had the child in the house when you visited her?'

Den shrugged. 'I didn't search the place,' he said. 'It's obviously possible.'

'So first thing to do is go back there. Don't give her any warning – just turn up quickly and quietly and give the place a good going-over. My hunch is the kid'll be there, safe and sound, and we can forget the whole thing by lunchtime.'

Den blinked. 'Yes, sir,' he said. 'I'll take Timms with me, shall I?'

'Good idea. Now, one or two more things, while I've got you here . . .' and he launched into an entirely unnecessary spiel about the difference between hearsay and hard fact, suspicion and actual evidence.

'There's nobody in,' Bennie Timms repeated, as Den hammered on the door of Penn's Crediton house.

'So what do we do now?' he demanded.

'Report back and then go on to North Staverton. It isn't too far from here, through the lanes. An hour, at most.'

'We're not breaking in here, then?' he said, a trifle wistfully.

'I don't think so. On what grounds? Weren't you listening to Danny Boy this morning?'

'I thought he'd been told personally by God that little Georgia was here in this house. Give the place a good going-over, he said.'

'Not enough direct evidence to warrant breaking and entering,' she insisted. 'Not by a long way. But we can check with him, if you like.' Den nodded and she made the call. Reluctantly, the DI told them to leave it for the moment, providing they could be completely certain the house was empty.

'How do we do that?' Den wondered.

They drove a short distance, parked the car, and walked back, one on each side of the street, examining the house from all angles and watching the windows for movement. Then Den went round the back while Bennie knocked vigorously on the front door. They waited five more minutes, listening hard. Not a sign of life could they detect.

'Okay, then,' he said, rejoining her at the car. 'North Staverton it is.'

Unfortunately, they quickly realised that they'd chosen the worst possible moment. Several cars were parked inside and outside the main gate to the Peaceful Repose Cemetery. As they cruised past, trying to find a space, Bennie drew Den's attention to a group of people walking slowly across the field, four of them carrying an unmistakable cardboard coffin.

'Bloody hell!' Den cursed.

'Well he *is* an undertaker,' Bennie chuckled. 'He must have to do this sort of thing fairly often.'

'He said he had two funerals today,' Den suddenly remembered. 'Damn it – we can't interrupt him now.'

'No,' Bennie agreed. 'So let's have a rethink. I'll call in and see if there's been any developments and we'll take it from there.'

Den didn't reply. She followed his direction of gaze and found its object: a sturdy young woman, dark-skinned and black hair neatly coiled at the back of her neck. She was working with Drew, standing on opposite sides of the grave, slowly lowering the coffin into it. There was something oddly ambiguous about the tableau: the dark clothes and sombre nature of the event clashed with the birdsong and fluffy clouds. Nobody appeared to be weeping, and yet everyone's movements looked slow and heavy. There didn't appear to be any minister of religion present, which gave the proceedings an ad hoc aspect, harking back to simpler times. 'Nice,' she murmured. 'Lucky it's not raining, though.'

'Or snowing,' Cooper added, with a short laugh.

Bennie made the call back to the station, asking for any news update on the Renton child, while Den turned the car and headed back towards home ground. A squawk of surprise came from his colleague.

'What?' he demanded.

She finished the call and turned towards him. 'We've missed some excitement at the farm. While everyone was busy outside, somebody new turned up and picked a fight with the Renton man.' She glanced at the note she'd automatically scribbled. 'A Mr Carlos Francisco Pereira.' She grinned. 'No prizes for guessing who he must be.'

Den got there in seconds. 'Father of Justine? First husband of Mrs Roma Millan?'

'I shouldn't be at all surprised,' she said.

At the last minute, the nasty daughter couldn't hold her tongue, the power of her dream apparently losing in the struggle with her lifelong prejudices. Watching her father's cardboard coffin being lowered into the shallow grave, she jabbed her elbow into her sister's ribs and said loudly, 'Well, I hope you're satisfied. This is a disgrace. It's indecent.' Drew and Maggs, holding tightly to the webbing that supported the coffin, hesitated. It was only just feasible for the two of them to lower a body into a grave, and it took all their concentration. Normally, it was a job for four men, but he and Maggs had become adept at doing it between them. Using cardboard, willow or even linen wrappings, instead of traditional heavy wooden coffins, made it a much lighter job. Generally, two or three relatives would assist. Mr

French's daughters, however, had turned up with only two young children, and showed no sign of getting involved.

'Carry on,' Drew muttered, and they slowly let the box drop.

'Shut up!' the nice daughter hissed. 'It's done now.'

'Mum!' chirped one of the children. 'I'm cold.'

The day was far from chilly, and the child well wrapped up, but Drew knew all too well that the emotion and trauma of a funeral affected the body much as a sharp east wind might do. All the more reason to get on with it, Drew decided.

The top of the unadorned brown of the cardboard seemed uncomfortably close to ground level when they'd finished. Drew always experienced a pang of anxiety at this point. He knew that a foot and a half of well-packed soil on top would protect the contents of the grave from any unpleasant consequences, short of an earthquake or major flood, and it certainly fitted with ecological considerations – but it looked alarming to people accustomed to the six feet of conventional burials.

Clearly, the nasty daughter was very well aware of this. Her lip was curled in disgust, her brows drawn together in a vicious frown. Drew quailed. She was going to make them bring him up again; insist on a cremation, cause all kinds of havoc.

'Jennifer,' the nice daughter said firmly. 'We've talked it all through, and you know full well that this is what Dad wanted. It's beautiful here – exactly the sort of thing he loved. Be glad for him, why can't you? And don't forget that dream you had.'

Her sister tossed her head. 'Well . . .' she said. 'I suppose it's done now.' The tension level fell instantly, as everyone exhaled together. Even the children seemed relieved. Drew reached for his spade, and nodded to Maggs to remove her lowering equipment.

'Would you like to scatter a handful?' he asked the sisters, carefully addressing them equally. Somewhat to his surprise, the disgruntled Jennifer grabbed the spade, and hefted a large clod of soil onto the coffin.

'Don't want to get my hands dirty,' she said. Her sister made a show of scooping up a double handful, and letting it trickle into the grave. Both children imitated her with some eagerness.

'Thank you,' said Drew swiftly. 'Maggs will take you back to the office, while I finish here.'

Roma had lied about the need to go to the shops. Justine's short-lived urge to do something had been infectious and Roma had been suddenly gripped by the compulsion to see for herself just what was going on at Gladcombe Farm. If the Renton man had lied, as Justine claimed and the wife was uncaring and irresponsible, Roma wanted first-hand demonstration of it.

She had no very clear idea of precisely where the farm was, but having accumulated Ordnance Survey maps of the South-West over several years, she was confident that she could find it. The triangle formed between Bridgwater, Tiverton and Minehead was an area she knew reasonably well. Small rural settlements like her own village of Pitcombe, and Drew's of North Staverton, abounded, connected by a mesh of small lanes clustering like a swarm of bees to the south of Bridgwater, thinning out as they approached the heights of Exmoor. Methodically, she examined the map, using clues dropped by Penn and Justine, until she located the farm. It was about twenty-five miles distant, and she paused to reflect on the realisation that her daughter had been living so close by for years and she had never known.

Pushing through her more immediate thoughts, as she drove, was the knowledge that it couldn't be much longer now before the central issue between her and Justine was confronted. The mere thought was terrifying and sent Roma's insides churning. She wasn't at all sure she could do it, however urgent the obligation might be. Perhaps what she was now doing was a kind of alternative, a way of letting her daughter know that she owed her something. By tackling the Rentons and establishing exactly what the truth of the matter was, she might at least find she'd taken that arduous first step in the long process of reconciliation.

She took a number of wrong turns, despite the map, cursing the inadequate road signs and the narrow lanes; so it was over an hour before she finally reached the farm. Not having an idea what to expect, she parked on the road at the end of the approach drive and continued on foot.

There was no sign of a police presence, which she found both a surprise and a relief. She had assumed that there would be an officer with the distraught parents, but that she would be allowed to speak to them in her capacity as Justine's mother. She even had a few placatory lines rehearsed in advance.

A newish Saab stood in the cobbled yard, but she could neither see nor hear anyone. The front door, with a yellow climbing rose growing in profusion over the porch, was firmly closed. She rapped the brass knocker vigorously.

Three long minutes later, the door opened. As unshaven man was standing there, the bright August light clearly causing him some difficulty.

He seemed to have just woken up, until Roma looked again and decided he had been recently punched in the face. Through slitted eyes and thickened lips he grunted, 'Yes?'

'Mr Renton? I'm Roma Millan, Justine's mother. I think I need to talk to you.'

'Erghhh,' said the man, rubbing his dark hair confusedly. 'Why would that be?'

'I want to know why you think my daughter would do anything to harm your child.'

He laid a square hand against his stubbly cheek in a gesture of weary annoyance. 'Because I let her take Georgia . . .' his voice quivered on the child's name and he closed his eyes, moving the hand to his sternum. 'I can only hope she's kept her safe somewhere. It's sending us crazy, not knowing . . . and now this madman turns up out of nowhere and starts a fight.' He began to close the door, obviously intent on keeping her out. A sudden idea had apparently entered his head. 'Your husband, he must be,' he accused. 'He says he's Justine's father.'

'What?' Roma was stunned. 'Carlos? He's been here?'

'Too right he has. Shouting and screaming. Says I must have harmed his precious daughter, calling me names.'

'But . . . how did he know?'

Renton shook his head tiredly. 'The police

contacted him when that friend of yours reported Justine missing. Routine enquiries, they said, but it seemed to annoy him.'

Roma could not repress a sudden smirk. 'It never did take much to do that,' she said, almost fondly. 'Where is he now? And why aren't there any police here?'

'They've taken him into custody,' said Renton with satisfaction. 'The place was crawling with cops a few minutes ago.' He looked around the yard in surprise. 'They were searching the barns and shippons. I expect they'll soon be back again. They don't seem to stick at anything for long, before changing their minds.' He frowned, as if trying to remember something. Roma thought he might be in need of medical attention.

'Shouldn't you see a doctor?' she asked, amazing herself at this lapse.

'I'll be all right,' he said. 'I'm not leaving here. They said they might send someone to have a look at me.'

'Meanwhile, there's still no sign of your daughter, I suppose?'

He shook his head quickly. 'Now, I don't want to be rude, but . . .'

Roma didn't flinch. 'Right you are,' she said to the closing door.

CHAPTER ELEVEN

Renton's dismissal suited Roma perfectly. She was free now to carry out the search of the farm that she'd been itching to undertake. She had always enjoyed looking for things, missing pens, magazines, equipment of all sorts. There was a meticulousness to her character that made her habitually note where she left things, where she observed them lying as she went about her work. She had an excellent sense of direction, and a nose for people's means of concealment. What's more, she admitted to herself, a child who'd been missing and possibly dead for over a week would be locatable by the olfactory sense, if nothing else.

All of which suggested that the police search

would surely have found Georgia if she'd been anywhere near the farmhouse or Justine's cottage. Not knowing the layout, or the extent of the property, she let instinct take over. To her left was a small orchard, containing ten or twelve mature apple trees, not the modern stunted user-friendly mutations, but good-sized tree-shaped specimens. She paused to admire the yellowish fruit on many of them. Automatically she swept her gaze around the edges in search of beehives. No orchard should be allowed to exist without bees; it was a criminal waste.

There were none, but the rapidly warming day – by this time almost noon – had brought other insects out, most notably wasps. Only a handful of apples had fallen off the boughs, but those that had were being hollowed out by sugar-seeking insects, their predations leaving brown ragged edges around the cavities they'd made. Roma kicked at one, hoping to kill a wasp in the process.

Beyond the orchard a stile led into a grass field, and she climbed nimbly over it. A path was worn diagonally across the field, ending in a small copse of trees in the far corner. Buttercups grew densely amongst the grass, as well as a scattering of meadowsweet. Roma wondered whether the Rentons were deliberately encouraging it to become a wild flower meadow. This and the orchard seemed out of harmony with her initial picture of them as busy professionals playing at being country dwellers. Perhaps they had more feeling for the environment than she'd given them credit for. Perhaps, she thought suddenly, they'd been victims of foot and mouth disease.

The ground was knobbly beneath the long grass, poached presumably by the feet of cattle walking on it in damp conditions. It all had an abandoned air, as if an abrupt change had been wrought. That would be it, she decided. All the animals slaughtered in one holocaustic day, and the man she'd just seen too flattened to risk restocking his land.

She admitted to herself that she knew nothing about the Rentons. The man had looked a lot more like a farmer than she'd expected, although with his face all battered he could just as easily have been a professional boxer. She grinned ruefully to herself at the thought that Carlos had done that. Renton must have said or done something to provoke him to violence, but Roma knew only too well that it need not have been much. Sometimes the mere angle of an eyebrow could set him off.

The grass was long and the path narrow. Roma found herself thinking how it would be for a small child to walk through this field, the grass up to her shoulder, and the flowers vivid to the clear young eyes. There'd be butterflies and birds, seed heads on many of the grasses, a world of colour and movement that would enchant a little girl. Letting her thoughts wander and her instincts flow free, Roma convinced herself that Georgia would have come to this field, perhaps with Justine, several times through the summer, to enjoy its animal-free glories. Roma knew, albeit vaguely, that farm animals did not always have a beneficial effect on pastureland. Without them, the truly wild flora and fauna could proliferate amazingly.

The copse was obviously an ancient one, boasting big woodland trees that might well have been deliberately planted in the first instance. A beech spread protectively, two oaks and a handsome holly had all grown to impressive size. Between them were younger saplings, a tangle of brambles, bracken, ivy. The field was being encroached, without fencing to mark any division between it and the copse. Instead, there were signs of a shallow ditch and above it a low bank, full of gaps and burrows made by animals, perhaps even badgers. Brambles ran riot along much of the ditch, forming a natural barrier that most people would hesitate to tackle.

The smell only gradually forced itself onto her attention. It might even have first wafted into her nostrils as she emerged from the orchard, but in the country you got smells, and learnt not to over-react to them. It wasn't until she reached the copse that she labelled it for what it was. Standing very still, she reminded herself of what she was looking for, why she was there. She had even been expecting to encounter this very stink. Of course, it was sure to be a sheep, trapped in the brambles somewhere, and dead of hunger and exhaustion. It happened all the time.

But her senses were operating independently of her mind. Closely examining the stretch of bank, and the hedges to her right and left, she noticed activity at a spot low down in one of the intact sections of bank. Darting in and out, there were wasps, hundreds of them, far more than Roma had ever seen in one place before. Cautiously, she moved closer. Despite knowing that wasps never attacked in force, it took strong nerves to approach such a mass of them. Without warning, the face of her own little brother, killed by bee stings, flashed into her mind. She hadn't given him a thought for years, had never felt any conscious grief or guilt or anxiety about what had happened to him. She'd been stalwart in her refusal to pretend to care, causing adults to draw back from her, disconcerted by her coldness.

'No escape,' she muttered to herself now. 'Everything connects.' It had taken her a long time to accept that a person's innermost processes operated on a level beyond conscious control, and that it was all right for this to be true. It was more than all right: it was instructive and reassuring. If her little brother's face was in her mind now, there must be a good reason for it, if only that the conjunction of a child and insects brought a rather obvious memory to the surface.

The smell, though, needed investigation, regardless of the wasps. It did seem to emanate from the same general direction as the boiling mass of insects, and a very nasty suspicion was rapidly forming. Was it true, she asked herself, that sugar-loving insects would be attracted to a dead body? The dead lion in the Bible which contained a bees' nest, was surely just a convenient space, the ribcage offering an ideal cavity for a swarm to set up home in? Surely the flesh wasn't used for food?

Below the wasps was a depression in the ground, part of the original ditch, filled with long grass. As Roma approached, the smell became appalling. It flowed into her stomach and made her involuntarily retch. Before she had seen anything, before the reality was lodged in her mind, her stomach had reacted.

The body was clothed in a skimpy summer outfit, leaving plenty of greenish flesh visible. It had been placed face down, as far as she could ascertain. Light brown hair covered most of the visible portion of the head. Crazily, the wasps were clustered on a point about a foot away. Something else had been dumped, alongside Georgia, and it was this that attracted the insects in such numbers. With her hand tightly over her nose and mouth, trying not to breathe, Roma bent closer to see what the wasps were eating. A sticky glistening mass was visible, streaked and splashed with various colours – red, yellow, green, purple. At the farthest edge Roma found a clue – a melted shape lying apart from the rest, which she gingerly prodded, oblivious of the buzzing wasps. It was like semi-solid jelly. She picked it up, slippery in her fingers, and held it in the palm of her hand.

It was a green jelly baby, melted after days in the sun and rain, so the shape was distorted, but still recognisable. There had been a great many more, tipped in a heap beside little Georgia's head, as if to offer her some consolation for being dumped lifeless in a dry ditch. The sweets had stuck together, blending their colours and sugary selves into one mass – a mass that would be irresistible to wasps, and other sugar-loving insects.

Roma backed away, without any further examination of the child. She looked around her worriedly. Had anybody seen her coming in this direction? What should she do now? No way could she go back to the house and tell the child's parents what she'd found. She would have to locate a telephone and call the police. Or somebody.

Anybody else would have had a mobile phone, she chided herself. They'd have made the call and then waited in the field for emergency services to congregate. Helicopter, police doctor, social workers, undertakers – and then stood modestly to one side. She felt reluctantly relieved that she did not have the gadget with her. Now she at least had time to think, as she cut across the field in the direction of the farm drive, climbing over a wooden gate and hurrying back to her car.

The child is dead, she repeated to herself. *There's nothing to be done for her. No need to panic.* And yet she was on the brink of panic. She looked around her anxiously, not wanting to be seen, especially by the Renton man. Not by any returning police officers, either – although she knew she must quickly inform them of her find.

She drove away jerkily, rubbing frequently at her nose, trying to expel the lingering stink that had somehow lodged inside it. Her hand was sticky from the melted jelly baby, which she had carried back with her and wrapped in a scrap of paper she found on the floor of the car. It was now on the top of the dashboard, an odd irrelevant piece of evidence. She was thinking; thinking almost to the exclusion of doing. Her head was full of the sight and smell of what she'd found, the extreme oddness of the pile of sweets; the incompetence of the police who obviously hadn't bothered to search beyond the farmyard and its buildings; if they'd done even that much. That was surely because they were so convinced that either Justine or Penn was responsible for the lost child, and still held her, alive and well, somewhere.

But behind and through and over all these impressions and suppositions was one big idea; so big and loud that it made everything else seem shadowy and evanescent. This idea was the reason she had turned and run, as if away from a piece of knowledge that could be left undisturbed. This idea arose inescapably from a memory of how Justine had always loved jelly babies far beyond any other kind of sweet. The idea was that Justine had, after all, quite obviously killed Georgia Renton.

She didn't phone the police when she got home forty-five minutes later and found Justine fast asleep in the spare room; she phoned Drew Slocombe. His second funeral of the day was barely over and he'd been indulging in a cup of tea and a bucketful of self-congratulation. He was entirely unprepared for what Roma had to say.

'Drew, I'm going to ask something terrible of you,' she began. 'Something I have absolutely no right to even suggest. But I can't carry it by myself, and there's nobody else but you who'd even hear me out.'

'Go on,' he invited warily.

'The little girl's dead. Been dead for days. Past any help from anybody. I found her an hour ago.'

She could hear him gulp, and try the find something to say. All he managed was a croak of astonishment.

'I've implicated myself dreadfully, leaving footprints and fibres and God knows what, so if the police are called out, they'll soon know I was there.'

'But they'll know your traces are more recent than when she died,' he said, having got his voice back with difficulty.

'Will they? Actually, that's not my main worry. The thing is, Drew – I'm convinced that Justine is going to be even more under suspicion than she is already. There's nothing about the body that would exonerate her, as far as I can see. And, Drew, I don't think I can be the one to make the phone call that might incriminate my own daughter. I realise it's stupid – that it's not going to make any difference in the long run. Not unless I'm planning to move the child and make a better job of hiding her once and for all. The thought did occur to me, I don't mind admitting, but I can't face it. She's very decomposed.'

'What do you want me to do?'

'Call the police.'

'Not the Rentons?'

'Would you be able to cope with that?' she wondered, before remembering his profession. 'I suppose you would. It doesn't matter which. That's up to you. I do understand what I'm asking of you – that you're sure to get much more deeply involved than you'd like. The police won't understand why it's you making the call, when up to now you've had no link with the missing child. I have absolutely no right to make such a demand on you.'

'It's all right,' he said. 'I understand. You'd better tell me where she is, then leave it with me and I'll try and work out the best way of informing them.' When she'd described the location, he snorted. 'Why on earth haven't they already searched all the fields? Wouldn't you think that'd be the first thing they'd do? How far is it from the house?'

'I would guess about a quarter of a mile.'

'Could Georgia just have wandered off on her own, and got lost? She might have died of exposure.'

Roma thought of the wasps, and the path

through the long grass, the stile and the orchard. 'I don't think so,' she said. 'Don't forget, the parents thought they knew where she was. The father waved her off with Justine. The mother cheerfully assumed she was with her granny on the Isle of Wight.'

'And nobody knows when Penn last saw her,' Drew said darkly. 'It's only looking so bad for Justine because nobody believes what she says about Penn.'

'Do you believe her?' Roma demanded.

'I'm not sure,' he replied carefully. 'Do you?'

'I did,' she said. 'Until this happened.'

Detective Sergeant Den Cooper knew he was making a hash of the whole case. He was going through the motions, but not according it his full and undivided efforts. When he thought about the small girl, missing now for a week, he should have been wrung out with concern for her. He should be meeting with the DI every few hours, pressing for assistance from other forces, or else handing the whole thing over to Exeter. He felt a strong disinclination to take it any further, wishing Drew Slocombe had never chosen Okehampton to report the missing Justine in the first place.

When Carlos Pereira had shown up, shouting for his daughter, maddened by the bland

286

unconcern of Philip Renton, it had thrown everything into even greater confusion. The uniforms had dragged him off Renton and taken him to the station. The forensic team had almost simultaneously finished bagging up their gleanings from the Metro and followed closely behind. Den and Bennie had been left unsure what to do, until Hemsley had ordered them back to base for yet another debriefing.

He wished it would all just stop. He didn't want to search for a missing child; he didn't want to find her dead and have to watch the wretched Rentons disintegrate. He would much rather never have heard of Justine Pereira or Georgia Renton. Except then of course he would never have met the delightful Maggs. And meeting Maggs was the only bright moment in a long spell of gloom.

Carlos Pereira was clearly not a fully functional person, although once in police custody he did calm down considerably. He could not coherently explain exactly why he'd driven down to Devon from his home in Derbyshire and launched an attack on the unsuspecting Renton. He would only say that he'd known something like this was coming. Justine had not been in touch as regularly as usual; she'd sounded depressed the last time she'd phoned him and laughed bitterly when he'd asked if she had boyfriend trouble.

'That's not quite the same thing as accusing her landlord of harassment,' Den observed mildly.

'Something was upsetting her,' said the man stubbornly. 'I begged her to tell me what it was, so that I could come and lend a hand. She always used to come to her Dadda when she had problems.' Pereira's Spanish accent was unmistakable, but he seemed to have complete mastery of the English language. His daughter was very like him in looks and Den wondered whether she'd inherited some of his instability as well.

'Well, sir, you've shown up at a highly critical moment,' Den told him, with a touch of exasperation. 'As you probably realise, we're in the process of investigating the disappearance of Mr and Mrs Renton's three-year-old girl. There's a strong possibility that your daughter is somehow implicated in the matter.'

Pereira stared wildly at him. 'Little girl? No, I know nothing about that.' His face contracted at a sudden painful thought. 'Justine wouldn't hurt a little girl. Not after losing her own baby.'

Den was slow to react. 'Pardon?' he said. 'When did this happen?'

'Five years ago,' the man supplied, his eyes sunken into dark shadow. 'It was terrible. A tragedy. Little Sarah, the light of our lives, the best darling child in the world. She died.' He clutched his heart dramatically. 'It was like the ending of the world. Poor Justine. She went wild – we both did – and then she started her pottery and calmed down, and took those rotten pills the doctor gave her and seemed to be getting better. I telephoned her every week and wrote to her and went to see her a few times. But now . . .' He sighed heavily, and rubbed his broken knuckles where he'd punched Philip Renton.

Even operating on autopilot, Den couldn't miss the obvious. 'How old was Sarah when she died?' he asked.

'Three. She was just over three. The same age as this child you say is missing.' He stared desperately at Den, the same thought quite legible on both faces. But then Pereira banged the door shut on it. 'No,' he said firmly. 'It's a coincidence. Justine would never do anything to harm a little girl.'

'I hope you're right,' said Den, unconvinced.

Drew asked for Detective Sergeant Cooper when he telephoned. He'd rehearsed various ways in which to give Roma's message, but they all sounded weak at best and positively obstructive at worst. Roma's behaviour – driving home, leaving an hour's interval between finding the body and reporting it – seemed almost culpably careless. This family – Justine, Penn and Roma – were rapidly seeming more and more strange. Disturbed, dysfunctional, devious: epithets rolled round Drew's head as he imagined the police reaction to his information.

He was, after all, an undertaker. He knew that there was a profound human need to gather up and protect the mortal remains of a deceased person. When it was a child, this need was all the greater. The image of a week-old body lying in a ditch, exposed to weather and animals and birds, was deeply distressing. The time between replacing the receiver on Roma's call and lifting it again to do her bidding and tell the police was little over two minutes. And even that felt much too long.

By some telepathic magic, Maggs came into the office just as Drew pronounced the name of Cooper and flew to his side, her eyes firing questions at him. In the wait for the policeman to be located, he refused to tell her anything, waving a finger across his face to indicate the need for patience. Finally they were connected. 'Cooper,' came a tired-sounding voice.

'Drew Slocombe. Listen, I've got some very serious news for you. Roma Millan – Justine's mother – went to Gladcombe Farm earlier today and found the body of a little girl. She's in a ditch, about a quarter of a mile from the farmhouse and seems to have been dead for some days. Roma's too upset to speak to you herself, so she asked me to do it.'

'All right,' came the steady response. 'Is she there now? Will she show us the place?'

'No, she went home again. I think she just acted instinctively. It came as a horrible shock to her.'

'Must have done. Tell her we'll collect her right away, take her back there and she can show us what she's found.'

'Can I come?' Drew surprised himself by the question. 'Me and Maggs. You'll need someone to remove the body anyway.'

'Steady on. That won't be until after the team's done its bit. Doctor, SOCOs, photographer – all that stuff.'

'I know. And I have urgent work here for another half-hour or so. But we can't help feeling involved, especially since Roma asked me to call you. I think she might need someone like me to be there. Somebody who understands her.' He wondered at his own temerity, his acute sense of wanting to protect the woman who everyone saw as so in control and domineering.

'I can't stop you if you decide to be there. Now, I'll have to go. This is going to need all available hands, in the house as well as outside. Sounds as if it'll be messy.'

* * *

Sheena Renton was home by five-thirty, a sudden surge of emotion sending her foot down on the accelerator, for no conscious reason. She arrived to find the farmyard so full of vehicles that she had to leave her car on the approach drive. Philip was standing by the house, the lowering sun shining full on him like a spotlight. As she ran to him, she saw that his face was bruised and swollen, giving him an appearance both sinister and pathetic.

'Have they found her?' she gasped breathlessly.

He met her eyes. 'We tried about fifty times to call you. Where have you been?'

'Driving. Just driving. What's happening here?' Her voice felt rough, emerging from a constricted throat. She stared around at the knots of people filling the yard, none of them quite looking at her. She recognised the tall detective and a short middle-aged woman with him who had the square shoulders of a police officer. There were at least four uniformed officers standing about.

'Philip, tell me. What the hell is going on?' She made as if to run to the single person she recognised, but her husband caught her arm.

'We have to stay here. They'll come and talk to us when they're ready. They only say there have been developments, up to now.'

'Developments? Why? What's happened?' She

felt light-headed, inarticulate, the only important questions endlessly repeating themselves.

'They told me to stay in the house. They wanted to keep me a prisoner in my own house. So I came outside.' His voice was much too loud. Many nervous glances came his way from different corners of the yard.

'For God's sake, we should do as they say. They have our best interests at heart. And what happened to your face?' She put up a hand to examine his injuries.

'What?' He brushed her hand away. 'What makes you think that?'

'It's our daughter who's lost,' she whispered, tears filling her eyes. 'Come on. We should go in.'

Philip sagged defeatedly and followed her back to the kitchen. They sat down at the table in silence. Sheena pushed the fingers of both hands through her hair and dropped her head, staring blankly at the scrubbed pine surface inches from her face. Her husband once again began to explore his own damaged face, slowly crisscrossing his cheeks, wincing as the bruises reacted, but making no effort to lighten the pressure of his fingers. Ten minutes passed, with occasional subdued sounds filtering through from the yard. Sheena resisted any temptation to look out of the window at what might be happening. Somehow over the past moments, she had understood, and no longer felt any impatience to know the unbearable truth.

But Philip was different. 'I can't stand this!' he burst out, and got up from his chair. 'I'm going to see what they're doing.' Sheena ignored him as he went out of the room.

He was back within seconds. 'There's another man here now. Looks like a doctor.'

'Oh, God,' she wept. 'They must have found her, then.' She stared blankly at him. 'But how . . . ?'

'We'll know soon enough,' he grated. 'All we have to do is sit here until they condescend to talk to us.'

Only then did Sheena grasp the reason for the surreal sense of déjà vu she had been experiencing since entering the yard. Men in uniform; silent stony faces; heart pounding; Philip almost crazy with the horror of it. 'It's like the foot and mouth all over again,' she whispered.

Philip's throat worked convulsively and she wondered for a moment if he was going to be sick. He said nothing.

Another twenty minutes passed, during which neither spoke a word. For Sheena time meant nothing. Her thoughts alighted on a string of unrelated topics, one after another. Images of Georgia meshed with memories from earlier times. She thought of Philip's father, pulling on his boots and cursing the weather. She heard again the muted explosions of the stun guns, killing scores of healthy cows. She smelt again the rotting carcasses that were not removed for an unbearable ten days. She thought of her husband, doing his best to carry on, dealing in safe undemanding bales of hay and straw, investing no emotion in them, a hollow man.

At last the waiting came to an end. She lifted her head as she heard footsteps in the hallway outside. The tall detective ducked his way into the room with them, his face grim. There were grooves around his mouth and nose, as if he'd been trying to escape an awful smell.

'I'm very sorry,' the detective began. 'But I have to tell you that we have found the remains of a child in a ditch a short distance from here.'

'No!' Sheena howled, wrapping her arms around her head as if to ward off a blow.

'We'll have someone here in a few minutes to sit with you,' he went on. 'She's just outside . . .'

'What does that matter?' Renton ground out. 'We don't need anybody like that.' He scowled at the floor near Den's feet. 'What happens now?'

Den cleared his throat. 'There'll have to be a positive identification and then a post-mortem. Until then, we can do very little.'

Renton dragged himself to his feet. 'I'll identify her,' he said. 'Let's get on with it.'

'Oh . . . no, not yet.' Den showed some alarm. 'She isn't – I mean, it would be better at the mortuary. Better, actually, if there was somebody less closely related.' He swallowed.

'There isn't anybody,' the man insisted. 'What's the matter? Won't it make your job easier this way?'

Den looked in vain for assistance. Nobody had followed him into the kitchen. There was no way he could permit the man to lay eyes on the horrible mess that had been his little girl. But he wasn't sure how to prevent him.

'I really don't think—' he tried again.

The sound of more people just outside the front door gave him hope of reprieve. 'Just a moment,' he muttered, and went to investigate.

Drew and Maggs were standing warily, looking around at the gathering in the yard. They smiled awkwardly at Den.

'Am I glad to see you,' he hissed at them, coming up close. 'You can probably help me on this.'

'All done then?' Maggs asked, eyes glittering.

'More or less. She's been dead several days and not nice. The thing is . . .' he spoke urgently, addressing himself to Drew, '. . . the father says he wants to identify her. Here. Now. I can't really

296

stop him if he insists, but he probably has no idea what it'll be like. You must get this all the time. What do I do?'

'Nasty,' Drew agreed. 'How bad is she? Smelly, I suppose.'

'Very. We've got her into a bag, just down there. Her eyes are gone, for a start. Well, you know.' Cooper put a hand to his mouth, wishing he could dispel the image from his mind.

'Give us a couple of minutes with her,' said Maggs. 'We can probably get her a bit better. Has the photographer been?'

'All that's been done hours ago. That's why we've made you wait for so long.' Cooper nodded at the crowded yard. 'It's a murder enquiry now.'

'Couldn't she have just wandered off and got lost?' Maggs asked.

'It's a tempting thought – but unlikely,' Den grimaced. Their eyes met, with layers of meaning.

'So we can remove the body, can we?' Drew had become briskly professional. 'I assume we're to take her to the Royal Victoria?'

'Once we've sorted the parents out,' Cooper assented.

'Go and see if you can talk him out of it. If he still insists, then give us the nod and we'll do what we can.'

'You know you can't do anything that might interfere with evidence?'

'Obviously. But we can wrap her up nicely and close her eyelids. Every little helps.'

Cooper went back into the kitchen, taking Bennie Timms with him. She'd been deep in conversation with Roma Millan, who had hovered for the entire afternoon, unable to tear herself away. The two women had formed a bond based on the tragic anguish of a dead child.

'Mr Renton,' Den began carefully. 'The undertakers are ready to transfer the body to the mortuary. Can I just repeat that we think it would be very much better if someone else could be found to identify her, or if you really do want to take it on, then wait until tomorrow morning.'

'No, I'll do it now. Where is she?'

'Philip?' Sheena raised her head from its slumped position on the table. 'Why?'

'Because it has to be done and if I don't do it now I may never find the strength again.'

'No, I don't mean that. Why did she kill her? Why in the world did Justine have to kill my baby?'

CHAPTER TWELVE

Maggs watched the slow dispersal of the various professionals, once the little body had been stowed in the back of the van, and Drew was having a final word with DS Cooper. One individual seemed to stand out, a solitary figure apparently lost in her own thoughts. Instinctively, Maggs went up to her.

'You must be Roma Millan,' she said quietly. 'All this is so awful, isn't it.'

'It doesn't feel real,' said the older woman. 'When you see death at close quarters like that . . . it's just a foul smell and extra work for everyone. That's all I can see.' She spoke dreamily, not looking at Maggs.

'Oh, but it's ever so much more than that,' the girl assured her earnestly.

'You think so?'

'Yes. Absolutely. You should talk to Drew about it.'

'I have, dear. More than once.' Roma seemed to shake herself, focusing finally on the girl in front of her. 'You're Drew's famous business partner, are you? He's told me about you.'

'And me about you. Pleased to meet you.' Maggs smiled. 'We don't have to hang about here any longer, you know.'

'You might not. I've got to wait for a lift home.'

Maggs didn't pause to think. 'Oh, we could take you. If you don't mind the van. And I suppose it might whiff a bit, come to think of it.'

'I could probably bear that.'

Maggs suddenly realised that the woman had been fighting back tears throughout their conversation. 'Anything rather than stand here for another minute.'

'That's sorted, then.' Maggs looked round for Drew. 'Oh, there he is. Drew!' she called. 'Can we go?'

His frown told her she ought not to be raising her voice. A hush had fallen over the yard from the moment Philip Renton had emerged from the house and been taken to identify the body of his child. The resulting howl had completely silenced everyone for some minutes.

Chastened, Maggs climbed into the van, inviting Roma to follow her. 'The middle seat isn't very comfortable,' she explained. 'You're better off by the door.' Drew came to the driver's side with an enquiring expression. 'I said we'd take Roma home,' Maggs explained. 'She doesn't want to wait around for the police.'

'Better tell them, then,' Drew said tightly. He beckoned DS Cooper over. 'Mrs Millan's coming with us, if that's all right,' he said softly. 'It looks as if you're not quite finished here.'

'Right. Thanks.' The detective seemed absent. His eye caught Maggs's and he stirred himself enough to give a friendly wink. It did little to ameliorate the distress etched on his features.

Roma became talkative in the van. 'They'll arrest Justine, of course. Everyone's convinced she killed the little girl now. I did the right thing, didn't I? I couldn't just leave her there, once I'd found her. I should never have gone looking for her like that. It was stupid of me – interfering old bat that I am. She'll never forgive me. Why should she? I betrayed her.' Tears dropped sporadically from the outer corner of each eye, to be dashed impatiently away.

'Everything's collapsing around me. Laurie's gone off, God knows where. That's a dreadful smell, isn't it. Do I have to come with you to the

301

hospital? It's an awfully long way in the wrong direction.'

Drew had the window open, hoping the air current would help dispel the noxious reek from the body in the back. 'We can take you first,' he offered. 'The Coroner trusts us not to tamper with the body.'

Roma wiped her eyes with a crumpled tissue. 'Just drop me in the village. Don't go to the house.' Drew knew better than to argue with her.

'They'll have to keep the mortuary open for us,' Maggs reminded him, with a glance at her watch. 'Sam isn't going to be too pleased.'

'There's isn't much of an alternative,' Drew said tightly. 'We can be there in under an hour, even via Pitcombe. If they'd called Plants, it wouldn't have been any quicker. We were on the spot, after all.'

'Poor little thing,' Roma murmured. 'I hope she didn't suffer. It conjures up some horrible images, doesn't it?' Drew and Maggs both knew what she meant.

'You don't really think it was Justine, do you?' Drew asked.

'I can't let myself think that, can I? I'm her mother. And you've seen her; she's so small and fragile. How could she have done anything like that?'

Drew remembered that Justine was a potter; it must take some muscle to throw clay on a wheel. She had big sinewy hands. Justine might be small, but Georgia Renton was a lot smaller.

'They'll be able to tell us much more tomorrow,' he said. 'After the post-mortem.'

Maggs felt the pressure of the older woman's arm and shoulder against her. It was shaking, although when Maggs glanced sideways at her there was no visible sign of the tremor. 'What am I going to tell her?' she burst out. 'She's there now, waiting for me. She doesn't know what's going on. I don't think I can bear to say the words.' She clutched her hands together. 'Isn't that stupid?'

Maggs turned to Drew. 'I can stay with her, can't I, and see if I can help. You don't need me to come to the mortuary.'

'Drew cleared his throat. 'Well . . .' he began.

'Of course you don't. It's not as if she's too heavy for you.'

'True.'

'But how will you get home?' Roma asked.

Maggs shrugged. 'I could stay the night, if that's all right with you. Drew can come and fetch me in the morning.'

Drew understood that a bond had instantly developed between the girl and the woman, and marvelled at Maggs's acuity. In anyone

303

else it would have seemed like impertinence, an invasion of the family at a time of crisis, but Roma seemed to grasp at the offer with undisguised relief. He knew better than to interpose his own misgivings.

'I suppose I could,' he agreed.

Justine met them at the door as they walked the few hundred yards from where Drew had set them down. 'Who's this?' she demanded, staring at Maggs.

'Her name's Maggs and she's staying the night,' said Roma shortly.

'Something's happened, hasn't it? Where have you been all afternoon? I've been phoning all over the place trying to find you.'

'Oh?' Roma showed a flash of curiosity. 'Who in the world would you have phoned? You have no idea who my friends are or where I'd be likely to go.'

'I tried Karen Slocombe and Aunt Helen and one or two people in your address book. None of them replied except Karen and she didn't seem to know anything.'

'I'm not surprised. It's Thursday.'

'So?'

'Bridge night,' Roma told her. 'They'll be wondering where I am. I never miss it.'

Justine hugged herself, waiflike in a baggy

cotton jumper. 'I thought you'd walked out and left me here, like Laurie.'

'Justine, something really dreadful has happened and I'm going to have to try and tell you about it. There's a good chance the police will be here in a little while, so we might not have much time. Maggs has very kindly offered to stay with us, because – well, because we might need her. We'd better go into the living room.'

'We should have some tea or something first,' Maggs suggested. 'It's ages since I had a drink, and I bet you're the same.' She thought back over the afternoon. Mr French's funeral seemed days ago already. She and Drew had finally set out for Gladcombe shortly before three. Now she looked at her watch to find it was well past seven. 'Gosh!' she exclaimed. 'No wonder I'm thirsty.'

'I'll make some tea then,' said Justine faintly. 'What about something to eat?'

Roma and Maggs shook their heads in unison. 'Not hungry,' they grimaced.

In the event, Roma's ominous preliminaries made it easy for Justine to guess the news. She wept as her fears were confirmed, the tears shaking free from her pinched little face. 'Oh, that poor baby,' she moaned. 'She was such a sweet little thing, so good and undemanding.' She crossed her arms tightly across her stomach and rocked herself. 'She must have been so scared, out in the fields by herself.'

Roma's voice broke harshly through. 'How do you know she was in the fields?' she grated, her face suddenly grey.

Justine frowned at her. 'She must have been, surely? They'd have found her if she was anywhere else.' Terror at her mother's tone dried her tears. 'My God! You think I killed her, don't you? You still think all this was me, that I made up the story about Penn locking me up.'

'Nobody said anybody killed her.'

'You didn't have to. I can see it in your face. You said the police would be coming. Coming for *me*, I suppose. Charged with murder, on the say-so of my own mother.' She laughed wildly and looked at Maggs. 'And you think so too. You're here to protect her against me, in case I strike again. Justine the mad murderer, not safe to be with.'

'Stop it,' Roma ordered in a shaky voice. 'You're not helping yourself, behaving like this.'

'Why should I help myself? Why should I care what happens to me? It was all falling apart anyway, only the pills keeping me going. And Georgia. She loves me far more than her mother, you know. That stupid cow barely even knows she's got a kid at all. She doesn't deserve such a little love as that.' She collapsed into weeping

306

again. 'I knew something terrible must have happened to her. I just hoped that somehow Penn had taken her and kept her safe. She knows Penn, so that would be OK.'

'But you knew she was out in the fields,' Maggs reminded her in a low voice. 'When you can't really know for sure, unless . . .'

'Unless I left here there, you mean. I was guessing, OK? Look, you've both got mud on your shoes and Ma's got a leaf in her hair. I just picked up the clues with realising. You both smell, as well.' She plunged her face into her hands, closing her fingers over her nose. 'That's her smell, isn't it? Something that's been dead for days. If that'd been in a house or barn, someone would have noticed. *Of course* she must have been outside somewhere.'

'So you still say you were abducted by Penn. Your cousin, my sister's daughter, did that to you?' Roma's face seemed to strain forward, hungry for the truth.

Justine nodded vigorously, her face still hidden. 'She did,' came her muffled voice. Then she raised her head. 'But I've been thinking about it, over and over. I don't believe she really meant to hurt me. It was almost as if she was *saving* me from something even worse.'

Maggs ventured a small laugh. 'You could say the whole story's so unlikely it has to be true,' she said to Roma. 'Don't you think?'

'If it is true,' Roma began, having taken a deep steadying breath, 'then Penn deliberately made fools of us. Drew, me – the whole thing about you being missing.' She tilted her head awkwardly towards her daughter, as if scarcely bearing to look at her. 'She pretended to be worried about you, when all along she'd left you to die of thirst. That's impossible to believe,' she sagged back in the armchair. 'It's just too bizarre.'

'She might have intended to come back and release me,' Justine suggested. 'Although . . . well, maybe if she'd given me a *fantastically* good reason, I'd have forgiven her. She didn't really hurt me too badly, apart from my wrists. She might even have known I could climb through my arms. We used to do it when we were little and I was always better at it than her.'

'Chloroform?' Maggs reminded her. 'That's serious stuff. Where would she have got it?'

'College, I suppose. They've got a big Natural Sciences department. They probably use it to kill rats and things for dissection.'

Roma stared hard at her daughter. 'Jelly babies,' she said, her voice icy.

Maggs barely stifled a giggle, while Justine shook her head in bewilderment. 'What?' she said.

'There was a big pile of jelly babies with the little girl. It had wasps all over it.'

'So?'

'Justine – you were always mad about jelly babies. You must have eaten thousands of the damned things. I'm quite sure you would have bought them for this little one.'

Maggs was suddenly aware of something unspoken between mother and daughter; some event or person they'd been thinking about, almost referring to but never quite permitting it into their discourse. It could only be the cause of their rift five years earlier, something that made one angry and the other fearful, too momentous for words, even now. Like a huge iceberg sitting there in the room, which they could look through, but which distorted their view of each other and which froze the normal emotions that mothers and daughters felt for each other.

Justine refused to defend herself against this new accusation. Instead she leant her head back and closed her eyes. 'I guess I'll just wait for them to come and arrest me,' she said. 'I'd rather explain myself to them than to you – at least they might keep an open mind.'

But Roma couldn't leave it there. 'Can't you see I *want* you to convince me?' she demanded with awful intensity. 'I want to believe you. That's the reason I went over there today, to see if I could find something that would confirm your story.'

309

'And didn't you? Wasn't a dead child enough?'

Roma shook her head miserably. 'Not when I saw the jelly babies,' she whispered.

'I think you should give her the benefit of the doubt,' Maggs asserted, her voice ringing loud. 'Don't judge her so quickly. There's obviously much more to the story than you've heard yet. We need to find Penn, for a start. We need to talk it all through from the starting point that Justine hasn't done anything wrong and see if we can make sense of it that way.' She sat back in her corner of the sofa, and gave Roma a stern look.

Roma sighed. 'Don't make us go through it all again,' she pleaded. 'I imagine we've got until tomorrow, anyway. I don't think the police are coming, after all.'

'They haven't got much evidence until the post-mortem,' Maggs agreed. 'We should probably all get an early night.'

'We should have something to eat,' Roma worried. 'I always forget about food when Laurie's away. If we don't have some supper we'll all be prowling around the kitchen at two in the morning.' She went off to the kitchen and neither girl did anything to stop her.

Penn thanked providence for the invention of mobile phones. Calls could not be traced – at least not without massive police pressure on the phone company – and could be made from discreet locations where nobody could overhear.

'Mum?' Relief flooded through her as the phone was picked up at the other end. 'Is everything all right?'

'Why shouldn't it be?' Helen's voice was slow and warm. 'I was just dozing in front of the telly with the cats.'

'Where's Dad?'

'He's gone to bed. It's half past ten – past his bedtime.'

'Mum?'

'What? It isn't like you to phone me. Is something the matter?'

'Have you seen Roma? Or Justine? Have you heard anything from them?'

'I dropped in on them on Tuesday, as it happens. Roma and Laurie, that is. I wouldn't expect Justine to be there, now would I?' she laughed.

'It might surprise you to know she's there now,' Penn said sharply. 'You must only just have missed her. So you don't know anything about what's been going on at Gladcombe?'

'What's Gladcombe?' asked Helen vaguely.

'The farm where Justine lives. Near Tedburn St Mary. Keep up, for goodness' sake.'

Helen tried to shake herself into a better focus.

'Penn, are you trying to tell me something?'

'Actually, I'm trying to ask you to do something for me. Things are rather difficult just at the moment. I've gone away for a bit. I thought you might have been trying to get hold of me . . .' she tailed off weakly.

'I've got your mobile number, haven't I? Or have you changed it again?'

'No, it's still the same.'

'So explain what it is you want. I don't have to go out anywhere, do I? Not at this time of night.'

'No, no. Tomorrow will do. But would you go to Pitcombe again and see if Justine's still there? If she is, tell her . . . well, tell her I'm really sorry. That I can explain what I did to her and it isn't as bad as it must have seemed. The trouble is . . . there's a chance that Justine's got some pretty serious problems just now, and I've probably made them worse for her.'

'I haven't understood a word of that,' Helen interrupted crossly. 'Why can't you tell her yourself?'

'I can't face her,' Penn admitted. 'She's going to be so furious with me.'

'Well, I suppose I could,' Helen conceded without enthusiasm. 'You want me to say you're sorry for whatever you did and there's a good reason for it. Is that right?'

'That's it.'

'And you're not going to tell me what it was?'

'It was too awful.' Penn tried to laugh. 'You might not even believe it.'

'Maybe Justine will tell me,' Helen said. 'Is there anything else? You are all right, aren't you?' she added belatedly.

'I'm fine. I just need a few more days . . .'

'I'll give you a ring when I've seen Justine, shall I?'

'Thanks, Mum,' sighed Penn. 'You do that.'

DS Cooper was amongst friends and colleagues, discussing the discovery of the dead child and feeling miserable. Worse than miserable, if he was honest with himself. A small child had died and been left to rot in a ditch – and Den could not find it in himself to seriously care. He made dutiful notes, asked the right questions, put due procedure into train, and it was as if the whole thing were experienced through a thick mist. His attention was somewhere else entirely. It was in fact in a number of other places, not one of them to do with his job as a police detective.

Primarily it was with Maggs. She had scarcely glanced at him the previous afternoon, leaving all the talking to Slocombe. At the end, when they might have managed a quick encounter, she'd marched over to Roma Millan and started talking to her instead. He could only conclude that she'd changed her mind about him; that what had initially seemed like a mutual attraction was now indifference on her part. He was poison where women were concerned, that much was obvious. And it shouldn't matter. The job should be enough, and his friends, and . . . and . . . at this point he was forced to admit just how hollow his life had become in the past year or so. There didn't seem to be anything to fall back on; he knew from close observation that it was this sort of thing that led to a downward spiral into booze and self-neglect and bitterness and depression. Sometimes it seemed that it happened to virtually all police officers sooner or later, so why should he be any different?

DI Hemsley was speaking, his voice getting louder, angrier. 'Cooper? I'm asking you about the Renton couple. Someone's going to have to give them the result of the post-mortem later this morning.'

'That'll be the Coroner's Officer, won't it. What's his name – Sharples?'

'Apparently he's on holiday. Some other chap's standing in for him, and hasn't got a very good name for dealing with families. Especially not

314

families of kiddies. I thought maybe you and Bennie . . . ?'

Den shook his head resignedly. 'Whatever,' he muttered.

'Because,' said Hemsley, even more loudly, 'we have to remember there's a lot of doubt about the truth of his story. The Renton man's. There's a lot that doesn't add up. Everything he's told us has been contradicted by the Pereira girl. And the way we found the child suggests that neither of them's giving us anything even close to the truth. So he needs to be watched, OK?'

'Right.' Den rallied somewhat. 'And we ought to be looking for Penn Strabinski. I think she holds the answer to most of this.'

'We're looking,' the DI nodded. 'But it's a needle and haystack scenario. She didn't even take a car, wherever she went.'

'Has anyone asked Roma Millan or Karen Slocombe if they know where she is?'

Hemsley shrugged and looked around the room. 'Today,' he asserted. 'We're doing that today. Good God, we only found the kid last night, after all.'

'Who . . . ?' Den wondered, looking at Bennie Timms and the three uniformed officers in the room.

'You, Cooper. Obviously. As soon as you've

been to the farm again. And you're doing that as soon as we hear from the mortuary.'

'Yes, sir,' sighed DS Cooper.

Maggs felt strange waking up in Roma's living room, where she'd spent the night on the sofa, wearing a pair of Roma's pyjamas. She'd been invited to use Laurie's bed, next to Roma's, but had politely declined. 'The sofa's fine,' she'd insisted. 'It's lovely and soft and plenty long enough for me to stretch out.'

Her thoughts were fragmentary and jumbled on this new day when everyone waited to know just how little Georgia had died. There were too many shadowy suggestions with no substance behind them. Not enough evidence, by a long way, and too many unadmitted secrets. She realised she hadn't wanted to wake up and face whatever might develop before this day was over.

Instead she let her thoughts drift to Detective Den Cooper, who was always there now, taking up whole big sections of her mind. She'd been amazed at the way her body had reacted at the sight of him, even in the midst of the gruesome events at the farm. Her heart had lurched, her skin had tingled, and minor explosions had gone off inside her head. It had been crazy and almost frightening. She wasn't that sort of person, for goodness' sake.

Desperately, she had tried not to look at him again, after that first shocking reaction. She'd been there to do a job, and so had he. If Drew had noticed what was going on, he'd be irritated, and probably sarcastic. She wasn't even sure he liked the tall policeman, which would make things very awkward if anything were to develop between Maggs and Den. So she kept away from him, squaring her shoulders and forcing her mind onto the job in hand. She'd gravitated towards Roma, clutching at the straw of the woman's evident distress. And that had worked. Roma had quickly diverted her attention, so that the image of Den Cooper and his almost irresistible wink had receded considerably throughout the evening that had followed.

The dog was curled on Maggs's feet at the end of the sofa, where it had been all night. 'She always sleeps in here,' Roma had said flatly. 'I hope you don't mind.'

As it happened, Maggs had a very soft spot for dogs, and spaniels especially, but she wondered what would have happened if she'd made an objection. Now she fondled its long ears and velvety nose. It was an extremely pretty dog, she noticed again. And well-behaved. 'It must be time you went out,' Maggs murmured. But the animal didn't seem to be in any hurry to leave its cosy nest. 'Don't blame you,' Maggs sympathised, pulling the duvet over her shoulders again. 'Let's just have another ten minutes, then.'

From the *Western Morning News*:

SWEET GEORGIA FOUND

The body of a young girl was found yesterday afternoon in a ditch at the edge of a field on the farm where she lived.

Police are treating it as a suspicious death, although they have no firm evidence until the results of the post-mortem are known later today.

Mr and Mrs Renton, Georgia's parents, are said to be devastated. Georgia attended a day nursery and Mrs Gloria Desmond said earlier this week, when Georgia was reported as missing, "She is a sweet little girl and we've all been very concerned about her. Already several children at her nursery have been asking 'Where's Georgia gone?'"

Investigations continue, with a fingertip search of the farm, and enquiries made throughout the area.

Our reporter has learnt that a young woman who also lived on the farm has been missing for some days. She was finally found and interviewed yesterday.

'Don't you love local papers?' Karen grimaced. 'It's not looking very good for Justine, is it?'

Drew shook his head, his mouth full of toast. He hadn't slept well and was bleary-eyed. A phone call had come at eight-thirty that morning from a man who wanted to pre-arrange his funeral as a matter of urgency. Drew had managed to stave him off till eleven.

'I'll have to tidy up yesterday's graves before this chap arrives,' he said. 'I didn't get a chance to do it yesterday. And I said I'd go and fetch Maggs from Pitcombe. I don't suppose . . . ?'

Karen smiled tolerantly. 'You want me to go and get her?'

'You'll have to take the kids as well.'

'I'll take Timmy. Steph's going to play with the twins this morning, providentially.'

'Thanks, Kaz. I owe you one.'

'No problem. I wouldn't mind a little chat with Maggs, as it happens. Girl talk,' she added mysteriously.

'I wonder what the post-mortem's going to find on the little girl,' he returned to the topic that had kept him awake for much of the night. 'There wasn't any obvious sign of anything too horrible. Although . . .'

'Don't tell me,' Karen shuddered. 'I can cope with most things, but murdered three-year-old girls is just too close to home.'

'Tell me about it,' he muttered grimly.

CHAPTER THIRTEEN

'Have you tried phoning Penn's mobile?' Justine asked her mother. 'Did she give you the number?'

Roma shook her head. 'She knows I loathe the blasted things.'

'I think I can remember it. Try it now. She might talk to you. Why didn't we think of this before?'

Maggs was wondering the same thing. 'Clever of you to have it in your head,' she marvelled.

Justine made a face. 'I was always good with numbers,' she said. 'They just seem to stick in my memory.' She wrote it down for Roma. 'Go on – see what happens.'

Roma obeyed, using the phone on the kitchen wall. 'I wish I could phone Laurie as well,' she muttered. 'He said he'd be in touch before now.'

'Let's worry about him later,' said Justine impatiently.

'It's making a peculiar noise . . .' Roma proffered the receiver. 'Listen.'

Justine took it cautiously. 'I don't want to speak to her,' she insisted. Then, 'It's switched off. We could text her, though, if only I had my phone here.'

'Use mine,' Maggs offered carelessly, fishing in her bag.

Roma wrinkled her brow. 'What does it mean – text her?'

'Mum, where have you been?' Justine groaned. 'I can send a text message and it'll be waiting for her next time she switches it on.'

'She won't believe it's from me, though, will she? She knows I wouldn't know how to do that.'

'Never mind that,' Justine thumbed the keys rapidly.

'What have you said?' Maggs asked, peering over her shoulder. Justine showed her the tiny screen.

Where R U? call roma asap. Lots going on here.

Maggs made a dubious face. 'D'you think she'll respond to that?'

'I have no idea,' Justine said. 'I can't claim to understand her at all any more. But if she speaks to anybody it'll be her Aunt Roma.' She glanced spitefully at her mother.

Maggs moved restlessly around the room, watching out of the window for Drew to come and take her back to North Staverton. It was already close to nine-thirty and her sense of something about to happen was getting stronger with every passing minute.

Then, between nine-forty and nine forty-five, three vehicles all appeared in the road outside Roma's cottage wall.

The first contained Helen Strabinski. She hesitated outside the gate, and seemed to brace herself before coming in. A fine drizzle had begun to fall, frosting her brown hair. Roma met her in the doorway, eyebrows raised. 'What on earth brings you here again so soon?' she demanded.

The second was Karen, with Timmy strapped into the back seat. When Maggs failed to appear immediately, she hooted the horn, evidently not wishing to get out of the car.

The third, causing Roma far more astonishment than Helen had, was Carlos Pereira, released from police custody first thing that morning, and looking dreadful. He was getting out of a dirty white car that Roma thought for a wild moment was the same one he'd been driving when she'd been married to him twenty years ago.

'Bloody hell!' she gasped. 'I must be dreaming.' She glared at him fixedly as he stood with one had on her front gate. 'Last time I saw him . . .'

'Was at Sarah's funeral,' came Justine's voice softly from behind her. 'Hello, Dad,' she called more loudly. 'Come in, why don't you? And Aunt Helen.' Justine seemed almost manic, flapping her hands at everyone to make them do her bidding. 'And who's that out there?' She peered through the drizzle at Karen. 'The woman in that car.'

'I don't know,' said Roma. 'I have no idea what she's doing here.'

'She's collecting me,' said Maggs, trying in vain to push through the small crowd on the doorstep. 'If you'll let me out, I'll get out of your way and leave you to your family reunion.' Suddenly she'd had more than enough of the lot of them – Millans, Pereiras and Strabinskis. 'She seems to be in a bit of a hurry.'

'But why is *Carlos* here?' Roma couldn't get beyond that all-consuming question. 'I thought he'd been arrested.'

'Let's go in, for heaven's sake,' Helen urged. 'I'm getting soaked out here. Carlos, come on in. Take no notice of Roma.'

Karen pipped the horn again and Maggs finally forced her way through to the garden path. 'Coming!' she shouted. At the gate she side-stepped the unshaven Carlos, thinking how sinister he looked. Thick black brows, untidy long hair and piercing dark brown eyes all gave him the appearance of a lawless gypsy. How Roma could ever have married this man was a mystery that would have to wait for another time.

'Who were all those people?' Karen asked, as soon as Maggs was in the car.

'Relations. The woman is Penn's mother. Must be your aunt, mustn't she?'

'Auntie Helen! Good grief, I would never have recognised her. She used to have much darker hair than that.'

'Dyed,' said Maggs succinctly. 'Stands out a mile.'

'No sign of Penn, then?'

'Nope. We've just texted her, though, telling her to call Roma, so she might get in touch. How's things back at the ranch?'

'Drew's tidying up yesterday's graves. And there's a man coming to book his own burial. That's why he sent me to fetch you. Was it awful? Drew told me what a state Roma was in. I wish I'd got a better look at them all, but I didn't want to stay long, with Timmy and everything.'

'You should get to know Roma better. She's a great character.' Maggs tried to relax, but still felt jangled. 'She can't decide whether to believe Justine or not.'

'She can't seriously believe her own daughter would murder an innocent child.'

'She doesn't want to. But she doesn't believe the story about Penn abducting Justine, either. And there's something about jelly babies. Seemingly that looks bad for Justine as well. There was some sort of sticky gloop close to the body. I wonder if that's what she's talking about. It had wasps all over it. Drew was quite scared of them, after his sting.'

'There's a piece in the paper about it – not that they can say much until the results of the post-mortem come through.'

'It must be finished about now,' Maggs realised. 'They start soon after eight.'

'They're not going to call Drew about it, are they? Nobody's gone so far as to suggest that he might be burying her.'

'Did you know Justine as a little girl?' Maggs asked curiously.

'Hardly at all. I saw her once, that I can remember, and I didn't really like her. We were both very young, but childhood impressions are hard to change. I thought she was sly. She told some sort of lie, I think.'

'So you think she's lying now as well?'

Karen gave a self-deprecating laugh. 'It isn't very rational, I know, but it really wouldn't surprise me if she was.'

'Well, I believe her,' said Maggs firmly. 'I think she's been deliberately set up by Penn. Framed. Everyone seems to have forgotten that the Renton man claimed he'd been having an affair with her. She hasn't even mentioned him, so I hardly think she's in love with him.'

'It doesn't follow,' laughed Karen. 'I mean – what about you and the policeman?'

'What about us?' Maggs said stiffly.

'He came all this way to see you the other evening and you went off with him. I saw the way you looked at each other.'

'He is nice,' Maggs admitted, with some relief. 'But it's complicated . . .'

'That just adds to the fun,' said Karen.

'Don't hold your breath,' Maggs told her. 'It'll probably come to nothing.'

Karen could get no more out of her. She was mildly disappointed, hoping for some girlish confidences. Serves me right, she thought. I should have known Maggs better than that.

The pathologist faxed the post-mortem findings through to Okehampton police station. 'Cause of death: dislocation of cervical vertebrae, rupturing spinal cord. No suggestion of strangulation. No indication of sexual assault. Contusion on the scalp, which did not bleed, suggesting that it occurred at the time of death or shortly afterwards. No other bruising found on the body. The child was small for her age, but healthy. Lividity would suggest that the body was placed in the ditch up to eight hours after the time of death. For some period between the time of death and being placed in the ditch, it lay on its side. Stomach contents reveal cereal such as "Ready Brek" recently consumed. No evidence of any broken bones at any point in her life. Death would appear to have resulted from a fall or sharp blow to the neck, consistent with an accident or a deliberate attack.'

'Accident!' breathed Den. 'Accident?'

'Someone panicked and hid the body,' Hemsley noted. 'Rather a long time later.'

'So the Pereira girl was babysitting the kid, let her fall to her death, and after dithering all day, carried her to the field and dumped her in a ditch. Sounds reasonable to me.' Den was warming to the idea that nobody had deliberately killed little Georgia. She hadn't suffered. She hadn't been frightened and hurt by someone she trusted. She'd fallen out of a tree, off a high wall, wherever she'd been playing, and landed fatally on her head. What happened afterwards didn't really matter. Did it?

'It's possible,' the DI nodded. 'Makes it a bit tricky for us. No evidence of foul play, but someone deliberately concealed the body. She didn't die in the ditch. That's an offence in itself, failing to report a death.'

'It's the sort of thing a woman would do, don't you think?' Den was trying hard to concentrate. 'Somebody who'd been left in charge by the parents and was petrified by what happened.'

'Supposition,' Hemsley dismissed.

'Can't we flush them out by issuing a statement that it wasn't murder, but an accident? Tell them to come forward, and there'll only be a minor charge against them?'

'We could try,' was the unenthusiastic reply. 'We're still left with a messy pile of blatant lies, however you look at it.'

Cooper clamped a hand to his brow, trying to think. 'Say Philip Renton was telling the truth. Justine drove the kid away. But she braked suddenly for something, sending the child – not strapped in – flying, broke her neck, left her in the car until it was dark, dumped her in the ditch and went off to hide somewhere as if the camping trip was still on.'

'Go and ask her,' Hemsley ordered him. 'After you and Bennie have seen the parents.'

Nobody heard the phone ringing at first, for the noisy discussion going on in Roma's living room. 'Telephone!' Justine shrieked at her mother, finally making herself heard. 'It might be Penn,' she added, more quietly.

Roma went into the kitchen to take the call, glad of the excuse to escape the overwrought scene.

'Roma? Is that you?'

'Laurie! Where are you? I've been worrying about you. You've been gone for ages.'

'It was only yesterday!' he protested – a claim she found impossible to believe at first.

'Was it?' she said uncertainly. 'It seems like weeks. We've had the most dreadful time here.'

'I thought you might. That's why I came away. It's feeble of me, I know, but I really am useless in a crisis.'

'They found that little girl. I'm afraid she's dead, poor little thing. All the world and his wife have been here since last night. It's absolute bedlam.'

'Have they arrested Justine?' He cut in urgently. 'Do they think she did it?'

'We don't know *what* they think. They haven't been in contact with us, although they know she's here. Laurie, will you at least tell me where you're staying, just in case I need to speak to you quickly?'

'Oh, well, I suppose I should.' He sounded reluctant. 'But don't tell anybody else. I came here for a bit of peace. And promise me you won't phone unless there's something really serious. I'm out a lot, anyhow, strolling along the seafront watching all the old fogeys. They make me feel positively youthful by comparison.'

'You'll come home soon, won't you?' She tried not to sound wistful. 'I expect everything will settle down in a few days, one way or another.'

'Don't worry, old love. I haven't gone for good, you know. Here you are then, make a note. I'm at the Elmcroft Hotel in Bournemouth. It's in the East Cliff area, a couple of roads back from the sea. But try and give me a couple of days' peace. Is that too much to ask?'

'I hope not,' she said.

Maggs was driving Drew slowly insane with heavy sighs and moony looks. She ignored him when he spoke to her and jumped every time the phone rang. 'They'd tell us what the post-mortem said if we phoned them,' he offered. 'Graham Sleeman's standing in for Stanley, while he's on holiday. He's an old friend of mine. He'll have spoken to the family by this time, anyway, so I can ask if they said anything about the funeral.'

'Mmm,' was all she replied.

He made the call, curious on his own account as to how the little girl had died. Sleeman was his usual inefficient self, rustling papers as if he'd never heard of Georgia Renton. 'Oh, here we are. Looks like an accident. That's what they've reported to the Coroner. No evidence of violence or foul play, except the body was moved at some time after death. Failing to report a death, I suppose.'

'Did you speak to the parents yet?'

'Nah. CID are dealing with it for me. Everyone knows I'm useless at that sort of thing.'

'You're useless at everything,' Drew told him, scarcely bothering to temper the truth with a friendly laugh.

Bennie and Den were disconcerted to find nobody in at Gladcombe Farm. Nobody responded to their knock on the door and when they went round to the back, where a muddy scullery had its own unlocked entrance, but a second bolted door through to the kitchen, they could discern no sign of life. Returning slowly to their car, they heard another vehicle approaching down the farm lane. 'Maybe they just popped out to the shops,' said Bennie. 'Or maybe they've gone to the doctor about the chap's bruised face.'

But the car when it did arrive contained only one young woman. 'Journalist,' said Bennie with certainty, and Drew believed her.

'Hiya!' the creature whinnied. 'Anything going on?'

'CID,' growled Cooper repressively. 'Mr and Mrs Renton aren't here. What do you want?'

'*Daily Chronicle*,' she beamed. 'Wondered if the parents had anything to say.'

'I thought they'd stopped this sort of crap,' Den told her. 'You're wasting your time anyway. As I said, they're out.'

'Funny. Gone to stay with friends, have they? Can't bear the painful memories?'

'Something like that. Now you'd better go. This is still the scene of a suspicious death and nobody's asked you to be here.'

'Suspicious death? Surely you've had the post-mortem results by now, and know what killed her?'

'No comment,' said Den, with a disgusted look.

'Hey, don't be like that. This is public interest stuff. Little girl found dead in a ditch a week after going missing. Only – what? – a few hundred yards from her house. We're not giving up on a story like that.' She looked carefully all around her, easily spotting the well-trodden track towards the orchard. 'That way, is it?'

'Leave it,' Den warned her. 'Forensics haven't finished with it yet. It's out of bounds.'

'So what's with this girl lodger or whatever she is? Why's everybody being so cagey about her? Has she been taken in for questioning? You ought to tell us, you know. We've a right to be kept informed.'

'No comment,' he snarled again. 'Now go away.'

Defiantly, the reporter got back into her car and reversed it at speed across the yard, already fumbling for a mobile phone as she headed back down the lane towards the road.

'So where are they?' Bennie queried. 'Don't they know they should stay put? That we'd be back this morning wanting to speak to them?'

'Search me,' Den snapped. He looked at the upper windows of the house, which stared implacably down at him. He felt a quiver of unease. 'You don't think . . . ?' he began.

'What?' She followed his line of gaze. 'That they've topped themselves in their grief? I doubt it.'

'We should have a quick look,' Den grimaced. 'This is Crediton all over again. Why's everybody avoiding us, do you think?'

Bennie did not respond to the feeble joke. 'We'd have to break in.'

'True. Best leave it then. Let the DI worry about it.'

'Right.' She sighed with relief. 'Now we're off to Pitcombe. Is that it?'

Cooper scratched his head. 'Is that what he said?' He looked at her blankly for a moment, forgetting the significance of Pitcombe.

'Come on, Den. Wake up, will you? Pitcombe's the mother of the girl who lives in the cottage here. We're to go and talk to them again, remember?'

'Yeah, yeah,' he nodded. 'I just didn't connect,

for a minute. It's not going to be a lot of fun, is it?' He made no move to return to the car, despite Bennie's attempts to shift him. 'They ought to be here,' he worried. 'Somebody should have stayed all night to keep an eye on them.'

'Well, they didn't. They probably insisted on being left alone.'

'But don't they want to know about the post-mortem?'

'I don't know, Den,' she said patiently. 'That's why we have to go and talk to the Pereira woman. See if we can get her to admit she dropped the kid on its head and panicked. Get the whole thing sewn up, once and for all. Plus we need to call in and tell them we've drawn a blank here.'

'Let's go then,' he said. 'I don't like it here, anyway.'

Philip Renton slowly left the barn behind the house, when he was sure the police had finally left. All his movements were heavy, whole minutes passing between one step and the next. Something in the house was urging him, finally identified at a ringing telephone. *Business*, he thought distantly. He should apply himself to business. It had stopped before he got to it, but a few minutes later it began again.

'Mr Renton? We sent two officers to tell you this in person, but they must have missed you. I

334

hope you'll understand if we tell you this over the phone . . .'

He was standing in the yard, fifteen minutes later, when Sheena drove in. She had been to the supermarket, hysterically tearing out of his clinging arms when he tried to stop her. And then, when she got there, she'd filled the trolley with all the things that Georgia had liked best, including a box of jelly babies. Standing in the check-out line, she suddenly saw what she'd done, staring at the Alphabet Spaghetti, the small seedless grapes, chocolate milk drink and bloody jelly babies. With a shriek, she'd thrust the whole thing away from her and run from the shop in tears.

Her husband didn't seem to be doing anything. He was just *there*. His bruised face was haggard, his hands shaking. Sheena found him repellant in his obvious distress. 'Have you been here since I left?' she asked.

He nodded, then recollected himself and shook his head. 'They phoned – about the post-mortem.'

'Phoned? Shouldn't they come in person? Why are they so insensitive?'

He shrugged weakly, unable to explain. 'Her neck was broken. They think she – she didn't suffer. It was quick, they said.'

'Broken neck? Like strangled? Is that the same thing?'

335

'No, I don't think so. More like a fall. Or a quick blow. Something like that.'

Sheena's face screwed up. 'I don't want to know.' She breathed quickly. 'Yes I do. I want to know. If I don't I'll never rest.'

'Rest,' he echoed, looking as if he was ready to sink to the ground and never get up again.

'Have they arrested Justine yet?'

'I don't know.'

'Wouldn't it be on the news? There'll be reporters here, won't there? Hasn't *anybody* been?' The thought that they might not have had any visitors seemed very bleak to her. Were they so antisocial, so disliked in the neighbourhood that nobody would come to offer solace at such a time?

'I think somebody came. I was . . . outside. They went again.'

'We'd better have something to eat.' She headed for the front door, fists tightly clenched. Inside, something was erupting and she couldn't let it. It had to do with Philip, his blank expression, his still unexamined confession about the affair with Justine. There was rage against him, acid in her throat, but she couldn't let it out. He'd lost his little daughter and was plainly suffering. All she could do was wait it out until they were both strong enough to decide what to do next.

*   *   *

Drew was relieved to find that Maggs's attention was aroused by the latest news. 'Accident?' she repeated. 'Are they sure?'

'Not completely. But that's the way it looks.'

'Poor little thing. But it doesn't explain anything, does it? Why was she left in the ditch? Do they think she was climbing a tree or something, and just lay where she fell? Dropping the bag of jelly babies?'

Drew was hooked. 'Jelly babies?'

'That horrible sticky mess with wasps all over it, beside the body. Roma says it was once a bag of jelly babies. And that was what made her really sure that Justine had killed the kid – though I didn't follow the logic, I must admit.'

'The body was moved,' Drew remembered. 'That's what Graham said. So somebody knew she was dead and tried to hide her.'

'It still looks like Justine, doesn't it.'

'I don't know.' Drew heaved a sigh. 'I still can't quite see it.'

'Nor me,' Maggs admitted. 'I like her, you know. She's obviously a mess in lots of ways, but she doesn't come across as *guilty*. I mean, if you'd done something like that, you'd have trouble living with yourself, wouldn't you?'

'Right,' he nodded. 'You've put your finger on it. That's what's been nagging at me. After all, we've seen what guilt does to people – that sunken look they get, when they think they should have done more for their husband or old mother.'

'That worried frown when they think they're going to be found out,' she chimed in.

He laughed. 'It wouldn't cut any ice in a court of law, though. People would say we were mad.'

'We probably are,' she said, before another thought struck her. 'You know who *does* look guilty?'

He gazed at her consideringly. 'Sunken eyes? Worried frown. Hmm . . .'

'Mr Renton!' she crowed. 'I only saw him for a minute, but he was the absolute picture of guilt.'

Drew began to shake his head. 'No, not him. That wasn't guilt; that was horror, grief . . . stuff like that. Poor bloke.'

'No.' Maggs slapped the table emphatically. 'I'm telling you – it was guilt.'

The day swirled on, phone calls flying back and forth, people talking confusedly, asking unanswerable questions of each other. Everyone experienced frustration at not having the whole picture available to them, including DS Den Cooper.

'Where's Mr Millan?' he asked Roma.

'He's having a few days on his own down

338

on the coast. I can assure you he has nothing relevant to contribute to this business. He's a lot better off out of it.'

'And where is Penn Strabinski?'

Roma shrugged. 'Nobody seems to have an answer to that.'

And where were the Rentons this morning? Den thought angrily, knowing Roma would have no answer to that one.

'Although,' Roma went on, after a brief pause. 'I did get a message from her this morning. Or rather, Justine did.'

'From Miss Strabinski?'

'Penn. For God's sake, call her Penn.'

He eyed her impatiently and waited for whatever was coming next. 'I'm not sure I should tell you,' she prevaricated. 'I'm sure she wouldn't want me to. But it does put Justine in a much better light.'

'Go on,' he encouraged.

'Well, Penn phoned my sister – her mother – and asked her to tell Justine that she – Penn – is sorry for what she did and that she'd explain everything. A bit mysterious, but we assume it's about the way she kidnapped Justine and left her in that place.'

'The place she says she wouldn't be able to find again?' Den couldn't resist adding.

Roma didn't rise to the provocation. 'Helen

came over this morning, which was good of her. She could have phoned.'

'She was just being nosy.' Justine had come quietly into the room. 'I suppose you've come to see me?' she said to Den. Bennie Timms was on a chair beside the fireplace, leaving everything to Cooper.

'The post-mortem report's come through,' he said. 'It isn't quite conclusive yet, but the initial suggestion is that the little girl died of a fall, or some sudden trauma of that sort.'

He and Justine stared at each other, each watching for clues to the other's thoughts. 'So she died quickly? Is that what you're saying?'

'So it seems. Of course we can't possibly get the whole picture. But it seems unlikely that she suffered any pain.'

'Thank God for that,' Justine breathed, tension draining from her shoulders and hands. 'I've had such terrible visions all night of how it might have been for her. She was such a sweet little thing. She had an awful life, really. We do treat children horribly, don't we?'

'Do we?' Bennie Timms spoke from the fireplace. Everyone looked at her.

'We make them fit our own selfish ways. They're at the mercy of our crazy beliefs or money-grubbing values.' Justine glared briefly at her mother as she spoke. 'They're completely

at our mercy. It's disgusting. I'm never going to
have any more, that's for sure.'

'Any more?' Bennie murmured.

'My little girl died,' Justine said aggressively,
as if expecting not to be believed. 'She was three,
as well. I'm sure you knew that – it must be
somewhere in your records.'

'You're not in our records,' said Den. 'You
haven't ever committed a crime, as far as we
know. But your father did say . . .'

Justine smiled, her expression a complex
tangle of exasperation and triumph. 'He would,'
she said. Carlos had taken himself off in his dirty
white car for a visit to a barber, directed by Roma
who showed no inclination to offer him any of
her own facilities.

Den drew himself up and hardened his heart.
'Miss Pereira, I do have to put it to you that you
were present at the death of Georgia Renton and
that you deliberately concealed the fact of her
death by placing her body in the ditch where it was
subsequently found. It is an offence to knowingly
conceal a death. Do you have anything to say?'

'Are you accusing me? Charging me?' She
frowned at him. 'Or just trying to get me to admit
something in front of witnesses?' Her composure
surprised him and he kept his eyes on her, saying
nothing further.

'I promise you,' she went on, 'I was not there

when she died. I can tell you absolutely nothing about what happened. But it does seem obvious to me that my cousin Penn must have known something about it.' She frowned more deeply. 'I think we'll find that Penn holds the answer to the whole thing, if we could just find her.'

Den looked at Roma, who had drifted over to the window, her back to the room. 'Mrs Millan? Have you any idea as to where your niece might be?'

'Not really,' she said in a low voice. 'Neither does her mother. Are you going to arrest Justine?'

'No, we're not going to arrest her at present, but the investigation will continue. There'll be a further forensic examination at the farm and some more interviews.' He addressed Justine. 'Would you be good enough to stay here for a few more days, or inform us of your movements if you leave?'

Justine nodded. 'You should find Penn,' she advised him.

'We'll do our best,' he agreed, with another glance at Roma.

Karen took Roma's phone call to the Peaceful Repose office, since Drew and Maggs were both at the top of the burial ground and out of earshot. After five rings it automatically switched through to the house.

'Is Drew there?' Roma demanded.

'I could call him. It'd take a couple of minutes.' She hesitated. 'I think he's doing some measuring.'

'Don't bother him then. He can phone me back. I've got another commission for him, if he's interested.'

Karen didn't find it hard to guess. 'You want him to look for Penn,' she said.

'Clever girl! That's exactly it. I'm probably going to sound barmy, but I've a hunch I know where she is.'

'So why not go and see for yourself?'

There was a silence at the other end. 'Can we just say I prefer not to?' Roma eventually said. 'There are at least two rather good reasons, but I can't really explain them at the moment.' Justine might be listening, Karen guessed.

'OK,' she said. 'I'll tell him and he can phone you back for more details.'

'And if he wants to take that young partner of his, I'd be more than happy,' Roma added. 'That girl's a real asset, isn't she?'

It had been a while since Karen felt jealous of Maggs, Even now, it wasn't exactly *jealousy* she assured herself. More a slightly wistful *might have been*. 'She's a marvel,' she said flatly.

Drew wasn't sure how he felt about this latest twist in his involvement in Roma's life. He kept coming up against the fact of Penn being Karen's cousin, when his strong inclination was just to drop the whole thing now that Georgia had been found. It had all turned very sour, with no comfortable outcome any longer possible. Penn had forfeited his loyalty by disappearing the way she did, leaving everyone to run around like headless chickens. Or, more accurately, stunned zombies. The full implications of the little girl's fate still hadn't really been absorbed. Drew hadn't heard any more news of the child's parents, but he assumed they were deep in grief and recriminations. He was intrigued by Justine and hoped she hadn't been responsible for Georgia's death. He was uneasy about Karen's disposition, which could take a downturn at any moment. But here she was now, urging him to maintain his involvement and return Roma's phone call as quickly as possible.

'It sounded as if she didn't want Justine to know what's happening,' she said briskly. 'So if she's funny on the phone, that'll be why.'

'Couldn't she just have told you the whole thing?' he grumbled. 'Save all this messing about.'

'Don't be silly – she needs to speak to you. She doesn't know if you'll do it. I think we really should try to find Penn, if my opinion counts for anything. She started all this; it's irresponsible of her to just go off and leave everybody else to pick up the pieces.'

Drew wholeheartedly agreed with that, at least. He supposed he could give up a Saturday to do what he could to bring the whole sorry business to a conclusion, if that was possible. It seemed too much to hope that Penn would just calmly explain to both Drew and the police exactly what had happened to Georgia, and when and how and why, but nothing would happen without her. The glaring problem was that Roma should disclose what she guessed about Penn's whereabouts to the police, and not to a totally unwarranted local undertaker. It would not sit at all well with Cooper and his team when they inevitably found out that their investigations had been deliberately obstructed.

Roma was indeed circumspect when he phoned. 'Is Justine listening?' he asked. 'Karen thought you might not want her to know what you're proposing.'

'It's not that. I just don't want you to jump to any premature conclusions. Approach with an open mind. I truly don't know where Penn is, but I do have a strong hunch. I could be making a stupid mistake.'

'Do I get my petrol paid?' he joked.

'Only if it turns out to be a wild goose chase. If not, you get the satisfaction of solving another case. Drew Slocombe, amateur detective, can add another notch to his notebook.'

'Ha, ha,' he said.

He noted down the few hints she could give as to where she wanted him to go, and agreed to set out early next morning with Maggs.

'I'll let you know as soon as we have anything to report,' he promised.

Maggs was puzzled but willing. 'Why doesn't she go herself?' she asked.

'Karen wondered the same thing. It's delicate, apparently. But all we have to do is find the Elmcroft Hotel in Bournemouth, walk in and ask for Penn Strabinski. Simple as that.'

'What if she's using a different name? What if she sees us and does a runner? Wouldn't it be better to stake the place out and wait for her to show herself? She's not likely to stay stuck in some dreary seaside hotel all day, is she?'

'Maybe we could go and have lunch there. It's probably open to non-residents.'

Maggs pulled a face. 'She might be having fish and chips on the seafront and we'd have wasted all that time and money. We'd better wait till we get there and decide then.'

'You're right,' he agreed, feeling suddenly cheerful. 'At least it sounds fairly easy to find.'

* * *

Putting the phone down, Roma closed her eyes and remained very still for a full minute. However you looked at it, she admitted, she had interfered. She had broken a confidence and that felt like a violent thing to have done. Worse than that, she would have to wait for several hours before she knew the outcome of her action. Waiting, for Roma, was very like being in hell. She would have to find some compelling distraction to pass the time.

From habit, her thoughts turned to the bees. All the honey had been taken off, the hives were clean and in good order; there was little danger of swarming and little hope of a new swarm turning up out of a clear blue sky, so late in the year. But seeing as how she was in an interfering sort of mood, she decided on a close inspection of the frames anyway. The weather was not ideal – a heaviness in the air that tended to make the bees tetchy – but that didn't worry her.

But before she could climb into her protective all-in-one suit, the phone rang. 'Oh, hello, Mrs Millan? You don't know me, but my friend saw the card you put up in the Pitcombe village shop. About bees? I've been at my wits' end, trying to find somebody to take ours away. They were my husband's, you see, and he died last month. I don't have any idea what to do with them.'

'Wasn't he in a club? Haven't you got any

beekeeping friends to help you?' Roma was incredulous. Normally people turned up in their own version of a swarm when they heard of a colony going begging.

'No, no. He was too ill for that. But he loved the bees. The thing is, the neighbour's little boy got stung yesterday and they've been saying some very nasty things. So in desperation I wrapped a blanket round them last night so they can't get out. Now I don't know what to do. My friend Irene came round to help and she remembered seeing your card. We were waiting on the doorstep of the shop this afternoon waiting for it to open after lunch, so we could get your number. Oh, do you think you can do something?'

Roma didn't hesitate. 'Give me your address,' she ordered. 'I'll come right away.'

Transporting bees wasn't as dangerous as it sounded, but it did have to be done properly. It should be done around twilight, or slightly later. But Roma was not inclined to wait, especially as the poor bees were already wrapped up and likely to suffocate if left much longer. Grabbing another thick blanket of her own, some rope, a thick wad of foam rubber and her suit and veil, she left the house without bothering to explain to Justine where she was going. She merely shouted up the stairs that she would be out for a while.

* * *

The woman met her at the gate of her house, hands worriedly clasped together. 'Can you manage?' she bleated. 'Will you need any help?'

'Well . . .' Roma paused. She wouldn't be able to lift a full hive into the back of her car without assistance. 'I'll need someone to help me lift them.'

'I'll do that,' the woman said, as if it was obvious. 'I'm not afraid of them. I just don't know what to do with them – and they seem to cause such a lot of trouble.'

'Have you taken off any of this summer's honey?'

The woman shook her head. 'I haven't touched them since Teddy died at the end of June. He'd been ill for a month or more, so nothing's been done to them in all that time.'

Roma felt a thrill at the prospect of a great quantity of honey just waiting for her, as well as real concern for the consequent weight of the hive.

From the bundled shape of it, she couldn't be sure of the type. 'Is it a National or a WBC?' she asked. The response was a blank stare. 'What colour is it? The hive, I mean.'

'Oh. Sort of brown. It's not one of those that looks like a clapboard house.' Roma considered this before understanding the analogy. A WBC hive comprised an inner set of boxes, one on top of another, with a casing of 'lifts' sitting in tiers, their lower edges slightly fluted. A WBC hive was almost always white. 'Good,' she said. 'Sounds like a National. Much less complicated to transport.'

Wearing the suit, and advising the woman to see if she could find one for herself, Roma delicately pulled back one edge of the enveloping blanket to locate the bees' entrance. If she could work quickly, very few of them would notice what was happening and escape through the briefly unobstructed opening. She pushed a strip of foam rubber into the orifice and pulled the blanket down again.

Then she rearranged the covering, tying it tightly with rope, hoping there was still enough air getting in to keep the bees alive.

The woman came back wearing a peculiar assortment of gabardine overall, battered bee bonnet and gardening gloves. 'This is what Teddy used to wear,' she announced. 'He hardly ever got stung.'

'That's fine,' Roma approved. 'They won't get out now, anyway. Do you want your blanket back when I've finished?'

'Not really.'

'We'd better be quick. They haven't got much air. I hope you're strong.' She hadn't been able to get her car closer than about thirty feet, the hive being in a far corner of a small back garden. Neighbouring houses clustered on all sides and

Roma could see why there'd been difficulties. In a busy summer there'd be twenty thousand bees coming and going all day long. Nobody could fail to notice that much activity.

The hive, when they lifted it, was disappointingly light.

'You're sure there are bees in here, are you?' Roma demanded.

'Oh yes. Definitely.'

'It doesn't feel as if they've been working very well. Never mind – I'll see what's what when I get them home.' The fleeting thought that she might be introducing a diseased colony into her own apiary was firmly dismissed. She wasn't going to abandon the project now.

They carried the bulky bundle awkwardly between them, walking crabwise. The car's hatchback was open and waiting, and they gingerly tilted their burden to get it in. Roma knew it was possible – she'd chosen the car with this very procedure in mind – but it was a tight fit. The relief was palpable when they had it securely wedged in.

The woman was effusive. 'Oh, it'll be so wonderful to be rid of them. I know Teddy loved them, but it was always a worry. I swell up terribly every time I'm stung.'

Roma stared at her. 'But you're not afraid of them?'

'Oh no. I always think it's such a shame that they die when they sting you. I mean, when you think of that, you can't really complain, can you?'

The logic gave Roma some pause. She'd never looked at it like that before.

'But you've just helped me carry a hiveful. What if we'd dropped it?'

The woman smiled. 'Don't you find, dear, that it's never the obvious danger that strikes? It's always something you couldn't have foreseen or protected yourself against. I suppose I'm more likely to be stung now, with the bees gone, than I was before. That's the way it goes, isn't it.'

There were elements of this philosophy that chimed with Roma's own viewpoint, but it sounded odd on another person's lips. 'I suppose it is,' she said. 'Thank you, anyway. I should pay you for them, by rights. The hive alone is probably worth quite a lot.'

'No, dear. I think I should pay *you*. You've just done me a great service.'

The drive home was uneventful, although Roma experienced a strong temptation to pick up a youth she passed who was trying to thumb a lift. She imagined telling him, just as he got out of the car, that she had a hive full of bees in the back. When she remembered that she would need someone to help her lift them out of the car, she almost went back for him. But she thought better of it. Justine would have to do it.

It was not easy to persuade her daughter. Only by letting her wear all the protective clothing did she manage it, first having fussily prepared a stable base for the new hive in a carefully selected position. As soon as it was in place, she sent Justine back into the house to take off the suit and pass it over to Roma. Then she ignited her smoker and embarked on an examination of her new acquisition.

The colony was in better condition than she'd feared, although not very numerous. There could be a variety of explanations for this: an old queen recently dying and the new one not yet properly into her stride. Varroa was a possibility, of course, although the departed Teddy had presumably treated them the previous autumn. The stop-start spring they'd had, coinciding with Teddy falling ill, might have meant short rations for the bees. All in all, she was pleased. There was still time before winter for them to gain in strength and numbers, with the help of sugar syrup and varroa medication. It was a sturdy, well-maintained hive, too.

And best of all, she had not given a thought for hours to Penn or the Rentons or even her errant husband.

CHAPTER FOURTEEN

As it turned out, the hotel was very difficult to find. The only map of Bournemouth they had was a sketchy one in Drew's road atlas. 'East Cliff,' Maggs kept repeating, as if she could conjure the area merely by saying its name. They eventually noticed a sign to that effect, on a road they were sure they'd already traversed, only to find themselves in a maze of leafy streets, rows of hotels tucked retiringly behind every tree. They drove slowly up and down, reading the name on every entrance, until Drew was furious with Maggs, Bournemouth and the world in general. Taking a turning at random, and then another, they suddenly found it, sitting smugly obvious. 'Elmcroft Hotel!' Maggs crowed. 'Can't miss it.'

'About bloody time,' Drew snapped. They'd used Karen's car, instead of the van, making good time until this last frustrating struggle slowed them down. It was ten forty-five when they pulled up in the street outside and considered what to do next.

'For a start, it's got two entrances,' Maggs pointed out. 'One here and one round the corner. We can't watch both of them unless we split up. And that means one of us will have to hang about in the street looking conspicuous.'

'So why don't we just walk in and find her?'

'Maybe we could. Even if she won't come with us, we can say we've seen her.'

'Roma wants us to talk to her. She wants us to take her home with us. We can't let her run off.'

'So how's about if I stick out my foot and trip her up, and then you do a flying tackle and pin her to the ground? Then we'll tie her up and bundle her into the car before she knows what's hit her.'

'Like she did with Justine, you mean?'

'So you believe her at last?'

'I don't know.' He shook his head. 'But I do know it's nice to have you paying attention again. I thought for a minute I'd lost you, yesterday.'

Maggs flushed dark and gave him a quick punch. 'Don't tease,' she ordered. 'It isn't nice.'

'Sorry. So we're going in, are we? Of course,

we don't know she's here at all. She might be in Aberdeen or Aberystwyth all along.'

'I bet she's here. I've got a feeling.'

'Just don't trip her up until I give the signal, right?'

They left the car where it was and walked side by side through the hotel car park and in through the front door. A small reception desk was positioned on the right, immediately inside. There was nobody behind it. Drew gripped Maggs's elbow and pushed her onwards, towards a collection of open doors at the end of the hall. A cursory inspection revealed a lounge, bar and dining room respectively. Almost without hesitation, Drew steered them into the lounge.

Three of the deep armchairs were in use, although the room was in silence. Three grey heads could be seen over the tops of newspapers. As the newcomers stood there, wondering what to do next, a copy of the *Independent* was slowly lowered. Drew met the eyes of the man behind it and the mutual gasp of recognition attracted the notice of the other two residents.

'Laurie Millan,' Drew exclaimed. 'My God!'

With an expression of suppressed exasperation, Laurie folded the paper. 'I might have know she'd send someone,' he muttered.

Maggs was looking from one to the other in

bewilderment. 'Who?' she hissed at Drew. 'Who did you say he was?'

'Laurie. Roma's husband,' he told her.

'Ah,' she said, as if this made perfect sense.

Drew went closer to the armchair, and smiled down at Laurie. 'Actually, she didn't say you had to come home,' he began. 'In fact, she didn't . . .'

The flurry of another person hurriedly coming into the lounge interrupted him. 'Laurie . . .' it began, in unsuitably ringing tones, attracting exhalations of disapproval from the other loungers. 'I thought I might . . .' She caught sight then of Drew and her jaw dropped. 'Drew!' she said faintly.

'Hello, Penn,' he greeted her. 'Fancy meeting you here.'

There was no need for Maggs to employ her tripping-up strategy. Penn sat down composedly in a chair close to Laurie's and waved Drew and Maggs to complete the circle.

'I assume Roma worked this out,' she said. 'I didn't think she would.'

'Neither did I,' put in Laurie. 'I find it strangely pleasing.'

'So what happens now?' Drew wanted to know. 'Everybody wants to ask you a lot of questions.' He addressed Penn almost apologetically.

'I expect they do, but they'll have to wait a bit. I'm not coming back yet.'

'She's missing me, is she?' Laurie asked wistfully. 'I'm quite ill, you know.'

Drew examined him closely. He did look drawn and weak. 'Is it something serious?'

'Oh, yes, quite serious. Roma can't cope with illness, as you've probably realised. It's a completely taboo subject with her. The pretending gets quite draining after a while. I came away to try and get some strength back for another bout.'

Drew recalled the conversation he'd had with Roma, less than a month earlier. She'd revealed something then of her feelings on the subject, causing Drew to feel a cocktail of emotions towards her: admiration, pity, protectiveness and a dash of impatience.

'It's not as if there's anything the matter with me,' she'd laughed weakly. 'But I know it'll happen one day and it horrifies me. *Really, really* horrifies me. I haven't had a single night for months now where I haven't woken up and seen death staring me in the face. Stupid, isn't it. I know why it is, too. It's because I'll soon be sixty. Exactly the same thing happened ten years ago. And there isn't a thing I can do about it, except to find someone like you to talk to. Do you know how rare a character you are, Drew Slocombe? How lucky I am to find you.'

Drew had held her hand lightly in his,

saying little, but conveying his exceptional understanding.

'That's ridiculous!' Maggs now protested. 'What happens when you can't pretend any more?'

'Who can say?' Laurie spread his hands.

'I think I can,' Penn offered. 'She'll punish you for it. She'll get angry and accusing and tell you you're doing it on purpose. That's how she was with Justine when Sarah was ill.'

Everyone waited and Penn had little choice but to elucidate. 'Justine had a little girl, Sarah, who developed acute myeloid leukaemia when she was only two. The doctors wanted to try a bone marrow transplant, but – well, it didn't work out.' Penn looked at the floor for a moment, chewing her lower lip, before continuing. 'It's more likely to match if you're a relative, of course. Roma refused to be tested. She said it was modern medicine gone mad, that it would only prolong the child's suffering and she would either recover of her own accord, or . . .'

'Or what?' Maggs demanded.

'Or everyone should accept the inevitable and let her die in peace. Which is what happened, but not without a lot of terrible fights. Justine blamed her mother for not doing more to help. Roma felt misunderstood. They haven't spoken since.'

Maggs narrowed her eyes thoughtfully. 'Where were you?' she asked.

Penn smiled tightly. 'I was in Poland,' she said. 'I only heard about it when I got back, a few months later.' She swallowed, as if something had stuck, and then changed direction. 'I gather Justine's shown up at Pitcombe now?'

'We fear those we hurt,' Maggs murmured, ignoring the last remark.

'What?' Drew asked.

'It's a quote I picked up from somewhere. It seems to fit, don't you think?'

'It's very true,' Laurie confirmed quietly. 'Roma's a very fearful person, deep down. She knows she tramples on people's feelings and then she steers clear of them – as she did with Justine. But the thing she fears most, of course, is death. Not like most people, in that let's-not-think-about-it sort of way. Real in-your-face terror. I think it's with her all the time – she can never understand how other people live so easily with it. She wants to force them to share her fear and they won't.'

'So why not do everything possible to save poor little Sarah from dying?' Maggs asked.

Laurie sighed. 'I wasn't there, but it's something about her associated loathing for the medical profession. She thinks they cover their own fear of death by telling lies and giving false assurances. She never thought Justine's little girl could hope to survive, whatever anybody did.'

'She's crazy,' Maggs concluded.

'Not at all. I first met her a few weeks after Sarah died, and she was in an awful state, but she wasn't crazy then and she isn't now. Poor Roma,' he finished sadly.

Yes, Drew silently agreed. *Poor Roma*. He watched all three faces, wondering why Roma hadn't made an opportunity to speak to Laurie as she had spoken to him. Did she know, he wondered, how well her husband understood her?

'Poor Justine, more like,' Maggs protested.

Drew patted her arm. 'Not really,' he said. 'The world would have been on Justine's side. And the child probably would have died anyway, as Roma said. No, I think my sympathies are with Roma. It's not her fault that she can't fool herself like practically everyone else manages to do. There's something terrible about being forced by your own clear-sightedness to confront the unbearableness of death, every single day. You ought to understand that, working with me,' he added lightly.

A sniff from Penn alerted them to her distress. 'Sorry,' she laughed weakly, dashing a hand across her eyes. 'It's been a pretty horrible week and now it's catching up with me. I'll have to go to my room for a bit. You're not rushing home again, are you?'

'Stay for lunch,' Laurie invited expansively. 'They do a very good grilled trout here.'

'Yes, do,' urged Penn. 'But count me out. I'll go and have a bit of a lie-down and see you later. After lunch.'

Drew understood that he wasn't being given any option, and nodded, keeping an eye on Maggs at the same time. 'See you down here at about two, then,' he suggested to Penn.

Den Cooper wasn't working that Saturday. He got up late, put a load of clothes in the washing machine and grilled himself some bacon. Then he did what he had wanted to do for days and composed a text message for Maggs.

Been thinking of u. Free tomorrow? Can talk shop or not as u like. Den

After all, she *had* given him her mobile number. She surely must expect that he would use it, despite her coolness on Thursday. He wished he'd been more inventive with his message; it was a weird means of communication that he still hadn't entirely got the hang of, but it did have advantages over a phone call. If she had changed her mind about him, she could simply ignore the message without having to make excuses. At least he'd tried. With a sigh, he admitted to himself that this didn't really count for very much.

For want of anything else to occupy him, his thoughts turned to the strange death of the child at Gladcombe Farm. Late the previous afternoon, a fuller pathology report came through, with blood analysis, description of clothing, and absolutely no signs of defensive wounds (even a small child would fight back, given the chance, it seemed), no petechiæ haemorrhages in the eyes, pupil dilation, lacerations, puncture marks. A long list of negatives, in fact. Only one small item seemed to be of interest: there were three wisps of hay attached to the clothes, and two in her hair. Little Georgia had, perhaps, been playing in one of the farm buildings on the day she died. Time – even date – of death had been impossible to pinpoint accurately, but the Ready Brek in her stomach clearly suggested that she had recently eaten breakfast.

Den ran through what he knew of the Renton family's normal routine, as well as what they'd originally told him about the Thursday on which they last saw their daughter. She wasn't going to her day nursery because Justine was taking her camping. Sheena Renton had left for work at seven forty-five, leaving her husband to give the child breakfast. She claimed to have seen Penn Strabinski driving through the farmyard at that same time. Then Philip had taken Georgia to

Justine's cottage while he got on with some work on his computer. It seemed that from Georgia's point of view it had been a break from routine in almost every respect.

Den wished he had asked more probing questions. *Where did Georgia think she was going – her Grandma's or camping with Justine? Did she not talk to her mother about it?* But then he remembered that Sheena had freely admitted that she had little time for conversation with her daughter. The change of plan had been effected without consulting her and seemingly without arousing any suspicions.

Neither parent could adequately describe the clothes the child had been wearing that morning. Philip had thought it was a green thing, a sort of light cotton dress. Sheena had shown no embarrassment in admitting she had no idea.

'She usually just chooses her own clothes,' she'd shrugged. 'If it's completely wrong, I make her change, but it's usually something OK.'

Den had made a mental note – promptly forgotten – to ask Bennie whether it was usual for a three-year-old to dress herself.

There were numerous holes, not just in the story, but in the police investigation as well. It had been slow to get going, slow to take the matter seriously. And then, almost before they could get started, Roma Millan, of all people, had found the body. There were loads of unasked questions; now probably never to be asked, because to judge from the post-mortem findings, it was never going to be a murder enquiry anyway. Even if Georgia had been dropped out of an upstairs window or killed while riding in a car that stopped too suddenly or placed on the back of a wild pony that had then bucked her off – any number of similar ideas started bubbling up as he let his mind range free – there was never going to be any evidence to prove it. *Something and nothing* came the phrase again. She hadn't even been stung by any of those bloody wasps, he sighed impatiently to himself.

The inquest, of course, was going to demand a lot more detail than a child with a broken neck left in a ditch for a week. Even if it concluded Death by Misadventure, as was perfectly likely, there would have to be a concentrated police investigation to discover just how she got into the ditch and why. And it remained more than possible that this aspect alone would be enough to tip the Coroner over into a verdict of Unlawful Killing. Den sighed. He wanted very much to abandon the whole thing here and now. If Justine Pereira had accidentally killed the child, then she must already have suffered agonies of remorse. If Penn Strabinski had been responsible, Den doubted whether anyone would ever get the truth out of her. Even if a local paedophile had got hold of the kid, she'd died before he could assault her. It didn't seem worth all the hassle, in Den's opinion. But then nothing seemed worth the hassle to him at the moment.

Laurie Millan was inscrutable over the hotel lunch, despite an apparent willingness to fill in some gaps for Drew and Maggs. 'You'll be wondering why Penn and I are here together,' he began. 'I assure you that the obvious explanation is the wrong one . . . at least . . . well, I suppose we are in a sort of alliance against Roma. She's so . . . dismissive, you see. She doesn't listen to any worries or difficulties. So I turned to Penn. And she had been having her own problems, poor girl, which she couldn't confide to her aunt or mother, so she came to me. I admit I was flattered.'

'Problems?' Drew encouraged.

'I'm afraid I can't disclose anything she's told me.' He turned his attention to his plate, carefully removing the skin of his trout and lifting a slab of pink flesh to his mouth. Maggs had opted for a chicken salad, but Drew also had the fish. They ate in silence for a few moments before a startling thought struck Drew.

'Er . . . you did know they'd found the body of the little Renton girl, didn't you?' he asked gently, unsure of the man's reaction.

Laurie lifted his head slowly. 'I saw it in the papers,' he said. 'Such a shame. One of my reasons for coming here was to escape that additional trauma. Were you . . . ?'

'Yes. Maggs and I removed her and took her to the mortuary.'

Laurie glanced at both pairs of hands, first Drew's, then Maggs's. People often did that, as if expecting some stain to be visible. 'I don't think I want to know any details,' he said.

'We should just add that it was Roma who found her,' Drew persisted. 'That wasn't in the papers, I suppose. And they're still not sure what happened to her.'

'Complicated,' said Laurie, taking a deep draught of the Chardonnay he'd ordered without consultation, as if it were unthinkable to eat trout with any other sort of wine.

'You don't seem very upset,' Maggs observed.

'It isn't exactly a surprise, you see.'

'Isn't it?' Drew leant towards him. 'Why's that?'

Laurie put his cutlery down. 'The truth is, I just don't have any emotion to spare for a strange child. I feel so tired all the time.'

'But what about Penn? Do you think she

367

might know what happened to Georgia?' Maggs pressed.

'I can't speak for Penn, but I can say she has made no mention of it to me.'

'I'm sorry this seems like an inquisition,' Drew smiled. 'Do tell us if it gets to be too much for you, but there's still a lot I don't understand. For example, how long have you and Penn been . . . allies?'

'A year or so. It really isn't anything to get excited about. Just an occasional lunch in town and a chat.' He replenished his glass without offering anything to his visitors – the only sign Drew could find of the man's antipathy.

Drew could see that Maggs was becoming restless. He himself had little idea of what they ought to do next, apart from telephoning Roma to tell her what they'd found. She wouldn't be surprised, he realised; she'd known that Laurie and Penn would be here together, which was doubtless the reason why she hadn't come herself. She hadn't wanted to embarrass them. She'd known of their alliance all along. Whatever else she might be, Roma was not a fool. And Drew did not believe that she was a bad listener, either. She heard everything that Laurie and Justine and others had to say; she just felt very differently from them on many issues. Drew himself did not share Maggs's outrage concerning little Sarah.

He had worked as a nurse, including a stint on the paediatric ward, and knew the horrors of leukaemia in small children. He agreed, to some extent, with Roma: the treatment could be worse than the disease, and after a certain point it was the best and bravest decision to leave the pitiful little thing to die. He remembered a family who'd insisted on doing just that and he had been deeply and permanently impressed by the whole process. It had led, in part, he later realised, to his career change soon afterwards. Knowing he had to leave nursing, he'd applied for a job with a funeral director in Bradbourne, becoming a coffin-maker, bearer and remover-of-bodies. Drew, like Roma, had gained an insight into the reality of death that few people appeared to share.

The meal over, they took coffee into the lounge and made small talk about the weather, much to Maggs's disgust. For lack of anything else to do, she took her mobile phone out of her bag, intending to call her mother with a rough idea of when she'd be home. 'You should do that outside,' Drew hissed at her, casting a worried eye over the somnolent residents who would almost certainly abhor mobiles.

'OK,' she shrugged, thumbing the tiny buttons as she got out of the chair. 'Oh!'

'What?'

'Nothing.' She flushed and then dimpled. 'Just a message.'

'From our friend in Okehampton, I suppose.'

'Shut up,' she mumbled, and left the room, gazing raptly at the minuscule screen in her hand.

'Boyfriend?' Laurie asked when she'd gone.

'She seems to be very taken with the police detective investigating the Renton business,' Drew said.

'You don't sound very happy about it.'

'It's her business of course. She's had boyfriends before, but they never last long. She's very committed to the business, you see.'

'I don't quite see the problem.'

Drew shook himself. 'There's isn't a problem. Good luck to her. Karen thinks it's perfectly sweet. But they're an odd couple, just the same.'

'Couples are generally odd, I find,' said Laurie with a twinkle.

Maggs returned ten minutes later and stood impatiently in front of Drew's chair. 'It's past two now,' she said. 'Shouldn't we be getting on?'

'Get on with what?'

'Seeing what Penn has to say for herself. Asking her what happens next – what she wants us to tell Roma.' She put her hands on her hips, bending slowly forwards to make sure Drew took notice. 'You know.'

370

'I'll pop up and see if she's awake,' offered Laurie. 'She hasn't been sleeping well, you see. She's upset . . .'

'And you won't tell us why,' Maggs accused.

'Perhaps she'll tell you herself when she comes down.' He levered himself out of the chair. 'Won't be long.'

Afterwards, Drew couldn't say for sure how long Laurie had been gone. Maggs thought it was almost fifteen minutes, but Drew felt it was less than that. They talked about Den Cooper, each aware that they couldn't permit taboo subjects to develop between them. Their relationship must be protected from any such nonsense. But it was an awkward, jerky little conversation, which neither of them enjoyed.

Laurie did not come directly back into the lounge. He went to the Reception desk, and called for assistance, loudly enough to be heard by most of the ground floor. 'Ambulance!' he shouted. 'Call an ambulance!'

Drew was by his side instantly, pulling at his sleeve, demanding to know what was wrong. Laurie finally turned to him, his face haggard. 'It's Penn,' he said. 'I think she's killed herself.'

Too stunned to go up to the room to see for himself until the ambulance had arrived, Drew never got close enough to make his own assessment of what had happened. Then

371

he hovered with Maggs in the corridor outside while a brawny female paramedic performed heart massage on a limp Penn Strabinski. She didn't persist long before backing away and shaking her head at her colleague. Two police officers turned up, taking an age to establish who everybody was and then summoning their own police doctor to certify life extinct. Laurie collapsed onto a fragile chaise longue in the hotel corridor, with Drew and Maggs clustering attentively beside him.

'She can't be *dead*,' he kept saying. 'What's Roma going to say? And Helen? Oh, God, poor Helen!'

The policemen muttered with the paramedics, made phone calls, consulted the doctor and wrote things down. They asked if anybody could identify the deceased and Drew stepped forward. After a long interlude, during which a police photographer materialised and took a dozen close-up flash pictures, two undertakers' men appeared and removed the body. This, for Drew, was the strangest part.

Laurie clumsily extracted a small notebook from an inside pocket and thumbed through it, eventually finding Helen and Sebastian Strabinski's address, having been asked for Penn's next of kin. Maggs had been watching the proceedings avidly as well as cocking a sharp ear for the muttered exchanges between the various professionals. Drew looked forward to hearing what she'd gleaned, once they were alone.

Which suddenly they were. Laurie was taken to his own room by one of the paramedics and treated for shock, the hotel manager disappeared and the last policeman departed.

'There was a hypodermic,' Maggs muttered. 'They think she injected herself with something lethal. She'd only been dead about twenty minutes or so when the ambulance arrived.'

'But Laurie must have been with her then.'

'Maybe.' She cocked her head to one side. 'Yes, maybe he was.'

'You think he *killed* her?'

'Before she could tell us anything. Maybe,' she added irritatingly.

'It's a terrible thing, however it happened. I mean, she's Karen's cousin, for heaven's sake. We're *involved* – I mean, *personally*.'

Maggs threw him a cynical look. 'You hadn't even met her until last week,' she reminded him. 'You barely even knew she existed.'

'I did. Karen's only got three cousins. I couldn't fail to know she existed.'

'Well, I don't think you're going to miss her particularly. Neither will Karen. But it's very nasty, I know,' she added hurriedly. 'And very mysterious.'

'It's got to have something to do with the Renton child. Don't you think?'

'Definitely,' she agreed.

'Like – Penn killed her and then committed suicide because she felt so guilty.'

'The obvious explanation,' Maggs agreed.

'A bit too obvious?'

'Maybe.'

Karen was completely emphatic on one point. 'Penn wouldn't have killed the little girl,' she insisted. 'I just know she wouldn't.'

'You can't be sure, especially as it looks like an accident. She could have panicked,' Drew remonstrated.

'I'll never believe it,' she said implacably.

Drew and Maggs had delivered Laurie home to Roma, but hadn't stayed. Drew had an uncomfortable feeling that he had somehow precipitated Penn's death, and was loath to stay and hear this accusation from Roma. Time enough for that when the police had done their part.

Maggs was subdued, riding home on her motorbike without any further discussion. Drew was in no doubt that she was yet again thinking about Den Cooper.

'I'll have to go and see Auntie Helen,' Karen worried. 'She must be desperately upset.'

'What – now?' Drew was alarmed. It was eight o'clock in the evening.

'No, no. Tomorrow. Drew, I can't help feeling this is somehow all our fault. Even if it isn't, we're deeply involved.'

'Yes, I know,' he said gloomily. 'That's what I said to Maggs. But we didn't start it. Penn came to us, remember. We didn't have much choice.'

'It feels as if we failed. As if she came to us because she was scared something would happen, and we never came up with the goods. We didn't do what she wanted us to.'

He shook his head helplessly. 'I don't know what else we could have done.'

'Probably we did too much,' she said, with a grimace full of pain.

Drew searched for some distraction. 'Did you know Justine had a daughter? Sarah. She died of leukaemia when she was three.'

Karen stared at him. 'What?'

'That's what the argument between Justine and Roma was about. Roma wouldn't cooperate with a bone marrow transplant and I guess Justine blamed her for the child's death.'

Karen took a while to digest this, aware that Drew had strong feelings on this sort of subject, aware of herself as the mother of a child of a similar age. 'Bloody hell!' she breathed. 'So Roma was a granny.'

Somehow Drew hadn't seen it from that particular angle. 'Is that significant?' he wondered.

'Only that she must have been appallingly torn. Justine's her only child. Her only hope of immortality lies with her and any children she has. That's usually a huge commitment. And she let it die.'

'I think she was convinced it would die whatever she did.'

Karen reached for Drew's hand. 'It scares me,' she admitted. 'Little girls dying.'

He followed her gaze to where Stephanie was playing outside the window. 'Me too,' he said.

CHAPTER FIFTEEN

If u arent busy, how about the seaside? This pm.

Maggs knew he'd recognise her number, so she didn't sign the message. The desire to see him was a nagging pain in her chest, drowning out everything else. He'd probably be working, anyway, now there was another death, despite it being Sunday. He'd have to ask lots more questions, and look at reports about Penn, trying to work out whether she really did kill herself. He would have to interview Laurie Millan, and probably herself and Drew.

The death of Penn was continuing to mystify Maggs, but in a low-level background sort of way. She wanted to talk to Den about it, to offer him her suggestions, such as they were, but more because of Den than Penn. She wanted him to think she was clever and concerned and mature. She assumed that he would be preoccupied by the matter and therefore she should discuss it with him.

Always inclined to go for the most dramatic explanation, she very much favoured the theory that Penn had been murdered. And although in that case, Laurie Millan had to be the prime suspect, there was just a chance that it had been someone else. If the doctor had been wrong about the time of death by five or ten minutes and if Laurie had gone first to his own room, or the Gents, before finding Penn, then there was every chance that someone could have slipped into her room before Laurie got there.

It was this fine-tuned scenario that she wanted to run past Den Cooper. And if it was true then she thought she knew the only possible person it could have been.

The post-mortem on Penn Strabinski, performed by special arrangement on Sunday morning, revealed poisoning by a large injection of local anaesthetic, of a type normally used for cattle and sheep. The only puncture wound had been found directly into the heart, which while possibly self-inflicted, was far more likely to have been administered by another party. Mild bruising on the thoracic area suggested that the deceased was held down firmly as the injection was given. Death would probably have occurred relatively slowly, but the effects of such a dose on a human heart were unpredictable. To the pathologist's knowledge, this was an unprecedented method of killing someone and he was unable to say with any certainty how long a time might have elapsed between the injection and the moment of death. The heart had suffered some damage from the needle itself, and the lungs had also been affected by the anaesthetic.

'Weird,' Den remarked to DI Hemsley, when he read the report. They'd both been called in to begin the investigation. Both were in Sunday mode, a long way from any excessive action. 'Must have been suicide, don't you think?' He was still trying to get to grips with the fact that Drew Slocombe and Maggs had been at the scene of death, and yet she could send a casual invitation to the seaside as if nothing had happened.

I am busy. Need to see you though. Drew too, he'd replied.

Hemsley pursed his lips. 'Funny way to top yourself,' he objected. 'With friends just downstairs. Doesn't seem very likely to me. Not with those bruises as well.'

'So it's a murder enquiry, is it?' Den sighed.

'That's what we have to assume,' the DI

concluded. Then he leant back in his chair and fixed Cooper with an unsettling stare. Den's heart began to flutter with apprehension.

'Cooper,' Hemsley began with unusual heaviness. 'I seem to be getting some odd vibes from you these days. I don't get any sense of *engagement* with the work. For all you care, children can get themselves killed, young women not safe in their own hotel rooms, and none of it seems to touch you. What's the matter with you?'

Den considered, but dismissed, the easy option. He'd worked with Danny Hemsley for years and owed him a modicum of candour. 'I'm a bit low, to be honest,' he admitted. 'Probably just a phase. Burnout, maybe. I'll be OK again in a bit.'

'Never mind burnout. It's woman trouble, isn't it? You haven't been right since the final rift with Lilah. Time you got someone new, mate. That's what you need.'

'As it happens, I'm working on that. It's very early days and it isn't going to be plain sailing, I can see already – but there is someone. It's just that she doesn't seem to be doing the trick, workwise.' He heaved a sigh. Putting it into words only seemed to make it all much worse. The truth was suddenly a lot bigger and blacker than he had admitted to himself so far.

'OK. Well, maybe you can take the rest of the day off. I'll arrange for this Millan chap to be taken to Taunton, and go and interview him there myself. He came within a whisker of being caught red-handed, as I understand it. We ought to see what he has to say for himself.'

'But . . .' Cooper felt a tremor of panic. He was being taken off the case! He was all the more agitated for knowing it was what he had wanted, only a day or so ago. Now it felt like a put-down. Worse than a put-down – it felt like the beginning of the end, and that was very scary.

'Make good use of it, that's all I ask. And be back here tomorrow, bright and early,' Hemsley added, before he dismissed him.

Laurie Millan had been warned by the police to make himself available the next day for questioning. There was no room for doubt that he was by far the most significant suspect in the matter of Penn's death. He had quavered repeatedly, 'I didn't touch her. You must believe me. I never laid a hand on her.' Only when reunited with Roma did he quieten down.

'Oh, God,' he trembled. 'I really thought they'd charge me with her murder.'

Roma refrained from questioning him, aware of his fragile condition. Instead, she put him to bed with a hot milky drink and a warm affectionate spaniel for his feet. Even in his traumatised state he noticed the change. 'Thank you, dear,' he breathed. 'This is very kind of you.'

She'd nodded wryly and said nothing.

Next morning the police came for him, requesting politely that he accompany them to the station to make a statement. They were solicitous, accompanying him gently in and out of the car, bringing him a mug of tea. But the questions were pointed.

'Could you please describe the exact nature of your relationship with Miss Strabinski?'

'How long were you intending to remain at the hotel?'

'Did you see anybody you recognised while staying there?'

'Please tell us, in your own words, precisely what happened between two-fifteen and two-thirty-five on Saturday afternoon.'

Hesitantly, Laurie talked them through those long twenty minutes. He'd gone to the lavatory first, on the ground floor, a little way from the lounge. Then he'd waited for the lift because Penn's room was on the second floor. It had been slow in arriving. There had been three people coming down in it. He had also heard voices on the stairs. There were still people coming out of the dining-room, too. In short, the hotel was relatively bustling.

He did not have a key to Penn's room – of course he hadn't. Why would he? So he knocked, gently at first, thinking she might be asleep, not wanting to give her a rude awakening. When she did not reply, he tried the handle and found the door unlocked . . .'

At this point, Hemsley looked up and frowned. 'Don't hotel doors lock themselves automatically when closed?' he asked the officer sitting next to him.

'Not at the Elmcroft,' Laurie said robustly. 'You have to turn the key on the outside. Too many people lock themselves out, otherwise. You have to remember we're talking about Bournemouth, where practically everyone is over eighty.'

Hemsley smiled tightly, and waved for Laurie to continue his account. Quite slowly, he explained, he had pushed the door open, calling Penn's name, wondering why she wasn't answering. The room had a short shadowy corridor between the door and the main area, where the bathroom had been added. He had assumed initially that she must be in the bathroom and therefore unable to hear him. He'd even tapped on the open door and called her name again. Only then had he stepped towards the bed and seen her. He thought she was asleep – obviously that was what he thought. But her eyes were open, her mouth drooling, her arms flung out. People didn't sleep like that. He'd approached her, with his head spinning with the impossibility of what he was seeing. He'd poked her, then shaken her, then lifted her up and tried to waken her.

He could tell no more than that. The rest was already documented. The rest they already knew.

'Thank you, sir,' they said. 'We'll just have that transcribed, if you'd wait a few minutes, and then perhaps you could read and sign it for us.'

At 9 a.m., Maggs was trying to read, out in the garden, her mobile close beside her. Her mother had been astonished at her early rising. 'But it's Sunday!' she'd protested. 'You never get up before eleven on a Sunday, unless Drew calls you out.'

'I'm going out,' Maggs explained. 'I hope.' She gave her mobile a little shake as if to ensure it was still working. 'But not with Drew.'

Her mother sighed. 'Oh, *I* see. Why do girls *still* wait for the man to make the call? Hasn't feminism made any headway at all?'

'Because,' Maggs explained tightly, 'you have to be sure he wants to go out with you. And that's the only way to do it. If I called him and persuaded him to do something he didn't really want to, I'd regret it later. Some things are best left the way they are.'

'Well it shouldn't have to be so complicated. And one-sided. It all seems ridiculously unfair to me.'

The phone beeped and Maggs's whole demeanour changed. She read the message in silence.

'Well?' her mother demanded.

'I'm not sure,' Maggs frowned. 'I think I'm supposed to wait for further developments or something. He says he's busy.'

'You could go back to bed,' her mother suggested.

But Maggs remained in the garden, leaving her mother to get on with her regular Sunday routine of seeing to all the house plants. There were at least a hundred, on every windowsill and several other surfaces, and they all needed their dead leaves removing, or their aphids destroying, or a new pot, as well as a good drink of enriched water. It all took well over an hour.

The phone warbled before she quite reached the point of despair. Den's voice came strongly down the airwaves as if he was standing next to her. 'Seaside then,' he said. 'Is your cozzie packed?'

'Of course.'

'I'll be there just after eleven.'

'You're sure you can find it?' Had she even given him her address, she wondered?

'Escott Way, Bradbourne, right? You told me when we were in the pub.'

'Did I? I'll wait outside for you. Number 42.'

'I'm on my way.'

They went to Weston-super-Mare and spent hours on the pier, then paddled, and sunbathed and talked and walked. They held hands, and then kissed and cuddled on the grey sand, oblivious of the families and couples and ice cream sellers all around them.

They spoke seriously about global warming and pollution and the future of the planet. They giggled over anecdotes concerning their mothers and the folly parents are prone to. They did not mention funerals or murders. Den showed her his trick of bending his legs until his feet were on his shoulders. She showed him her double-jointed thumbs. He built her a castle of stones and shells, which she decorated lavishly with seaweed.

They ate scampi and chips at a kiosk and then drank Bass in a nearby pub. He drove her home at ten, each of them wondering how time could possibly pass so quickly.

'Tomorrow the police will have to interview

you about Penn Strabinski,' he said regretfully as they sat in the car outside her house. 'It won't be me – I'm too far away.'

'Don't talk about that,' she flashed. 'Don't spoil the day.'

'Sorry.' He stroked her cheek wistfully. 'I'll phone you. Early. You and Drew.'

'Fine,' she nodded, before sinking into one last long goodnight kiss.

Monday was different in countless ways. Maggs looked at Drew, the burial field, the sparse settlement that was North Staverton, with completely new eyes.

'Right,' she said, as soon as she was in the office. 'This is the first day of the rest of our lives. You know that, don't you?' She regarded Drew sternly. 'We need to sort this Penn Strabinski business out, once and for all. It's getting in the way. It's making Den depressed.'

'And we can't have that, can we?' Drew tried to keep his tone light. 'So how are we going to do it, then?'

'He's going to call this morning. We'll have to be interviewed again.'

'Obviously, now they've got the post-mortem results.'

Den's call came at nine-thirty, and Drew handed the receiver to Maggs. She conversed for ten minutes, while Drew diplomatically removed himself to the field. She came to find him, eyes sparkling.

'Listen to this!' she cried. 'They want to interview us both again, you first, then me. Den and his boss, Danny, are coming up here later on . . .'

Drew interrupted impatiently. 'Maggs, there's work to do here. Look at all these letters. We've got to send accounts out for last week, and another reminder for the Grants. I'm officiating at the crem tomorrow, in case you've forgotten. I should really have gone to see the family on Friday. I'll have to go today.'

'You mean you forgot them until now,' she accused.

'Sort of,' he admitted. 'They'll be wondering where I've got to.'

'I seem to remember you grumbling about vicars who left it till the last minute,' she said.

'OK, OK. Anyway, I'll go this morning. You'll have to hold the fort here.'

'Fine, so long as you're back by twelve. It'll all fit perfectly well, don't fuss. Although I *might* have to make a few phone calls. Drew – you realise how seriously involved we are with the police case, don't you? You don't seem to have taken it on board.'

He leant towards her in mock earnestness.

'Maggs, believe me, I am deeply serious about it. But I'm even *more* serious about my livelihood here. I know I can be of no further help to the police, and I don't intend to make any more attempts to solve the case single-handedly without them.'

'Double-handedly, you mean.'

'But if you want to keep on at it, I'm not stopping you. I haven't forgotten that it was me who brought you in on it in the first place. And now you've got such a personal commitment to it as well . . .' he clasped his hands together in a parody of congratulatory ardour, '. . . who am I to get in your way?'

'Shut up,' she said. 'Or I won't tell you what else Den told me.'

'I haven't got time to listen now, anyway,' he said. 'Wait until I get back.'

Over a lunch of bread, cheese, salad and fruit, provided by Karen, Maggs filled him in on the rest of Den's information. 'Penn was injected into the heart with some kind of local anaesthetic. The sort they use on animals.'

'Did she do it herself?'

'Doubtful, they think.' She watched his face, wondering how much attention she was getting, and finding the answer unsatisfactory.

'Drew, I've got a few ideas as to what might

have happened. Not just to Penn, but the little girl as well. Do you want to hear them?'

He chewed for a moment. 'Go on, then.'

She was interrupted before she could start. A car pulled up outside the office and two uniformed policemen emerged from it. 'Here we go,' Drew realised. 'Time for your interview. Or did you say I was to go first?'

'You first. Don't worry, mate, I'll see yer all right,' she growled. 'Every visiting day, without fail – I'll be right there, with yer favourite cakes.'

'Don't let the children forget me,' he pleaded.

'Not a chance. We'll sit them in front of the video where you're burying that old vagrant, every blessed day. Don't you worry about that.'

The police were at the door. Drew struggled for composure as he opened it. Maggs was snorting behind him. 'This is very generous of you,' he said. 'Providing transport, I mean.'

'All part of the service, sir,' said one of the men genially. 'We're to use the Taunton office, for convenience. It's a long way from here to Okehampton. All we need is a statement and a signature.'

'And you're bringing me back, then collecting Miss Beacon?' He could hardly believe the trouble they were taking.

'That's it, sir. No sense in disrupting your business if we can avoid it.'

Maggs watched them go and then tapped in another text to Den.

How goes it? I have ideas. Ring me, office, soon.

Cooper and Timms spent most of Monday morning in Crediton. Den's mood, like Maggs's, was transformed. 'What's happened to you?' Bennie marvelled, as he whistled in the car.

'Oh, nothing much. Had a nice day at the seaside yesterday, that's all.'

This time they used the keys that had been found in Penn's handbag and let themselves into the small terraced house. No neighbours appeared to challenge them, and nothing stirred once they were inside.

Wearing rubber gloves, they rapidly examined every room. In the living room, Den lifted the phone and keyed 1471. It had become standard procedure in recent years, with sometimes remarkably helpful results. He stared at the number he'd jotted down, with the date and time beside it. 'She doesn't get many calls,' he commented. 'This goes back to the middle of last week.'

'Everyone uses mobiles these days,' Bennie said. 'Presumably her friends all know she's away.'

Den continued to stare at the number. 'It looks familiar.' He fished out his notebook and flipped through a few pages. 'Yes! It's Gladcombe Farm.'

'The Rentons or Justine?'

'Rentons. Justine's cottage hasn't got a phone.'

He then pressed the Redial button for good measure. The phone was answered promptly. 'Elmcroft Hotel. How may I help you?' chirruped a female voice.

'Oh!' Den feigned surprise, thinking quickly. 'Is that the Elmcroft Hotel in Edinburgh?'

'No, sir. We're in Bournemouth.'

'Oh dear. Silly me. I'm sorry to have troubled you.'

'What was all that about?' Bennie demanded.

'She called the hotel, that's all. Nothing very surprising about that, I suppose.'

There was nothing untoward about the contents of the house downstairs. It was uncluttered, tidy, much as Den remembered it from his earlier visit to Penn. Upstairs they found a supply of contraceptive pills in three unopened packs. 'We knew she was on the Pill,' said Bennie. 'There was half a pack in her handbag.'

'How thorough are we being?' Den asked, never happy about rifling through personal belongings.

'Fairly. Letters-and-diaries thorough, but not

dirty-washing-and-dustbins,' she suggested.

'Right.' They opened drawers and cupboards, looked under the bed, reached up to the top of the wardrobe and medicine cabinet, opened jewellery boxes and suitcases. They found in a small overnight bag a meagre collection of letters, minus envelopes, held together by a rubber band. Also in the bag was a long T-shirt of the sort used for bed, a pair of socks, a bottle of expensive perfume and a toothbrush in a plastic bag.

There were five letters in total, each one only a single sheet of notepaper. They were unsigned, undated and with no address.

Should be fine for Wednesday. J has to go into town. We'll have plenty of time, sweetheart, and can use the house for a change. I know it might be awkward for you to get away, but you can say you're sick, can't you? Roll on the holidays, eh!

You won't need to nag me about you know what, either, because I've got a plan. I've been speaking to a chap who's just back from Krakow and says my ideas would work out fine. So we'll get there yet, you just see. You know I want it as much as you do — it's just that these things take time.

Sorry it's been so long. Not my fault,

honestly. I'll make up for it on Wednesday,
with knobs on. Don't forget to leave the car
in the usual place.

'It's an assignation,' said Bennie unnecessarily.
'It looks quite recent. Not at all faded, anyway.'

'Where's Krakow?'

'Poland, I think.'

'Her father's Polish,' Den remembered. 'It
couldn't possibly be from him, could it?'

Bennie's eyes widened. 'Hardly,' she spluttered,
before reading it again. 'Well,' she amended, 'it
doesn't actually mention sex in so many words,
does it.'

'And people do sometimes have sex with their
fathers,' Den said conscientiously. Bennie slapped
his arm and made a hissing sound. 'Sorry,' he
grinned.

'*We can use the house for a change,*' Bennie
murmured. 'It certainly sounds like sex. But it
could just as easily be a game of ping-pong, or
making bait for fly fishing, or . . .'

'Trimming bonsai trees or framing pictures,'
Den contributed. 'Or about five million other
things.'

'It sounds like sex to me,' said Bennie.

'Why didn't the bugger sign it?' Den grumbled.
'Better have a look at the others.'

The other letters were even briefer and all

named a day and a time for a meeting. Endearments were sprinkled liberally and one made reference to a 'delicious perfume'.

'It has to be a married man, scared to use the phone because everything's itemised, waiting for a moment when the wife is sure to be out,' Bennie concluded.

'I think you're right,' Den said. 'So I wonder who J is.'

He phoned Maggs as soon as he read her latest message. 'We found some letters at Penn's house,' he told her, well aware that he was breaching strict rules of procedure. 'Love letters, by the look of them, arranging meetings that sound like . . . er . . . well, a love affair. Possibly with a married man. Mentions a person called "J". That's it, basically. You realise I shouldn't be telling you. Bennie was with me this morning, so I couldn't phone then.'

'That's OK,' she forgave him lingeringly. 'Now listen to this—' she confided several of her thoughts and some of her intentions. He shivered at her courage and sheer youthful energy.

'I almost wish you hadn't told me any of that,' he said. 'I'll have to pretend I never knew about it, if it goes wrong. I suppose I don't need to tell you not to take any silly risks? And keep me posted.'

'No, sir. Yes, sir. Thank you, sir.'

His responding laugh was half-hearted and she was left wondering whether he was always so melancholy or only when he had a new girlfriend.

Den was left in an agonising dilemma, torn between his duties as a police officer and his profound admiration and awe in the face of Maggs's outrageous plans.

Immediately after work, having sailed through her police interview with perfect composure, Maggs went on her motorcycle to Roma Millan's in Pitcombe. She trotted up the path as if she was one of the family.

'Come on, both of you,' she ordered Roma and Justine. 'We're going out. Bring a camera and a tape recorder if you've got one. And some sort of bell or whistle. Something that makes a really loud noise.'

'Tape recorder?' Roma looked blank. 'I haven't got one.'

'There's the video camera,' Laurie suggested. 'The one the boys gave me for Christmas. The battery might be flat, though.' While he fetched it, Roma produced a large handbell from a cupboard. 'Laurie uses this to summon me down from the field,' she grinned.

The little red light on the video camera

advised them that the battery was alive and well, and Maggs grabbed it enthusiastically. 'Great!' she crowed. 'The very thing.'

Roma drove, with Maggs next to her and Justine in the back. Maggs spent the entire journey coaching them in what they were going to do. At first Justine protested, partly afraid, partly appalled by the strength of Maggs's argument.

'Do as she says,' Roma ordered. 'She's right. It's obvious when you think about it. Why haven't the police realised?'

'They haven't been trying,' said Maggs. 'Not really. It was always a something and nothing case to them.'

'It won't work.' Justine shivered apprehensively. 'I know it won't.'

'We keep at it until it does,' said Maggs. 'But I think you'll be surprised.'

They parked under some trees and walked quietly up the track, Maggs in the lead. With no sign of life in the house, they made quickly for the big stone barn and scuttled inside. 'Are you sure they're in?' Roma hissed. 'I didn't see any cars.'

'They keep them round the far side of the house,' said Justine. 'I'll go and have a look.'

Furtively she skirted the yard and disappeared from sight. A minute later she reappeared, thumb emphatically raised. 'They're both there,' she breathed, when she was safely back inside the barn.

'Right – ladder,' Maggs ordered. A lightweight metal one was found standing against the wall leaning its top few rungs against a suspended floor about eighteen feet off the ground. As far as they could see, there was very little stored on the upper level. Justine's brief moment of exhilaration seemed to evaporate as they stood back and gazed upwards. 'Oh, God,' she whimpered. 'It's terribly high.'

'Hold on, now,' Roma tapped her on the back. 'Don't spoil everything.'

'Let me just fix the camera somewhere,' Maggs puffed, halfway up the ladder. 'Probably at the top here, with a bit of hay to hide it. I hope I remember to set it going.'

'Lucky they haven't got a dog,' Roma commented. 'Or they'd have been out here by now.'

'We'd have handled a dog,' Maggs boasted confidently. 'There's no stopping us now. Right, Roma, come on up.'

It took a further couple of minutes for them to get themselves settled and then Maggs called down to Justine, 'Your turn! Give it hell.' Justine bent and picked up the bell from the floor and began to ring it with all her might. The noise was deafening. She walked to the barn door and kept on ringing until she saw the farmhouse door begin to open. Retreating quickly, she gave one last peal for good measure, dropped the bell and shimmied up the ladder, until her face was just level with the upper floor.

Philip and Sheena Renton appeared together in the barn doorway. 'What the—' shouted Philip. 'Who's that?'

'Daddy! Penn! What are you doing?' cried Justine in a little-girl voice. 'Oh, Daddy, why have you taken your trousers off? And Penn looks funny.'

Roma, in mock rage, appeared at the top of the ladder. 'Bloody hell, child, what are you doing here?' She made a lunge for Justine, who ducked and made a masterful impression of falling off the ladder, skimming down it and collapsing in a heap at the foot.

Maggs was now just visible, hand over her mouth. 'Philip! My God, what have you done? Georgia! Get up, Georgia!'

She started down the ladder with some caution, Roma calling after her, 'Don't touch her. Wait for me.'

At the bottom, Maggs and Roma stood together, arms wrapped around each other. 'She's dead,' growled Roma. 'I can't let Sheena know what happened. We can't tell her about us yet. It's too soon. Look, Penn, why don't we just fit Justine up? Make it look as if she was responsible.'

'But how?' Maggs turned trustful eyes upwards. 'How could we do that?'

'Let me think. Look, cover her up for a bit, and we'll leave her until we've thought of something.'

A cry of outraged horror came from Philip Renton, at the same time as his wife stepped further into the barn, towards the still-crumpled heap that was Justine. It was as if she really believed it was her dead daughter. She turned back to her husband. 'Is it true?' she screamed. 'Is this what happened?'

'N-no, of course not,' he blustered. But his face was deathly white and the fight seemed to have drained out of him.

'It is,' said Sheena more calmly. 'You pushed her off that ladder and broke her neck.'

'I didn't push her. She slipped. I never touched her. She was only halfway up, too. She never even saw anything, just heard us up there. She should never even have hurt herself, but she landed awkwardly, I suppose.' He buried his face in his hands and Maggs went slowly up the ladder again to retrieve the camera.

'Thank you,' she said to Philip, pressing a button. 'I think I've got all that quite nicely.'

Sheena was kneeling beside Justine, who had

roused herself to a sitting position. They were both looking at Philip. The light in the barn was poor, with the sun almost setting outside. 'You utterly loathsome bastard,' Justine said, almost conversationally. 'Your own child, and you just dumped her like a piece of rubbish. You must be subhuman to do a thing like that. You can't even claim it was all done in a panic. You left her here all day, thinking it all through, right down to the bag of jelly babies. And Penn . . .' she choked on her rage. 'Penn helped you.'

'She had the jelly babies anyway,' Renton muttered. 'I only threw them down beside her to get rid of them.'

'So where's Penn now?' Sheena cut in shrilly. 'This is as much her doing as Philip's. She should be here. I want them both to pay for what they've done.' Her face was dark with fury.

Roma gave her a long look. 'Penn has already paid, as I think you know perfectly well.'

Maggs stepped forward, the camera still in her hand. 'We think you know exactly what's happened to Penn. We think you knew, or guessed, what happened to Georgia as well. Then you took your revenge on your husband's mistress.'

Justine crawled forwards on hands and knees across the hay-strewn floor as if grief and fury had removed her ability to walk. 'You two are

401

the sickest pair of useless parents I've ever met. That poor innocent little girl, stuck with you two and never complaining. Frightened to shed a tear in case it drove you even further away. And Penn making it all a hundred times worse. I wish you were both dead, I really do.'

The effect of her words could perhaps have been predicted. The Rentons drew closer together, Philip stretching a hand out to his wife. He spoke directly to Roma. 'Sheena doesn't know that Penn's dead. She hasn't heard any news or seen anyone for days.' He stood limply, his hand failing to connect with his wife. 'I was trying to protect her, you see, from knowing what I'd done. That's all.'

Nobody spoke as they tried to make sense of his claim. 'If she'd known, she'd have lost me as well as Georgia. And we've had so much loss here . . .' He subsided into harsh sobs.

'So,' Justine began, with no hint of softening in her tone, 'why did you tell her you were having an affair with me? How was that going to help?'

'In the long run she wouldn't have believed it. I was buying time.'

'You were telling one stupid lie after another, until nobody knew what to believe,' Maggs corrected him. 'You weren't thinking about the future at all – the long run. You were just scared shitless and said whatever you thought would save your own skin.'

He shook his head helplessly. 'You don't understand,' he whimpered. 'That piece of play-acting just now – it wasn't *at all* like that. It was Penn's idea, most of it. She thought we were going away to Poland together, to start a new life. I kept telling her I couldn't leave Georgia, not with Sheena so busy all the time. I said we'd have to take Georgia with us. She pushed the ladder; *she* made Georgia fall.'

'We don't believe you,' said Justine icily. 'That isn't what you said just now.'

'I believe him,' said Sheena quietly. She looked round at all the faces. 'Did somebody say that Penn is dead? How can that be?'

'Murdered,' said Maggs. 'On Saturday. I wonder where you two were at the time?'

'I was in town, at the office,' Sheena remembered. 'Philip was here all day.'

Maggs tightened her grip on the video camera before she spoke. 'You weren't here, were you, Mr Renton? You were in Bournemouth with a hypodermic syringe full of high strength local anaesthetic. You injected it into Penn's heart, fully intending to kill her.'

He followed his wife's gaze, from one face to another. 'They killed all the cows, you know, in this very barn. Shot them, one by one, while they just stood and waited. They weren't panicked or scared, even when they could see their friends dropping to the floor. It was a sea of death. We dragged them outside with the tractor and they went rotten before anyone would let us bury them. My father hanged himself a month later.'

Sheena put a hand to her throat, retching, her face greenish in the dim light. 'So Georgia was just another cow,' she gasped.

'We loved those cows,' Philip said simply. 'Looked after them like princesses. The line went back fifty years.'

Roma glanced at Maggs, meeting her eye. 'We're getting out of our depth here,' she murmured. 'Don't you think?'

Maggs nodded and extracted her mobile phone from her pocket. Deftly she operated the keys with her left thumb, sending a brief message. 'That should do it,' she said.

'You did kill Penn then, did you?' Roma persevered, making everyone else wince at the unkindness.

But Renton was beyond unkindness. He was slumped against an upright beam supporting the overhead floor. Sheena was holding him, a hand pawing uselessly at his chest.

'Leave them,' Maggs said, making a flapping motion towards the door. 'They're not going anywhere. We did what we came to do.'

The threesome slowly left the barn and went to sit in Roma's car. 'Can't say I feel much sense of triumph,' Roma admitted.

'Wish I had something to smoke,' said Justine. 'I feel awful.'

'I doubt if it counts as a confession,' Maggs worried. 'Even though I got it all on camera. He didn't actually say he'd killed Penn, did he?'

Roma and Justine looked at her in confusion. 'You switched the camera off,' said Roma.

Maggs grinned sheepishly. 'No, I switched it *on*. I forgot all about it for the bit on the ladder. Just as well really. The last part was much more interesting.'

'It *was* a confession. Surely it was. At least – he didn't *deny* it,' said Justine.

'Maybe,' sighed Maggs. 'We'll have to see what Den thinks. He should be here soon.'

CHAPTER SIXTEEN

Den thought it was all a bewildering mess when he and Bennie arrived at Gladcombe. Sheena would not let go of Philip, who seemed to be sunk into a catatonic state from which nobody could retrieve him. 'We'd better search the house,' Den decided.

In the kitchen, in a cupboard under the sink, was a large bottle of the same local anaesthetic as had been found in Penn Strabinski's body. There was a pad beside the telephone with 'Room 32, Elmcroft Hotel' written on it. The handwriting on that and other items found around the house, matched that in the letters found in Penn's bedroom.

'Mr Renton, I'm afraid you're under arrest,'

Den muttered to himself before going into the living room and formally charging the man.

In the light of his precarious condition, a secure vehicle was summoned and Philip was eventually driven away to a closed psychiatric ward in Taunton. Sheena had to be forcibly disconnected from him.

'I still think it might have been her who murdered Penn,' Roma insisted mulishly to the others in the car.

'I don't think so,' Maggs said. She was still glowing from Den's admiration, which had been unstinting once he'd grasped what she'd achieved.

Roma drove them all back to Pitcombe through the dark country lanes. 'Summer's nearly over,' she said wistfully. 'It always goes so quickly.'

'It's not over yet, by a long way,' Maggs said from the back seat. 'September's usually lovely.'

'I hate September,' Roma gloomed.

'Sarah died in September,' Justine said.

'Exactly,' said Roma.

The atmosphere in the car was subdued and the conversation lapsed. The image of the wreck that had been Philip Renton was an unpleasant one and even Maggs couldn't sustain her sense of triumph for long.

'Did you know he was such a mess?' she asked

Justine, shortly before they got back to Pitcombe.

'Not really,' she said softly. 'But I'm not altogether surprised. He's been through a lot, after all.'

'Not as much as you have,' Maggs reminded her. 'It must have been dreadful.'

'Let's not talk about that,' Roma pleaded and Justine murmured her agreement.

Maggs managed a full minute's silence before trying again. 'I think you should. It's obviously sitting there between you, spoiling things for you both. It's such a waste. Mothers and daughters are supposed to be friends.'

'This sounds like a counselling session,' grumbled Justine. 'I've had my fill of them, thanks.' At the wheel, Roma made a *tch* of disapproval.

'You can tut,' Justine snapped. 'But there wasn't anyone else I could talk to. My child *died*, Mother. You don't just brush yourself down and get on with things when something like that happens.'

'I thought *my* child had died, a few days ago,' Roma said softly.

'Oh? And how did that feel?' Justine was aggressive.

'I have no idea how it *felt*. I was worried, angry. I've been worried and angry more or less since you were born, so it was nothing unusual. I'm angry now at what it's done to Laurie.'

'None of it is my fault,' Justine wailed. 'When will you see that?'

'I didn't say it was. I never said it was your fault. I'm not that stupid. I know I was the adult and you were the child. It was down to me to try and get it right. But the task was beyond me.'

'You should never have had me,' Justine said. 'Not with that man. Anyone could have told you it was an impossible mix. There's scarcely a sane person on either side of the family.'

'Except Helen.'

'Right. Poor old Auntie Helen.' Justine sniffed back the threatening tears and kept her tirade going. 'So what the hell did you *expect*? You never blamed *him*, did you? My father. You never confronted the horrible mess that you two made of your marriage. No wonder I went off and got pregnant with someone I met in a nightclub and never saw again.'

'You honestly think that was a rational thing to do?'

Maggs felt a compelling mixture of embarrassment and fascination. There was often something heightened and genuine about a conversation inside a car that you rarely found elsewhere. For one thing, the participants couldn't easily escape from each other. They had to see the thing through to an acceptable conclusion. There were only three or four miles to go, though, and

Maggs worried that they would need more time than that.

'I don't blame you for Sarah dying, you know,' Justine choked out, after a brief silence. 'You think I do, but I don't. I wish now that I'd listened to you and not subjected her to all that horrible medical stuff. They turned her into a *thing* at the end. She smelt of them and their rotten drugs, she cried most of the time, she was nothing but skin and bones. I really wish I'd had the courage to snatch her away and take her home with me to die. But you always hogged all the courage, didn't you Mother? You were the only one brave enough to reject their whole package. You were the one who faced up to Sarah dying, to losing her forever. You've always been so appallingly brave, haven't you? And you've no idea how terrifying that is to other people.'

Roma parked the car beside the wall of her cottage and made no move to get out. 'Brave?' she whispered. 'Is that how you see me?'

'We all know – we've all seen – how you confront your demons. We know how scared you are sometimes, but you deal with it. You carry on. You march out there with a flimsy stick and wave it in the face of the monster, while the rest of us huddle in the cellar and pretend everything's perfectly all right. You make us all aware of what cowards we are.'

Ah, thought Maggs. *Now I understand why Drew likes her so much.*

'Well, I'm sorry,' said Roma faintly. 'But I don't know what I can do about it.'

'Just go a bit easier on us lesser mortals, that's all. Leave us to our delusions and comfort blankets. Let poor Laurie wallow sometimes, without having to put on a brave face whenever you're around.'

'How do you know about Laurie?' Roma sat up straighter.

'He told Penn a lot about himself. They had a few sessions together in a pub or somewhere. She told me some of it. She kept me informed quite well, really. Poor Penn – we haven't been thinking about her as much as we should. Her death is probably the most terrible of them all and yet we've scarcely even mentioned her.'

'Time enough for that,' Roma said, with a pleading note. 'If Laurie was as fond of her as you seem to be saying, I'm going to have a job on my hands, aren't I, trying to put your advice into practice.'

Justine began to say something and then changed her mind. 'Yes, you are,' she said.

Den Cooper wasn't required for long at the Somerset police station, so he went back along the endlessly tedious M5 to Okehampton, where he wandered outside into the warm street. As he always did, he gazed to the south-east where Dartmoor bulked darkly in the near distance. Although no great rambler, he'd enjoyed a few long moorland walks and carried the knowledge of it inside him – a place to escape to, to get lost in, if things became too heavy.

They were pretty heavy now and he groaned inwardly at the prospect of another lonely evening in his flat. It was not quite nine o'clock. He'd have to kill at least a couple of hours before he could decently go to bed. And he badly wanted somebody to talk to. Somebody with a fresh robust view of life and the horrible things that happened. Somebody who would cut through all the twisted and chaotic emotions that had been knotting themselves tighter and tighter inside him for the past months. Maggs would have been more than willing to give it a try, but he had no intention of inflicting such a weight on her, at this point. Maggs was for fun and optimism and lightness of being.

Without really thinking, he pulled his crumpled notepad out of his pocket and flipped a few pages. Yes, the number was there and his mobile was in another pocket, fully charged. He phoned the number.

A woman answered. 'Is Drew there?' he asked.

'I'll fetch him,' she chirped, with no discernible reluctance. There was even a generosity in her voice that warmed him.

'Hello?' came Drew's voice.

'Oh, hi. Cooper here. Look, I know it's late and this is a lot to ask, but I was wondering, would you meet me for a jar somewhere?'

'What? Where are you?'

'Okehampton. But if we met in Honiton or somewhere it's only be about forty-five minutes for both of us. We'd have time for a couple of pints. It's just . . .'

Drew understood. He'd heard pain in all its many guises by this time. 'OK,' he said. 'Do you know a likely pub?'

Cooper named a small village on the A30 which boasted a single hostelry.

Drew arrived first, shortly before ten and for a few minutes he worried that the detective had had an accident, speeding along the dual carriageway around Exeter. Then a Cavalier swept into the tiny car park and the tall man climbed out.

Aware of limited time, by mutual consent they chose a corner table close to a large fireplace and examined each other's faces. 'We haven't really got to know each other through this, have we?' Drew began. 'But I gather you've made quite an impression on Maggs.'

413

'She's quite a girl,' Cooper nodded. 'But that isn't what I want to talk about.'

'No. I wouldn't be the right person.'

'And I haven't come to talk about Penn Strabinski or Roma Millan, either. Except as they relate to my job, which I suppose is seeing that justice is done.'

'Right. Funny thing, justice.'

'Is it true that Roma was dismissed for slapping a kid in her class? She really lost her job over that?'

'So it seems. She wouldn't defend herself, which actually made the whole thing more protracted, oddly enough. She suffered much more than she let on, I suspect. She lost an incredible amount; not just her job.'

Cooper nodded. 'Respect, confidence, a sense of purpose, structure . . .'

'Exactly. It sounds as if you've been thinking about it.'

'She slapped a brazen little bastard, probably leaving only a faint mark on his cheek and a dent in his ego for two minutes and who might in the process have learnt that there's a limit to what you can get away with. Thirty years ago it would have been completely unremarkable, even approved of. So why do I feel like a fascist for even thinking like this?'

'I don't know. Why do you?'

'Because it affects *me*. I'm not allowed to slap vile little buggers who have no idea how to behave, either. And that Renton man can casually push his kid off a ladder and kill her and probably would have got away with it completely if he hadn't been crazy enough to murder his girlfriend as well.'

'No,' Drew protested. 'He wouldn't have got away with it. Didn't you see his face last week? He's been in agony since it happened. He's never going to escape the image of that child with her head flopping loose, and he doesn't even *want* to. He went to look at her rotting body. He insisted on doing that when you tried to stop him. You don't have to worry too much about justice. It has a way of taking care of itself.'

Den shook his head miserably. 'You're not helping,' he sighed.

'Explain the problem, then.'

'My job,' said Cooper again. 'I don't think I can do it any more. The police aren't really about the things I thought we were about. We all do our best, but we get so easily distracted. We get all agitated about completely the wrong things. Half the laws in this country are ludicrous, to start with. What's the point of killing ourselves trying to enforce them when nobody really believes in them? It makes us look like idiots or worse.'

'Bloody hell,' breathed Drew. 'This does sound bad.'

'It's bad,' confirmed Cooper and took a long swig of his pint.

'So what would you do instead?'

The tall man looked at him with a frown. 'Instead?'

'Yes. You're telling me you want to quit the police – so what would you do instead?'

'I can't quit the police. I mean . . . is that what I said?'

'Isn't it?'

Den finished the drink and stared numbly at the empty glass. 'That feels scary,' he admitted. 'I never considered any other kind of work.'

'There's plenty out there. You're single, fit, intelligent. The world's at your feet.'

Den laughed bitterly. 'I don't think so.'

'Look. I did it. I was working as a nurse and suddenly realised I couldn't hack it any more. A bit like you, really. It just wasn't right, somehow. So I flipped through the Situations Vacant and found an ad for an assistant at an undertakers. I was only there a year before setting up on my own. You've got to follow your gut feeling, otherwise why be alive at all?'

'Precisely,' said Den through gritted teeth.

'Well, I can't tell you what to do. Either you've got the nerve or you haven't. But in my experience there's nothing more scary than forcing yourself to stick at a job you don't believe in. It deforms you in the end and diminishes you.'

'It was all right for you; you knew what you wanted to do, what was right for you.'

'I didn't know until I saw that job ad. I'd never have come up with it in a vacuum. It would never even have occurred to me.'

'So I should read the job ads?'

'It wouldn't hurt. Have another pint?'

'Thanks. Maybe I'll get done for drunk driving and have it all settled for me.'

'Too easy, mate. It doesn't work like that.'

An hysterical Sheena Renton visited her husband early next morning and pleaded to be allowed to stay all day. The ward staff were forced to enlist a social worker and a doctor to deal with her. When they failed to calm or distract her, they asked if there was someone they could call, someone she'd be able to stay with until things were sorted out.

'Justine,' she whimpered. 'I want to see Justine.'

Justine came without argument, curious to see what was happening and very much aware that she had more than a little in common with Sheena now. They were given a small dark side room and left alone. Each woman

417

was shocked at the appearance of the other.

'You look terrible!' Sheena gasped, shaken into rationality for a moment.

'So do you.' Justine managed a ghastly smile. 'Death does that to people – even the ones still left alive.'

'He did kill Penn, didn't he?'

'And Georgia, I'm afraid, though probably by accident. I don't think anyone will believe his claim that Penn did it.'

'But why leave her in that ditch for so long? Pretending he didn't have an idea where she was?'

'Sheena, he wasn't thinking straight. He's really not well, is he? He hasn't been right since his father died. You know – well, maybe you don't – but when somebody dies, it brings back terribly strong memories of previous deaths. It must have been like that for Philip. When Georgia fell off the ladder in that same barn where his cows were killed and his father hanged himself, he must have completely flipped. He'd have done anything to avoid going through those same feelings again. I think he threatened Penn, told her it was all her fault, that he was going to tell you it was her that did it. And then somehow she made him see that that would mean you finding out about her and him. And he really didn't want that. That's the secret he was most desperate to keep, from start to finish. He doesn't want your marriage to break up. That would be the final straw.' She spoke quickly, breathlessly, pouring out the explanation as convincingly as she could.

Sheena sobbed, breaking down without warning, wrapping her arms around her head as she had always done when upset.

'Listen,' Justine pressed on urgently. 'I could be wrong, but I think I do understand. He promised Penn all kinds of wild things: running away together, even leaving the country. She's been hankering to live permanently in Poland for years now. And with farming the way it is, there'd have been some attraction in the idea for him, too. But I doubt very much if he'd ever have gone. Or if he did it would be in his own good time, perhaps thinking he could persuade you to go as well. Personally, I'm convinced he'd never have found the nerve.'

'No,' sniffed Sheena. 'He wouldn't. It would mean selling the farm and he'd never have done that. It's all he's ever known.'

'So when Penn managed to calm him down, she must have dreamt up the idea of making it look as if I'd gone off with Georgia on a camping trip – which meant I would have to be disposed of, and your mother-in-law told of a sudden change of plan. The thing that puzzles me is why

419

she kept saying it was for my own good when she locked me up in that awful little shack.'

'What?' Sheena frowned bleary bewilderment.

'Did you never hear what happened to me? Well, it doesn't matter now. The point is, they needed to make it look as if I'd gone off with Georgia, but it got stupidly complicated when it came to the cars. I guess they decided to dump mine somewhere it would never be found, and he was too lazy or scared to make a decent job of it.'

'Perhaps he intended to kill you, too and make it look as if an intruder had done it,' Sheena suggested, almost casually. 'And Penn wanted to save you, seeing you're her cousin and her friend.'

A cold shiver ran through Justine at the way this new idea had been presented. As if Sheena knew even without thinking about it what Philip could be capable of.

It made all too much sense. 'So she was doing the best she could for me in the circumstances. Funny, though. Even now I don't feel a bit grateful to her.'

'I hate her!' Sheena exploded. 'She's taken everything from me.'

'She's paid the price,' Justine murmured. 'Don't forget that.'

'No.' Sheena shook her head wildly. 'By

letting him kill her, she's won. He'll go to prison for years and years, if he ever recovers enough. You haven't seen how he is. He's got worse since yesterday. Like a zombie, just staring at nothing. It's as if he's not there any more.' She sobbed again, louder than before.

'You think Penn just lay there and let him kill her?' Justine couldn't let the story fizzle out now. She gripped Sheena's arm and shook her. 'Sheena! Stop it. It'll help to talk about it and we both need to understand.' She swallowed a surge of tears of her own, thinking of dead children and a lost cousin. 'Maybe we need each other, too,' she added.

Sheena turned a desolate face towards Justine. 'To Philip it would be just like when they killed his pigs: a needle full of poison, quick and simple. It's *exactly* the way he'd choose to kill somebody. He wouldn't even have to think about it.'

A sudden noise outside the room reminded them that they would have to rejoin the real world before long. 'The police will never understand why he did it, will they?' Sheena went on. 'Unless I tell them.'

'I think there might be someone else who knows even more than we do,' Justine realised slowly. 'Someone they'll have interviewed by now.'

Sheena showed no curiosity as to who this might be. Instead she was staring hopefully at the door and when it opened, she was out of her chair, straining to hear that she could go back to her husband's side.

'Yes,' the woman nodded. 'You can have a few minutes with him. But we'll be moving him in a little while, to a specialist unit. I'm afraid the doctors can't do anything for him here.'

Sheena elbowed the woman out of the way, forgetting Justine completely. A second woman in police uniform was hovering outside the room and stepped aside as Sheena pushed past.

'Well,' said Justine, 'this looks like my marching orders. I hope I did what she wanted.' She watched the receding figure with some resentment.

'Don't take it personally, luv,' said the policewoman.

'No. Right. Well, I'll be off now.' But she only took a couple of steps before turning back. 'So they think Philip's going to get better?' she asked. 'I mean, people don't stay like that for long, do they?'

'Probably not, Miss,' came the reply. 'If you ask me, he's better off the way he is. His future isn't exactly rosy, after all.'

'You don't think he's *pretending*, do you?'

'Who can say, Miss?'

* * *

422

Justine had borrowed her mother's car, and now she sped home at a reckless pace. She put a tape in the player, turned up loud to keep her awake. Suddenly sleep seemed immensely attractive, an escape from the grief and confusion on every side.

It had been nearly two weeks now since she'd been separated from her anti-depressants and for several days she hadn't given them a thought. Life had been so strange during the time, it was almost like being on some sort of hallucinogen. But since Thursday, when Roma had found little Georgia and the uncompromising reality of the situation had forced itself through to her, she'd felt as if she was finally coming alive, after five long years. Even the scenery seemed to gain a dimension – trees were aggressively vivid as she passed them; faces revealed emotions and thoughts that she had not previously noticed. Without her drugs it was as if a film of gauze had been torn away from her senses and she was seeing things as they actually were for a change.

How would this affect her pottery, she wondered. Would her bold stark designs be too much to take now? Would she prefer small intricate shapes and patterns instead? It was an intriguing and disturbing question.

But it was also an avoidance of much more

urgent questions. And as she had already said to Sheena, there was only one person who seemed likely to have some of the answers.

Laurie was in the garden, a tall glass of fruit juice by his elbow, the dog at his feet. He wore a light open-necked shirt and a pair of khaki shorts. The informality was somehow endearing, as if he was making an effort to keep up with the world. His pale legs were sparsely sprinkled with grey hairs, his feet were in blue socks and leather sandals.

'She's told you all about last night, I suppose?' Justine opened the conversation, having remained quietly at his feet, playing with the dog's long ears for a moment.

'It sounded like something out of *Girl's Annual*,' he commented. 'You were lucky nobody got hurt.'

'Philip Renton killed Penn, you know. There's no doubt about that.'

Laurie said nothing, sinking his head on his chest and fixing his gaze on Lolly.

'You knew she was having an affair with him, didn't you? Did you also know she was there when Georgia died? Did she tell you before or after you went to Bournemouth with her? Did you know she was dreaming of running off to Poland with him?'

'Justine!' Her mother's voice rang out, full of

424

rage, the special school-mistress tone impossible to withstand.

The girl looked round quickly. 'What?' she muttered.

'Leave him alone. How dare you?' Roma was standing on the patio, a few feet away.

Justine took a deep breath. 'I have every right to know. You seem to forget that Penn assaulted me. I think Laurie knows all about it, and why she did it.'

'She was a very dear girl,' Laurie mumbled, suddenly very old. 'I can't believe she's dead. She never deserved that.'

Justine laughed bitterly. 'When did *deserving* have anything to do with it? Did my Sarah deserve to die? Or poor little Georgia?'

'Laurie didn't know what Penn had done,' Roma said, walking towards them. 'Nobody did.'

Justine looked from one to the other. 'I don't believe you,' she said. 'Just more lies – there's been nothing but lies since this began.'

Laurie moaned quietly. 'I didn't know, Justine. I admit that Penn lied to me. I don't think she meant any harm by it. But she told me that Sheena had killed the little girl.' He raised his eyes slowly to meet Justine's. 'And I believed her at the time.'

Justine looked wildly at her mother. 'What?' she demanded. 'What does he mean?'

Roma took a step backwards, waving a hand as if to dissipate the question. 'Don't ask me,' she protested. 'What do I know about it?'

Laurie cleared his throat. 'There are different kinds of truth,' he murmured. 'Different methods of killing someone. Different ways in which a person can be responsible.'

'Oh, for heaven's sake,' Roma pleaded. 'Don't go all philosophical on me.'

Justine flopped down on the grass and covered her eyes with a pale forearm. 'I'm tired,' she said. 'I can't do this now.'

'Let it go,' Laurie advised. 'It's the only way.'

Roma sucked in a hissing breath, but said nothing.

All three knew that however much they might wish it, the story hadn't finished yet.

CHAPTER SEVENTEEN

Karen followed Drew up to the bedroom when he came in that evening and went to change his clothes. The weather was warming up relentlessly, the air heavy and sultry.

'I do feel strange,' she said. 'I can't really pretend to be bereaved, when I hardly even knew Penn – but I suppose I am in a way. And it's so much worse that she was murdered. It seems so terribly cruel.'

'I know,' he sympathised. 'I feel much the same. She was so young, for one thing. Even if she hadn't been related, we'd feel sad about that part of it.'

'And it's even more confusing because we don't know whether she was good or bad,

I mean she *might* have killed that little girl. I don't suppose we'll ever know for sure. And that'll stain her memory for everybody. Even poor Aunt Helen isn't totally convinced of her blamelessness and she still doesn't know half the story.'

'I don't think we do, either. Maggs seems to have taken over the detective aspect of things in the past few days. I've been too busy to listen to every detail of what's been going on.'

'She's having a romance – that's what's going on,' smiled Karen. 'It's very sweet, isn't it.'

'It would be if I thought he'd be any good for her,' Drew said sourly. 'As it is, the chap's already going through a crisis – trying to start a new relationship at the same time must be asking for trouble.'

'Come on, Drew. Life doesn't work like that. You don't settle one dilemma all nice and tidy and then start the next thing. It comes in a great big jumble. Look at us last year – everything happening at once. It goes like that.'

'Yeah, I know,' he sighed. 'But I hate to think of Maggs getting caught up in someone else's mess. She's always been so direct and clear-sighted about everything.'

'Then she's probably exactly what he needs,' said Karen.

* * *

Roma couldn't rid herself of the feeling that everybody but her had begun to accept that there was little more to be said on the subject of the Rentons and Penn. Despite the welter of practicalities to be sorted out between Sheena and Justine and Helen, the horror of Penn's funeral still had to be faced and the abiding misery surrounding the death of little Georgia. Nobody seemed to be asking questions any more.

Nobody, that is, except Roma. And because Laurie was so stuck in grief and sickness, she couldn't address any of them to him. Helen was distraught at the loss of Penn, and Justine had put up the shutters for the foreseeable future. Which only left one person.

Or so she thought. When a battered white car rumbled its way towards her garden gate, she had to revise her opinion. Here, astonishingly, was another person she might be able to talk to. Someone who had some explaining to do of his own.

She intercepted him at the gate and steered him back towards his car. 'Not here,' she hissed at him. 'We can't stay here. Drive back the way you came and we can stop at the Swan. She stared hard at the car. 'Carlos – it *isn't* the same one, is it?'

He laughed, the same high peal of pleasure she had always enjoyed. 'No, no, it isn't the same one, but it's very like it. That was a good car. I'm glad you remember it.'

Inside it was filthy, so much so that Roma hesitated before sitting on the muddy seat. 'What have you been doing in it?' she demanded.

He glanced around vaguely. 'Nothing special.'

He drove them to the pub and waited for Roma to fetch the drinks, as he'd always done. She felt a pang of unease at the way the years fell off her shoulders, leaving her thirty-five again, with her handsome Spanish husband who was so obviously going to be a rich and famous artist.

'Are you still painting?' she asked him, carrying the beers back to their table in the garden.

'Off and on,' he nodded. 'When I feel like it.'

'Not making any money, I suppose?'

He grinned, 'Hardly any.'

'Carlos, why did you hit Philip Renton like that? Haven't you calmed down at all, in all these years? Are you still as crazy as ever?'

He rolled his eyes and bared his teeth, ran fingers through his thick black hair. 'What do you think?' he growled.

'I think it's all an act. What did you have against the man?'

He drooped suddenly. 'It was Penn,' he confided. 'She phoned me and said Justine was in trouble, but I was never to tell anybody that

430

she'd told me about it. Now the poor girl's been killed, I suppose I can break the secret.'

'When was this?'

'Oh.' He flapped a hand. 'A weekend. *Last* weekend. I mean the one before last. I had to drive down here on a Sunday, with the thousands of stupid trippers and their horrible caravans. I hate this part of England.'

'Yes, I know. You always did. So what did Penn tell you?'

'She told me to go to a derelict house, off the B3151 . . .'

'You can remember where it was?' Roma interrupted excitedly.

'Who could forget the B3151?' he demanded. 'It's poetry.'

'All right. So you went. On the Sunday.'

'The car broke down,' he admitted. 'And I couldn't find a garage, so I had to wait until Monday. And then it took them hours to fix it, so it was in fact *Tuesday*, when I reached the place. But I found it, yes, and it was empty. All the windows downstairs were boarded over, but the clever girl had made a way out upstairs.'

'Carlos, does Justine know that you went there to find her?'

He shook his head emphatically. 'Penn told me not to tell anybody. I haven't really had any words with Justine, even when I came to your

431

house on Friday. You don't let me stay for long, remember?'

'I didn't let anybody stay for long. I'd had just about enough by then.'

'Poor Roma. Never mind. You're very strong – you'll get over it all.'

'That's what you said before,' she remembered. 'When we got divorced.'

'And I was right. Now you have that sweet old man to keep you company.'

'He's not so old,' she said automatically. 'Only seventy.'

'Of course,' he agreed. 'And I am a child of fifty-eight.'

'You're a witness to Justine's story,' she mused. 'And Penn sent you to rescue her before she could starve to death.' She eyed him doubtfully. 'How did she know where to find you?'

'She was Justine's cousin and her friend!' he reproached. 'They came to visit me. She had one of my cards. I give *everybody* one of my cards. I have hundreds of them printed every year. I am the easiest person in the world to find.'

Roma laughed weakly. 'Oh Carlos!' she said.

'So then,' he went on, as if the story still had a long way to go, 'I was worried and angry. What should I do? Was Justine all right? Where had Penn gone to? Should I go home again? I did not have Penn's telephone number and the stupid Directory person said she wasn't listed. Of course, I could have mis-spelt her name. It's much too foreign to be sure how to spell it. But I had the number for Mr Renton, so I called him, and pretended that I knew nothing of what was going on. I asked him if I could speak to Justine. That's all. And guess what he said to me.'

Roma shook her head.

'He said Justine was a bloody little criminal, who had kidnapped his baby and was being searched for by the police.'

'Did he know who you were?'

'Oh yes. I said I was her father, planning to come and visit her. He said I should be ashamed of myself for raising such a person. And other things.'

'He knew she hadn't taken Georgia,' Roma said in puzzlement. Then her face cleared. 'His wife must have been listening. It was all an act for her benefit.'

'Anyway, that's why I smashed his face for him. Nobody says such stuff about my girl. And there was also the matter of the police.'

'Explain.'

'I called Barney, you see . . .'

'Barney?'

'My lodger. He cleans my house and looks after me, instead of paying rent. He takes messages for me too.'

Roma was dumbfounded. 'Carlos, he sounds more like a valet than a lodger. Or a gay lover.' She fixed him with a probing look.

'Whatever.' He waved the details away. 'Barney told me the police had telephoned asking if we knew where Justine might be. So then I knew the Renton man had told his lies to the cops and I had to bash him for it. Simple.'

'You devil,' she said, unable to conceal the admiration. 'Now they think you're a loony, loose on the community.'

'Mostly I am just a loony,' he admitted regretfully. 'A sad and harmless loony.'

'But they let you go, in spite of the bashing,' she noted. 'Have you got to face charges? Is there a court case coming up?'

He gave her a superior look. 'Roma, I am told by your sister that Mr Renton is Penn's killer. I hardly think he's going to prosecute me now, is he?'

'Probably not,' she sighed. 'You were always a lucky bugger.'

Somehow, she realised, the conversation had been hijacked from the outset, and she was not going to find an opportunity to explore the areas of the story which remained stubbornly grey.

'Carlos – why did you come to see me?'

'Just for old time's sake,' he smiled. 'And because I think we are forever tied together,

through our girl, and the little grand-daughter . . .'
His eyes filled, without warning, and Roma, to
her horror, felt hers do the same. Blindly, each
reached for the other's hand. 'That little girl
should have been spared to grow up and make
us all happy.'

'She'd be eight tomorrow,' Roma whispered.
'I've been trying so hard not to remember the
date, but it's cut into my heart forever.'

'And Justine's too,' he said.

'And Justine's too,' she agreed.

Maggs gave Drew a full day before she confronted
him. 'You and Den had drinks together, didn't you?
On Saturday night? Why didn't you tell me?'

'It had nothing to do with you,' he defended
hotly.

'Well it has now, because he told me all about
it. How he's thinking of quitting the police and
wants something else to do.'

'So? Why are you so cross about it?'

'Because you should have said something.
We have to find him another job. And I was
wondering . . .' her glance strayed to the burial
ground. Drew got her meaning instantly.

'No! Don't be silly. There isn't anywhere near
enough work. You know there isn't. And . . .'

'You don't like him,' she finished sadly. 'It's
all right. You can say it.'

'I do like him, Maggs. He's a great chap. But not many people want to work as an undertaker. Have you suggested it to him? Don't pretend it was his idea.'

She shook her head. 'No. I wanted to run it past you first.'

'Well it's daft. Believe me. He'd be the first to agree.'

'Maybe,' she said grudgingly. 'But he's got to find something. He's really had it with the police, you know.'

'I know,' Drew nodded.

Detective Inspector Hemsley was packing up whatever notes he had concerning Mr and Mrs Renton, to dispatch to the Superintendent of the Devon Constabulary. There were very few loose ends remaining, as far as he could see, as far as the facts were concerned. It should never have been a matter for the Okehampton police anyway. He had been both appalled and entertained by the extraordinary story of the undertaker's assistant and the video camera, hearing it from top to bottom in Exeter.

He paused, and re-read his words. Would they ever know the full truth, he wondered. Even if Renton recovered his wits, as he was already showing signs of doing, there was no guarantee that he would ever disclose his true motives and intentions. According to the officer watching over him in hospital, all his talk was of cows and sheep and pigs and the stink of their rotting bodies.

Hemsley, like Cooper, could never forget the ravages of the foot and mouth outbreak, sweeping like a modern pestilence through people's lives, shaking all their certainties and filling their souls with such shame that many found it beyond bearing. The balance of Renton's mind was surely impaired beyond complete recovery as a result of the horrors he had witnessed.

No wonder, he thought, in a moment of terrible desolation, *no wonder Cooper wants to get the hell out of this.*

Den could feel the ground tilting beneath his feet, tipping him out of his secure rut as surely as if he'd stepped onto a ski slope without knowing how to stop. After years of unquestioning identity as a policeman, he was now actively trying to change. Despite all the wise advice of centuries – always run *to* something, never away – he was going to escape into a void. He had no debts, even some modest savings; he was ready, even anxious, to sell his flat, which would bring in a little bit of positive equity. He had his health and the backing of an unbelievably good woman. It might be a void, but it was a rose-tinted one.

But first, for his own peace of mind, he had to tidy up one or two loose ends. He had to go and visit Roma Millan.

She came to the door carrying a small white plastic bucket with a close-fitting lid. 'Oh, sorry!' she exclaimed. 'I was just going to feed my new bees.'

'Don't let me interrupt,' he said easily. 'I'll come with you, shall I?'

'If you like. You're not scared of them, then?'

'Should I be?'

'Of course not.'

They walked across the field behind Roma's house, Den suddenly apprehending how similar the layout was to Drew Slocombe's property. There seemed to be some hidden but promising message in this.

'We'll be releasing your niece's body today,' he said. 'Her mother will be wanting to arrange the funeral.'

'I'm not sure *wanting* is quite the right word, but yes, it'll have to be done. Poor Penn. She was a lovely girl, you know. I don't think we'll ever understand what went wrong.'

'Mr Inspector believes that Mr Renton has been mentally ill ever since the foot and mouth outbreak. It led to the loss of all the stock and his father's suicide.'

'That doesn't explain anything, really, though. Does it?'

'I don't know. I think perhaps it does. He must have had a big influence over Penn. Women fall for damaged men – have you noticed? It seems to be in their nature.'

'Even me,' said Roma in a low voice. 'Though I'd never have put it quite like that.'

'I had a girlfriend,' he confided. 'We were going to get married. Then she left me for a farmer. It was as if he hypnotised her. It all came apart after a little while and we had another try, but it never really worked again.' He sighed. 'I still dream about her sometimes. How it all might have been.'

'But I think Renton still loves his wife,' Roma mused. 'Justine says so, anyway. It makes Penn seem terribly *irrelevant*, somehow. As if she died for nothing.'

'Everybody dies for nothing,' Den said angrily. 'How can it ever be for something?'

'People think it is, though, don't they? Suicide bombers; somebody saving another person; making a political point.' They'd reached the apiary and Roma handed him the tub of sugar syrup. Then she slowly lifted the lid of the new hive and peered in. Evidently all was well. Taking the feeder from Den, she suddenly turned it upside down. Slow drips of syrup fell through

439

the nylon mesh in the centre of the lid. Quickly she popped it inside the hive and replaced the roof. Den continued their talk as she stepped away from the hive.

'They're fooling themselves,' he said.

'You're right,' she agreed. 'Tell me, why did you come here today?'

He rubbed his long cheek thoughtfully. 'It sounds daft, I suppose, but I've had the feeling all along that this business has really been about you. I wanted to see if I could work out how.'

She turned a stricken face up to him. 'Surely not?' she breathed.

He laid a hand on her shoulder, squeezing gently. 'I didn't mean it to sound like that. I was just tracing back the connections and that's the way it seemed. But I don't know it all – not by a long way. And I'm not talking about blame, either. After all, hardly anybody sets out to do deliberate harm.'

'Don't they? Is that what you believe?' she asked him.

'Don't you?'

She told him, then, about little Sarah and her own implacable stand. About Justine's breakdown and her, Roma's, inability to face her daughter again after such hurt. 'So is that where it all began?' she asked him. 'Is that why Penn died? I feel bad, but not quite *that* bad. I really can't see how it could be so.'

'Only if Penn did deliberately kill little Georgia,' he said. 'And why would she do that?'

'You've lost me,' she frowned.

'Penn remains a mystery. Even if Renton recovers enough to tell us everything, we probably still won't understand her. How did she really feel towards Justine? And you? Was she simply manipulating everybody, or was she in thrall to Renton and doing what he told her?'

'We've got visitors,' she noticed. Three people were coming out of the french windows at the back of the house, waving towards her. Roma put a hand to her throat.

There were two men and a woman. The latter had honey-coloured hair and a broad face. 'My God!' breathed Roma. Surely it was Penn, returned from the dead?

'That's Mrs Slocombe,' Den murmured. 'With your husband and Drew.'

'She looks just like Penn,' Roma said weakly. 'It's like seeing a ghost.'

They sat together, the five of them, on the patio. Laurie fetched cold drinks and Pringles. The air was heavy with imminent thunder. Drew and Karen explained they'd left their children playing with Jane-in-the-village, who had twins and was always a popular change of scene. Roma and Den said little, feeling a sense of interruption.

'Having a party?' came a cold little voice from the living room. Justine stood inside the french windows, looking out at the scene.

'Join us,' Laurie waved an arm like a traffic policeman, trying to usher her out. Slowly she obeyed.

Drew, as always uneasy in a prickly atmosphere, tried to dispel the gloom. 'Karen wanted to meet Roma,' he said. 'And Laurie, of course. So we decided to drop in. Never dreamt we'd find Cooper here,' he laughed.

'It's a long time since I last saw Karen,' Justine said slowly. 'Not that there's any reason why we should see each other. It's not as if we're related.' She examined Karen for a long moment. 'You look like Penn,' she said. 'Doesn't she, Mother?'

'I thought I'd seen a ghost just now,' Roma admitted shakily.

'Yes,' Justine nodded. 'So did I. Horrible.' She shuddered.

'Sorry,' said Karen, trying not to sound huffy.

'Not much of a party, really,' Justine observed. 'More like a wake. Or a post-mortem.'

Den plunged in, aware of violating something fragile. 'We were talking about Penn – wondering why it all happened the way it did.'

Justine met his eyes for several seconds and

he glimpsed a deep abiding agony in them before looking away.

'You should ask Sheena,' she said. 'She understands.'

Everyone looked at her then. Drew was the first to speak. 'She's going to stick by him then, is she?'

'Oh yes,' Justine blurted bitterly. 'Yes indeedy.'

'Justine.' Karen leant forward. 'Did Penn *really* kidnap you?'

Exhaustedly, Justine nodded. 'That's really what did it, in the end.' Meeting Den Cooper's eyes again, she spoke directly to him. 'She was a match, you see,' she muttered, so indistinctly that he misheard her.

'A smash?' he repeated in puzzlement.

'A *match*. Tissue type. Penn and Sarah were the same.'

Roma made a gurgling sound of disbelief.

'That's right, Mother. You needn't have worried about getting yourself tested, after all. Penn had the test, but then buggered off to Poland before the results came through. I couldn't contact her. Nobody had the address. And Sarah only had a few weeks left.'

'But why didn't you ever say?'

'Because by the time the results arrived, you'd convinced me that it wasn't worth all the

443

pain and misery and false hopes that the whole process would have let us in for. I *agreed* with you, Mother, and you still won't let me tell you that. You were so convinced you knew what I was thinking and feeling, you wouldn't listen to anything I tried to say.'

'But, Penn. How could you ever forgive her?'

'She punished herself so much that in the end she was in a worse mess than I was. We comforted each other. But then there was Georgia and I realised what Penn was really like.'

'Which was what?' asked Den.

'A coward. Always running away, lying to herself, me, everybody. She knew she'd never be able to face a bone marrow transplant, so she left the country. But she had the test because she was afraid of my reaction if she didn't. I didn't find out for ages that she was having an affair with Philip. They must have been so careful to make sure I wasn't around.'

Den remembered the 'J' in Renton's letter, who had to be out of the way before they could use the house.

Justine went on, ignoring his slight intake of breath. 'She spent her whole life dodging unpleasantness, until she had everyone else thinking *they* must be crazy.'

'So you killed her?' suggested Den reluctantly. 'Was it *you*?'

Justine smiled and shook her head. 'No. Philip did it. I knew right away, as soon as I heard she was dead. I think he did it for Georgia, mainly, in the end. Penn's cowardice killed that little girl – I believe she kicked the ladder away when she heard someone coming up. She thought it was me. And then she made up that stupid plan of abducting me. I could have died in that hovel for all she cared.'

'Well, no,' Roma corrected her coldly. And she recounted her conversation with Carlos. 'Penn would never have deliberately killed anybody.'

'She and Renton made a fine pair, didn't they,' said Drew.

'I don't think any of us comes out of it very well,' said Roma sadly. Laurie reached over and gripped her hand. She clung to him like somebody drowning. Den and Maggs caught each other's eye, locked in a long gaze.

'Come on,' Drew said to his wife. 'Time to go home.'

If you enjoyed *The Sting of Death*, you'll love
our other books by Rebecca Tope . . .

'One of the most intelligent and thought
provoking of today's crime writers'
Mystery Women

'The classic English village mystery
is alive and well'
Sherlock Magazine

'Exciting, humorous and topical'
Crime Time

'Rich in psychological insight . . . Tope is
particularly skilled in creating interesting
and unique characters'
Deadly Pleasures

THE COTSWOLD SERIES

To order visit our website at
www.allisonandbusby.com
or call us on
020 7580 1080